TRACING OLD NORSE COSMOLOGY

VÄGAR TILL MIDGÅRD

VÄGAR TILL MIDGÅRD 16

Tracing Old Norse Cosmology

The world tree, middle earth, and the
sun from archaeological perspectives

Anders Andrén

Nordic
Academic
Press

NORDIC ACADEMIC PRESS

The project 'Roads to Midgard – Old Norse Religion in Long-term
Perspectives' was financed by the Bank of Sweden Tercentenary Foundation.
The publication of *Tracing Old Norse Cosmology* has been made possible with grants
from the Bank of Sweden Tercentenary Foundation.
ISSN 1650-5905

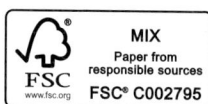

MIX
Paper from
responsible sources
FSC
www.fsc.org
FSC® C002795

Nordic Academic Press
Box 1206
221 05 Lund
info@nordicacademicpress.com
www.nordicacademicpress.com

© Nordic Academic Press and Anders Andrén 2014
Typesetting: Aina Larsson/Sättaren i Ängelholm
Jacket design: Jacob Wiberg
Jacket image: 'Borr's sons' © Peter Hupfauf/BUS 2013
Print: Livonia Print, Riga 2014
ISBN 978-91-85509-38-6

Contents

Preface

This book has been on its way for a long time, too long actually. My interest in studying cosmology from archaeological perspectives started in the 1990s. First I published investigations of Christian cosmology in urban and rural settings (Andrén 1998b, 1999, 2000b), although I conducted parallel fieldwork at the Iron Age ringfort of Ismantorp on Öland in 1997–2001. My interests in pre-Christian aspects of cosmology were more pronounced during 2000–2007, when I co-directed the interdisciplinary project *Roads to Midgard – Old Norse Religion in Long-term Perspectives* at Lund University. My professional move to a position at Stockholm University in 2005 meant a lot of new work and responsibilities, but also an important broadening of my chronological horizons. I have been increasingly engaged in the international scene of Scandinavian studies as well. From colleagues in folklore studies, the history of religion, literary studies, and philology I have deepened my interdisciplinary understanding of ancient Scandinavia.

Other projects (Andrén 2010, 2011a, 2011b) have interrupted this book, but now that it is finally finished, I owe many people my sincere thanks. Although the project *Roads to Midgard* no longer formally exists as an active network, the book is published in the series of the project, since many of the ideas and preliminary investigations were formed within this inspiring environment. Therefore my first and warmest thanks go to my co-directors Kristina Jennbert and Catharina Raudvere and to the participants, Stefan Arvidsson, Åsa Berggren, Maria Domeij, Ann-Britt Falk, Peter Habbe, Ann-Mari Hållans Stenholm, Ann-Lili Nielsen (who sadly died in 2008), Gunnar Nordanskog, Nina Nordström, Heike Peter, Jörn Staecker, and Louise Ströbeck.

During my fieldwork at Ismantorp, Mats Blomhé was my closest collaborator, who cheered up the working days with his knowledge and quiet humour. Other indispensable participants during the fieldwork were David Andrén, Henke Fallgren, Lotta Fernstål, Roberto Grassi, Bent Gregersen, Peter Pedersen, Magnus Pettersson, Jack Simonsen, and Klaus Thorsen. In Stockholm, I have encountered a large and very inspiring scholarly environment. In this context, I would like to single out for my warmest thanks Kerstin Cassel and Susanne Thedéen, who have read and commented some of the chapters, and Torun Zachrisson, who has read the whole book, and has given many comments from her immense knowledge of Iron Age Scandinavia. I started looking at the Bronze Age following a kind invitation to Copenhagen from Klavs Randsborg to be the examiner for Flemming Kaul's doctoral thesis. In further studies of cosmology in the Bronze Age and Iron Age, I have had rewarding discussions with Kristian Kristiansen and Lotte Hedeager as well.

In the international world of Scandinavian studies, I have met many colleagues with a passion for and profound knowledge of the ancient Nordic world. I am deeply indebted to Terry Gunnell who has read the whole book, and commented on the content as well as the language. My profound thanks go to Margaret Clunies Ross as well. She was a very considerate host during a sabbatical in Sydney in the spring of 2006, and has read the whole book with a critical – but friendly – eye. In Sydney, I also had interesting discussions with Peter Hupfauf concerning possible ways of using Old Norse traditions in art. Finally, Olle Sundqvist has been kind enough to read the whole book, and to share his insights on the issue of religion.

During three other sabbaticals, my scholarly horizons have been broadened in other directions. In 2009–10 at the Swedish Collegium for Advanced Study in Uppsala, the daily discussions, above all with Philipp Lepenies and Björn Wittrock, gave me new insights into different areas of humanities and social sciences, with clear relevance for this study. During the winter term in 2010–11 in Heidelberg, Thomas Meier and Roland Prien introduced me to Late Antiquity and the early Middle Ages in central Europe. During excursions and ongoing discussions, I had to revise several of my preconceived ideas about these periods. During a second period at the Swedish Collegium for Advanced Study in Uppsala in 2013, I had the pleasure of working with John Lindow, Steve Mitchell, and Jens Peter Schjødt. They have not read my text, but daily discussions with them have helped me reconsider some important aspects of my ideas.

As always, Alan Crozier has patiently followed my attempts to write English. I warmly thank him for recasting one chapter from Swedish to English, and for revising the whole book in the final stages. My editor Annika Olsson has been an invaluable collaborator throughout the production of this book. Not least her humour and firm deadlines finally brought this book to an end.

I am not sure that my family will be really interested in this book. My children, Rasmus and Sara, having two archaeologists as parents, have chosen to follow their own pursuits. But I hope that this book in a tangible way will show my passion to them. Sanne, for reasons of principle, is not interested in my 'northern barbarians', but it is a privilege to have her as a colleague and partner. Above all, I appreciate her humour and strange interest in writing archaeological texts during summer vacations.

Anders Andrén

Figure 1. The rune stone at Karlevi in Vickleby on Öland. The monument, from about the year 1000, commemorates one Sibbi Fuldarsson, who was a sea-warrior ruling 'over land in Denmark'. The text includes the oldest attested skaldic verse in *dróttkvætt* and the oldest attested Scandinavian form of the term *Jǫrmungrundr* ('mighty ground') as an expression of the world (see Andrén 2007b) (photo by the author).

CHAPTER I

Old Norse cosmology as an archaeological challenge

> Young were the years when Ymir made his settlement,
> there was no sand nor sea nor cool waves;
> earth was nowhere nor the sky above,
> chaos yawned, grass was there nowhere.

This is the famous description near the beginning of the Icelandic Eddic poem *Vǫluspá* (*The Seeress's Prophecy*) of the empty void before the creation of an ordered world. The following stanzas tell how the gods gave everything in the world its name and right place, how they built ritual sites and made precious objects, and how they blew life into the first humans from two pieces of wood. After descriptions of the world tree and the first war between the two families of gods, the Æsir and the Vanir, the poem ends with the death of the god Baldr and the destruction of the world, Ragnarok (Ragnarǫk), literally 'the destiny of the gods'. However, the poem states that after Ragnarok a new 'eternally green' world will come from the sea, and in the grass the children of the old Æsir gods will find 'the wonderful golden chequers, those which they possessed in the ancient times' (*Vǫluspá* 59, 61).

The ordered world in *Vǫluspá* was usually called Midgard (Miðgarðr), meaning 'dwelling place in the middle' (Simek 1993:214). This concept was known not only in Iceland, where *Vǫluspá* was composed probably in the eleventh century (McKinnell 2008), but also in other areas of the Germanic-speaking world. As early as AD 370, in Bishop Wulfila's Gothic translation of the Bible, the same concept is rendered as *midjungards*. Other later but similar forms are known from Saxon, Old English, and Old High German. In Scandinavia, the earliest reference to Midgard comes from a runic inscription on a boulder at Fyrby in

Södermanland in central Sweden, dated to the early eleventh century (de Vries 1957:372–3; Vikstrand 2006). An alternative name for the world, Jormungrund (*Jǫrmungrundr*) meaning 'mighty ground', also existed. It is recorded in *Grímnismál* 20, but also in *Beowulf* 859 and on the famous rune stone at Karlevi on Öland in eastern Sweden (Fig. 1) from about the year 1000 (Simek 1993:180).

Today, notions of an ordered universe are usually framed by the concept 'cosmology'. The word, meaning 'knowledge of good order', was first coined by the German Enlightenment philosopher Christian Wolff (1679–1754) in his *Cosmologia Generalis* from 1731. Since then, the word has been given many different uses and meanings. One of the modern uses of the word is anthropological, being a general concept of different culturally constructed worldviews. Cosmology in this sense usually includes fundamental notions regarding time and space, the structure of the universe, the creation of the world, borders between supernatural powers and humans, origins of social groups, divisions between men and women, fate and death, ethics, and the criteria of truth. In several cultures, these different cosmological aspects are linked to one another in a cosmological system, as in the case of the Chinese principles of *yin* and *yang* (for example Douglas 1966; Geertz 1973; Clunies Ross 1994:42 ff.; Raudvere 2004).

Cosmology is accordingly a modern concept, like the concept of religion itself. Both words are modern attempts to define certain aspects of human action and human thought in time and space. Cosmology is not necessarily connected to religion, but in most pre-modern societies religious myths provided answers to many of the fundamental cosmological questions. A coherent worldview is seldom presented in these myths, and should not be expected, since cosmology is a modern concept. However, some general principles can often be deduced from the narratives (Raudvere 2004).

Cosmology can also be connected to rituals, since ritual sites and monuments in many cultures seem to have been modelled in accordance with aspects of different worldviews (Widengren 1969:340 ff.; Sundqvist 2004). In that sense, cosmology is a concept situated between the concepts of myth and ritual, since it can be connected to both. This conceptual location of cosmology is important, especially in current reconsiderations of ritual, myth, and religion.

Previously, myths were regarded as the core of religion, whereas rituals were often perceived as passive expressions of myths and actions designed to maintain a cosmological order (Eliade 1958). In recent decades, however, these perspectives have been challenged in anthropological criticism of the implicit Judeo-Christian background of many religious studies (Smith 1987; Asad 1993; Bell 1992; Humphrey and Laidlaw 1994; Rappaport 1999; Habbe 2005). Religion is no longer defined as theology, but is viewed much more as changing social practice, associated with a religious transcendental discourse. Myth and ritual are understood as two different but interrelated social categories. As a consequence, ritual is not necessarily regarded as a representation of myth, but can be apprehended as a formalized act that in itself creates meaning. Instead of merely maintaining a cosmological order, ritual is also seen as a transformative act. Besides, ritual is not regarded as necessarily religious, since it can refer to other – legal, political, and social – discourses (Nilsson Stutz 2003; Habbe 2005). Myth, meanwhile is still regarded as an important narrative, but in recent years above all its social functions have been underlined (Meulengracht Sørensen 1993; Clunies Ross 1994; Lindow 1997a).

Nonetheless, in those cases where ritual and myth can be related, cosmology may still play an important intermediate role. Cosmology is never limited to a single medium, but is usually played out in different myths as well as in ritual sites. This interface does not necessarily lead in a single direction. Ritual sites might be expressions of cosmological ideas, but it is also possible that the sites and monuments themselves created and reinforced cosmological notions. For example, the divine abodes of Old Norse gods and goddesses were expressed through, but also modelled on, the large halls that the political elite in Scandinavia used in the Iron Age (Hedeager 2011:148 ff.).

Still, since current ritual theory is above all based on the theory of practice (see Bourdieu 1990), questions concerning the history and meaning of rituals in long-term perspectives are to a large extent lacking in today's debate. Similarly, it is noteworthy that material culture plays a minor role in much current ritual theory, since objects are conceived of as symbols in a traditional semiotic, sense. This means that objects are viewed as 'empty symbols', without any fundamental importance for the understanding of religion (Kyriakidis 2007). However, in recent religious studies inspired by cognitive science, material culture has been fully incorporated into investigations of religion. A good example is the work of Johan Modée, who underlines the fundamental role of objects, buildings, and places in religion. According to Modée (2005), without them, religion is not conceivable and would not exist as a social practice.

Cosmological aspects of Old Norse religion

Old Norse religion is the conventional name for religious traditions in Scandinavia before the conversion to Christianity in the tenth and eleventh centuries. Pre-Christian religion in Scandinavia was above all based on ritual practice and oral traditions, although runic writing has been used in northern Europe since about AD 200. This means that almost all written accounts of these religious traditions are external, written either by Christians referring back to their pagan past or by foreigners from ethnographical perspectives.

Most written accounts of Old Norse religion come from the rich and varied medieval Icelandic literature. The mythological world is summarized and explained in *Snorri's Edda*, a poetic manual written by the Icelandic chieftain and skald (poet) Snorri Sturluson (1179–1241) in the early thirteenth century. He based his knowledge on a large corpus of skaldic poems, some lost, some preserved in fragments, and some extant in their full length. The most important surviving mythological and heroic poems are collected in the *Poetic Edda*, which was written down and edited in the early thirteenth century, although some of the poems were composed earlier. Besides, references are repeatedly made to the pagan past in many of the Icelandic sagas from the thirteenth and fourteenth centuries. Apart from the Icelandic literature, the Danish scribe and historian Saxo Grammaticus wrote extensively about Scandinavia's pagan past in his Danish history (*Gesta Danorum*) from the early thirteenth century. Descriptions of Scandinavian ritual practice are also known from accounts by the Arabic diplomat and geographer Ibn Fadlan (922) and by three German clerics and historians, Rimbert (*c.*870), Thietmar of Merseburg (*c.*1010) and Adam of Bremen (*c.*1075). Besides, the Old English poem *Beowulf* (probably tenth or eleventh century) includes references to worldviews in ancient Scandinavia. Cosmological ideas, of more or less clear pre-Christian origin, are scattered across many of these texts. Above all the *Poetic Edda* and

DE NI VERDENER.

Figure 2. A reconstruction of the Old Norse worldview with nine worlds. (After Magnusen 1825, photo by Jens Östman, Kungliga Biblioteket, Stockholm.)

Snorri's Edda, but also skaldic poetry, contain descriptions and words connected to past worldviews.

Many aspects of Old Norse religion that can be covered by the modern concept of cosmology have been studied. A major field of research concerns the basic construction of the world. Most scholars have underlined the fragmentary, contradictory, and ambiguous notions of the pagan worldview in extant sources (Gurevich 1969; Hastrup 1985; Davidson 1988:167 ff.; Schjødt 1990; Clunies Ross 1994:42 ff., 2011; Brink 2004; Wellendorf 2006). The scattered nature of the evidence has been explained at least partly in terms of oral culture, which is usually characterized by regional and social variations. Nonetheless, much effort has also been put into understanding the basic structures that appear to lie behind these scattered remains. Some scholars have tried to harmonize what is known into more coherent images (Fig. 2), whereas others have tried to discern the different historical or regional horizons that may be detected in the sources.

The ritual aspects of Old Norse cosmology have been another main field of research. Place-name scholars have been able to show how the abodes of deities were present in the human world in the form of ritual sites with sacral place-names linking them with specific gods or goddesses. In some cases, such as the island of Selaö in central Sweden, practically the whole divine universe was present in a specific small area (Brink 2001, 2004; Vikstrand 2001, 2004). Other ritual aspects are reflected in the cosmological structure of the religious and political centres of the Iron Age, the so-called central places. Elements in the early descriptions of Gamla Uppsala have long since been considered to be expressions of central cosmological ideas, especially the references to a well, a tree, and a hall. Similar discussions have also been connected to Helgö, Gudme, and lately other central places (Widengren 1969:340 ff.; Alkarp 1997; Andrén 1998b:148; Hedeager 2001; Gunnell 2001; Sundqvist 2004; Zachrisson 2004b, 2004c).

Human and social aspects of Old Norse cosmology have also been studied. Above all, cultural models including issues such as the idea of society, the origins of humans, honour, ethics, healing, food, and the relation between humans and animals have been investigated (Dumézil 1973; Meulengracht Sørensen 1993; Clunies Ross 1994; Hedeager 1997, 2004, 2011; Jennbert 2004, 2011; Solli 2004).

The chronological and spatial horizons of Old Norse cosmology

Although the Old Icelandic texts have been used for a long time in studies of early Scandinavian worldviews, some fundamental methodological issues are raised by the nature of the rich and highly varied literature from Iceland. The texts are medieval Christian literature, and show how authors in thirteenth-century Iceland interpreted the pre-Christian oral culture of Iceland and Scandinavia. A basic question is therefore how we should view the relationship between the narratives, the authors' society in the thirteenth century and later, and the pre-Christian society in which most of the narratives are placed retrospectively (see Meulengracht Sørensen 1977; Habbe 2005). Do these texts merely present a 'fantasy religion', created by classically learned authors in a diaspora culture who were looking back to an imagined homeland, or do the Icelandic stories contain elements based on social practices and worldviews that existed in a pagan past? Due to the multidisciplinary character of Old Norse studies, the answers to these questions vary quite considerably.

Today, most philologists, historians, and literary scholars underline the medieval Christian character of Old Icelandic literature, partly as a reaction against earlier views that tended to take the literature as representations of pagan customs and beliefs. The main arguments against using the texts in reconstructions of a pagan past are the many similarities between the Icelandic texts and contemporary Christian narratives, as well as the distance in time and space between medieval Iceland and prehistoric Scandinavia (Lönnroth 1965; Olsen 1966; Meulengracht Sørensen 1977; Clover and Lindow 1985; Düwel 1985; Krag 1991; Clunies Ross 1994, 1998). Consequently, this position has led scholars away from discussions of the pagan past to other interesting studies in which medieval Icelandic culture and literature have a value in their own right (for instance, Meulengracht Sørensen 1993; Clunies Ross 1994; Lassen 2011).

In contrast, many historians of religion and place-name scholars still emphasize the common non-Christian traits of many elements in the Icelandic texts (Steinsland 1991, 2005; Schjødt 1999a, 2009; Näsström 2001a; Sundqvist 2002; Brink 2004). Although these scholars acknowledge the huge source-critical problems involved, they nonetheless try to reconstruct a pagan past by comparing elements in the Icelandic texts with other kinds of evidence. This strategy includes comparisons with older descriptions of the Germanic peoples or Scandinavians in Roman, German, and Arabic sources, older runic inscriptions from Scandinavia, the etymology of various words, comparisons with other non-Christian Indo-European religions, and sometimes references to the phenomenology of religion. These comparisons show that many details in the Icelandic texts appear to have some relation to a pre-Christian past.

Nevertheless, these comparative methods pose problems of their own. The chronologically and geographically scattered statements given in earlier texts about Germanic tribes and Nordic peoples and their customs are sometimes too easily combined into a homogenized picture of their religious traditions. Since the comparisons are drawn from many different sources, periods, and places, the image of Old Norse religion often tends to be set outside time and space. Possible changes over time as well as regional variations have often been lacking in comparative accounts (see, however, McKinnell 1994; DuBois 1999; Brink 2007; Schjødt 2009; Andrén 2012; Nordberg 2012; Gunnell forthcoming).

The methodological issues are especially problematic in Georges Dumézil's influential reconstruction of Indo-European mythology. Old Norse religion plays an important role in his work, since Dumézil assumes that Old Norse religion represents an archaic and unchanged religious tradition on the periphery of Europe (Dumézil 1958, 1973). His position has been criticized by many (Renfrew 1987; Drobin 1989; Clunies Ross 1994), and, from an archaeological perspective, the assumption of an unchanged periphery is hard to reconcile with the fact that Scandinavia was constantly interacting with other parts of Europe throughout prehistory. Besides, Dumézil's tripartite mythology is too simple to correspond to the complex grammatical structure that is found in Indo-European comparative linguistics. Although Dumézil connects the mythology with the social structure, his reconstruction remains outside time and space. Due to their general character, his ideas can in a sense be applied everywhere and nowhere.

Furthermore, the methods used in historical linguistics mean that linguistic proximity is emphasized at the expense of geographical proximity. Various Indo-European languages have been drawn into the argument as self-evident points of reference in studies of pre-Christian Norse religion, regardless of the geographical location of the languages

(Dumézil 1973; de Vries 1956, 1957). At the same time, nearby Sámi and Finnish areas have often been ignored, despite the extensive cultural encounters with these regions. In recent years, however, some studies have started to include these connections (see Lindow 1997b; DuBois 1999; Price 2002; Bertell 2003, 2006; Brink 2004).

Archaeology and Old Norse cosmology

Archaeology currently plays an increasing role in the study of Old Norse religion and cosmology, but the discipline has not always been a central part of Old Norse studies, due to changing perspectives on the complex interface between texts and material culture, as well as varying views of the interpretive possibilities of material culture. The role of archaeology in the research field largely runs parallel with the theoretical trends within archaeology itself.

The first professional museum curators and archaeologists, such as C. J. Thomsen and J. J. A. Worsaae, were well versed in Old Icelandic literature, since it had become important in creating a Scandinavian identity and history with the Romantic movement of the first half of the nineteenth century. We therefore find some references to the Old Norse world in their works, for instance in the interpretations of gold bracteates (Thomsen 1855; Worsaae 1870). However, the first thorough archaeological study of Old Norse religion was a survey of pagan rituals and beliefs among the Scandinavians, written in 1876 by Henry Petersen, *Om nordboernes gudedyrkelse og gudetro i hedenold: en antikvarisk undersøgelse*. In this work, some of the fundamental links between objects and references in the Icelandic texts were examined for the first time. Petersen's contemporary, Hans Hildebrand, used a similar approach when he identified for the first time certain small T-shaped silver amulets as representations of Miollnir (Mjǫllnir), the hammer of the thunder god Thor (Þórr) (Fig. 3; Hildebrand 1872). Nonetheless, as in other historical archaeologies (Andrén 1998a), the conventional method for a long time tended to be a rather simple 'matching game' between words and objects. Consequently, archaeology played a rather passive, secondary role in the study of Old Norse religion, often reduced to illustrating motifs in the texts.

In the first half of the twentieth century, the Old Icelandic literature preserved its role as a mental background for archaeological interpret-

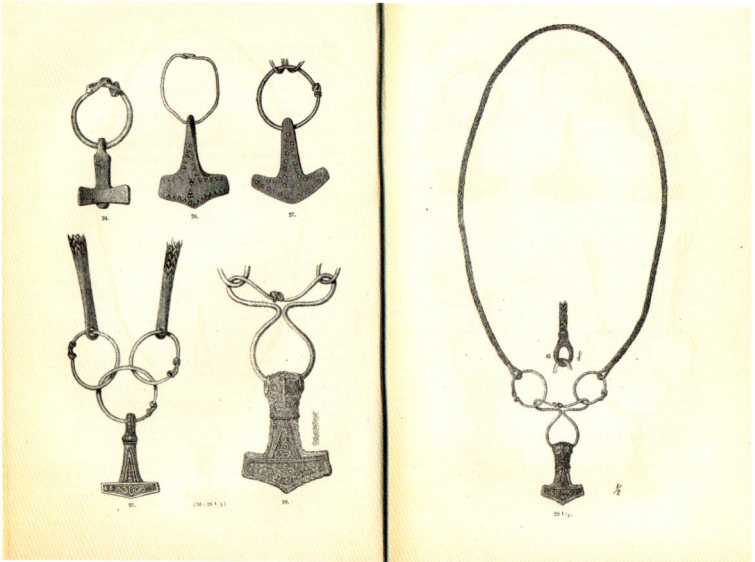

Figure 3. T-shaped silver amulets, for the first time identified as Thor's hammer Miollnir. This identification is today fully internalized in scholarship as well as in popular culture. (After Hildebrand 1872:52–3.)

ations of the Iron Age, and above all for the Viking Age in Scandinavia. This is especially clear in the work of the more historically oriented archaeologists, such as A. W. Brøgger, Birger Nerman, and Sune Lind-qvist (for instance, Brøgger 1916; Nerman 1941, Lindqvist 1945). In their studies, however, Icelandic textual references were used more to illuminate archaeological problems than to contribute to a general understanding of Old Norse traditions. In that sense, Scandinavian archaeology during the first half of the twentieth century followed the principles later outlined by Christopher Hawkes in a famous article from 1954, on 'the ladder of reliability' in this tradition (Hawkes 1954). According to him, archaeology in general could primarily be used to study technology, to a lesser extent economy and social organization, and only with great difficulty religion and mentality. Religion was more of a residual category for things that could not be explained otherwise. It was only when support came from additional texts that archaeology would be able to say anything more substantial about thoughts and beliefs.

During the 1960s, 1970s, and early 1980s, the so-called processual archaeology turned away from issues of religion, on account of the neo-materialistic and neo-evolutionary aspects of this tradition (Trigger 2006:386 ff.). Consequently, very little archaeological research was carried out in the field of Old Norse studies during these decades. The focus was instead on landscape, settlement, economy, and social organization. Above all, the archaeology of landscape and settlement made its breakthrough. Important results included new perspectives on land use, settlement structure, and hierarchies of settlements (Ambrosiani 1964; Lindquist 1968; Myhre 1972; Hyenstrand 1974; Carlsson 1979; Widgren 1983; Hvass 1985; Berglund 1991).

It was only with the cultural turn in the 1980s and 1990s, which has been labelled in the discipline as post-processual or contextual archaeology, that ideology, mentality, and to a lesser extent religion returned as important research issues (Hodder 1986; Insoll 2004). In this tradition, material culture is viewed as an active element in constant negotiations and renegotiations between people. Meaning can be ascribed to artefacts, settlements, and landscapes, which can sometimes represent complex ideas. As in many other human sciences, interpretation has been placed centre-stage in archaeology.

This interest in ideology, mentality, and religion in archaeology means that totally new results concerning pre-Christian Scandinavian religion have been achieved in recent years (see, for example Bennett 1987; Andrén 1989, 1993, 2007a; Engdahl and Kaliff 1996; Hedeager 1997, 2011; Kaul 1998, 2004; Price 2002; Solli 2002; Andrén et al. 2006; Andersson and Skyllberg 2008; Carlie 2009b; Bäck and Hållans Stenholm 2012; Svensson 2012). For example, it is now possible for the first time to have a serious discussion about the occurrence of ritual buildings in pre-Christian Scandinavia on the basis of concrete physical evidence from the Iron Age (Nielsen 1997; Larsson 2004). A part of this trend is that the Old Norse tradition in general – and not only the religious aspects – has provided analogies for archaeological interpretations. As a result, parts of Scandinavian prehistory have become very historic.

In the last decade, however, a reaction against the optimistic views and the relativism of some interpretations in contextual archaeology can be discerned. Now the materiality of objects is underlined, instead of meaning (Olsen 2003, 2010; Glørstad and Hedeager 2009). The searchlight is being directed at what material culture does to people rather than what it means. Consequently, religion is again less in focus in some archaeological research, although issues of materiality and biographies of objects are well-suited to a dialogue with ritual theory, which underlines the social meaning rather than the mental meaning of rituals (see Lund 2009).

The new focus on materiality has clearly opened up other perspectives in archaeology, but issues of meaning will not disappear. Many results from processual archaeology have been integrated into contextual archaeology, and a similar confluence will probably take in the current theoretical shift. The critique of optimistic and shallow interpretations in contextual archaeology is sometimes well-grounded, but I still find the search for mental or religious meaning important in archaeology. Especially the metaphorical potential of material culture is worth studying in relation to religion, an issue that I will explore to some extent in further down. Besides, in the different historical archaeologies in particular, the dialogue between material culture and worldviews has been studied for a long time (Andrén 1998a). These studies are usually based on thorough contextual analysis of the material culture, but are in dialogue with written sources.

Although that dialogue will be continued, the relationship between Old Icelandic texts and material culture will remain complicated. The distance in time and place between thirteenth-century Iceland and Iron Age Scandinavia means that the texts never contain descriptions of actual contexts that can be studied archaeologically. Instead, it is always a question of other non-direct relations. The indirect relationship between the two nonetheless also has constructive causes, since the common background for the written word and materiality is oral tradition. As many scholars have stressed, oral tradition is both changeable and rich in variation (Clanchy 1979; Ong 1982; Herman 2005). An extant text is therefore only one possible variant of a narrative. Material culture related to the same narrative can thus represent yet further versions, meaning that the relationship between artefacts and texts will always be provisional.

Thus, the use of material culture in the study of pre-Christian Norse religion is not uncomplicated. Furthermore, the changed view of ritual means that it can be difficult to ascertain from material traces of ritual-

Figure 4. The chancel and apse of the Romanesque church at Vä in Skåne. The paintings in the vault of the chancel depict a divine choir of angels singing the psalm *Te Deum,* according to the banderoles. The images and the texts show how the chancel vault can be interpreted as a representation of heaven, being part of the Christian cosmology. (Photo by the author.)

ized acts whether the rituals were connected to a religious discourse or not. The element of variation in the oral tradition also means that the identification of different motifs and figures can never be any more than provisional (see Price 2006). At the same time, the fundamental, active role of materiality in all oral culture means that artefacts can be a truly primary source for narratives, conceptions, and patterns of action in ancient Scandinavia. Objects and images could be used as mnemonic devices for composing new variants of the narratives in the form of ekphrasis (Clunies Ross 2005:54). While cosmological perspectives are sometimes merely hinted at in mythical or heroic narratives, the worldview can be depicted in a highly systematic way in material culture, for example in settlement, buildings, and artefacts. Recurrent formalized acts at one and the same place may even show concretely how certain patterns of action were maintained for generations, in that the place and the acts were part of the collective memory. Consequently, the use of material culture in the study of Old Norse religion and cosmology has a great potential.

It is clear that in many cultures, different aspects of worldviews are expressed through material culture. Objects and buildings may have been designed according to ideas about the structure of the world, and settlements as well as whole cities may have been laid out according to cosmological principles. Good examples from literate societies are Chinese cities planned as prototypes of the universe, Hindu temples constructed as the world mountain, and Romanesque churches (Fig. 4) built as expressions of Christian history from the Creation to Judgement Day (see Wheatley 1971; Fritz and Mitchell 1987; Krautheimer 1942; Deichmann 1983:89 ff.). Material culture can also be used to express worldviews in oral cultures such as the layout of Navaho houses (Aveni 2008:111 ff.) and the design of tattoos in Polynesia (Gell 1993). In several cases, it seems that the material representations of different cosmologies are more systematic than they are in the narrative references. This raises the question of whether material expressions of different cosmologies could not only trigger systematic thinking about the world, but in some sense could be regarded as the source of cosmological ideas. Material culture, accordingly, did not only represent ideas, but partly formed the material basis for these ideas.

The material aspect is above all underlined in cases where cosmologies were connected with ritual space, such as Hindu temples, Romanesque churches, and prayer rugs. In these instances, the different categories of ritual and myth all but merge into a single category, in ways that current ritual theory does not really take into account. In that sense, cosmology can be categorically placed between ritual and myth, making it an ideal point of departure for investigating fundamental myths as well as important rituals.

Three archaeological studies

The three following studies are all focused on central cosmological elements in the Old Norse worldview – that is, notions of the construction of the world. The first study, 'In the shadow of Yggdrasill', is a revised translation of a Swedish text published previously (Andrén 2004). It is an archaeological investigation of a question raised by a central figure of thought, the world tree, in Icelandic mythology. As I will show, the idea of a world tree seems to have developed gradually over time, to reach the notion recorded in the medieval Icelandic narratives. The second investigation, 'A world of stone', proceeds from the opposite position; in other words, it starts out from an analysis of an archaeological monument. The text is based on a preliminary report of the fieldwork at the site (2006). It is an investigation of the notion of Midgard, and its possible creation as part of the cultural encounter with ordered cosmologies in the Roman Empire. The final essay, 'Whirls, spirals, and horses', was also written specifically for this volume, but a summary of the text has been published recently (Andrén 2012b). It is based on images from the Bronze Age and Early Iron Age, and concerns solar aspects of a cosmology that had almost completely disappeared before the Viking Age and early Middle Ages. The essays are ordered in a cosmological sequence, starting from the middle of the world and proceeding to the sun, which was seen as the main celestial figure moving around the world. In the conclusion, some aspects of Old Norse religion and cosmology in long-term perspectives will be considered.

Figure 5. The oak at Norra Kvill in Rumskulla in Småland. It is believed to be more than a thousand years old. (From Wikimedia Commons.)

CHAPTER 2

In the shadow of Yggdrasill
The tree between idea and reality
in Scandinavian traditions

A distinct figure of thought in Old Norse cosmology is a world tree standing in the middle of the world, with a huge crown reaching up to heaven and with roots going into different parts of the world. The meaning, function, and historical background of this world tree have been extensively debated by textual scholars. Usually, however, archaeologists have been absent from these debates, probably because this central cosmological idea has been regarded as falling outside the realm of material culture (see Hawkes 1954). Such a position can nonetheless be questioned, since cosmologies have often been represented and enacted in the material culture of many societies in different parts of the world (see, for instance, Krautheimer 1942; Wheatley 1971; Rykwert 1988; Andrén 1998a). Therefore, there are good general arguments for undertaking an archaeological study of the Old Norse world tree.

This transcultural phenomenon – that worldviews can be represented in material culture – illustrates several aspects regarding the concept of material culture. Although the tangible and silent materiality of things has been underlined in recent debates (for instance Olsen 2010), it seems as if material culture is an umbrella term for highly varied and heterogeneous things (Hodder 1994). Some of these things may have representative qualities, others may not. But material representations should not necessarily be viewed as symbols in the linguistic sense of de Saussure, meaning that there always is an arbitrary relation between form and content. Instead, material representations can be regarded as 'concrete symbols', linking function and meaning in different ways. In that sense, there can be complex connections between the mental world and the experienced human world. This means that, in relation to the Old Norse world tree, there may have been complex interactions between mythological trees, real trees, and representations of trees. In order to study this figure of thought archaeologically, it is therefore necessary to discuss each of these forms in which the tree appears.

Mythological trees

The ash of Yggdrasill, which stands in the middle of the world, with its crown reaching heaven and its three roots extending to the different parts of the world, is a well-known element in Old Norse cosmology (Fig. 6). In textbooks on the pre-Christian religion of Scandinavia there is normally a description of the world tree, its attributes and inhabitants (see, for example, de Vries 1957:380 ff.; Ström 1961:97 ff.; Näsström 2001:27 ff.). There is also a more specialized literature about the tree, its mythological significance, and the meaning of its name (Steinsland 1979; Simek 1993:375–6; Kure 2006). With few exceptions, these modern commentaries and interpretations are often somewhat homogenizing, since aspects of trees with other names are often added to the description of Yggdrasill. All the same, it must be admitted that this homogenizing tendency can be detected as early as the works of Snorri Sturluson, since in *Gylfaginning* he already attributes elements to Yggdrasill, which have been borrowed from other contexts. From other parts of *Snorri's Edda* and from the *Poetic Edda* and occasional skaldic verses it is clear that we can count references to at least three mythological trees, namely, Yggdrasill, Mimameid, and Lærad, which may all be viewed as representing three different aspects of the idea of a world tree.

Yggdrasill is mentioned most frequently, but the name is controversial. The most common interpretation is that the name means 'Odin's horse', which is a poetic metaphor (kenning) for 'gallows', referring to how the god Odin (Óðinn) hanged himself in the world tree. Suggested interpretations such as 'the terrible tree' allude to the same motif, but there is also a completely different but less likely interpretation, according to which the name of the tree means 'the yew support' (Simek 1993:375–6).

The different parts and attributes of Yggdrasill are stated most clearly in *Vǫluspá* 19, 47, *Grímnismál* 29–35, 44, and *Gylfaginning* 14–15, where the description is largely based on *Vǫluspá* and *Grímnismál* (Steinsland

VERDENSTRÆET YGGDRASILL.

Figure 6. A reconstruction of the Old Norse world tree. The Icelandic scholar Finnur Magnússon (1781–1847) was the first to visualize Yggdrasill. His understanding of Old Norse cosmology has had a long-lasting effect on scholarship and popular culture (see Clunies Ross 2011). (After Magnusen 1825, photo by Jens Östman, Kungliga Biblioteket, Stockholm.)

1979; Simek 1993:375–6). According to these Eddic poems, the ash Yggdrasill is a tree at the top of which sits an eagle. Four stags browse on the buds in the crown of the tree, and dew from the leaves drips all over the world. A dragon and countless serpents gnaw at the roots of the tree, while a squirrel runs up and down the trunk, carrying malicious messages between the eagle in the crown and the serpents at the roots. The three roots of the tree reach all over the world, and under the roots are humans, the giants, and the realm of the dead, Hel. Beside the tree are the well of fate or Urd's well (Urðar brunnr) and the hall of the women of destiny of the Norns (nornar). According to *Vǫluspá* 19, the tree is showered with 'shining loam' (*hvítaauri*). Snorri states in *Gylfaginning* 15 that the Norns take this liquid from the well and pour it over the tree, so that the branches will not dry out. The seat of the speaker or reciter of the assembly (*þular stóll*) is placed at Urd's well according to *Hávamál* 111, whereas the god Thor holds court with the other Æsir at Yggdrasill according to *Gylfaginning* 14.

Snorri also states in *Gylfaginning* 14 that Yggdrasill has three roots, but he tells us instead that they reach the frost-giants (Hrímþursar), the dark realm of the dead (Niflheim) and the gods 'in heaven', in an attempt to harmonize different poetic accounts of Yggdrasill. According to *Vǫluspá* 47, Yggdrasill 'groans' on the eve of Ragnarok, but its fate in connection with the destruction of the world is not clearly expressed in the poem. Most scholars assume that the tree burns up along with the rest of the world (Hallberg 1952). Some think that a new tree grows up after the end of the world (Steinsland 1979), while others believe that there may have been a world tree in each preceding age of the world (Schjødt 1992).

Three further details are normally associated with Yggdrasill in accounts of the Nordic world tree. Under 'the radiant, sacred tree' (*undir heiðvǫnom helgom baðmi*), according to *Vǫluspá* 27, there is Heimdall's hearing or sound (*Heimdallar hljóð*), which may refer to the ear of the god Heimdall (Heimdallr) or to the horn Gjallarhorn, which he blows at Ragnarok (Simek 1993:135–6). According to *Hávamál* 138–41, Odin hangs himself on a 'windy tree' (*vindgameiði*) for nine nights in order to acquire knowledge of the runes. *Vǫluspá* 2 mentions furthermore the mighty 'measuring tree' (*mjǫtviðr*), which is associated with nine worlds or nine preceding ages (Schjødt 1992). Many interpret these expressions as further descriptions of Yggdrasill, but the three poems do not explicitly state that they are referring to this particular tree. Yet another allusion to Yggdrasill could possibly be found in the note about eagles sitting on the branch of the ash in *Helgakviða Hundingsbana* II:50 (Hofsten 1957).

A different tree that is not mentioned so often is Mimameid (Mímameiðr), which can be interpreted without ambiguity as 'Mimir's tree' (Simek 1993:216). It is described in the late *Fjǫlsvinnsmál* 20 and 24 as a deciduous tree that spreads its branches out over the world. An obscure passage states that the fruits of the tree should be borne 'on fire' to sick people and 'women suffering in secret', which perhaps refers to curative smoked fruit or roast nuts and acorns (Hofsten 1957). Sitting in the tree is a cock, which may only be killed by a sword and which then falls down into the halls of Hel. The sword is made by Loptr, another name for the god Loki, and is kept in a chest with nine locks by Sinmara, wife of the fire-giant Surt (Surtr). The reference to Surt also invokes associations with Ragnarok, since according to *Vǫluspá* 47, 52–3, Surt plays a crucial role in the destruction of the world (Simek 1993:303–4). Mimameid is attested only in *Fjǫlsvinnsmál*, but the tree must be connected to Mimir's well (Mímis brunnr), which is mentioned in *Vǫluspá* 28. Snorri states in *Gylfaginning* 14 that Mimir is a wise man because he drinks from the well with the aid of Gjallarhorn. It was also in this well that Odin sacrificed one eye in order to attain wisdom. At Ragnarok, Odin will also acquire advice from Mimir's head, according to *Vǫluspá* 46, *Gylfaginning* 50, and *Ynglinga saga* 4, 7. The scattered details about this particular tree can perhaps be juxtaposed with the information given in *Vafþrúðnismál* 45 about Hoddmimir's wood (Hoddmímis holt), which may be interpreted as the tree trunk in which the two humans Life (Líf) and Lifthrasir (Lífþrasir) survived Ragnarok (Simek 1993:154–5). This interpretation hints that part of the tree somehow managed to escape destruction in the fire at the end of the world. The cock in Mimameid has meanwhile been regarded as a parallel to another cock, which, according to *Vǫluspá* 42, sits in the gallows tree (*galgviðr*) in Jǫtunheim, the world of the giants (Steinsland 1979:130).

A third tree, Lærad (Læraðr), is mentioned in *Grímnismál* 25–6 and hence also by Snorri in *Gylfaginning* 38. The meaning of the name is uncertain; suggested interpretations include 'damager', 'protector', and 'giving liquid' (Simek 1993:185). This tree stands by Valhall (Valhǫll), the hall of the slain warriors, and a goat and a stag gnaw at its branches. The goat stands on the roof of Valhall, and from its horns comes the mead that the heroes in Valhall (*einherjar*) drink. From the crown of the stag, water drips down into the well Hvergelmir ('the bubbling cauldron'), which is the source of all rivers (Simek 1993:185, 166–7). In addition to these three trees, we read in *Vǫlsunga Saga* 2 that in the middle of the hall of the Volsungs there was a large oak called 'children trunk' (*barnstokkr*), which may indicate that women gave birth under the tree. Odin had stuck a sword into the oak and only Sigmund, son of Volsung, could pull it out (de Vries 1957:385).

In Old Norse cosmology, then, the tree stands out as a distinct but complex figure of thought. I therefore think that we should not regard Yggdrasill as the 'true' world tree, but should consider Yggdrasill, Mimameid, Lærad, and Volsung's tree, and possibly 'the sacred tree', 'the windy tree', 'the measuring tree', and 'the gallows tree', as variations on a common tree theme. Some of the names seem to be poetic variations only, whereas other names were probably linked to different myths in which different aspects of the figure were emphasized. In part, the various names seem to reflect ideas about trees in different suprahuman worlds (Steinsland 1979). What the different versions have in common is the connection with Odin, who hangs himself in 'the windy tree', probably sacrificed his eye in Mimir's well, lives near Lærad, possibly has given his name to Yggdrasill, and is the divine ancestor of the Volsungs. At least two of the trees are moreover linked to Odin's search for knowledge (Schjødt 2004), namely, the knowledge of the runes that he acquired by hanging himself in 'the windy tree' and the wisdom attained by the possible sacrifice of an eye, in Mimir's well. Urd's well at the roots of Yggdrasill is likewise associated with knowledge and wisdom. Perhaps the statement about the mead flowing from the goat that stands on the roof of Valhall can also be viewed as an echo of an alternative myth about the origin of skaldic mead, and hence the art of poetry (Drobin 1991).

Alongside Odin, the gods Thor and Heimdall can also be connected with the world tree. According to Snorri, Thor holds court with the Æsir at Yggdrasill (*Gylfaginning* 14) and saves himself from a flooded river by pulling himself out of the water with the aid of a tree trunk (*Skáldskaparmál* 18; Simek 1993:20–1). As noted above, Heimdall's ear or horn Gjallarhorn can be found at Yggdrasill, and Heimdall also winds Gjallarhorn at Ragnarok. The interpretation of the name Heimdall is disputed (Ström 1961:133 ff.; Simek 1993:135–6; Cöllen 2011). Some scholars interpret it as 'he who lights up the world', while others believe that the meaning is 'world tree' or 'world pillar' (Cöllen 2011). The latter interpretation fits well with the god's by-name Hallinskidi (Hallinskíði, meaning 'the leaning split log' or 'the forward-leaning staff') given in *Gylfaginning* 26. In this sense, Heimdall himself may be seen a personification of the world tree or the world pillar, which could explain his diffuse role in the Nordic myths.

Apart from these divine links, there is also a clear relationship between the tree and human beings. According to *Vǫluspá* 17–18, the first humans were Ask ('ash') and Embla (meaning disputed; Josefsson 2001). In *Gylfaginning* 8, Snorri also says that they were made from two tree trunks which had floated ashore. Odin and two other gods, according to *Vǫluspá* 18 and *Gylfaginning* 8, gave these tree trunks human life by adding 'breath' (*ǫnd*), 'spirit' (*óðr*), 'vital spark' (*lá*), and 'fresh complexions' (*góðr litr*) (Steinsland 1983; Simek 1993:21). In a similar way, the only two people who are said to survive Ragnarok probably derived from a tree trunk. As mentioned above, Líf ('life') and Lífþrasir ('he who strives for life') hid in Hoddmimir's wood, according to *Vafþrúðnismál* 45. Similar ideas about a connection between trees and human life recur in *Qrvar-Odds saga*, which mentions that the hero rejuvenates himself by living as a 'tree-man' for a period (Simek 1993:20–1, 74, 335). One also notes that in *Vǫluspá* 1 humans are called 'offspring of Heimdall' (*mǫgo Heimdallar*), which may also allude to the same relationship between trees and man, especially if Heimdall is perceived as a personification of the world tree or world pillar. Indeed, the link between humans and trees is so prominent that the world tree and the well at its roots have recently been interpreted as a metaphor for the male and female sex organs (Kure 2002; see also Josefsson 2001).

The world tree, in other words, stands out as a central but ambivalent figure of thought in Old Norse cosmology. It was related to fundamental questions about the creation and structure of the world, about the origin of knowledge and the descent of man. The tree stood in the centre of the world, surrounded by the creatures and powers inhabiting the earth, and through its trunk it connected heaven, earth, and the underworld (Schjødt 2004). Concepts such as time and place, destiny and death were thus associated with the tree (Clunies Ross 1998:245).

The idea of a world tree or a world pillar in the middle of the world is not unique to Old Norse cosmology. Thanks above all to the classic study by Uno Holmberg, *Der Baum des Lebens* (1922–3), the Old Norse world tree has long been discussed in relation to many parallels in much of Europe and Asia. The Old Norse world tree has thus been incorporated into a general discussion in the history of religion about the world pillar, the *axis mundi* (Eliade 1958).

The boundary between world tree and world pillar is fluid, since they can both be perceived as 'functional alternatives' in early cosmologies. Åke Hultkrantz nevertheless believes that there are certain structural differences between the two forms. The world tree alludes chiefly to the link between heaven, earth, and the underworld, while at the same time the tree is often seen as a representation of a god. The world pillar, on the other hand, bears up the heavens, and in several traditions its top is attached by a nail to the 'immobile' Pole Star. The idea of a world pillar was most common in circumpolar cultures, whereas the idea of the world tree was more prominent outside the Arctic and subarctic area. In certain cultures, for instance among the Sámi, there were beliefs about both world tree and world pillar (Hultkrantz 1996).

The Old Norse figure of a world tree beside a well shows general similarities to 'the tree of life' or 'the tree of knowledge' (Fig. 7), and to paradisal rivers of milk and honey, recurrent themes in many ancient traditions in the Near East, not least in the description of the Garden of Eden in the Old Testament. In certain other details, too, the Old Norse idea of the world tree finds striking parallels in European and Asian traditions concerning both world trees and world pillars (Holmberg 1922–23; de Vries 1957:382 ff.). An eagle sitting at the top of the crown is also found in the Persian 'eagle-tree', while stags and a goat are associated with the world tree in both Persian and Assyrian traditions. A squirrel, acting as intermediary in a battle between a bird and serpents, is found in both Greek and Indian myths. A dragon lies at the root of the cosmic tree in several Siberian traditions, while shamans move between the seven or nine worlds connected to the world tree or the celestial axis. Other Siberian myths mention a milky liquid found in a spring under the world tree or dripping from its branches over the first humans. Even such a particular detail as Snorri's description of a root that reaches heaven has parallels in the idea of an *arbor inversa*, that is, an upside-down world tree. The belief is attested in Indian myths about

Figure 7. A gravestone from Ekeby on Gotland for one Olof of Ekeby, who died in 1316. The central image shows how the Christian cross could be regarded as the Tree of Life. (After Hildebrand 1898–1903:455.)

trees, as also in Siberian 'shaman trees' and in Sámi sacrificial rituals involving tree trunks with their roots turned upwards (Coomaraswamy 1938; Edsman 1944; Mebius 1968:61 ff.). In certain Siberian myths, the upturned shaman tree symbolized the upper celestial world (Mebius 1968:151, 2003).

The similarities between notions of a world tree and world pillar in Europe and Asia have led to extensive discussions of the age and origin of the idea. Sophus Bugge argues that the parallels above all with the Near East simply show that the idea of the world tree was introduced with Christianity, and that it is an expression of the syncretistic society in which Old Norse literature was created (Bugge 1881–9:399 ff.). Although many scholars agree that there may be Christian elements in the Old Norse idea of the world tree, most believe that the idea is 'primeval', since the parallels show such a wide geographical and cultural spread (see, for instance, Ström 1961:98; Steinsland and Meulengracht Sørensen 1994:31). From a diffusionist perspective, Holmberg (1922–3) argues that the idea originated in the Near East and India, from where it spread over Asia and Europe. Jan de Vries (1957:392) claims instead that the idea is 'pre-Germanic', but nevertheless Indo-European, based on linguistic parallels. Björn Collinder (1926), on the other hand, regards the Arctic and subarctic regions as the source of the idea. Thede Palm (1948:121) is thinking along the same lines when he suggests that the Old Norse concept of the world tree and its shamanistic features were conveyed via Sámi culture. Åke Hultkrantz (1996) has recently arrived at a similar view, arguing from an ecological perspective that the world pillar represents an archaic circumpolar worldview, of Mesolithic or even Palaeolithic origin. The question of the history and meaning of the Old Norse world tree is thus disputed, and its relation to people's lived world in the distant past is obscure.

Real trees

The discussion of mythological trees in relation to real trees has mainly followed two lines. On the one hand, there are various forms of 'holy trees', which can be regarded as a more or less obvious representation of the cosmology. On the other, there are 'farm trees' or 'guardian trees' of later times, which can be perceived as a fundamental element in the cultural landscape, from which the figure of the 'world tree' may have derived part of its inspiration.

The link between the cosmological trees and ritually important trees in the real world has long been of interest in Scandinavia. The frequently cited but controversial example is Adam of Bremen's account of the tree 'always green, winter and summer' (*semper viridis in hieme et aestate*), which stood 'near the temple' (*prope illud templum*) at Gamla Uppsala (Adam of Bremen IV, scholion 138; see de Vries 1957:382; Hultgård 1997). His description has long been questioned (most recently by Janson 1998), but it has a parallel in the independent *Hervarar Saga*, which also speaks of a 'sacrificial tree' (*blóttré*) at Gamla Uppsala (Sundqvist 2002:131). The tree at Gamla Uppsala could therefore be viewed as a ritual focus for the site and as a representation of the Old Norse

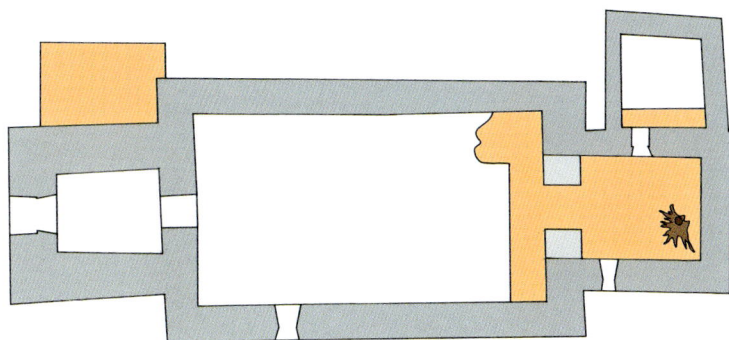

Figure 8. The Romanesque church at Frösö in Jämtland, with the extent of the excavations (in yellow) and the investigated birch root (in brown) from the Viking Age. The birch root was found by the altar of the church, indicating a cosmological continuity at the site. (Plan by the author, based on Almqvist 1984:122 and Hildebrandt 1985, 1989.)

world tree (Sundqvist 2004; Warmind 2004). The excavated remains in Frösö church of a birch root surrounded by deposited animal bones (Fig. 8) provide yet further support for the argument that votive trees, probably with cosmic associations, existed in Viking Age Scandinavia (Hildebrandt 1985, 1989; Iregren 1989; Näsström 1996; Andrén 2002:322).

The idea of a link between the world tree and later guardian trees is old, going back to the ideas of, above all, Wilhelm Mannhardt that pagan relicts were preserved in European folk culture and that the fertility cult was the fundamental element in pre-Christian religion (Mannhardt 1875:54; de Vries 1957:382). He saw the origin of the Old Norse world tree in a fertility cult focusing on guardian trees and a generally 'animated' nature. Although later historians of religion have not accepted Mannhardt's vegetative cult, many do stress the link between guardian trees and world trees (see, for instance, Ström 1961:97; Steinsland and Meulengracht Sørensen 1994:30). The relationship between latter-day guardian trees and the Old Norse world tree is nevertheless problematic as regards source criticism, since all the information on guardian trees is based on records of folk traditions from the seventeenth to the nineteenth centuries. These records show that each guardian tree was very closely related to the farm and its inhabitants. The fate of the tree was virtually synonymous with the fate of the people and the farm. That was why it was often forbidden to break off branches or to damage the tree in any way. It was also common that votive offerings were made at the tree in connection with childbirth and marriage (Palm 1948:60 ff.; Vikstrand 2001:283). The more or less explicit argument for seeing a link between these modern guardian trees and the world tree of Old Norse mythology is based on certain structural similarities, such as the link between humans, destiny, and trees.

The question of whether there were corresponding guardian trees for settlements in pre-Christian times is difficult to answer, but the best argument for their existence is that the names of various trees occur in place-names from the Iron Age. Sigurd Fries (1957), in his study of Nordic tree-names, has pointed out that trees in pre-Viking Age place-names with the generics -hem and -vin are always in the singular. In Viking Age place-names ending in -by, on the other hand, the specific is usually in the plural, although singular forms do occur. Just under 25 per cent are singular forms in Swedish names ending in -by with trees as the specific. The plural forms always refer to stands of several trees, but Fries believes that the singular forms can also refer primarily to more than one tree, as a kind of abstraction. Yet Fries does not dismiss the possibility that the names may have referred to individual trees. The best argument is that there are a number of single-element names such as Ask (ash), Ek (oak), and Krokek (crooked oak), which seem more clearly to have referred to important individual trees. In the Mälaren area these single-element names are always found in central Iron Age districts of great antiquity (Vikstrand 2001:275, 2004). In other words, the place-names suggest that both during and before the Viking Age there were important trees that were so closely associated with farms and villages that they served as the basis for the names people gave to places (see Brink 2001). What is interesting in this perspective is that by far the most common tree-name among the pre-Viking Age names ending in -hem is the ash (Fries 1957), which thus suggests associations with the Norse world tree.

It was not unique to Scandinavia that individual trees were of great importance in people's lives. Evidence of sacred trees at places of assembly and cultic sites can be found, for example, in Celtic, Slavic, Saxon, and Greek traditions. Medieval Irish sources state that an ash on Mount Uisnech was the holiest tree in Ireland. The mountain was believed to be in the centre of Ireland, and was therefore the scene of large annual gatherings. Other places in Ireland were also associated with single ashes, oaks, and yews (Maier 1997:272, 275–6).

A Slavic equivalent to Gamla Uppsala and Uisnech may be Szczecin (Stettin) in Pomerania. According to the German monk Herbord's description from the 1150s, there was a large oak and a spring beside a 'temple' with idols (Słupecki 1994:73, cf. Sundqvist 2004). Carolingian sources show that in Saxony there were likewise sacred trees with ritual associations. There is a particularly explicit record of the holy 'Jupiter oak' (probably 'Thor's oak') in Geismar (Hessen), which the Anglo-Saxon missionary bishop Winfrid (St Boniface) ordered to be chopped down around 720 (Palm 1948:49 ff.). Before this, classical writers with their descriptions of the Celtic druids hint at a connection between humans, knowledge, and trees. The druids always performed their rituals with oak leaves, and the Latin word *druida* probably derives from a Celtic word meaning 'he who has knowledge of the oak' (Maier 1997:98–9, 211).

In classical Greece there were numerous special trees with ritual functions and mythological references. A recurrent feature was that important trees grew at major sanctuaries, as was the case with the olive tree on the Acropolis in Athens (Birge 1994). In certain instances the trees could be associated with the myths, since they were believed to mark the birthplace of gods and goddesses, for example, Hera on Samos and Apollo and Artemis on Delos (Marinatos and Hägg 1993). In other cases the ritual functions of the trees were particularly obvious, as with the oaks of Zeus in Dodona (Lauffer 1989:197 ff.), where an oracle spoke through the rustling of the oak leaves. The tenacious importance of the holy trees in Greece is particularly clear at Dodona (Fig. 9). The site with its oaks is mentioned as early as in the *Iliad*, probably from the eighth century BC, but even for Homer the oracular cult was ancient, said to be 'Pelasgian' ('pre-Greek'). For more than a thousand years the oracular function of the oaks was maintained, and it was not until AD 391 that they were cut down, when a bishop's see was established on the site. Dodona has been excavated, and the site of the oaks was found to be walled off by a small enclosure, which had been renewed several times (Lauffer 1989:199). Many of the surrounding buildings were much more monumental, which means that the most important place at Dodona does not stand out very clearly in archaeological terms.

Figure 9. The peribolos wall around the site of holy oaks at Dodona in north-west Greece. New oaks were planted within the walls during the twentieth century. (Photo by the author.)

The number of more or less 'sacred trees' could be multiplied with the addition of both European and non-European examples, since the tree seems to have had a virtually universal metaphorical potential (Rival 1998). The background to the prominent role of the tree is probably at once practical and cognitive. In the pre-industrial world, trees were a crucial resource for human activity and survival. Houses, boats, and tools were all made of wood, and leaves from pollarded trees were important fodder for livestock in some areas. Besides, trees in the form of fuel were necessary for all kinds of human transformation of nature, such as cooking, pottery, metal production, and cremation. From a cognitive perspective it is also important that certain species of tree can reach a very great age, such as yew, oak, and ash (see Fig. 5). The oldest examples in northern Europe today are at least 1,000 years old, some perhaps even 1,500 years (Österman 2001; Bevan-Jones 2002). Both now and in the past, old trees were therefore a kind of constant in the landscape, going far back beyond human memory. The trees have 'always' been there, and will 'always' be there. They had become a kind of 'natural place' (Bradley 2000) in the same way as rocks, mountains, and water, but with the difference that they were alive and growing. As growing species, trees were connected to the underworld by their roots, but also reached out towards heaven via their crowns. The wide-ranging practical uses for trees, along with their potential age and their growing structure, thus enabled them to serve as important metaphorical elements in the landscape. How important they were and the meaning they were assigned, however, were determined by the historical context.

Generally speaking, trees have been important elements, often with mythological associations and ritual functions. Even in Scandinavia there are occasional records showing that rites were connected to trees. Moreover, place-names with a tree as the first element suggest that particular trees had special relations to both settlements and people. But despite their great significance, the real trees are an almost insoluble archaeological challenge. We know that the trees existed, but at present we often lack techniques with which to detect them convincingly. All that remains are some important but highly random finds such as the tree root under Frösö church. Instead, archaeological investigations of the tree motif have to follow other paths, namely, representations of trees.

Representations of trees

In Scandinavia, as elsewhere, three different forms of representations of trees can in principle be studied: (*i*) tree trunks, logs, and posts; (*ii*) pictures; and (*iii*) monuments built of earth and stone.

The use of trunks and posts proceeds from the idea of *pars pro toto*, meaning that parts of a real tree have been used as a reference to more metaphorical trees. One such possible tree representation is the common custom of burying dead people in tree trunks or wooden containers. The oldest clear evidence of this practice in Scandinavia comes from the Danish oak coffins from the Early Bronze Age (Fig. 10), dated by dendrochronology mainly to the fourteenth century BC (Jensen 2002:186). But there are also more diffuse and indirect traces of probable tree-trunk coffins from the Late Neolithic (*c*.2400–2000 BC, see Lomborg 1973:112 ff.). In the Late Bronze Age and Pre-Roman Iron Age (1200–1 BC) cremation graves gradually took over and the tree-trunk coffins disappeared. But the association between dead people and trees was preserved, as the cremated human bones were sometimes placed in wooden vessels sealed with resin (Granlund 1939). From the

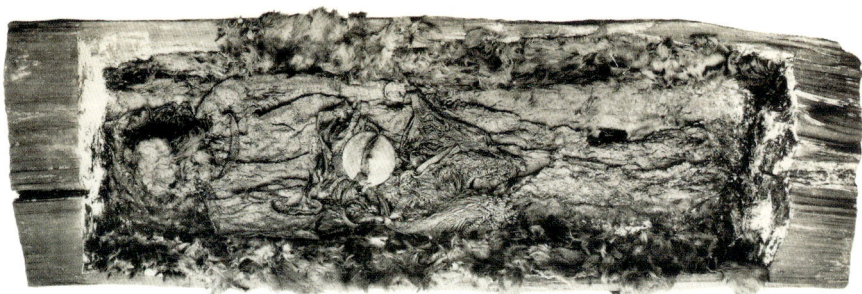

Figure 10. Oak coffin found in a Bronze Age mound at Egtved in Jutland. The oak coffin contained a young woman who, according to dendrochronology and preserved flowers, was buried during the summer in 1370 BC. (After Thomsen 1929, table xi).

Roman Iron Age onwards (AD 1–400), inhumation was reintroduced parallel to cremation graves, and in several cases there is indirect evidence that the dead were once again buried in tree trunks (Voss and Ørnes-Christensen 1948; Andersen et al. 1991:31–2). The end of this mortuary practice comes with early Christian tree-trunk coffins of ash, oak, and lime from several places in southern Scandinavia. In Lund this type of coffin can be dendrochronologically dated to the period AD 990–1050 (Mårtensson 1976).

If tree-trunk coffins and resin-sealed vessels are considered as representations of trees, mortuary practices as well as worldviews can be placed in new perspectives. The tree-trunk coffins in particular could be given meaning by being associated with the idea that the first humans were made from two logs which floated ashore, and that the only two people to survive Ragnarok were hiding in a tree trunk (see the discussion of Hoddmimir's wood above). From this point of view, the tree-trunk coffins could be seen as reflecting the idea that death was a return to man's original vegetative form or as a rebirth comparable to the regeneration of the world after Ragnarok. At the same time, the early certain and possible datings of tree-trunk coffins mean that aspects of the world tree idea could be very old in Scandinavia.

When it comes to standing posts and logs, they may have represented either the world tree or the world pillar, but bearing in mind that these conceptions were 'functional alternatives', the specific references are less crucial in this context. There are, however, few clear archaeological examples in Scandinavia of posts or tree trunks with cosmic associations. The best example is a post placed on a central terrace near the main building at the central place at Helgö. Around the post, ritual deposits from the period 550–800 have been found, including several layers of clay. Torun Zachrisson (2004a, 2004b) has interpreted these layers of clay as counterparts to the 'shining loam' that the Norns poured over Yggdrasill according to *Vǫluspá* 19 and *Gylfaginning* 15.

Otherwise the ritual use of piles and posts is chiefly known from written sources (Drobin and Keinänen 2001), especially from Arabian descriptions from the tenth century. Ibn Fadlan records how Scandinavian merchants sacrificed food and drink to a tall wooden pole with a human-like head beside the Volga, while Al-Tartushi describes how the inhabitants of Hedeby hung up animal sacrifices on poles outside their houses (Wikander 1978; Montgomery 2000). Indirect evidence of posts and poles with ritual functions comes from the prohibition of the worship of 'staves' and 'stave enclosures' in the laws of Eidsivathing and Gotland, dated to the eleventh and thirteenth centuries, respectively (Holmbäck and Wessén 1943:207, 292; Olsson 1976; Nilsson 1992). Certain staves were clearly associated with the Old Norse pantheon, which is evident from place-names like Nälsta, meaning 'Njärd's staff' and connected with a possible goddess Njärd (Vikstrand 2001:95, 294 ff.). The by-name of the god Heimdall, Hallinskidi ('the forward-leaning staff'), could be apprehended as indirect evidence that posts with cosmological associations existed. Some scholars have taken high-seat pillars as possible representations of the world tree or world pillar. In particular, statements that 'divine nails' (*reginnaglar*) were hammered into the pillars have been regarded as an analogy to the world pillar, which was fixed by a nail to the 'immobile' Pole Star (Simek 1993:262–3; Drobin and Keinänen 2001).

These mainly indirect pieces of evidence are corroborated by a number of non-Scandinavian parallels involving posts as representations of the world tree or world axis. The best-known example comes from the Carolingian conquest and conversion of Saxony. In the Saxon stronghold of Eresburg (present-day Obermarsberg) stood Irminsul (*Irminsūl*, 'the great pillar'), which was described as a 'world column'. After the conquest of the stronghold in 772, the post was destroyed and

Figure 11. Obermarsberg from the north. The Saxon hillfort of Eresburg was situated on the site of the modern Obermarsberg. The Gothic church with its tower is clearly visible at the top of the hill. The church replaced a Carolingian church which was built on the site of the world pillar Irminsul. (Photo by the author.)

replaced by a church, by order of Charlemagne. Later the Carolingian church was replaced by a Gothic church, which is still preserved and located at the highest point of Obermarsberg (Fig. 11). The location of the church shows that Irminsul stood at the highest point of Eresburg (Palm 1948:75 ff.; Best et al. 1999; see Sundqvist 2004).

Irminsul is known only from written sources, but in Russia there are clear archaeological parallels from the same time, for example, in Perynia south of Novgorod, in Pskov, and in Tushelma near Smolensk. The common pattern is large posts or post-holes, surrounded by circles of pits, graves, or smaller posts. Several of these structures have been found in the centre of fortresses, pointing towards contexts similar to Irminsul (Słupecki 1994:122 ff.). Another archaeological example is a large post found east of the main hall at the Anglo-Saxon royal site of Yeavering in Northumberland (Hope-Taylor 1977).

These examples come from a time corresponding to the Scandinavian Late Iron Age, but both archaeological and ethnographic records show that posts and logs as representations of trees have occurred over a very long time. A very early example is 'Seahenge', which was recently found in a marshy area in eastern England. The structure consisted of a circle with a diameter of about 5 metres, composed of 55 small stakes. In the middle of the circle was a large tree trunk placed with the roots upwards. The monument can be dated by dendrochronology to 2050 BC, that is, the transition between the Neolithic and the Bronze Age in England (Pryor 2001). The upside-down construction arouses immediate associations both with Snorri's description of Yggdrasill and its one root in heaven and with other examples of the *arbor inversa* in Sámi, Siberian, and Indian traditions. As a contrast to the early Seahenge, there are also modern records of posts as symbols of the world axis, both from the Sámi of north Scandinavia and from central and northern Asia (Holmberg 1922–3). In certain parts of Siberia almost every farm had a post with an image of a bird at the top. The bird, which often symbolized an eagle, was often placed on a special little platform on top of the pole. The posts were often square in cross-section and were sometimes decorated with seven or nine grooves to mark the different worlds that surrounded the world tree. It is also worth noting that the sky-post, among the Sámi and certain ethnic groups in Altai, was supposed to be raised obliquely (de Vries 1957:388), which can be associated with Heimdall's by-name as the 'leaning' log or staff.

Archaeologically speaking, posts as representations of trees are a potentially copious type of source material, but they are difficult to interpret, above all in the form of post-holes. Only through context can ordinary posts be distinguished from special posts. The post on Helgö is just one such example where the context clearly marks its special status. There are presumably similar archaeological examples that might be noticed in the future.

Another form in which trees are represented is in images. In Scandinavia there are no explicit pictorial motifs of trees until the rock carvings of the Bronze Age and the Early Iron Age. However, images of trees are uncommon, as is clear from the fact that Østfold and Bohuslän, despite their high density of rock carvings, have only about twenty examples (Hygen and Bengtsson 1999:118–19). The question whether these pictures represent an idea of a world tree is difficult to answer, especially since it goes together with the larger problem of the general meaning of the rock carvings (see, for instance, Kaul 1998, 2004; Goldhahn 1999; Hauptman Wahlgren 2002). The only thing that might indicate cosmic trees are certain features in the depiction and composition. All the rock images of trees seem to depict coniferous trees, probably spruce or yew, and a possible background for this selection is that coniferous trees were uncommon during the Bronze Age. Therefore, they were perceived as very special – evergreens in a landscape otherwise dominated by deciduous trees with vegetation that followed the changing seasons. Some images, moreover, show a standing person at the top of the tree, a motif with direct contemporary parallels in central Europe (Hygen and Bengtsson 1999:118–19). A few rock carvings also depict a capercaillie or black grouse sitting at the top of a tree. These pictures arouse associations with the cocks in the 'gallows tree' and in Mimameid. In short, although trees seldom occur in rock carvings, the petroglyphs do not seem to depict just any tree; these are trees with distinctive characteristics and special associations with humans and birds.

For the Iron Age, pictorial representations of trees are likewise not common. They are mostly confined to motifs on Gotlandic picture stones, textiles from the Oseberg grave, and the Överhogdal tapestry. But these images give a clearer impression of being representations of mythological trees than the earlier rock carvings. Scenes with people hanging in trees occur on the picture stone from Lärbo Stora Hammars (Fig. 12) (*c.* AD 800, see Andrén 1993) and on one of the Oseberg tapestries (*c.* AD 830). The motifs arouse associations not only with Odin hanging himself in 'the windy tree', but also with the hanging victims at Gamla Uppsala described by Adam of Bremen (Solli 2004; Sundqvist 2004, 2010; Warmind 2004). As I will discuss in Chapter 4, the image of a tree on the large Gotlandic picture stone from Sanda (*c.*400–550) in particular can be pointed out as a possible depiction of the Old Norse world tree (see Fig. 47).

A possible more formalized tree representation is the mushroom-shaped image, to which I will return in Chapter 4. It is a recurring image known between the Early Bronze Age and the Migration Period. This form is above all attested on bronze razors, rock carvings, and in the form of ceremonial axes from the Bronze Age. However, a gilded silver pendant from Vännebo in Västergötland (see Fig. 48; Salin 1904:157) as well as the form of the Gotlandic picture stones (see Myrberg 2005) also arouse associations with the earlier images.

To sum up, pictorial representations show that the tree played a cer-

Figure 12. A person hanging from a tree. Detail from one of the picture stones from Stora Hammars in Lärbro on Gotland, now in the open-air museum in Bunge. (Photo by the author.)

tain part in the human conceptual world, at least from the Bronze Age onwards. But it is not until pictures from the fifth century onwards that we find associations with mythological and ritual trees in the form in which they are known from Old Norse sources. These images of trees, moreover, are so few that it is not possible to perform any detailed spatial or chronological analyses.

The third form of tree representations, and the one best suited for an archaeological study of the world tree idea, comprises monuments built of earth or stone. The classical example of this form of representation is the 'Jupiter columns' erected in the Roman period, above all in the southern Rhineland (Fig. 13). The columns are sometimes covered with oak leaves and crowned with a figure of Jupiter, and they often include symbols of the compass points and winds. The columns can be perceived as Roman interpretations of sacred Celtic oaks, and thus hybrid forms of Roman and Celtic religion (Müller 1975; Bauchhenss and Noelke 1981).

In Scandinavia, I believe that similar representations of trees should be sought among Iron Age graves, especially among those with a geometrical exterior in the form of circles, rectangles, triangles, and pointed ovals. The varied grave forms have attracted attention for a long time, but the different external shapes have primarily been used to give general datings for graves and cemeteries (Ambrosiani 1964; Hyenstrand 1974). Scholars have also assumed that the characteristic geometrical forms had different symbolic values (for example, Hyenstrand 1984; Bennett 1987), but relatively few have focused on the specific meaning of the shapes. Grave forms which have been examined from this perspective

Figure 13. Partially reconstructed Jupiter column, standing in front of the Römisch-Germanisches Museum in Mainz. (Photo by the author.)

include stone ships (Crumlin-Pedersen and Munch Tye 1995; Artelius 1996), certain barrows (Zachrisson 1994; Johansen 1997), and stone circles (Bergström 1979).

Pointed ovals, for good reasons, are referred to as 'ship-formed stone settings' or 'stone ships', and it should likewise be possible to detect 'tree settings' or 'stone trees' among Iron Age graves. In my opinion it is above all the three-pointed stone settings (also called tri-radial cairns or 'tricorns' on account of their concave sides) that could be described as 'tree settings' (Fig. 14). These have previously been interpreted as expressions of the three main Old Norse gods, Odin, Thor, and Freyr

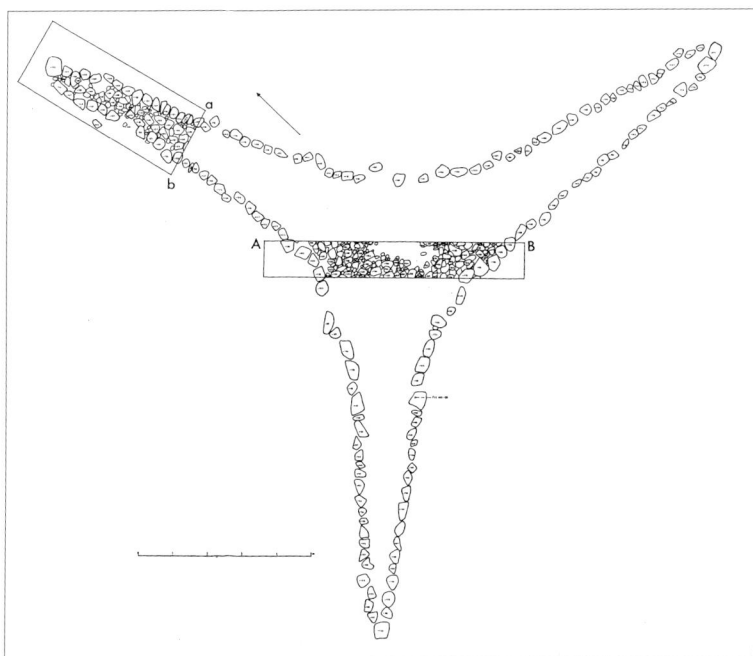

Figure 14. Three-pointed stone setting at Bjärsgård near Klippan in Skåne. (After Strömberg 1963:157.)

(Sjöborg 1822:54 ff.; Strömberg 1963), but I believe that an abstract interpretation like this does not consider the more concrete and 'representational' character of the external grave forms in the Iron Age. A more concrete interpretation of the tricorns would radically change our potential to investigate tree symbolism from an archaeological point of view. In present-day southern Sweden alone there are about 900 three-pointed stone settings from the Iron Age (Strömberg 1963; Slöjdare 1973; Hyenstrand 1984; Carlsson 1990).

The archaeology of 'tree settings'

There are four arguments for interpreting the three-pointed stone settings as 'tree settings': one semiotic, one typological, and two contextual. The semiotic argument proceeds from the unambiguous ship

49

Figure 15. Three-pointed stone setting at Seby in Segerstad on Öland. (Photo by the author.)

symbolism of ship-formed stone settings. Distinctive stones as stems of the ships, and sometimes stones to mark thwarts and masts, show that the pointed oval stone settings were built to represent ships. There is moreover a written reference, from the rune stone at Tryggevælde on Sjælland, which states that the widow had a 'ship' (*skaiþ*) erected in memory of her late husband (Moltke 1976:182). Stone ships, in other words, show that the geometric figures in the varied language of graves did not correspond to abstract principles, but instead were 'representational' images of central phenomena in Scandinavian culture. Stone ships were erected from the Late Bronze Age until the Viking Age, which also shows that the forms of representation could be in use for a very long time, but probably with varying meanings (Crumlin-Pedersen and Munch Tye 1995; Artelius 1996). The example of the stone ships thus opens the semiotic possibility that other graves with geometric shapes were constructed as representations of important cultural phenomena. Besides stone ships, this applies at least to 'tree settings' (three-pointed

Figure 16. Three-pointed stone setting at Herresta in Odensala, Uppland. The monument no longer exists, but it had a huge monolith in the centre, standing about 3 metres high. (After Dybeck 1865, figure 16.)

stone settings) and 'house settings' (rectangular stone settings, sometimes with convex long sides). In this context, however, I shall confine myself to discussing only 'tree settings'.

The typological argument is based on the similarity in the shape of three-pointed stone settings and descriptions of Yggdrasill. The mythological tree is described in two different contexts as having a crown, a trunk, and three roots which reach out to other worlds. Tricorns can be built up of earth, of a mixture of earth and stone, or entirely of stone (Fig. 15). Irrespective of how they are built, they often consist of long, narrow points ending in a distinctive stone. In addition, there is sometimes a central stone, which in certain cases has the shape of a monolith (Fig. 16). In some Norwegian examples two stones are placed in the centre (Grav Ellingsen 2003). In several excavated monuments a post-hole has been found in the centre, showing that a wooden post could also have stood in the middle. In other words, the three-pointed stone settings may be viewed as representations of the trunk (sometimes of wood, sometimes of stone) and three roots (sometimes of earth, sometimes of stone) of the world tree. The contextual arguments are based on the placing of the three-pointed stone settings and their content. They are primarily found in Iron Age grave-fields, but in some parts of southern Sweden more than 30 per cent of tricorns are solitaries, showing no connection with any other visible graves. When found in burial grounds, normally just a few three-pointed stone settings occur in each one, and it is not uncommon that there is just one tricorn in a cemetery even when it contains many graves (Slöjdare 1973; Carlsson 1990; Myhre 2005). The tricorns, singly or as groups of a few, are often located at the highest point of the burial ground (Fig. 17). A single three-pointed stone setting can also be the centre of a burial ground, surrounded by distinct groups of graves (Stylegar 2006). In certain cases they are the oldest monuments in the cemetery (for example Petré 1984), and in several other instances they have deliberately been covered by later graves or they themselves overlie earlier structures (Hållans Stenholm 2006; 2012). The occurrence of three-pointed stone settings inside and outside burial grounds clearly demonstrates that they represented special monuments in time and place. In several cases they seem by their date and placing to have been the starting point or the spatial focus of the cemeteries. The special character of the three-pointed stone settings is further underlined by examples from south-western Norway. Two tricorns are found at *tun* sites, which are discussed in the next chapter, whereas several are found close to churches. One exceptional case is the church at Avaldsnes on Karmøy, which was probably erected on the site of a tricorn. Two monoliths marking two of the points are still standing in the churchyard, one of them being very close to the church wall (Hernæs 1999; Myhre 2005).

In view of the special character of three-pointed stone settings, the finds they yield are surprisingly simple. At least 120 examples have been excavated in Scandinavia, but only about 65 per cent of these have yielded cremated bones and grave finds (Arbman 1940; Ramskou 1951, 1976; Skjelsvik 1951; Kivikoski 1963; Strömberg 1963; Slöjdare 1973; Carlsson 1990; Grav Ellingsen 2003; Myhre 2005). The objects are normally very basic, and in only about fifteen cases do we find the type of objects traditionally used to determine the sex of the buried person. These objects primarily indicate men's graves, but double graves with both

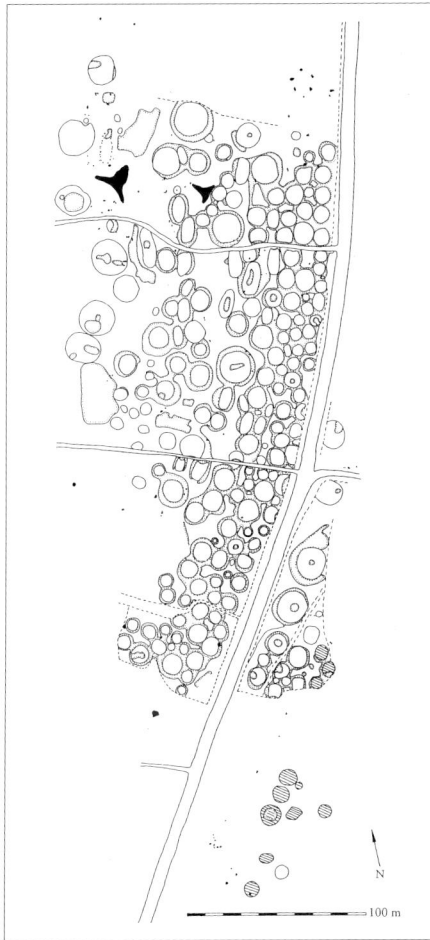

Figure 17. The Kånna Högar burial ground in Småland. The grave-field is dominated by grave mounds, but in the north-western part of the site there are two three-pointed stone settings. The larger one is situated on the highest point of the burial ground. (After Svanberg 2003:190.)

men and women also occur (Slöjdare 1973:13 ff.; Carlsson 1990:28 ff.; Grav Ellingsen 2003; Myhre 2005). About 35 per cent of the excavated three-pointed stone settings contain neither human bones nor grave finds, and in some of these 'empty graves' all that is left are hearths and charcoal layers with no remains of cremated bones (Carlsson 1990:27; Grav Ellingsen 2003). The question is whether these monuments were graves at all in the conventional sense, and therefore the tricorns have long been discussed in terms of 'cultic structures' (Strömberg 1963). A particularly clear example showing that tricorns did not just mark

53

graves can be found on Helgö, where a tricorn was placed on the terrace mentioned above (with its ritual deposits) where a post had been
raised. Since the centre of the tricorn corresponds to the location of
the earlier post, the stone setting may have been a new representation
of a world tree or world pillar on the site (Zachrisson 2004a, 2004b).
Based on these four arguments, then, I would interpret the three-
pointed stone settings as 'tree settings', that is, as representations of trees.
This means that it is also possible to conduct a more systematic study
of tree symbolism in pre-Christian Scandinavia from an archaeological
perspective. Tricorns occur primarily in southern and central Sweden
and in southern and central Norway. There are occasional sites with
tricorns in Denmark and Skåne, in western and northern Norway, and
along the Norrland coast in Sweden. Tricorns are found on the Åland
islands, but none in mainland Finland, nor in the agricultural districts
of Jämtland, Härjedalen, or Dalarna, nor on the islands of Gotland
or Bornholm (Ramskou 1951, 1976; Skjelsvik 1951; Kivikoski 1963;
Strömberg 1963; Glob 1967; Slöjdare 1973; Hyenstrand 1984; Carlsson
1990; Grav Ellingsen 2003; Myhre 2005). Outside Scandinavia, a few
three-pointed stone settings have recently been found in eastern Northumberland, probably dating to the Late Bronze Age (Ford et al. 2002).
     In Scandinavia, three-pointed stone settings are very clearly con-
nected to Iron Age cremation customs. Those three-pointed stone
settings which contain burials are all cremation graves (Slöjdare 1973;
Carlsson 1990; Myhre 2005), with a single exception from the village
of Danmark in Uppland (Rundkvist Westholm 2008). At Birka there
are about 70 tricorns, occurring only in areas with cremation graves,
while inhumations on the island are geographically separate from the
tricorns (Arbman 1940; Gräslund 1980). The link with cremation graves
can also partly explain the uneven distribution of tricorns in Scandinavia. When graves appear in southern Scandinavia during the Late
Iron Age, they were usually inhumations. This means that three-pointed
stone settings are found only in areas or at sites where cremation was
practised, for example, in northern Skåne and in Danish cemeteries
with cremation graves, such as at Lindholm Høje in northern Jutland
(Ramskou 1951, 1976; Strömberg 1963; Carlie 1994).
     The excavated three-pointed stone settings which can be dated belong
to the period from the Late Roman Iron Age to the Viking Age (200–
1050 AD). During this period the form of these monuments changed;

instead of having only slightly concave sides the triangles began to be built with more strongly curving sides and distinctly marked points (Carlsson 1990:18 ff.; Myhre 2005). This typological change means that the origin of tricorns can probably be sought in examples of stone triangles with perfectly straight sides, which generally date from the Pre-Roman Iron Age to the Migration Period (500 BC to AD 550). The straight triangles often have larger stones marking the three points and the centre (see Grav Ellingsen 2003). They could therefore also be viewed as a form of 'tree settings'. Apart from the shape, stone triangles share other similarities with the tricorns. Stone triangles never make up grave-fields of their own: they occur as single monuments in cemeteries. In some cases, moreover, the triangles are among the oldest structures in the cemetery and are at the highest location (Andersson 1996). Like the three-pointed stone settings, they are most common in southern and central Sweden and in central Norway, and they are clearly associated with Iron Age cremation customs (Hyenstrand 1984:81 ff.).

Triangular stone settings also occur among the so-called lake graves, that is, graves situated by lakes in northern Scandinavia, far away from the traditional agricultural districts. The lake graves, which range in date from the start of our era until the Viking Age, are connected to the hunting grounds in the interior of northern Scandinavia. Their cultural background is disputed (Österman 1994; Ramqvist 2007), but some sites with triangular stone settings contain deposits of elk and reindeer antlers. Since these features have been connected to Sámi burial customs, some of the triangular stone settings in northern Scandi-navia may have represented hunters and gatherers of Sámi background (Mebius 1968:96; Zachrisson 1997).

To sum up, the interpretation of tricorns as 'tree settings' means that tree symbolism persisted for over 800 years. But if we also include the stone triangles, the chronological span can be extended back another 700 years. The stone triangles in the hunting grounds also open the possibility of a Sámi connection. In view of this, the question is how the meaning ascribed to these monuments may have varied in time and place.

The semiotics of the 'tree settings'

Stone tricorns and triangles may thus be generally interpreted as representations of trees. But the concrete meaning of these monuments has no doubt varied through time and place, in the same way as stone ships had changing meanings (Crumlin-Pedersen and Munch Tye 1995). Clues to the specific meaning of 'tree settings' should be sought in a combination of their 'representational' character, their connection with cremation, and the local contexts. Crucial aspects in the local contexts are the size and design of the monuments, their special placing, and their content. In the following, I provide some examples of possible cosmological, ritual, and social meanings of the 'tree settings'. I will do that solely with the aid of the three-pointed stone settings since these are better documented than stone triangles, even though similar meanings can probably be ascribed to them.

The fundamental meaning of three-pointed stone settings can be construed as 'trees', and apart from this association with trees, the link with Iron Age cremation customs is a common feature of the tricorns. Interestingly, this was also an aspect stressed in local traditions about three-pointed stone settings in the middle of the nineteenth century. Richard Dybeck states about a tricorn in Södertörn that 'the old people say that much fire used to burn in the tricorn, and that the fire is still not completely extinguished, although it is only seen on certain nights' and that this 'old folk notion' survives 'in the whole country' (Dybeck 1865:25–6, my translation).

When it comes to the more specific meaning of the tricorns, several different scenarios can be outlined. Cosmological significance could be argued for some three-pointed stone settings standing alone, and unconnected to other graves. Sometimes they are highly monumental, stoutly built, with a distance of up to 25–30 metres between the points. They could be used to mark actual trees of a more or less 'sacred' kind, especially if they have no grave and originally lacked a central stone. The marking of a tree in these cases need not have had any connection with burials, and an example of this situation is the tricorn on the central ritual terrace on Helgö (Zachrisson 2004a, 2004b).

In other contexts, cosmological as well as ritual meanings to the three-pointed stone settings can be suggested. Many cemeteries contained only one tricorn, often in an elevated or central location. Such a

Figure 18. The burial ground at Borre in Vestfold. All the famous royal mounds at the site consist of cremations from *c.* AD 500 to *c.* AD 1000. The mounds are placed as a kind of semicircle around a large three-pointed stone setting, which can be viewed as the centre of the burial ground. (After Liestøl 1975; see Myhre and Gansum 2003:52–3.)

three-pointed stone setting can be regarded as the centre of the cemetery, or the focus of the cremation rituals performed at the site. The actual tricorn could have marked a real tree or a post, or it might have been a representation in stone of a tree connected with the cremations on the site. Bearing in mind that some three-pointed stone settings contain only large layers of charcoal, they could thus have marked the site of the actual fire, perhaps evoking associations with the world tree and its fate at Ragnarok. A good example of a centrally located three-pointed stone setting is at the Borre cemetery in Vestfold (Myhre 2003), where the well-known huge burial mounds with cremation graves are placed in a semicircle around a large tricorn, which may have been the ritual centre of the site (Fig. 18). A comparable context, but with a real tree as the focus, is Frösö. Before the church was built there, the excavated birch stood as a votive tree at the centre of a burial ground of barrows (Rentzhog 1987).

Social meanings must also have been ascribable to the three-pointed stone settings, since many cemeteries comprise several small tricorns and some of these monuments contain graves as well. On a general level, these monuments could mark the graves of persons connected with ideas about the world tree, the origin of knowledge, the creation of man, and the fate of the world after Ragnarok. The three-pointed stone settings could thus have marked the graves of different types of religious specialists with particular knowledge of the world (Sundqvist 1998, 2007). An argument for this interpretation is that some tricorns contain iron rings with pendants in the shape of a Thor's hammer (Slöjdare 1973:15, 28; Carlsson 1990:28). Long ago, Nils Henric Sjöborg touched on the idea of religious specialists, as he believed that certain three-pointed stone settings could have been graves for 'sacrificial priests' (Sjöborg 1822:55 ff.). But the three-pointed stone setting may also have marked persons connected with the local village tree or farm tree, to which modern-day guardian trees in some sense correspond. The tricorns in these cases could have marked the connection between person, tree, and settlement, especially for a person who 'founded' a farm or village with the trees belonging to it. Since a person like this had in a way 'created' the world from a local perspective, there could also have been associations with the world tree of the myths.

It is thus likely that several different specific meanings could exist for three-pointed stone settings in the same place. An example of prob-able parallel meanings for three-pointed stone settings is Birka, where virtually all of the over 70 tricorns are small or very small, while of the 17 excavated monument 13 are graves (Arbman 1940). Following the discussion above, these ought to mark the graves of persons who had special connections with trees and ideas about trees. The four 'empty' three-pointed stone settings are in three different burial grounds and may have symbolized the world tree or world pillar in these ceme-teries. In Hemlanden, the biggest grave-field at Birka, besides two of the 'empty' small tricorns, there is also a very large freestanding tricorn

(Arbman 1940, plate I, square N8). This big three-pointed stone setting has not been excavated, but it can probably be interpreted as having been a special focus for cremation rituals in the cemetery. If the small 'empty' three-pointed stone settings marked standing posts, the big three-pointed stone setting could have marked an actual tree or perhaps the site of a central pyre for cremations in the cemetery.

The world from the view-point of 'tree settings'

Place-names referring to solitary trees clearly show that trees were important during the Iron Age in Scandinavia. However, as archaeological objects, trees are truly evasive, and only through the interpretation of three-pointed stone settings as tree settings can we get a glimpse of the importance of the tree. Accordingly, this interpretation has consequences beyond the monuments themselves and the burial grounds where the tricorns are located. In the following I will provide some hypothetical arguments about trees in Iron Age settlements, on the basis of three-pointed stone settings.

Our perception of Iron Age settlement and its relation to Old Norse cosmology can be affected by the interpretation of three-pointed stone settings as well. Traditionally, the solitary farm was regarded as the basic unit of Iron Age settlement in Scandinavia. The solitary farm was therefore viewed as the background to the Old Norse idea of Midgard, as the place of humans in the world (de Vries 1957:272). Archaeological excavations in recent decades, however, have shown that Iron Age settlement was much more complex and varied. It could consist of solitary farms, but also of loosely composed villages (Fallgren 1998, 2006), densely built villages (Hvass 1988), estates (Skre 1998), and large, permanent, central places (Hårdh and Larsson 2002). Yet despite the breadth of variation in settlement, the question remains: what was the basic unit? Was it the farm, the village, or the estate? The three-pointed stone settings, interpreted as a representation of a tree, could shed new light on this debate. Since tricorns do not occur in all cemeteries in any area, their distribution shows that certain cemeteries, and hence indirectly certain settlements, were associated with trees and ideas about trees, while others were not. This difference could be apprehended as a contrast between, on the one hand, settlements with trees or representations of trees which were perceived as 'the centre of the world' and, on the other hand, settlements which lacked these associations. In social terms, the difference could be expressed as an estate (with tree and three-pointed stone settings) versus its subject farms (without tree or three-pointed stone settings). This perspective accords well with many of the monumental tricorns in the Mälaren valley as well as in Rogaland and Trøndelag. They mostly occur in cemeteries with large barrows, which in other contexts are usually pointed out as expressions of large farms and estates in the Iron Age (Hyenstrand 1974:22, 1984:79 ff.; Grav Ellingsen 2003:75 ff.; Myhre 2005).

Another field of study, which could be renewed with the aid of three-pointed stone settings, is the relationship between settlement and cemetery. Traditionally, this has been viewed as an uncomplicated one-to-one relationship – that is to say, that one settlement used one burial ground. This is the assumption underlying a great deal of the cemetery-based settlement archaeology (for example, Ambrosiani 1964; Hyenstrand 1974; Wijkander 1983). The excavations of recent years have shown, however, that the situation is more complex, with settlements without graves, with settlements that used several burial grounds simultaneously (Petré 1984), or grave-fields used by several different settlements at the same time (for example, Liljeholm 1999). The latter relationship, in particular, could be illuminated by cemeteries containing several contemporary three-pointed stone settings. An illustrative example is a large Viking Age burial ground at Stora Dalby in central Öland (Beskow Sjöberg 1987:80 ff.). The burial ground contains eleven three-pointed stone settings, which could represent several different villages using the grave-field at the same time. This interpretation is supported by the fact that the cemetery, which is the only securely attested Viking Age cemetery in the area, is surrounded by several villages with names ending in -stad and -by. The burial ground at Stora Dalby may in this way have been a district cemetery in the Viking Age, and thus a forerunner of the medieval churchyards.

A third discussion point, on which the three-pointed stone settings could provide new perspectives, is the relationship between cemeteries, settlements, and place-names. Comparisons between settlements and place-names are often made today on a very general level, since there is a serious risk of circular argument, for example, in attempts to date place-names archaeologically (Lönn 1999; Vikstrand 2001, 2013). However, in contexts where three-pointed stone settings can be interpreted as marking the graves of people who 'founded' a settlement with a 'village tree' or 'farm tree', these monuments could allow new angles on the discussion. In several cases, the three-pointed stone settings belong to the oldest stratum of graves in a continuously used cemetery. The tricorns, as expressions of a newly founded settlement with a 'village tree', could then be used to date the adjacent settlement and the name it bears. An example is the cemetery at Lunda on the island of Lovö, where the oldest graves can be dated to the Migration Period (400–550), among them two three-pointed stone settings (Petré 1984). The name Lunda for this place could thus go back to the fifth century. In other cases there are three-pointed stone settings, which were placed over older graves, suggesting a breach in continuity and a renewal of burials and settlement as well as the place-name. An example of this situation is the totally excavated burial ground at Fiskeby in Östergötland (Lundström 1965, 1970). The cemetery was used continuously from the end of the Bronze Age, but during the Viking Age (800–1050) two tricorns were placed right over graves from the Early Iron Age. The tricorns can be interpreted as a new occupation of a cemetery that had been used for a long time, and may thereby have alluded to a renewal or new foundation of an adjacent settlement, which may also have been given a new name. The name Fiskeby could thus be dated by means of the three-pointed stone settings to the Viking Age, even though the cemetery as a whole originated in the Late Bronze Age.

A fourth area where this interpretation of tricorns could influence archaeological perceptions and future excavations is Iron Age settlement and its relation to real trees. Three-pointed stones-settings may have been built around special trees or referred to some kind of 'farm tree' or 'village tree', while trees in place-names simultaneously emphasize the crucial significance of real trees in Iron Age society. It is therefore essential to develop techniques for looking for real trees, and to discuss which indirect traces might hint at the existence of important trees in a settlement.

Trees may have been surrounded by constructions in various ways, such as by cairns, stone settings, and tricorns. An example can be taken from the remains of an Iron Age village at Valsnäs on Öland (Fig. 19). Between stone foundations of the farms, which can be dated to the Late Roman Iron Age and Migration Period (200–550) there is a small solitary three-pointed stone setting (Stenberger 1933:94). Since graves

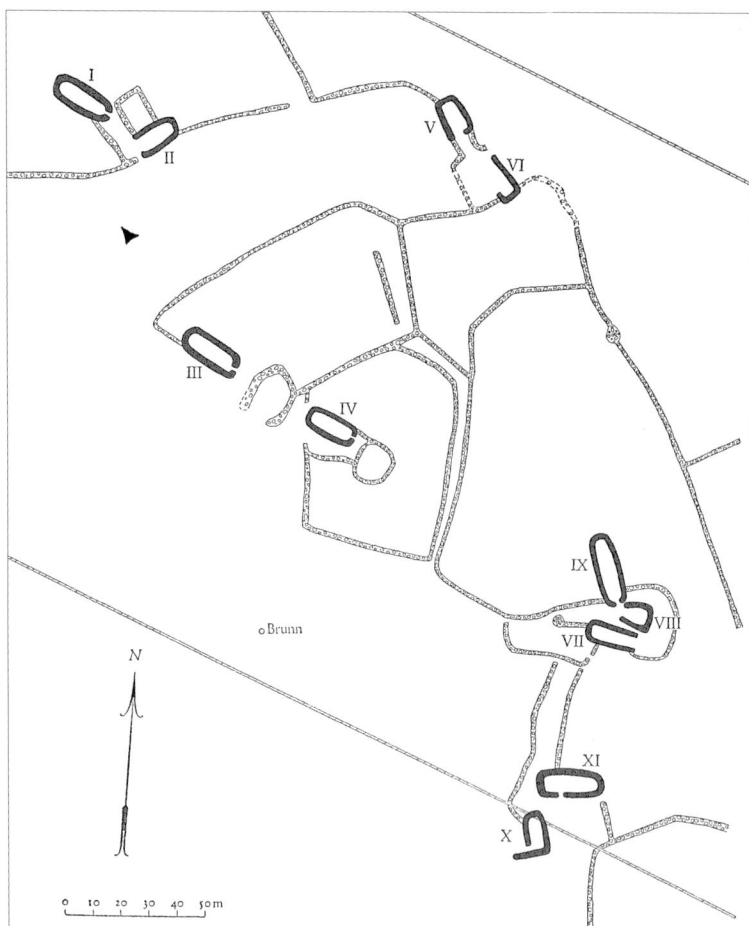

Figure 19. Remains of an Iron Age village at Valsnäs in Löt on Öland. In the western part of the village there is a three-pointed stone setting. Since graves on Öland normally were located at some distance from the settlements, this three-pointed stone setting is probably not a grave, but more plausibly marks a village tree. (After Stenberger 1933:94.)

were usually put on the periphery of these villages (Fallgren 2006), this centrally placed tricorn must have had a different function, most probably marking the 'village tree'.

The location of trees may also be detected by means of absences, because people due to the holiness probably avoided everyday activities around the local tree. The totally excavated Jutlandic village of Hodde from the late Pre-Roman Iron Age (150–1 BC) could be an example of this (Hvass 1985). The village consisted of farms grouped around an open green, which has been interpreted above all as a place where the village livestock was rounded up. But the open place was not uniform. Large parts of the area contained finds and pits, but an area to the south-west lacked pits and finds, but included a cremation. The area totally lacking finds beside the cremation grave could have marked the site of a central tree on the green.

Another possible way of finding indirect traces of trees is based on the supposition that settlements were organized in relation to an important tree, which means that the site of a central tree should be obvious from the organization of a settlement in time and place. An example of this context could be the totally excavated Jutlandic village of Vorbasse (Hvass 1988; see Holst 2004). The settlement consisted of a village with farms moving a short distance every generation from around 100 BC until around AD 1100 (Holst 2004). The successive movement of the settlement was inscribed in a large circle, and the centre of this circle was a small rise in the otherwise flat landscape. The circular movement may have been dictated by a 'village tree' on this spot, which thus could have marked the continuity of settlement, although the farms were founded and refounded every generation.

The tree in Old Norse religion

In this investigation I have tried to show that a conceptual figure such as the Old Norse world tree can be discussed and studied from an archaeological perspective. But the question is what new insights this archaeological survey has yielded in relation to the debate about the world tree in the historical study of religion.

As we have seen, Bugge regards the Old Norse world tree as a Christian idea, while most other scholars perceive the world tree concept as a very archaic stratum of pre-Christian Scandinavian religion, without specifying more closely what this could mean in terms of absolute dating. Opinions about the historical origin of this figure of thought are likewise divergent. Mannhardt sees the guardian tree and the 'primitive' cult of animated nature as the original model for the world tree, but without stating where this idea came from. For Holmberg, the 'civilizations' in India and the Middle East are the origin of the idea of a world tree or world pillar. De Vries claims instead that the figure of thought belongs to the original Indo-European conceptual core of Old Norse religion. He moreover believes that the idea of the world tree is a variant of a more primordial notion of a celestial axis, with the post-built house as its ultimate model. In contrast, Collinder, and after him Palm and Hultkrantz, point to the circumpolar area as the source of the idea of a world pillar, which could therefore have been communicated to Scandinavians via the Sámi. Hultkrantz declares that the idea goes all the way back to Mesolithic and Palaeolithic round huts with a central post.

Archaeology can scarcely provide any unambiguous answers in this debate, but can be used to put cosmological phenomena in temporal and spatial contexts. When it comes to chronology, an exceptional find like Seahenge suggests that a notion of an upside-down world tree existed in north-western Europe as early as 2050 BC, at the transition from the Neolithic to the Early Bronze Age. In Scandinavia, both oak coffins from the fourteenth century BC and rock carvings indicate a metaphorical link between humans and trees. The indirect traces of tree-trunk coffins in the Late Neolithic (2400–2000 BC) hint at similar ideas from the same time as Seahenge. Certain features of the world tree idea may thus have been very old.

On the other hand, the stone triangles (500 BC – AD 550) and the tricorns (AD 200–1050) are evidence of a successively formalized representation of the Old Norse world tree over more than 1,500 years. It is not until the period from the Late Roman Iron Age to the Migration Period (200–550) that the cosmic tree found a shape that can be recognized in Old Norse literature. It was expressed through the increasingly marked points of the tricorns and through the cosmic image of the Sanda stone (see Chapter 4).

As for the relationship between the idea of the world tree, real trees, representations of trees, and people, there are also certain tendencies that should be highlighted. Real trees are difficult to detect archaeologically, but occasional finds, along with indirect hints and place-names referring to particular trees, underline the central role of trees in relation to the estates and central places of the Iron Age. These trees and posts may be viewed as both models for and representations of the world tree, since the mental world and the real world must have influenced each other in constant interplay. If my hypothesis about Vorbasse is correct, the possible central tree surrounded by a continuously moving settlement could be viewed as an analogy to the various world trees that were associated with the ages of the mythic world. The nine worlds which, according to *Vǫluspá*, surrounded the 'measuring tree' (Schjødt 1992) can thus be perceived as both spatial and temporal if one uses Vorbasse as a model.

The idea of a connection between people and trees may have emerged in the same way in interaction between trees, tree symbols, and graves. Hollowed-out tree trunks were used as coffins perhaps as long ago as the Late Neolithic, and at least in the Early Bronze Age, and once again starting in the Roman Iron Age when inhumation was resumed in southern Scandinavia. Stone triangles and three-pointed stone settings, on the other hand, can be associated with the custom of cremation from the Pre-Roman Iron Age until the Viking Age (500 BC – AD 1050), above all in those parts of Scandinavia where inhumation remained uncommon in the Iron Age. In these links between graves and tree symbols it is possible to see both a source of inspiration and an expression of the idea of humankind's vegetative origin. In the same way, there may have been an analogy between trees and death in the mental world as well as in the real world. Before the construction of the church over the birch at Frösö, the tree stood as a focus for the surrounding barrow cemetery, just as certain three-pointed stone settings were the central points of grave-fields, for example, at Borre. The placing of the birch and the single three-pointed stone setting can therefore be said to correspond to the mythical tree Lærad that stood by Valhall, which was not just Odin's residence but also the realm of the dead for fallen warriors.

To sum up, I believe that archaeology above all can demonstrate a complex picture of the Old Norse idea of the world tree, which cannot be reduced to a primordial and unchanging idea. Instead, it is possible to sketch an alternative and more complex scenario for this particular figure of thought and its history. Since trees have been of great significance everywhere, the basis for the idea of a world tree must be sought in the huge metaphorical potential of trees, as 'unchanging' but growing constants in the landscape and as a fundamental source for human activity. This universal basis has then been activated differently in various historical contexts. The striking similarities in detail between the Old Norse world tree and ideas about trees in other parts of Europe and Asia indicate some form of historical connection, but how this should be perceived is not obvious.

An archaic stratum in the figure of thought is perfectly possible, especially with Seahenge in mind and its parallels with Old Norse, Sámi, Siberian, and Indian traditions. In the Bronze Age, the oak coffins and the trees depicted in rock carvings hint at ideas about trees with special relationships to humans and birds. The background to these ideas is obscure, but like a number of other phenomena in the Early Bronze Age they may derive from central Europe (Lomborg 1973:112 ff.) and ultimately from the eastern Mediterranean (Kristiansen 2004; Kristiansen and Larsson 2005). In the Iron Age, there was a general spread in the expressions of world trees, in the form of stone triangles and three-pointed stone settings. This spread can probably be linked to the custom of farm trees or village trees, as suggested by pre-Viking Age place-names. But it was not until the period 200–550 that the expressions for the world tree became so formalized that they resemble the descriptions in Old Norse literature. Bearing in mind that this period is characterized by distinctly Roman hybrids in Scandinavian society, it is therefore highly probable that the figure of thought of the Old Norse world tree was crucially influenced by the Roman and Late Roman world, including early Christianity. The similarities to representations of trees in the Mediterranean area and the Middle East may therefore be due to cultural encounters. A result of these interactions may have been that motifs from classical traditions, such as the tree of life and the tree of knowledge, were incorporated into existing Old Norse traditions.

The question of a possible association between Old Norse and circumpolar traditions is difficult to answer with the aid of archaeology. The sometimes striking parallels in the ideas of a world tree suggest that there are connections, but the historical contexts of these parallels are unclear. A relationship between Sámi and Old Norse conceptions about trees is suggested by the triangular stone settings that are found among the so-called lake graves in northern Scandinavia. But since stone triangles occur earlier in the Scandinavian agricultural districts than in the hunting grounds, the parallel grave forms suggest rather that this form of expression was transmitted from Scandinavian to Sámi culture.

In other words, from an archaeological point of view, the Old Norse idea of a world tree seems to be a hybrid, or a figure of thought with many roots. It was gradually built up, partly through interaction with other areas over a long time, partly through interaction between the lived and the thought world. The practice of using real trees and representations of trees has both influenced and been influenced by the conceptual world. In the world of myth, likewise, we cannot find any uniform idea of the Old Norse world tree, since the myths are clearly variations on a theme. The tree has different names, partially different attributes, and occurs in different mythic contexts. These variations may be viewed as expressions of the narrative structure of the myths, but they can also be perceived as expressions of the hybrid character of the figure of thought. The variations, in other words, may be regarded as marking the idea of the world tree as composed of several elements, differing in their origin, history, and context.

Figure 20. The south-west gate at Ismantorp ringfort. This gate is the narrowest of the nine gates that give access to the ringfort. (Photo by the author.)

CHAPTER 3

A world of stone
Warrior culture and
Old Norse cosmology

'Ismantorp fort is undeniably one of the most interesting of Öland's prehistoric defensive structures and one of the most remarkable ring-forts in our country as a whole.' This is how the Swedish archaeologist Mårten Stenberger (1898–1973) begins his description of Ismantorp in his classic dissertation on Öland in the Early Iron Age (Stenberger 1933:235, my translation). Archaeologists often declare their finds to be unique and sensational, but in this case Stenberger's words are fully justified. Ismantorp fort, located in the middle of the long, narrow island of Öland in the Baltic Sea, is amazingly well preserved. Even after one and a half millennia it still presents visitors with a ring-wall four metres high, surrounding almost a hundred fully visible house foundations of limestone. Nine gateways in the wall give access to the fort (Fig. 20), and at its centre there is a small open place.

This remarkable ringfort has been described, measured, and interpreted since the 1630s. Archaeological excavations have been conducted at the end of the nineteenth century and during the first four decades of the twentieth century. After extensive clearance of thick vegetation in and around the fort in the 1940s, the site has been a popular tourist attraction, and the ruin fires the imagination so strongly that it has even figured in a Swedish detective novel (Mårtenson 1987). In archaeological terms, the fort is remarkable because the ruin is so well preserved yet we know so little about the site. The old excavations have yielded very few results. No occupation layers or datable objects have been found, only scattered animal bones and pieces of charcoal.

Although our knowledge of the place is slight, the generally accepted interpretation was formulated by Stenberger nearly ninety years ago (Stenberger 1925, 1933:236 ff.; cf. Näsman 1997). He believed that Ismantorp served as a place of refuge in times of unrest during the Migration Period (400–550). Moreover, Stenberger claims that it was used as a central cultic site, since the nine gates were not suitable for defending a fort. In his interpretation, he refers to late Slavic strongholds from the eleventh and twelfth centuries, which functioned as places of refuge as well as ritual sites. One of the examples, Rethra/Radegost, a stronghold that has never been localized, is even described as having nine gates (Stenberger 1925, 1933:241–2; Słupecki 1994:51 ff.). Stenberger's words contain a fantastic possibility. If his hypothesis is correct, the well-preserved fort of Ismantorp could give us a total picture of a pre-Christian cultic site. The monument could thus play a crucial role in the discussion of pre-Christian ritual and religion, but the interesting thing is that Ismantorp never assumed that role. Neither archaeologists nor historians of religion refer to the fort in connection with Old Norse religion. The reason for this silence is largely due to Stenberger himself. In the absence of direct evidence for ritual activities, he never generalized his interpretation of Ismantorp. Instead the interpretation remained an ad hoc explanation of a remarkable ruin.

To renew the discussion about Ismantorp, I revisited the ringfort in 1997–2001. The circumstances of these visits are different from those encountered by Stenberger when he did his fieldwork in the 1920s and 1930s. The nearby and contemporary ringfort of Eketorp was totally excavated in 1964–74, and the results of those excavations are an important point of reference for Ismantorp (Borg et al. 1976; Boessneck et al. 1979; Borg 1998). In addition, the archaeological discussion of forts has changed character in the last few decades. The very concept of 'ringfort' or 'hillfort' (Swedish *fornborg*) has been questioned, and the variation in these structures in both time and place has been stressed. The connection of the forts with wars and periods of unrest has also been criticized for being stereotypical. My visits have not found any support for Stenberger's interpretation, but they have made it possible to put Ismantorp in other contexts which are at least as relevant for the discussion of both Scandinavian forts and the character of Old Norse religion.

A biography of Ismantorp

In this connection it is only possible to give a brief account of the fieldwork in 1997–2001, which was carried out in collaboration with Kalmar County Museum. In view of the disappointing results of previous excavations, a great deal of effort was expended on general surveys. Firstly, a new detailed plan of the fort and the topography was drawn up, based on rectified aerial photographs (Fig. 21).

The fort at Ismantorp was built on a dry moraine hillock, which rises just a few metres above a flat landscape with large shallow bogs and wetlands. The distances to the nearest settlements, both in the present and in the past, are one to two kilometres. The site was never permanently inhabited, because no occupation layers have been found either inside or outside the ring-wall.

The fort consists of a drystone limestone ring-wall 410 metres long with nine gates. Three of these openings, in the south, the west, and the north-east, are wide main gates, and from each a street leads directly to the centre of the fort, which consists of a triangular square. Outside two of the main gates there are special outworks, consisting in the north-east of a low rampart of earth and stone and in the south of a zone with closely placed granite boulders. In both cases the openings in the outworks are displaced counter-clockwise in relation to the gates in the ring-wall. The six smaller gates are narrower and in the final phase of the settlement they have no direct communication with the centre of the fort. Moreover, one of the smaller gates leads first into a house situated on the inside of the wall, and from this house into a narrow lane beside the building.

Inside the ring-wall, a total of 95 houses were built, 49 of them against the wall, 45 in three blocks in the centre and one small semi-circular building in the centre. Of the 49 houses along the ring-wall 5 were built parallel to the wall and not radially from it like the rest of the houses. Judging by joints between the foundations, the houses were built in several stages. At least two main phases of the settlement can be discerned, although they are not possible to date in absolute terms. The first phase consisted of all the houses along the ring-wall and nine small groups of houses in the interior, placed so that all the nine gates communicated with the centre of the ringfort (Fig. 22). In the second phase, further houses were irregularly built between the nine groups

Figure 21. Aerial photo of Ismantorp ringfort. (Photo by Metria, Norrköping.)

of houses, thereby creating three main blocks and three main streets linking the main gates with the centre.

It has not been possible to ascertain the functions of the houses on the basis of the few finds. On the other hand, differences in building methods, which are also known from the historical settlement on the island, can be used to classify the houses broadly into different categories (see Stenberger 1933:93, 104–10). Based on the historical analogies, 55 houses with gable foundations can be interpreted as dwellings and workshops, while 39 houses without gable foundations were probably byres, stables, barns, and stores. The different types of houses can be found in all parts of the fort (Fig. 23).

The areas inside and outside the ring-wall were searched by metal detector and georadar. The metal detector survey only yielded modern objects, whereas the georadar survey basically confirmed a few anomalies that were already visible as shallow depressions. From the results of these surveys, excavations were conducted during two seasons. Test squares were dug in the central parts of ten houses in order to obtain charcoal for dating. Besides this, seven smaller trenches were dug in the open areas between the houses. In the test squares and the small trenches, some charcoal was found, as well as a few sherds of un-decorated Iron Age pottery, a few pieces of iron slag, and small pieces of burnt animal bones from sheep/goat, cattle and horse (Sigvallius 1994).

Of special interest in this context are two trenches that were opened in the centre of the ringfort (Fig. 24). The centre of the fort consisted of a triangular open place with a small semicircular house at its eastern end. In the middle of the open area a large pit was discovered, containing earth, charcoal, and unburnt cattle bones. Alongside the pit was a fireplace, and beside the fireplace a bow of an iron fibula of Haraldsted type was found which dates from the middle of the fourth century to the end of the fifth century (Norling-Christensen 1957; Brinch Madsen 1975). Close to the large pit was a lancehead without its socket, deposited in a small pit. With its rhomboid form the lancehead can be dated to the sixth century, according to parallels in a weapon deposit at Balsmyr on Bornholm (Nørgård Jørgensen 2009).

At the east end of the central square the semicircular house was partly excavated. The excavations revealed that the house had been partially destroyed, leaving only impressions of some of the foundations in the ground. Probably the destruction was deliberate, since all other houses are well preserved. In a small pit towards the middle of the house was found a narrow arrowhead with triangular cross-section, but without the point (Fig. 25). Judging by parallels on Gotland, it can be dated to the fifth or sixth centuries (Nerman 1935, fig. 599–600). East of the semicircular house a dugout post-hole was discovered, with stones scattered around the post-hole showing that it had once been stone-lined. The post had been placed between the small house and the houses in the eastern block of the fort.

The nine gates are oriented towards the large pit in the central

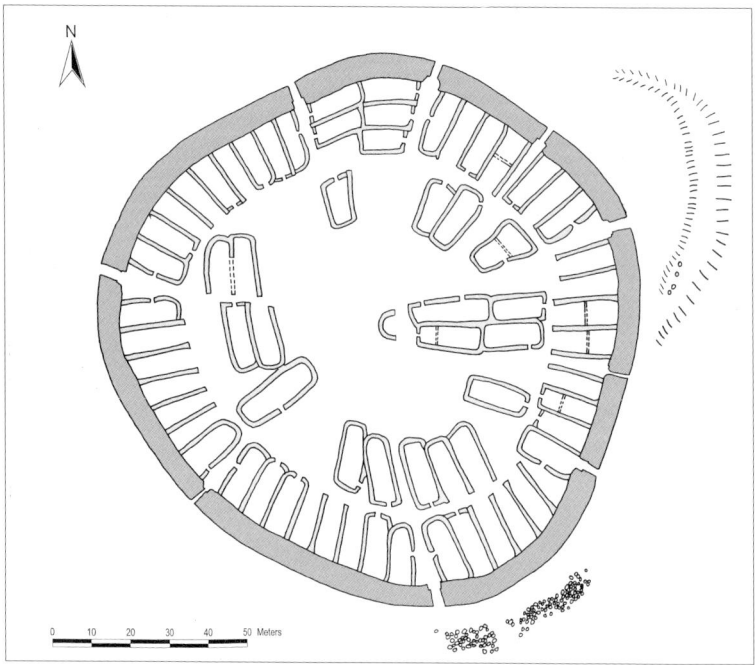

Figure 22. Reconstruction of the first phase of Ismantorp ringfort. The reconstruction is based on a rectified aerial photo (see Fig. 21) and on joints between different house foundations. In the first phase all nine gates had access to the centre of the fort. (Plan by the author.)

square, which shows that it was the original geometrical centre of the fort. However, the small semicircular house and the post on the east side of the square were also part of the centre. The two partly destroyed weapons, deliberately deposited in small pits, indicate that small-scale weapon deposits took place in this centre (see Nørgård Jørgensen 2009), but they scarcely correspond to the large-scale rites that Stenberger envisaged in his interpretation of the fort.

The dating of the three objects can be confirmed by eight overlapping radiocarbon datings of charcoal. In order to avoid the possibility that the firewood was old in itself, for instance a trunk of oak several hundred years old, only samples of twigs of hazel, sallow, and willow were used. With a 68.2% probability (1 sigma), six samples from several houses can be dated from AD 240–390 to 430–600, and with a 95.4%

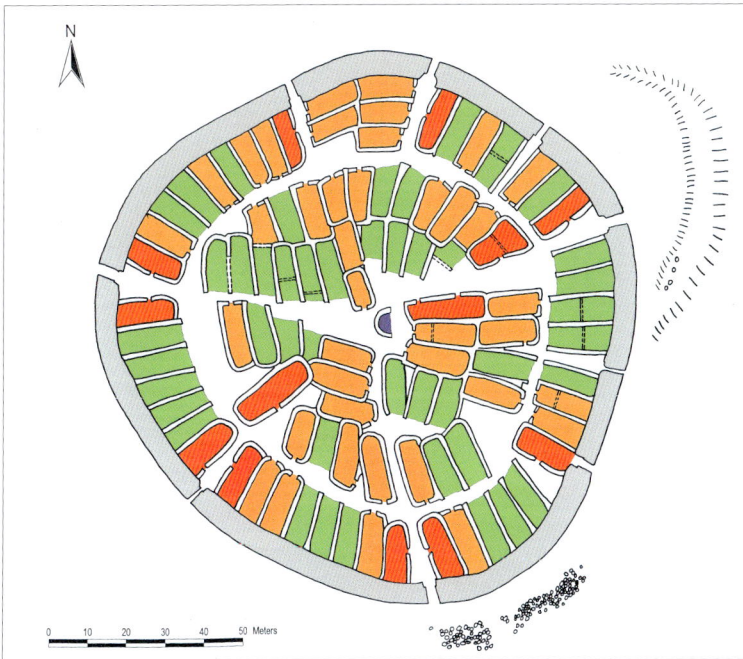

Figure 23. Reconstruction of the second phase of Ismantorp ringfort, showing different types of houses. The reconstruction is based on a rectified aerial photo (see Fig. 21). The function of the houses is not possible to determine from the few finds. Instead their construction can give some indication of their different functions. Houses with gable foundations and gable doorways (orange) can be interpreted as dwellings and workshops, whereas houses with doorways on the long side of the houses (red) seem to have had special functions. Most of them flank the gates as some kind of gatehouses. Houses without gable foundations (green) were probably byres, stables, barns, or stores. The semicircular house in the centre (violet) is unique in its shape as well as in its location. (Plan by the author.)

probability (2 sigma) they can be dated from 130–430 to 420–640. One sample from the pit in the central square can be dated with 1 sigma to 410–560 and with 2 sigma to 340–620, whereas a rubbish heap outside one house can be dated with 1 sigma to 430–610 and with 2 sigma to 430–640. The objects and the radiocarbon datings show that Ismantorp was primarily in use in about 300–600.

The ringfort was reused later. An Arabic silver coin (Stenberger

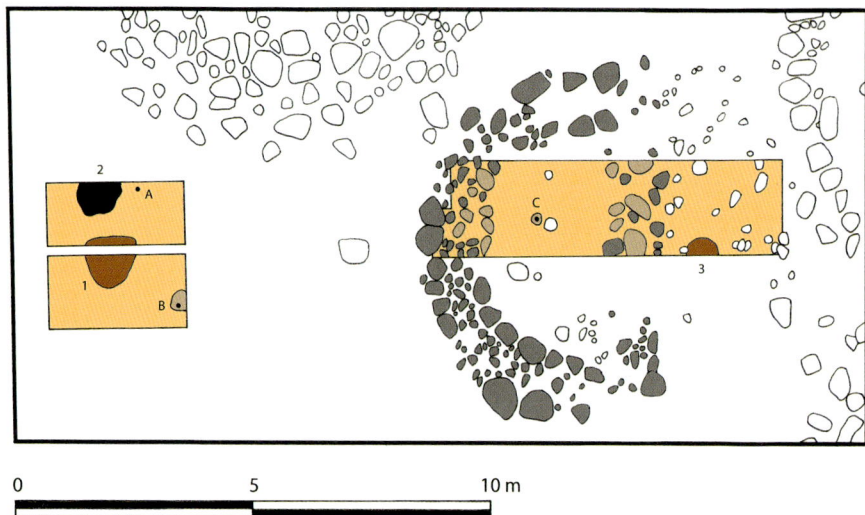

Figure 24. Plan of excavations at the centre of the ringfort at Ismantorp. To the left is a trench in the open triangular place, with a large pit (1), a fireplace (2), and the find spots of an iron fibula (A) and a lancehead (B). To the right is a trench through the semicircular house east of the open place. In the trench was found an arrowhead (C) and a post-hole (3). Besides this, areas with fine humus without till were discovered. These areas probably represent impressions of large stones that have been removed. The preserved visible stone of the small house (grey) and the impressions (light brown) together form a small semicircular house, with a straight east wall. Directly to the east of the house was the post-hole. (Plan by the author.)

1933:239) as well as a small smithy and eleven overlapping radiocarbon datings from the tenth to the thirteenth centuries indicate some form of activities in the historical ruin. Ismantorp was not radically rebuilt during this time, as four other forts on Öland were, but probably most of the gates were blocked and a few houses were rebuilt during this period.

After this reuse, there is no documented activity until the seventeenth century. The modern traces represent local hunting and early visits by antiquarians, archaeological campaigns, and modern tourism. Unfortunately, the original name of the fort is long since lost. Its present name derives from the nearest village, which has a typical place-name reflecting medieval colonization, with the ending *torp* (new settlement) (Hallberg 1985:52).

Figure 25. Finds from the excavations at the centre of the ringfort: from left to right, (A) an iron fibula, (B) a lancehead, (C) and an arrowhead. (Photo by the author.)

Thanks to the fieldwork in 1997–2001, it is possible to outline the history of the fort over a period of 1,700 years. Here I shall concentrate on the first 300 years. Important questions to answer are how the fort was used during this time, and why it was given such a strange design. The answers can scarcely be sought in the fort itself and the few finds encountered there. Instead the site must be compared with those in other parts of Öland as well as in the rest of Scandinavia.

Ölandic comparisons

Ismantorp is just one of many ringforts from the Iron Age on Öland. Fifteen of these are still relatively well preserved, whereas three only are known from older maps and antiquarian sources (Stenberger 1933:213 ff.; Wegraeus 1976; Näsman 1981, 1997, 2001; Fallgren 2008). According to the latest survey (Fallgren 2008), three of these ringforts are different in design and location, and can be dated to the late Pre-Roman and early Roman Iron Age, that is, around 200 BC – AD 200. The primary use of the other fifteen ringforts, including Ismantorp, can be confined to about AD 300–650, although most finds can be dated to the period 400–550 (Fig. 26). Some of the sites were subsequently reused from the tenth to the thirteenth centuries. Ismantorp is one of the oldest forts, belonging to a group of at least three ringforts with activity from the fourth century. The early dating of Ismantorp fits well with the experimental and irregular design of the settlement, compared to Sandby (Viberg et al. 2012) and the second phase of Eketorp (Näsman 1976b), which were evidently built according to more explicit models around 400 AD.

The fifteen ringforts on Öland vary in design and size. Bårby is a semicircle placed on a limestone cliff, Treby consists of three small circles in a row, and Lenstad has a semicircular wall around half of the ring-wall, whereas all the others are circular or oval in shape. The smallest forts have a diameter of up to 60 metres, a middle group have a diameter between 60 and 100 metres, whereas the largest group, including Ismantorp, have a diameter of over 100 metres. The largest ringfort is the irregular Gråborg, with a diameter between 160 and 210 metres (Fallgren 2008). The state of preservation of Ismantorp is unique, but virtually every element in the fort can be found in one or more of the other contemporary fourteen ringforts on the island.

Outworks with large granite boulders outside the main gates, as at Ismantorp, are also preserved at Löt and Sandby, and are probably incorporated in the early medieval outer ringwalls at Eketorp and Gråborg. Three main gates, as at Ismantorp, are preserved or attested at Eketorp, Gråborg, Löt, Sandby, and possibly Mossberga (Borg et al. 1976; Tegnér, G. 2008; Viberg et al. 2012; Stenberger 1933). Even the seemingly unique and inexplicable nine gates in the ring-wall of Ismantorp have their counterparts on the island. The first small fort at Eketorp was built in around 300, consisting of a polygonal ring-wall with nine corners (Weber 1976a). The fort had only one gate, but the figure of nine was inscribed in the shape of the ring-wall. Even the large Gråborg seems to have had nine gates in its oldest phase, from about 300. The fort was radically rebuilt in the twelfth and thirteenth centuries, when the ring-wall was reinforced and three gates were converted into gate towers (Stenberger 1933:228 ff.; Tegnér, G. 2008a). In the first half of the twentieth century, a fourth gate in the earlier ring-wall was found, indicating another design of the ring-wall in the Iron Age. In order to investigate this older plan, I made a thorough analysis of the masonry of the earlier ring-wall in 2003, with the help of digitized aerial photos, provided by colleagues from the Gråborg project (see Tegnér,

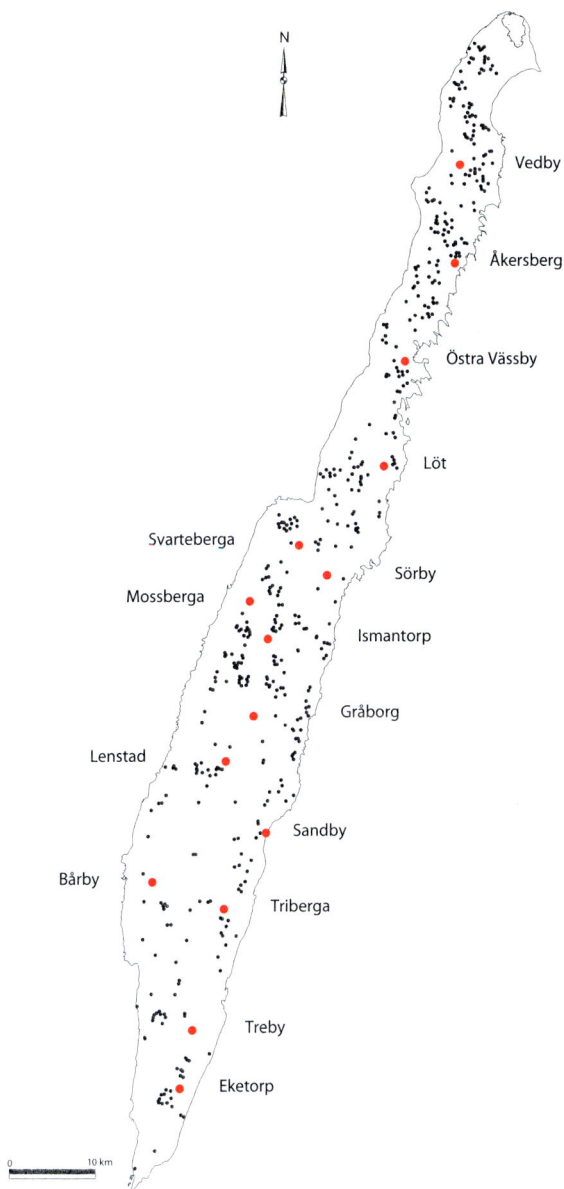

Figure 26. Map of Öland with ringforts from *c*. 300–650 (red dots) and ordinary settlements from *c*. 200–700 (black dots) (after Fallgren 2006:24 and 2008:125).

G. 2008b). During this fieldwork, I found five more walled-up gates, two between the west and south gates, two between the south and east gates, and one north-east of the west gate. Evidently, Gråborg also had nine gates in the Iron Age. Inside the rings-walls, dense settlement is preserved or can be attested in eleven cases (Fallgren 2008). Despite the many house foundations, most ringforts seem to have been used only temporarily, since graves in the surroundings are lacking, as are real cultural deposits inside the walls, although some objects have been retrieved from the different sites. The only clear exception is the second phase of Eketorp (around 400–650), which has been interpreted as a fortified village due to cultural deposits with many objects (Edgren 1979; Näsman 1981).

From other ringforts come accidental finds, such as Roman gold coins from the fifth century, bronze fibulas, and gilded relief brooches of silver (Stenberger 1933:213–55; Palm 2008). The relief brooches found at Mossberga and Sandby indicate the presence of high-ranking women, possibly with the religious function of a seeress or a *vǫlva* (see Magnus 2001b, 2004). Possible ritual objects include gold-foil figures from Eketorp, a bronze figure of a sitting man found under a stone in the centre of the ringfort at Mossberga, and a bronze figure of a standing woman from Svarteberga (Stenberger 1933:246). Traces of violence and warfare are also present. At Eketorp, arrowheads and extensive burnt layers were found close to the southern gate (Weber 1976b:105–106). At Sandby, two skeletons have been found inside the threshold of two houses (Viberg et al. 2012), whereas weapons such as arrowheads, spearheads, and lanceheads have been discovered in several forts (Stenberger 1933:213–255).

The origins of the objects from the forts attest to different forms of contacts around the Baltic Sea, to Gotland, Bornholm, Skåne, Denmark, and Prussia. Further away, connections with the late Roman or Byzantine Empire are visible in the shape of gold coins and glass vessels (Herschend 1980; Näsman 1984; Magnus 2004). In many ways, the finds from the forts mirror those from the contemporary graves and hoards on Öland.

It is uncertain whether any original name of an Ölandic ringfort has survived. Eketorp in the early medieval phase seems to have been called Gräsgård (Vikstrand 2007), but four forts – Åkersberg, Svarteberga, Mossberga, and Triberga – have names with the ending -*berga*.

This compound is very common for hillforts or settlements close to hillforts in eastern and central Sweden, indicating that these names might be original.

Alongside the ringforts, Öland is also known for its well-preserved traces of ordinary agrarian settlement from the same period, that is, about AD 200–700. Mårten Stenberger conducted the first investigations in the 1920s and 1930s (Stenberger 1933:85 ff.), but the most recent analysis of this agrarian settlement and its relation to the ringforts has been done by Jan-Henrik Fallgren (Fallgren 1993, 1998, 2006, 2008). According to his survey, 1,300 foundations are preserved or known from the outlands of the historical villages on the island (see Fig. 26). The ruins are in many cases still surrounded by abandoned fields, meadows, and cattle paths, all bordered by stone enclosures. The stone foundations correspond to perhaps 1,100 farms, situated in large and loosely organized villages. However, many more farms must have existed, but have been destroyed, because they were located too close to the historical villages and their arable land.

Based on the number and size of the houses, Fallgren has divided the farms of Öland into three different size classes, which also hint at the social order on the island (Fallgren 2006). Over 90 per cent of the stone-foundation buildings consisted of small farms with one or two houses, up to 20 metres long. About 8 per cent of the known settlement consisted of medium-sized farms, with three slightly larger buildings. Finally, there is a small group with decidedly large farms or estates. Accounting for less than 2 per cent of the known stone-foundation buildings, these farms consist of four or five houses, which can be up to 55 metres long (Fig. 27). Often there are also workshops and special free-standing hall buildings (see Herschend 1997) at these sites. In each village, there was normally just one larger farm, and these were chiefly located in the bigger villages with ten or so farms (Fallgren 2006).

The total number of houses in the contemporary ringforts is not known, but has been estimated as 'at least 1,000' (Fallgren 2008:124), which is probably too low regarding the inner space in some of the largest ringforts, such as Gråborg and Löt. A figure around 1,200 is more plausible, meaning that most of the inhabitants of the island could have been housed in the ringforts during periods of warfare. However, the ringforts were not refuges in the passive sense that they only reproduced the organization of the agrarian settlement. Instead,

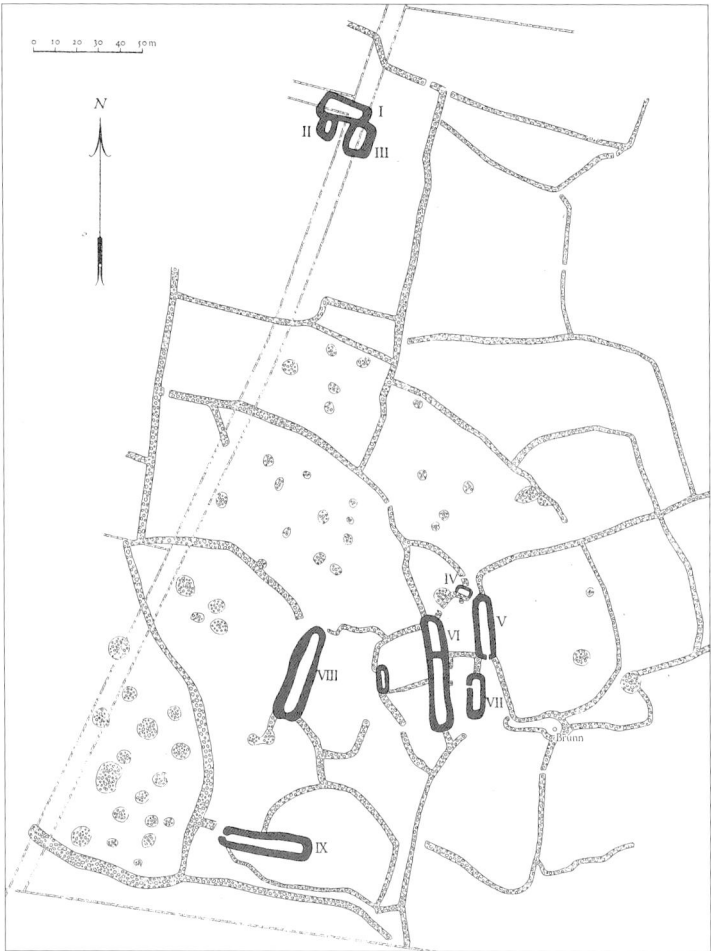

Figure 27. Remains of a village from c.200–550, with house foundations and stone enclosures at Rönnerum in Högsrum, about 2 kilometres west of Ismantorp ringfort. The inhabitants of the large farm or manor (houses IV–VII) were probably among the initiators of the building of the ringfort. (After Stenberger 1933:99.)

the location of the forts as well as their design clearly distinguished them from the surrounding settlement. This means that the ringforts must have represented an organization that was partly different from the agrarian settlement.

All the ringforts were placed in outland between the settlements; the smaller ringforts in outland between villages, and the larger ringforts on commons between regions of settlement (Fallgren 2008). Normally, the forts, as in the case of Ismantorp, were situated one or two kilometres away from the surrounding settlements. The forts were nevertheless clearly related to these settlements, since the main gates in several forts were directly facing the closest neighbouring villages. In Ismantorp the three main gates moreover had the same orientation as the three main roads in the surrounding agrarian landscape.

The forts and the villages were thus linked to one another, but at the same time they represented two different ways of organizing a settlement (Fallgren 2008). The obvious ranking of the farms and the tendency to build houses around enclosed yards emphasized hierarchy and enclosure in the unfortified settlements. The forts themselves were enclosed, but the houses inside the forts were relatively small and of equal size, and not placed in closed yards. Inside the ring-walls, the principles of equality and openness are therefore emphasized in the architecture. This combination of enclosed ring-walls and equal-sized houses inside the walls indicates military principles behind the ringforts.

The location of the ringforts between several different settlements must have meant that the initiative to build the forts came from several different villages at the same time, primarily from the large farms that dominated the villages. A collective initiative like this from several different estates could explain some of the differences between the unfortified and the fortified settlement. The forts were erected in outland on a kind of neutral periphery between the settlements, and the equal-sized houses toned down the competition between the estates. Instead the ringforts themselves represented a military order that for periods could replace the social order in the villages.

An interesting aspect of the links between the ringforts and the agrarian settlement is the observation that the size of each ringfort seems to correspond to the number of farms in the area around the fort (Näsman 1997; Fallgren 2008). This means that behind the larger ringforts were larger and more complex networks of high-ranking families from the large farms than there were behind the small ringforts. An outstanding case was the large Gråborg, which must have been the most central place on Öland during periods of war – perhaps representing a petty king of the island (see Näsman 1997).

To sum up, the Ölandic comparisons show that Ismantorp is not as unique and unusual as Stenberger claimed. The fort may be extremely well preserved, but in all other respects the site is deeply rooted in distinct Ölandic patterns. This applies both to other forts and to the relations between forts and ordinary settlement. Ismantorp therefore need no longer be treated as the great exception, which requires different or special explanations. Instead, the well-preserved ruin can be assigned a greater and in many ways more interesting role in the discussion of ringforts.

Scandinavian forts

The fifteen Ölandic forts are just a small proportion of the over 1,500 ringforts and hillforts registered in Scandinavia (Engström 1984, 1991; Taavitsainen 1990; Olausson 1997; Mitlid 2003, 2004). In the Baltic Sea area there are forts on Bornholm, Öland, Gotland, along the east coast of Sweden from northern Småland to central Norrland, around Lake Mälaren, and in south-west Finland. In western Scandinavia, forts are found along the coasts of Sweden and Norway from northern Halland to Trøndelag, in the provinces around Lake Vänern and in the interior of southern Norway. Ringforts and hillforts are thus found in areas of mixed landscape where farming country alternates with areas of forest. In the large plains of southern Scandinavia and in the agricultural districts of central Västergötland and western Östergötland there are virtually no forts.

The form of the forts varies according to the local topography. Ringforts where the walls totally surround the interior of the fort are found above all in flat terrain, as on Öland and partly on Gotland. The most common solution, however, was to place hillforts on cliffs and hills, with walls built along the least steep sections. The walls in these cases are often semicircular. A recurrent feature is the peripheral location of the forts in relation to contemporary settlement. As on Öland, the forts are usually built in outland and common land, some distance away from cemeteries and settlements. In many cases they are situated on later boundaries between parishes or hundreds. Several forts are also located facing lakes or seashores, and only a small group are placed close to settlements and cemeteries (Gihl 1918; Törnqvist 1993; Olausson 1997; Wall 2003:62 ff.; Mitlid 2004).

The link between certain forts on Öland and the place-name Berga and -*berga* ('rock, mountain, hill') has many parallels in other parts of Scandinavia. Besides many hillforts are related to place-names like Borg, -*borg* ('fort'), and Sten, -*sten* ('stone'). In certain cases the forts themselves have these names, while in other cases it is a nearby settlement that bears one of the names (Karlsson 1900; Gihl 1918; Johansen 1997; Wall 2003:167 ff.; Wahlberg 2003).

The Scandinavian forts generally date from the Late Bronze Age (*c.*1000 BC) to the Early Middle Ages (*c.* AD 1300), but the majority of the excavated sites belong to the period 200–700, and above all the period 400–550 (Olausson 2009, 2011), in other words, exactly the same time as the forts on Öland. There are both similarities and differences between the contemporary Scandinavian and Ölandic forts. Many ringwalls are similar in structure to the walls of Ölandic forts, with step-like ledges on the inside. Unlike the Ölandic forts, however, timber structures, sand, and clay were used in the construction of many hillfort walls (see, for example, Boman 1982; Engström 1984; Olausson 1997; 2009). Outworks with zones of closely spaced granite blocks are common, and as on Öland the openings in the outworks are shifted counter-clockwise in relation to the gates in the main wall. On the other hand, there are rarely more than one or two gates in the forts. An exception is Torsburgen on Gotland, which is one of the biggest ringforts in Scandinavia, with a circumference of about 4.5 kilometres. At least twelve entrances lead to this huge fortified plateau (Engström 1984). The characteristic density of buildings in the Ölandic forts, on the other hand, has no counterpart, although terraces with up to twenty houses occur at some hillforts in Uppland (Fig. 28; Olausson 1997; 2009). Occupation layers with pottery, food remains, craft waste, and the occasional dress artefact have also been found in some forts in Södermanland and eastern Östergötland, whereas finds of weapons are rare (Schnittger 1913; Nordén 1929, 1938; Olausson 1997, 2009). Analysis of animal bones from one site indicates that the hillforts with settlement remains were primarily used during the summer seasons (Olausson 2009:53). Yet the majority of forts lack cultural deposits and finds, so they can best be described as 'empty places' established directly on bare rock (see Wall 2003:139).

Opinions about the forts are sharply divided, and, generally speaking, interpretations of them alternate between modern concepts of politics, economics, and religion (Johansen and Pettersson 1993; Flygare 2000;

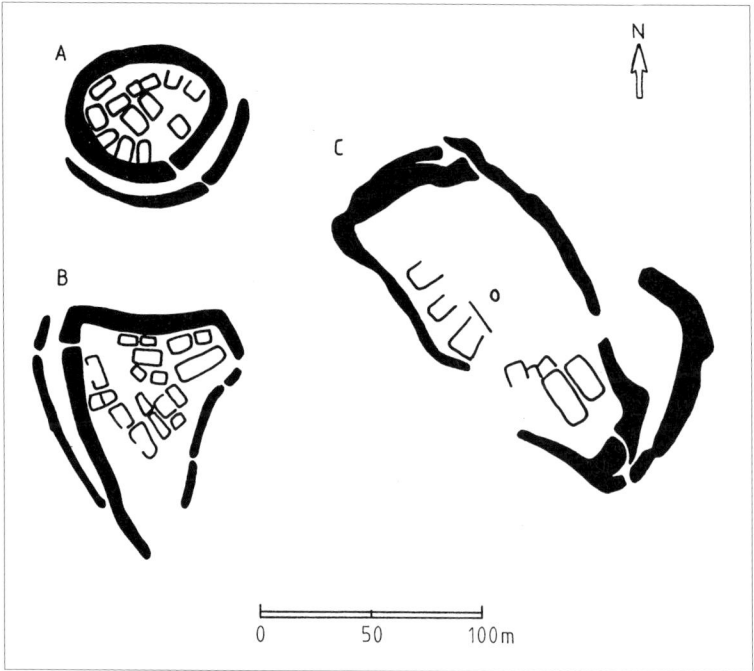

Figure 28. Plan of hillforts in Uppland, with terraces for houses, at Broborg (A), Darsgärde (B), and Runsa (C). (After Olausson 1997:159.)

Wall 2003; Ystgaard 1998, 2003; Olausson 2009). There are clear parallels to similar discussions about forts in Britain and Ireland (see, for example, Hill 1993; Stout 1997; Alcock 2003:179 ff.). The different views in the Scandinavian debate are due to the fact that the words used, such as the Norwegian word *bygdeborg* and the Swedish word *fornborg*, cover completely different types of structures built in very different historical contexts. In addition, the character of 'empty places', with few or no finds, means that many forts lack clear contexts. As a result, the forts are open to diametrically opposed interpretations.

Ever since the antiquarian tradition of the seventeenth century, the predominant interpretation has been that hillforts and ringforts are ancient structures providing defence against some form of military threat. However, opinions about the purpose of these fortifications have varied widely. The most common interpretation is that the forts were intended for defence against external enemies (for example Rygh 1882; Schnittger 1913; Stenberger 1933:213 ff.; Näsman 1997), but others view them as an expression of inner conflicts (Nordin 1881; Nihlén and Boethius 1933:24, 66; Olausson 1997, 2009; Skre 1998) or as bases for waging aggression outwards (Schnell 1934; Stenberger 1964). They have been regarded as places of assembly for weapon-bearing men (Mitlid 2003), but also as places of refuge for the non-fighting part of the population (Nordén 1938:338; Nerman 1941:155). Some scholars believe that the forts were fortified farms or defensive structures built at estates on private initiative (Ambrosiani 1964:12, 177; Olausson 1997, 2009; Skre 1998; Stylegar 1999). Others instead argue that the forts were expressions of small political units, preceding the medieval Swedish and Norwegian realms (Myhre 1966:193, 1987; Hyenstrand 1981; Damell 1993; Damell and Lorin 1994).

In opposition to the general military interpretation, various alternative views were expressed throughout the twentieth century. With particular reference to the astonishingly civilian character of the finds from several forts, some scholars have stressed the role of these sites as fortified dwelling places, as specially demarcated places of production (Hyenstrand 1984:89 ; Törnqvist 1993), as temporary places of assembly for a population chiefly subsisting on animal husbandry (Anjou 1935), as delimited spaces for people with power and with sacred and esoteric knowledge (Hegardt 1991), and as specially demarcated district centres, associated with the exchange of gifts and meetings with strangers (Cassel 1998:129 ff.). The ritual functions of forts have likewise been emphasized in several different contexts. The arguments for the ritual interpretations are that graves have been found inside the walls of some forts, that large erratic boulders with cup marks are found in a few forts, that the weak walls and many gates in some forts (for instance, Ismantorp) are not suitable for defence, and that sacral place-names can be associated with some forts or the nearby historical settlement (Gihl 1918:81; Nordén 1929, 1938; Stenberger 1933; Schnell 1934; Johansen 1997). From these perspectives, ringforts can be perceived as socially enclosed assembly places where judicial functions, cult, and initiation rites were performed. The walls would then not have been built against enemies, but instead would have marked holy places or symbolic fortifications, intended not just for men but also for women (Johansen 1997; Wall 2003). As holy places, the forts have also been viewed as images of Old Norse cosmology (Johansen 1997; Aannestad 2004; see also Sjöborg 1822:128).

It is scarcely likely that agreement can be reached about the function and meaning of forts, since the words *bygdeborg* and *fornborg* are umbrella terms for monuments from such different times and places. Broader and more neutral concepts, such as 'henged mountains' or 'enclosed spaces' have been introduced to account for the variations of the ancient monuments (for example, Johansen and Pettersson 1993; Wall 2003). However, these concepts may also be viewed as attempts to 'demilitarize' the forts, since these efforts are connected to a more or less unconscious desire to define war out of Iron Age society. Since war is not desirable today, it becomes undesirable in the past too, and thereby excluded from the discussion of interpretation (Keeley 1996; cf. Carman 1997; Vandkilde 2003, 2006).

I would not hesitate to view many forts from the period 200–700 in martial contexts, for several reasons. The stout walls and outworks of granite boulder from that period are on the whole difficult to understand in anything other than a primarily military context (Fig. 29), although the forts may have had other secondary functions as well (see Olausson 1997, 2009). Weapons that are found in forts are few, but archaeologists have actually found arrowheads, spearheads, lances, and sword details in several forts. The non-martial finds are not a direct argument against a military interpretation, since the maintenance of an army at the time required a distinct 'civilian' element in all military troops (Albrethsen 1997).

The military interpretation can also be supported by analogies with similar, contemporary forts in Scotland (Alcock 2003:119 ff.). About ten named and identified forts, according to statements in annals from 681 to 870, were subject to siege (*obsessio*), fire (*combusta*), or destruction (*distructio*) in connection with acts of war (Alcock 2003:144, 180 ff.). In these historical texts, then, forts occur in obvious military contexts. Of special interest is that burning down a fort was the ultimate sign of conquering a hillfort in Scotland (Alcock 2003:183 ff.), which fits very well with the walls of many hillforts in Sweden having been burnt several times and in some cases completely destroyed in 'ritual obliteration' (Olausson 2009:59). In some cases the hillforts have been so heavily burnt that parts of the walls have melted. These vitrified walls have been interpreted as deliberate measures to strengthen the walls

Figure 29. Section of the hillfort at Rällinge on Fogdön in Södermanland. The main wall is up to five metres high and is partly surrounded by large boulders. (Photo by the author.)

(Kresten and Ambrosiani 1992), but the Scottish analogies rather speak in favour of a final destruction of a conquered hillfort.

A further argument for a military interpretation is the link between forts and the place-name elements *-berga* and *-sten*. In several heroic poems in the *Poetic Edda* these elements are specifically associated with fighting. The prose text between stanzas 18 and 19 in *Helgakviða Hundingsbana* II mentions that warriors 'were sitting up on a cliff' (*sáto á biargi*) when they met an enemy army. The mythic places Arastein and Frekastein are also mentioned in *Helgakviða Hundingsbana* II:21 and 26, and in the prose texts between the stanzas 13–14 and 18–19, as well as in *Helgakviða Hundingsbana* I:14, 44, and 53 and *Helgakviða Hiǫrvarðssonar* 39. The hero Helgi Hundingsbani rests after a battle at Arastein, whereas he travels with a large navy to Frekastein, where several of his opponents are killed in a violent battle. But Frekastein is also the scene of negotiations between warring parties. The portrayal of Frekastein in these poems is thus very apt as a description of the function of the forts as military structures.

Although the military perspectives are fundamental, I believe that other aspects of the forts should be considered too. The lack of forts in the plains of southern Scandinavia shows that they were not essential to the warfare of the time. Forts were absent in areas with large and densely settled villages, but they were built in areas where settlement consisted either of single farms or of small villages and loosely organized larger villages (see Fallgren 1993; Riddersporre 1995). Forts were thus constructed in areas where the intimate and everyday interaction of the large villages of the plains did not exist. The forts thus seem to have met a special social need in areas where settlement and land use were more divided (see Wall 2003). Apart from this social dimension, the ritual and cosmological features that some scholars have detected in the forts must be reinvestigated. But the military and religious elements need not be viewed as being as separate as they are often claimed to be; they are more likely to have been different aspects of the function of forts. Instead of demilitarizing the ringforts, I think that the character of war itself should be redefined.

Outlines of an early Scandinavian martial culture

Only in recent years have war and warfare been more thoroughly debated in archaeology (for instance, Randsborg 1995; Nørgård Jørgensen and Clausen 1997; Carman and Harding 1999, Jørgensen et al. 2003; Otto et al. 2006, Vandkilde 2006, Hedenstierna-Jonsson 2006; Holmquist Olausson and Olausson 2009). Many important aspects of war have been underlined, such as its social and political consequences and the ritualized nature of much pre-modern warfare. Still, war as a historical phenomenon is an elusive activity. In some cases we can find the actual sites of warfare, such as battlefields (Schlüter 1997), burned hillforts (Olausson 2009:57), or burned and destroyed hall buildings (Herschend 1997). In other cases, traces of violent and bloody acts of war are found, such as mass graves of the slain (for example Thordeman 1939–40; Kjellström 2005). For the distant past, however, warfare can chiefly be traced by indirect means, and this applies particularly to Iron Age warfare. Apart from hill forts, Scandinavian warfare can, above all, be studied through weapon deposits, boathouses, and *ringtun*.

A good window on the culture of war is undoubtedly provided by the weapon deposits. These consist of weapons, riding equipment, personal objects, clothes, and slaughtered animals deposited in shallow

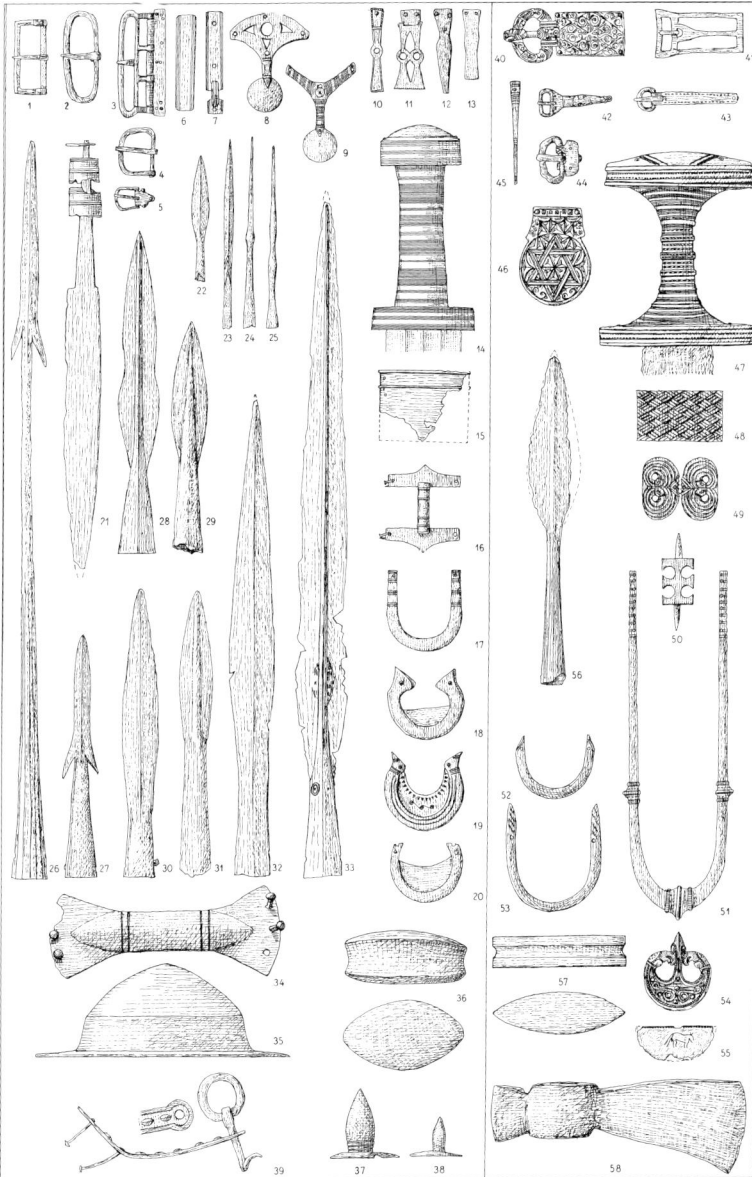

Figure 30. Selection of weapons and other objects deposited at Ejsbøl near Haderslev in southern Jutland during the fourth and fifth centuries. (After Ørsnes 1988, table 48.)

lakes (Fabech 1991b; Randsborg 1995; Ilkjær 2000; Jørgensen et al. 2003; Nørgård Jørgensen 2009). Weapons were deposited in lakes, bogs, and fens in the Late Bronze Age as well as in the early Middle Ages, but the large finds of often deliberately destroyed weapons all belong to the Iron Age, starting with Hjortspring from about 350 BC (Randsborg 1995). Around thirty sites of weapon deposits have been found, most of them in present-day Denmark and southern Sweden, although there are two known sites on Öland and a few in central Sweden (Fig. 30). Thus, the weapon deposits are primarily located in the agricultural districts of southern Scandinavia, which lacked hillforts. A recurrent pattern is that weapons were deposited in the same place on repeated occasions, but often at long intervals. About fifty deposits at the thirty sites are known for the period 200–600, and only three large deposits are known from 350 BC to AD 150 (Fabech 1991b; Kaul 2003; Ilkjær 2003).

Complete weapon deposits, representing war booty of fully equipped armies, have only been found in a few places from about AD 200 to the late fourth century or about AD 400 (Nørgård Jørgensen 2009). One example is Illerup Ådal in central Jutland, where roughly 10,000 weapons were deposited on just one occasion at the start of the third century. The find may represent a defeated army of an estimated two or three thousand men (Ilkjær 2000). Extensive, but not complete, weapon deposits have been discovered in several locations from the first century to about AD 475. Selected smaller deposits comprising mostly weapons can be dated from the beginning of our era to about AD 600. From this time until the twelfth century only single weapons were deposited in water (Lund 2009; Nørgård Jørgensen 2009).

The spectacular war booties from AD 200–350/400 have been interpreted as expressions of wars on a larger scale and a more centralized military organization than before. The early deposits, such as Hjortspring, contained fewer weapons and more diverse and personal martial equipment, reflecting small bands of individually equipped men (Randsborg 1995). From around 200, on the other hand, weapons became very standardized, which suggests that they were made in a few 'weapon forges' and distributed from there to a more professional and trained group of warriors (Ilkjær 2000; Kaul 2003).

It has been possible to reconstruct the organization of these groups of warriors, above all thanks to Jørgen Ilkjær's detailed analyses of the weapons from Illerup (Ilkjær 1997, 2000; cf. Randsborg 1995). He is able to sketch a military hierarchy consisting of three different levels of warriors – 'private' foot soldiers, mounted 'officers', and mounted 'commanders'. The armed warriors (89 per cent) were equipped with mass-produced lances, spears, and shields, while the officers (9 per cent) more often carried individually designed swords, shields, and belts with bronze mountings. The commanders (2 per cent) were equipped with artfully designed swords, shields, belts, and equestrian gear with gilded silver mountings, and some of them also had chain mail and decorative Roman helmets of silver. It is also to this military elite that objects with animal ornamentation and runes can primarily be linked. A similar tripartite army organization was found in the Roman army (Pauli Jensen et al. 2003) and can also be traced in the Pictish war organization in north-eastern Scotland (Alcock 2003:149).

Several scholars have studied the origin of the defeated armies using more personal items such as combs, strike-a-lights, and wooden vessels (Randsborg 1995; Ilkjær 1997, 2000; Pauli Jensen 2009). This allows us to glimpse the outlines of different lines of conflict in the Scandinavia Iron Age. Jørgen Ilkjær asserts that the defeated armies in the second century came from northern Germany, in the third and fourth centuries from northern Germany, western Sweden, and southern Norway, and in the fifth century from Öland, Gotland, and eastern Sweden. Ilkjær believes that the weapons were deposited close to the scene of the fighting, and consequently he sees the origin of the weapons as the origins of military attacks directed against Denmark. This large-scale scenario with a succession of different sources of aggression against Denmark has been criticized, however, because it rests to an excessive extent on some selected Danish finds. If the Swedish weapon deposits had also been included, the picture would presumably have been more complex (Nicklasson 1997:159 ff.; cf. Nordqvist 2007). In addition, there are smaller finds of weapon deposits along the south coast of the Baltic Sea, which could further complicate the picture (cf. Müller-Wille 1999, 2001).

Ilkjær's analyses are important, but they can be criticized on one decisive point, which means that the entire question of the direction of aggression must be reappraised. He views the repeated deposits of weapons in the same place as a military pattern of recurrent aggression against Denmark. At a conference in 2001, I proposed that the Scandinavian weapon deposits instead should be compared with war booty

Figure 31. Marble frieze of Roman war booty from the second century AD, found in Ephesus. (Photo by the author.)

in Greek, Celtic, and Roman areas, being inspired by Ida Östenberg (from a manuscript later published as Östenberg 2009). These ideas were taken up by some colleagues (Jørgensen 2001; Lund Hansen 2003a), but have also been criticized (Herschend 2003:312 ff.; Fabech 2009). Since I have only briefly touched upon them elsewhere (Andrén 2007a), I will expand the arguments here.

In Greek sanctuaries such as Olympia and Delphi, at sacred Celtic sites, and in Roman triumphal processions (Fig. 31), war booty from distant campaigns was assembled (see Baitinger 1999; Cunliffe 1997; Östenberg 2009). This war booty varied considerably according to time and place, but could comprise captured enemies, weapons, personal belongings, parts of ships, treasure from conquered regions and symbols of conquered land, such as trees and animals. Many of these aspects are present in the Scandinavian weapon deposits, such as weapons, personal objects, ships (Ørsnes 1988; Ilkjær 2000; Rieck et al. 1999), treasure in the form of golden arm-rings (Hagberg 1967a, 1967b), and possible symbols of conquered land, such as numerous sticks and branches of trees (Rieck et al. 1999). The recurrent weapon deposits in the lakes of southern Scandinavia must therefore be considered as following a ritual pattern, with clear contemporary continental parallels. Besides, many of the shallow lakes with weapon deposits were used for other ritual deposits, such as pottery, animal bones, and humans, before as well as after the weapons were thrown into the lakes (Pauli Jensen

2009; Monikander 2010). The Scandinavian sites could thus be seen as holy places to which parts of the war booty were brought on different occasions. The location of weapon deposits thus tells us nothing about where the fighting took place. This means that the battles could have been fought anywhere between the sites of the war booty and the place of origin of the defeated armies. The lines of conflict were presumably much more complicated than in Ilkjær's reconstructions. It is therefore perfectly possible that the densely populated and economically dominant southern Scandinavia in many cases may have been the point of departure for the attacks (cf. Nicklasson 1997:159 ff.), and that battles could have been fought in western Sweden and southern Norway, or on the islands in the Baltic Sea and in eastern Sweden.

Another expression of the war culture during this time is found in the boathouses or *naust* along the coast of Norway (Myhre 1997), which were probably based on Roman models (Grimm 2001). Around 150 large boathouses from the Iron Age and Middle Ages have been registered, above all in western and northern Norway (Fig. 32). The medieval boathouses are scattered along the coast, often right beside the places that were central in the medieval naval organization of the *ledung*. The boathouses from the Iron Age can be dated to the period *c.*150–700, but unlike the medieval *naust* they are located in several smaller concentrations along the coast. They therefore represent a network that is separate from the medieval naval organization (*skeppslag*). Bjørn Myhre takes them to be expressions of a less stable naval organization, with boats and warrior retinues connected to changing chieftains or commanders. Along the 250-kilometre-long coast from Lindesnes to Bergen alone, Myhre claims that 90 boathouses, for vessels of 15–30 metres length, may have been used during the period 150–700 (Myhre 1997). The large number of *naust* means that a very large navy with warriors could be mobilized from just a small part of the Norwegian coast. The boathouses thus represent a new military organization on a large scale, similar to the warrior units behind the contemporary south Scandinavian weapon deposits.

The Norwegian coastal area is also the setting of the particular *ringtun* or *tun* sites (Storli 2000, 2001; Stylegar and Grimm 2003). The word *tun* refers here to a cluster of houses placed around an open space in a circle or oval with one or two openings. In several cases the gables of the houses open out towards the yard (Fig. 33). The layout and

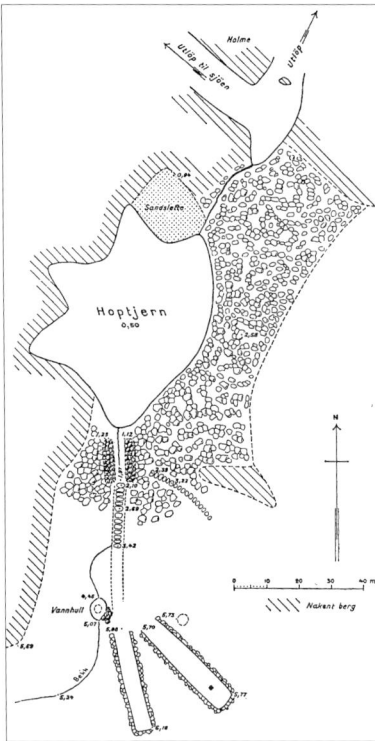

Figure 32. Two boathouses at Nes on Karmøy. (After Myhre 1997:170.)

design of the houses show several similarities to the buildings in the Ölandic forts, but, unlike these, the *tun* sites lack walls (see Stenberger 1933:260–1). Around 25 sites are known, from Jæren in the south of Norway to Lofoten in the far north. Like the ringforts, the *tun* sites are usually placed in the outland between different settlements, although closer to other ancient remains. There are often large cooking pits, fireplaces, and large burial mounds. Several *tun* sites are moreover linked to the place-name element -*leik*, which means 'play' but also 'training for war'. The finds are few and modest, but the sites were often used on different occasions over a long time. The general time framework for the *tun* sites is between AD 200 and 850.

The interpretations of the *tun* sites are as numerous and varied as those of the Scandinavian ringforts and hillforts. They have been interpreted as forts, barracks, military exercise grounds, amphitheatres,

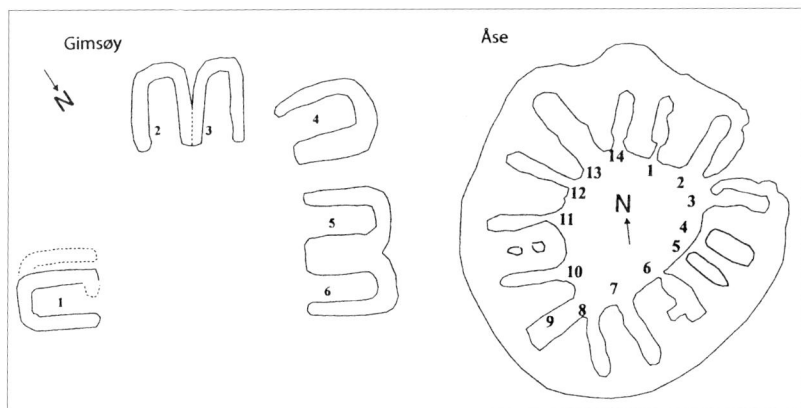

Figure 33. *Ringtun* on Gimsøy and at Åse on Lofoten. (After Storli 2001:94.)

and overnight lodgings for boat crews, but also as villages, sites of legal assemblies, and sacrificial sites (Storli 2000, 2001). Since the end of the 1970s, political interpretations have dominated, especially when it comes to the north Norwegian *tun* sites (see Johansen and Søbstad 1978). In the most recent scholarly treatment, they are regarded as places of assembly for the warrior retinues of the aristocracy (Storli 2000, 2001; Stylegar and Grimm 2003). Since the sites are located in outland, Inger Storli interprets them as neutral meeting places, where the landowning elite could gather on equal terms. She views them in connection with drinking ceremonies, which were necessary for creating a sense of community in a band of warriors not held together by bonds of kinship. The *tun* sites were abandoned when more supra-regional leadership was established, in Rogaland in the sixth and seventh centuries, and in north Norway at the start of the ninth century. The age of the *ringtun* and its probable military functions show once again that the time around 200 was an important turning point for the Scandinavian culture of war.

Studies of Scandinavian martial culture have been characterized by national divisions in the debate, which follow modern political boundaries and archaeological specialities. The weapon deposits have above all been studied in Danish archaeology, the forts have chiefly been a Swedish, Norwegian, and Finnish concern, while the boathouses and *tun* sites have been discussed almost exclusively in Norwegian archaeology. Like several other scholars, I believe that these martial phenomena should be viewed together, since they are all expressions of the same war culture in Scandinavia during the period 200–600/700 (Näsman 1988, 1997; see Nicklasson 1997:170). In concrete terms, the weapon deposits, forts, boathouses, and *tun* sites can be regarded as different aspects of the same conflicts in Scandinavia (Fig. 10). The forts in Sweden and Norway as well as the Norwegian boathouses and *tun* sites were the direct origin of some of the defeated armies found in the Danish weapon deposits (cf. Engström 1991:275; Stylegar and Grimm 2003).

War as ritualized action

The ringforts and hillforts, the weapon deposits, and the boathouses as well as the *tun* sites underline that warfare was an important and constant part of Iron Age Scandinavian society, above all during the period 200–600/700. Therefore, it interesting that in one of the few contemporary descriptions of Scandinavia, written by the Ostrogoth historian Jordanes *c.*550, recurrent wars are emphasized. He writes in his *Getica* that five peoples in southern Scandinavia living in the fertile plains 'are disturbed there by the attacks of other tribes', that four tribes are of 'a race of men bold and quick to fight', and that three tribes 'live like wild animals in rocks hewn out like castles (*castelli*)'. The term *castelli* has been interpreted by some scholars as a reference to the contemporary forts (Lund 1993:281 ff.).

The character of this warfare is not described in any detail. However, analogies with Britain and Ireland after the Roman period can show how war was a constant feature in society, but also that different forms of warfare existed. Based on anthropological studies of war (for example Haas 1990), Guy Halsall has examined statements about war in the Anglo-Saxon Chronicle and other historical works (Halsall 1989; 2003). He shows that war and violence were endemic in Anglo-Saxon England (450–1050), involving everything from private blood vengeance to large-scale war. In the same way, Leslie Alcock has studied war in the Celtic parts of Britain and Ireland, above all in Scotland (Alcock 2003:119 ff.). In both areas it is possible to see a clear distinction between ritualized war and large-scale war.

Ritualized warfare involved small-scale acts of war, such as annual plundering campaigns and raids conducted by aristocratic groups.

Through these martial acts, political leaders could gain access to prestige goods such as slaves, cattle, and horses. On the other hand, the conflicts did not change the basic balance of power. In ritualized war, there were clear norms, which meant that the combatants could jointly choose the place of battle, that parts of the plunder could be returned, and that the fighting could be replaced by tribute and concluded with an exchange of hostages, the swearing of oaths, and the establishment of ties of friendship. Generally speaking, the parties were expected to fight fairly, based on a kind of warrior honour (Halsall 1989). In Ireland, Scotland, and Wales it was part of the initiation of a new king that he and his followers should mount a cattle raid on a neighbouring kingdom. In early medieval Welsh laws, it was furthermore regulated that a king was allowed to plunder outside his kingdom once a year for a maximum of six weeks (Alcock 2003:119 ff.)

The large-scale wars, on the other hand, lacked the code of honour involved in ritualized combat. The major wars were big and bloody, and could mean that entire population groups were killed and replaced by others. The conflicts could change the balance of power, by shifting the boundaries of political units and allowing the rule over an area to be wholly or partly taken over by another king. In the whole Anglo-Saxon area, large-scale wars are mentioned roughly every three years, but for each individual kingdom a large-scale conflict occurred roughly every twenty years (Halsall 1989). In Scotland, major campaigns and battles occurred at roughly similar twenty-year intervals in the period 570–870 (Alcock 2003:131 ff., 180–1).

Ever-present war meant that there was a warrior culture, as is clearly expressed in Old English and Irish literature. This warrior culture is evidenced in the poems of praise to warriors and their weapons, and also in descriptions of how quarrels between warriors could suddenly arise. Otherwise, it was a tendency in Britain and Ireland that the kings gradually tried to restrict small-scale ritualized war, such as feuding and plundering, through legislation and tributes.

Despite the constant presence of war, there are no finds of weapon deposits and virtually no forts in Anglo-Saxon England during the period. In contrast, the Celtic regions have many forts. In Scotland alone more than a hundred forts have been dated to the period 200–850 (Alcock 2003:179 ff.), that is, exactly the same period as many of the Scandinavian forts. In Britain there is thus the same contrast as in

Scandinavia, between flat plains without forts and more forested and mountainous areas with forts. This shows that Scandinavian weapon deposits, forts, *ringtun*, and boathouses were not necessary expressions of war, but were used as markers in special contexts. They may be viewed as special manifestations of the warrior culture of the time. They thus constitute a kind of social and ritual filter, through which war can be detected. In the plains of southern Scandinavia, with large and densely populated villages, war was expressed through very large weapon deposits in a few select places. In the more forested and mountainous areas in the rest of Scandinavia, with single farms and more loosely organized villages, war was instead expressed through many forts located within short distances.

As in Britain and Ireland and in many other parts of the world (Otto et al. 2006), the actual warfare in Iron Age Scandinavia may have been large-scale wars as well as ritualized wars. Indications of large-scale wars are above all the very large weapon deposits from AD 200–400. Ritualized warfare may have been expressed in the smaller selected weapon deposits from the first century to around 600. Ringforts and hillforts as well as boathouses and *tun* sites could possibly be connected to both forms of warfare.

In the much later Icelandic literary tradition, there are several echoes of ritualized warfare in Scandinavian society (Price 2002; Nordberg 2003). Hints of predetermined and marked battlefields are found in the *Poetic Edda*, for example in references to small islands or fields marked off with hazel rods. In several skaldic poems and Icelandic sagas there are mentions of berserks (*berserkir*, meaning 'bear shirts') and ulfhednar (*ulfheðnar*, meaning 'wolf skins') as groups of specially initiated warriors dressed in animal skins (Simek 1993:35, 338–9; Lindow 2001:75–6; Näsström 2006; Hedeager 2011). Exactly what the terms berserks and ulfhednar meant is a matter of controversy (Simek 1993:35; Näsström 2006), but most scholars agree that they designated some kind of ecstatic warrior role associated with the war god Odin. The terms also show how war was associated with 'the wild' and especially with savage and feared beasts of prey. The earliest reference is found in the skaldic poem *Haraldskvæði*, composed in the late ninth century. However, warriors like these are depicted as early as around 600, on matrices for making helmets, at Torslunda on Öland (Fig. 34). Remains of bearskins in graves are also known from the whole of Scandinavia in the period 150

Figure 34. Bronze matrices for producing helmet plates, dated to c.600, found at Björnhovda in Torslunda on Öland. The two matrices illustrate a warrior between two bears and a 'wolf warrior' together with a one-eyed warrior with a helmet (Odin?). Both images call to mind the concepts *berserkir* and *ulfheðnar*. (Drawings by Bengt Händel in Sandwall 1980:24–5.)

BC – AD 1050, although they appear in female as well as male graves (Petré 1980; Ström 1980; Nicklasson 1997; Hedeager 1997, 2004, 2011).

Other expressions of the wildness of war are hints from the much later Icelandic literary traditions that initiation rites for warriors comprised meals of raw meat from wild animals (Schjødt 1999b; Näsström 2001a; Sundqvist and Hultgård 2004). The acts of war themselves were also perceived as wild, since slain enemies in skaldic poetry are conventionally described as feeding wolves, eagles, and ravens. The wildness of war is moreover evident from many of the martial names for men, based on the names of wild animals -*arn* ('eagle'), -*björn* ('bear'), -*ormr* ('serpent'), -*svín* ('wild boar'), and -*úlfr* ('wolf'). Several scholars have pointed out the striking similarity between these men's names and contemporary animal ornamentation, depicting eagles, serpents, wild boar, and wolves (Werner 1963, 1966; Müller 1968; Beck 1986; Hedeager 1997, 2004, 2011; Nordberg 2003; Domeij Lundborg 2006). However, the personal names based on wild animals are older than the animal art, since a name such as Widuhundar ('wood hound', probably a metaphor for 'wolf') is attested in a runic inscription from Himlingøje on Sjælland as early as the early third century (Krause and Jankuhn 1966:i. 32–3). The berserks and ulfhednar, together with the men's names associated with wildness, have been linked by scholars to war bands as well as some form of warrior shamanism (Erä-Esko 1965; Müller 1968; Haseloff 1981; Roth 1986; Hedeager 1997, 2004; Gaimster 1998:48 ff.; Price 2002; Sundqvist and Hultgård 2004). The violence of war and the associations with wildness may explain why the objects in the war booty were so deliberately destroyed. The particular deposits in the shallow lakes can be regarded metaphorically as traces of ravenous beasts of prey that ate up the booty, leaving only tattered remains. In the same way, the placing of the many ringforts and hillforts in the outland between settlements can be perceived as wild places appropriate for the equally wild wars. The forts were thus mentally in the same wild landscape as the men in bear shirts and wolf skins, and the men bearing names of beasts of prey.

War and cosmology

Judging from the late Icelandic texts, warfare in Scandinavia above all seems to have had mythological associations with Odin (Hedeager 1997, 2004, 2011; Schjødt 1999b; Price 2002; Nordberg 2003). However, the recurrent figure of nine at Ismantorp, Eketorp, and Gråborg points towards more general connections between war, rituals, and cosmology. The same numerical symbolism is found in graves, artefacts, and ritual sites from at least the Pre-Roman Iron Age to the Viking Age, that is, from about 500 BC to AD 1050 (see for instance, Äijä 1999; Rundkvist 1996, 2001; Svensson 2012).

The clearest parallel to the Ölandic ringforts are circles of standing stones (Sw. *domarring*) that marked cremation graves from about 500 BC to about AD 550 (Fig. 35; Jaanusson 1966; Lundström 1976; Leube 1979; Hyenstrand 1984:73 ff.). Stone circles are known in southern and eastern Norway, in southern and central Sweden, on Öland, Gotland, and Bornholm, and along the south coast of the Baltic Sea in present-day Poland and Mecklenburg-Vorpommern. They normally consist of an uneven number of stones, mostly five, seven, or nine stones, but the number varies regionally. In most provinces of Sweden, the most frequent number is seven stones, although circles with nine stones are common in all areas. Stone circles with nine stones, however, predominate on Öland and in Skåne as well as in Mecklenburg-Vorpommern (Leube 1979; Hyenstrand 1984:73 ff.).

Figure 35. Circle of nine standing stones at Norrby in Hallsberg in Närke. Apart from the usual number of nine stones, this circle is also constructed in relation to cardinal points. The tallest stones are erected in the north, whereas the shortest ones are placed in the south. (Photo by the author.)

On Öland, all excavated stone circles are dated to the period AD 1–550 (Arne 1938). They are mostly built up of round boulders, lying directly on the ground or placed on three or four small underlying stones. In cases where the stone circles have a central stone, on the other hand, it is a standing stone (Arne 1938). Kerbs linking the stones in the circles are mentioned in earlier antiquarian sources, but today they are not preserved or visible at any site. The form of these stone circles shows great structural similarities to the Ismantorp fort. The central pole, the nine gates, and the ring-wall at Ismantorp are paralleled by the central stone, the nine boulders on their underliers, and the kerbs of the Ölandic stone circles. Even the houses in Ismantorp can be said to correspond to the area in the stone circles where charcoal and burnt bones of humans and animals were scattered inside the ring of stones. Since the stone circles are widely distributed chronologically and geographically the recurrent figure of nine at Ismantorp, Gråborg, and Eketorp must refer to a spatial design that is otherwise mainly known from grave contexts. In view of the placing of burnt human bones in stone circles, this depiction must be connected to ideas about humans and their place in the world (see Bergström 1979; Andrén 2004).

Another parallel to the nine gates at Ismantorp as well as the stone circles is knobbed or ribbed bronze rings (Rundkvist 1996, 2001). These bronze rings are often decorated with nine knobs or ribs. In present-day

Sweden, about sixty rings are known in regions facing the Baltic Sea from the late Pre-Roman Iron Age to the Merovingian Period (about 150 BC – AD 750). However, more than half of the rings come from Öland. They are dated to the Migration Period (400–550) and all except four are furnished with nine or eighteen knobs or ribs. One ring with nine ribs was actually found in the ringfort of Lenstad. Martin Rundkvist, who has investigated the rings, underlines the similarities to the stone circles. Judging by graves in central Europe, this kind of ring was worn by women, hanging in their clothes. Given the recurring number nine and the connection with women, Rundkvist interprets the rings as amulets used in connection with pregnancy (Rundkvist 1996). However, a large neck-ring of similar design has been found somewhere in the parish of Torslunda on Öland. This bronze ring is furnished with nine knobs decorated with silver inlay, and has been dated to the Migration Period as well (Holmqvist 1951:116). Therefore, the bronze rings may have had more general significance connected to the number nine.

We can glimpse how this world was perceived from the echoes in the Icelandic literary tradition, where the figure of nine was a recurrent unit for time, place, and transformation (Simek 1993:232–3; Gansum 1999:459 ff.). According to *Vǫluspá* 2, the 'measuring tree' was surrounded by nine worlds or preceded by nine ages (see Schøjdt 1992); Odin hung for nine nights in the world tree (*Hávamál* 138); the god Heimdall was the son of nine mothers (*Hyndluljóð* 35), who probably correspond to the nine daughters of the sea god Ægir; from Odin's or Baldr's gold ring Draupnir there fell eight rings every nine nights (*Gylfaginning* 48; *Skáldskaparmál* 33); and at the end of the world (Ragnarok), Thor, after his fight with the Midgard Serpent, managed to take nine steps before he fell down dead (*Vǫluspá* 56, *Gylfaginning* 50).

The figure of nine also occurred in rituals. Thietmar of Merseburg and Adam of Bremen in the eleventh century mention that large sacrificial feasts were held every nine years for nine days at Lejre and Gamla Uppsala (Nordberg 2006). At Gamla Uppsala, nine men and nine male animals of seven different kinds of animals were sacrificed (Sundqvist 2002, 2004). These descriptions have been questioned, but they can partly be confirmed by a much earlier rune stone from Stentoften in Blekinge, where the figure of nine is associated with animal sacrifices.

This text from the seventh century states that 'with nine bucks, with nine stallions, Haþuwulf gave a good harvest' (Santesson 1989; Sundqvist 2002). The figure of nine can thus be seen as an expression of a kind of cosmological and ritual perfection, and connected to transformations from one stage to another (Brink 2004; Sundqvist 2010).

The structural similarities between stone circles, Ismantorp, and the mythical and ritual figure of nine means that the graves and the fort may be regarded as images of Old Norse cosmology. The stone circles and Ismantorp were thus concrete symbols in the same way as the three-pointed stone settings that I discussed in the previous chapter, the difference being that the three-pointed stone settings signified only the world tree while the stone circles and the fort expressed the worlds around the world tree. For Ismantorp this cosmological interpretation means that the post in the centre of the fort and the nine gates corresponded to the world tree at the centre of the world, surrounded by nine different worlds (see Sjöborg 1822:128).

The cosmic dimensions at Ismantorp are very clear, but it is perfectly possible that simpler forts likewise display associations with the Old Norse worldview, as Birgitta Johansen (1997) has suggested. The world was called Midgard, and according to *Grímnismál* 41 the gods made Midgard from the eyelashes of the primeval giant Ymir, and according to Snorri's *Gylfaginning* 7 Midgard was a fortress. Ismantorp, like many other Scandinavian forts, thus had cosmic associations. Yet this connection between war and cosmos is not confined to the Norse worldview; it is also found outside Scandinavia.

Models and parallels

In view of the dating of Ismantorp and the other forts on Öland, it is natural to turn to the Roman Empire and the Roman army in search of models. Stenberger suggested early on that the distinctive Ölandic forts may have been imitations of Roman models (Stenberger 1933:255 ff.). Joachim Werner believes instead that the forts on Öland were inspired by late classical Byzantine fortified villages and strongholds (Werner 1949:267–8.), while Frands Herschend and Ulf Näsman draw attention to Roman models for a special portcullis gate at Eketorp (Herschend 1985; Näsman 1989). Some forts in the Mälaren valley are also believed to have been built in imitation of Roman models (Olausson 1997, 2009).

The significance of the Roman Empire in northern Europe has long been noticed in Scandinavian archaeology, yet recent studies show that the Roman finds do not reflect simple 'imports' or passive influences from the empire (Hedeager 1979; Lund Hansen 1987; Ekengren 2009). Instead, the Roman objects were used actively as markers by socially and politically dominant groups in Scandinavia. Beyond the artefacts, Roman links can be detected in a number of different spheres, not least in the culture of war.

Around 300, more than a hundred years after the Marcomannic Wars (166–72, 177–80), the Roman warfare and defensive strategy had changed (Johnson 1983; Le Bohec 1994; Southern and Dixon 1996; Bachrach 1997; Schnurbein 1997; Fischer 1999:138 ff., 2000:207 ff.; Mackensen 2000:213 ff.; Schmidts 2000:219 ff.). Before the wars, the defence of the empire was chiefly based on a fortified border with ramparts, forts, army camps, and large garrisons, planned to fixed principles. After the wars, the Romans instead gradually created a deep defence with forts and fortified towns in a wide border zone. Over time, the fortifications were increasingly adapted to the terrain and thus became irregular. At the same time, warfare changed from battles in open land to siege warfare around fortified sites. The changes in the Roman army and its warfare can also be detected in the structure of the Roman army camps. Most of the geometric rectangular Roman fortresses had disappeared by 300, although some forts of rectangular shape were still built during the fourth century, such as Deutz, Boppard and Alzey in the Rhineland and Fenenpuszta in Hungary (Fischer 1999:138 ff.; Oldenstein 2009). Instead, many smaller forts were built, with high walls and towers. These forts could be square, trapezoid, round, or oval, but they could also be totally irregular if they had to be adapted to the terrain.

The classical Roman camps or fortresses were built as large squares or rectangles with slightly rounded corners (Fischer 1999:48 ff.). They were divided into four parts by two main streets, *cardo* and *decumanus*. In the middle of the camp there was normally a *principia*, or headquarters building, where standards, ensigns, weapons, and the regimental treasury were kept. Grouped around the headquarters were the commander's residence, barracks, stables, storehouses, field hospital, kitchens, and latrines. The fortresses were built according to the same principles throughout the empire, thereby creating a common spatial framework for the multicultural Roman army (see Schnurbein 1997). Unfortu-

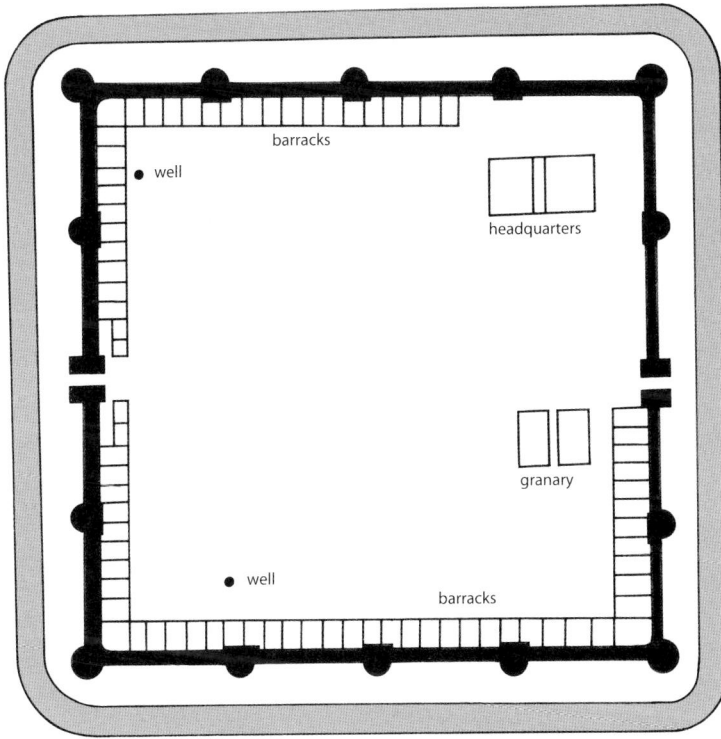

Figure 36. The late Roman fortress of Alteium (modern Alzey) between Mainz and Worms. The fortress was established in 367–70, and is one of several late Roman rectangular fortresses in the Rhineland. It was used by the Romans for only about thirty years, then rebuilt twice before it fell out of use in the late fifth century. (Plan by the author, based on Oldenstein 2009:268.)

nately, little is known about the design of the late classical fort, and the spatial principles are unclear in most cases. However, at the rectangular Deutz the caserns were still built in rows, whereas the barracks were built along the walls in Alzey (Johnson 1983; Oldenstein 2009). This place later became a political centre in the Burgundian realm in the fifth century (Fig. 36). Alzey as well as many of the other late Roman forts can be regarded as models for Ismantorp and the other ringforts on Öland. It is not necessary to search for a single model, since the

Ölandic ringforts should rather be viewed as local reinterpretations of the contemporary Roman forts.

The meaning of the distinctive design of the classical rectangular Roman fortresses has been studied in detail by Joseph Rykwert (1988). Based on Latin texts describing the ceremonies for the foundation of towns and garrisons, he is able to show that the places expressed the Roman cosmology, with the division of the heavens into four parts, and the connection between heaven, earth, and the underworld. The places were moreover perceived as images of Rome, even though the capital did not have a regular plan. The role of representation is particularly clear from the foundation ceremonies, which everywhere in the empire were based on the myth of Romulus founding Rome. The rituals included taking omens from flying birds, purifying the area by fire, and marking the centre of the world with the aid of a pit, which also symbolized the opening into the underworld. From the pit, garrisons were planned and simultaneously demarcated from the outside world by a furrow ploughed with a team of oxen. The foundation pit in the centre has actually been found a few times, for example at the legionary fortresses at Nijmegen in the Netherlands and at Inchtuchil in Scotland (Pitts and St Joseph 1985:59, 78). The classical Roman camps, in other words, expressed how the military order was incorporated in a larger cosmological model, which applied all over the empire. The possible meaning of the late Roman forts is not known to the same extent. However, due to the close link between war and religion in the Roman Empire (Rüpke 1990; Gustafsson 1999), as well as the foundation of some new rectangular fortresses in the fourth century, it is highly likely that the older cosmological order survived in some form.

This association between cosmology, fortification, and military organization was not confined to the Roman Empire. The best-known example after the Roman Empire comes from eighth-century Saxony, as mentioned in the previous chapter (Palm 1948; Best et al. 1999; Vikstrand 2001). In 772, the Carolingian army conquered the Saxon fort of Eresburg, where according to several different sources there was a large wooden pillar in the fort, which Charlemagne had chopped down and replaced with a church. The pillar, which was called Irminsul ('the great column'), should be regarded as a representation of a world pillar at the centre of the world. The Carolingian church no longer exists, having been replaced by a later church built at the highest point of what is today called Obermarsberg. The location of the church shows that Irminsul must have been placed at the highest point on the plateau where the fort stood. Eresburg was thus a heavily fortified stronghold but at the same time a representation of the world, with the world pillar erected at the highest part of the fort (see Fig. 11).

It is possible that the Slavic strongholds from the eleventh and twelfth centuries, which Stenberger used in order to interpret Ismantorp, may be viewed in a similar context. The Slavic forts were more permanently occupied than the earlier Scandinavian forts, and their central ritual functions were more pronounced (Słupecki 1994). At the same time, they were powerful strongholds with obvious cosmological associations. As we have seen, the fort of Rethra had nine gates, and, as at Ismantorp, these can be interpreted as symbolizing nine worlds. A narrow gate in the east led out to a nearby lake 'which looked truly terrifying' (*visu nimis horribile monstrat*, Thietmar of Merseburg VI, 23, in Słupecki 1994:52). In view of this wording, perhaps this gate can be perceived as a special 'death gate'. The association between organization of war and cosmology is also clear from other forts, which Stenberger does not mention. In the main Pomeranian stronghold at Szczecin (Stettin) there is mention of a temple but also a large oak and a spring, which can be connected with the idea of a world tree with a spring at its root. And at the centre of the main stronghold at Pskov in western Russia, the remains of a large post have also been found, arousing associations with a world pillar (Słupecki 1994:72 ff., 152). Thus the association between cosmology and the organization of war reflected a general pattern in the Roman as well as in the post-Roman world.

Back to Ismantorp

The background to the ringfort must be sought in the clear changes in Scandinavian martial culture that took place from the third century onwards. Before this, armies had consisted of smaller groups summoning individually equipped men, but from around this time the armies became bigger and more hierarchically organized, with mounted commanders. This military elite controlled the mass production of weapons and probably also the more professional training of soldiers. Like other contemporary changes, the new military organization must have been based on Roman models. Similar to other Roman elements in Scandinavia, it was not a straightforward adoption, but instead a process of conscious selection and reinterpretation (cf. Ingemark 2003). Aspects of a Roman martial culture were probably introduced by Scandinavian soldiers who had served in the Roman army. But the new military order could scarcely have been established without local negotiations. The location of the forts in outlands between different settlement areas indicates that they were built on a collective initiative, and that the army leaders thus had only temporary power during the actual campaigns. The large finds of weapon deposits in similar ways reflected collective rituals after martial campaigns.

Viewed from this perspective, it is possible to understand the meaning and function of Ismantorp as one of the distinctive Ölandic ringforts used between 300 and 650. In Ismantorp it is possible to see how Roman models were incorporated and reinterpreted in a Scandinavian context around 300 (Fig. 37). The foundation ceremonies for Roman towns and camps were partly adopted at Ismantorp. The rituals included determining the centre of the world by digging a pit, which simultaneously marked the opening into the underworld. From this pit the towns and garrisons were laid out, after which the pit was filled and covered. In the middle of the open area in Ismantorp there was a corresponding pit, which was the geometrical centre of the fort, since the nine gates were oriented towards it. Unlike the Roman foundation pits, however, this pit was open for a longer period.

From their foundation ceremonies, the Romans planned square or rectangular towns and camps with two crossing axes. The builders of Ismantorp instead constructed a virtually round fort with nine gates. The Roman cosmology, with a quadripartite sky, was thus translated to an Old Norse worldview with nine different worlds surrounding its centre, each world being represented by one gate. The local model for this design was the older and contemporary stone circle with nine stones. As mentioned earlier, one of the small gates was connected to a house. This strange construction can be viewed in cosmic perspectives as the way to a realm of the dead, either Hel or Valhall, which both surrounded the world tree. The gate could thus have served as a *Helvegr*, a special road used only to carry people to the grave (de Vries 1956:194).

In the middle of the Roman camps there was normally a headquarters building, the courtyard of which was placed over the original foundation pit. At Ismantorp the pit was retained in the open area at the

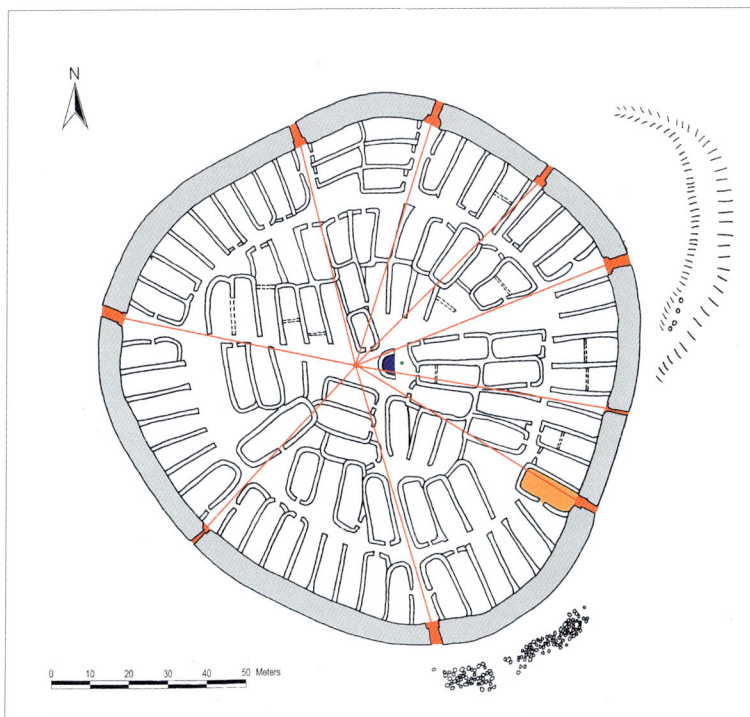

Figure 37. Reconstruction of Ismantorp ringfort, with possible cosmological references: the nine gates (red) and their orientation towards the pit in the centre (red lines), the house in front of the south-east gate (orange), the semicircular house in the centre (violet), and the post east of the house (green).(Plan by the author.)

centre, evoking associations with the well of fate or Urd's well, which according to *Vǫluspá* 20, and *Gylfaginning* 14 was located in the middle of the world beside the world tree (Simek 1993:236–7, 342). The post at the eastern end of the open area can be regarded as the representation of the world tree or world axis, whereas the small semicircular building may have staged the dwelling of the Norns, which according to *Gylfaginning* 14 was located beside the world tree. In the small house a seeress or a *vǫlva* may have been active, evoking associations with the mythical Norns. Several Roman sources mention seeresses as important to Germanic troops already in the first century AD (Simek 1993:356–7; Dobat 2009), and the exquisite relief brooches in two of the Ölandic ringforts have can be interpreted as marking the presence of high-ranking women with ritual capacities (Magnus 2004). No traces of large-scale rituals have been found in the centre of the fort, but the pit, along with the small building and the post, possibly provided the framework for other rites, such as the initiation of warriors and divinations before campaigns. The lancehead and the arrowhead deposited in small pits in the centre could thus be traces of such rites.

In the Roman camps, all the other buildings necessary for the army were constructed around the headquarters. The buildings were mostly grouped according to their various functions, so that the stables were grouped in one place, the barracks in another, and so on. At Ismantorp there were likewise different types of houses around the centre of the fort, but they were not separated according to function in the same way as the buildings in the Roman camps. Some of the buildings at Ismantorp, like the buildings in the Roman army camps, must have been intended for the followers, who may also have included women.

Many of the Roman camps became permanently occupied, and moreover attached to a less regulated civil settlement outside the fortifications. Ismantorp and most other Scandinavian forts from this period lacked this feature. Most of them were built in the outland far from cultivable land, so they lacked the conditions necessary for becoming permanent settlements. In addition, they were mentally speaking in a wild or liminal landscape, which suited the wildness of the Scandinavian martial culture. Ismantorp, like many other forts, must therefore be regarded as a kind of military resource, built by the estates in the surrounding settlements.

The exact function of Ismantorp is difficult to determine, due to the general lack of finds. However, various martial functions are the most plausible. The place could have been used periodically for training warriors and for the initiation of new warriors. It could also have been the scene of feasting and drinking ceremonies intended to reinforce the bonds between warriors from different settlements, in the same way as the Norwegian *tun* sites functioned. The ringfort could have served as a place of assembly for external campaigns or as a base for defence. It may have been used in full-scale wars, but was probably used mainly for recurrent plundering raids and ritualized wars. It is therefore possible that livestock, horses, and slaves from raids could have been gathered and divided in places like Ismantorp. The impressive monument moreover signalled that the surrounding settlement and their estates were well organized in military terms. The fort could thus have had an outright deterrent purpose.

Since the unique ringforts on Öland are located at fairly regularly intervals (see Fig. 26), several scholars have tried to reconstruct large-scale military divisions of the island (Hofrén 1948; Näsman 1997). Such ideas are quite plausible, due to the parallels between the size of the forts and the size of the surrounding settlement (Fallgren 2008). However, these divisions should not be viewed in too territorial a perspective, by using medieval military divisions as analogies (see Näsman 1997). Therefore, the forts should also be regarded as potential military resources, built and used in relation to the changing power positions of the estates in the surrounding area, as an analogy to the clusters of early boathouses along the Norwegian coast. The ringforts need not have been used at the same time; they could have been activated according to the prevailing political situation within an area. Such non-centralized initiatives could thus explain the low level of activity in Ismantorp as well as the short distance of only five kilometres between Ismantorp and Mossberga.

The ringfort at Ismantorp can be regarded as a hybrid form, with Roman elements incorporated and reinterpreted in a new context. This new creation was and remained unique to Öland, since the island's ringforts took on a highly distinctive character. There may be several reasons for this. The Roman-influenced hybridization of southern and central Scandinavia was not a uniform process, since circumstances differed in this politically and socially divided area. The different Roman phenomena should instead be regarded as individually adapted strategies by different local elites to demarcate themselves *vis-à-vis* the rest of the population, through Roman-inspired traditions and expressions. The Roman features could thus have taken on a highly local or regional character, and been given a wide variety of expressions. Densely settled ringforts were constructed only on Öland, boathouses and *tun* sites only along the Norwegian coasts, while Sjælland is particularly known for burials with rich Roman finds.

The special design of the Ölandic ringforts may also have to do with the fact that the island was strategically situated on the main sailing route along the eastern coast of the Scandinavian peninsula. The island represented a border zone between, on the one hand, a south Scandinavian area with large villages and weapon deposits, and, on the other hand, an east Scandinavian region with single farms, small villages, and hillforts. On Öland, there were both weapon deposits and ring-forts, but also large, loosely organized villages. This border location, which was also expressed through the styles of contemporary dress ornaments (Høilund Nielsen 1991), may have had the result that the island was heavily militarized (Näsman 1997; cf. James 1997). Perhaps part of Öland's economy was based on the fact that the island did not just produce cereals and livestock, but also soldiers. In view of Öland's strategic location, it is also possible that the densely settled forts, like the Roman camps, contributed to the creation of a common cultural framework for the Ölandic warrior groups, even if the individual warriors came from different cultural backgrounds (see Andrén 2011c).

Ismantorp and the other distinctive Ölandic forts were built in the fourth and fifth centuries, but they successively lost their primary functions in the sixth or early seventh centuries; the same can be said of many of the other Scandinavian forts. During the same period, collective weapon deposits were replaced by the depositions of single weapons (Nørgård Jørgensen 2009). The martial organization introduced in the third century was based on negotiations between different aristocratic families, and the military leaders probably only enjoyed temporary power associated with the actual campaign. From the fifth century, however, it seems that some of these war leaders gradually extended their power in a more lasting way. Signs of this shift in power are that a few forts became more permanently occupied in the fifth and sixth centuries, for example, Eketorp on Öland and Runsa in Uppland (Wall 2003; Olausson 1997, 2011). In this way, the power that the war leaders had only exerted during certain short periods became permanent. In the fifth and sixth centuries, the concentration of power thus led to a new form of leadership (Skre 1998; Näsman 2008; Olausson 2009). With this more permanent political elite, the military organization was to a higher degree based on retinues of warriors attached to a leader by oaths of personal loyalty (Nørgård Jørgensen 1997). At the same time, power and control over warfare was strengthened in the same way as in England and Scotland, so that the recurrent, chiefly ritualized raids gradually disappeared. In the long run, there was thus no longer a need for weapon deposits, forts, or *tun* sites where power relations between different aristocratic groups could be negotiated and renegotiated in more or less ritualized acts.

Ismantorp and Old Norse cosmology

Ismantorp was neither a place of passive refuge nor a central ritual site. Instead, it functioned as an occasionally used army camp inscribed with a cosmological meaning. The fort is a good illustration of how pre-Christian religion in Scandinavia was not necessarily a separate religious sphere but an integral part of people's practice. This also applies to such a special world as the martial culture of the time. As cosmological representations, Ismantorp and the contemporary stone circles are the oldest known depictions of the Old Norse worldview, as it is known in later texts. Cosmologies need not necessarily correspond to systematic and well-ordered figures of thought, but general ideas about the world can become a clearly structured universe in special circumstances. I believe that this is what happened at Ismantorp and the other Ölandic ringforts. In the encounter with Roman culture and its distinct worldview, Old Norse cosmology became more explicit and more systematic than before.

Earlier hillforts may very well have had cosmological associations. A good example is the hillfort at Odensala in Uppland, where different deposits around the walls seem to have expressed an anthropocentric worldview. In the centre of the hillfort were only deposits of human bones, whereas animal bones were deposited further away from the centre, and cereals were deposited on the periphery (Olausson 1995). However, it was only in the encounter with Roman culture that such a worldview was systematized into something partly new. Ismantorp was a hybrid based both on Roman models and on local traditions in the form of stone circles. In the Roman encounter, ideas about the world that were expressed in burial contexts were used for the martial settlement of the Ölandic ringforts. This encounter between Roman and Scandinavian culture engendered some of the features that would later characterize the Old Norse tradition in the Icelandic texts.

Figure 38. Early picture stone in the fabric of the church at Bro. This part of the church was built *c.*1300. (Photo by the author.)

CHAPTER 4

Whirls, horses, and ships
Solar aspects of Old Norse religion

Ever since 1902, it has been clear that Scandinavian religion in the distant past was sun-oriented. That year, several extraordinary bronze objects were found in a bog outside the village of Trundholm in northern Sjælland. It turned out that they could be put together to form a carriage of six wheels, with a partly gilded bronze disc drawn by a horse placed on the carriage (Aner and Kersten 1976). This motif of a horse drawing a sun-disc with a string from its neck is also known from contemporary bronze razors and rock carvings. These recurring solar images show how the sun played a central mythological and ritual role in the Bronze Age. It is much more uncertain whether Old Norse religion in the Iron Age had a similar solar orientation, or if the importance of the sun disappeared at the end of the Bronze Age or vanished gradually. Some aspects of a solar motif were nonetheless clearly still known 2,600 years after Trundholm, since some of the lays in the *Poetic Edda* and Snorri Sturluson in his *Edda* mention how the sun and the moon are drawn by two horses over the sky, and how the personified day and night ride over the sky after horses. However, in the Icelandic tradition these celestial phenomena are reduced to faint figures without any role in the mythological narratives. Somewhere between Trundholm and Reykholt the sun lost much of its ritual, mythological, and narrative importance, but it is not known when and why.

Early picture stones on Gotland

I will reconsider the changing solar aspects of Old Norse religion, starting midway between Trundholm and Reykholt, with the early picture stones on Gotland. They are part of an extraordinary pictorial tradition on the island, which can be followed over nearly a millennium. About 475 picture stones with different designs were erected on Gotland from the Early Iron Age until about 1100. Above all, the large monuments from the early Viking Age (750–900) have attracted scholarly attention for a long time. They are covered with vivid images, which have been linked to motifs in Icelandic myths and heroic narratives, for instance Odin on his eight-legged horse (Lindqvist 1941), the smith Volund (Vǫlundr) (Buisson 1976), and scenes from the Volsung cycle (Andrén 1993; cf. Staecker 2004).

The early picture stones have attracted less interest, because they are much more formalized (but see Guber 2011). These monuments contain fewer, and less vivid images, which are repeated over and over again. Above all, the stones are covered with large whirls, ships and antithetical pairs of smaller spirals, horses, riders, warriors, and snakes or dragons. Ever since Sune Lindqvist's large corpus *Gotlands Bild-steine* (1941–2), the early picture stones have been assumed to be grave markers, because lower parts of such stones as well as ornamented kerbstones have been found in graves. The monuments have been dated on stylistic grounds to the Migration Period – the fifth century and the first half of the sixth century AD. Due to this early dating, the images have been regarded as more difficult to interpret, being much more remote from the Icelandic tradition than the later monuments.

The round central figures on the early stones have in general been understood as sun representations. Already in the early twentieth century, Gabriel Gustafsson and Fredrik Nordin interpreted the large whirl at the top as a sun symbol and the ship at the bottom as a death ship (Lindqvist 1941:91). Lindqvist, however, was very hesitant in his interpretation of the early picture stones in his corpus. He argued that the round geometrical figures were perhaps depictions of shields. His main argument against Gustafsson and Nordin was that whirls, spirals, rosettes, and other figures on the Gotlandic stones actually occur in early Christian art in southern Europe at the same time (Lindqvist 1941:91 ff.). Hilda Ellis Davidson returned to solar interpretations of the early stones, with extensive chronological and geographical comparisons. She also understood the main round image to be the sun and the ship a ship of the dead (Gelling and Davidson 1969:139 ff.). Later on, she modified this idea in an interpretation of the complete stone from Sanda, which she saw as a representation of the Nordic cosmos. Davidson proposed that the large whirl was a symbol of the turning cosmos, whereas the two smaller spirals were the sun and the moon. A tree on a horizontal line she interpreted as the world tree, a creature underneath as a serpent of the depths, and a ship as the surrounding ocean (Davidson 1988:168 ff.). Since then, no one has tried to interpret the early Gotlandic picture stones systematically. Many scholars have accepted the idea of the sun and a ship of the dead (Nylén and Lamm 1978:15, 22; Althaus 1993; Andersson 2001), sometimes putting the images in a Celtic context (Görman 1998). Others have interpreted single motifs, above all a dragon and a man (Nylén and Lamm 2003:30 ff., 186; Raudvere 2004; Myrberg 2005; Ney 2006; Ragnarsson 2011).

Although Lindqvist has a point about the early Christian parallels, he does not take into account that the form and the Christian content of the models did not necessary follow each other. Late Roman and early Christian models might well have been incorporated into local non-Christian contexts in a process of hybridization. Since most of the large whirls and some of the smaller spirals have very distinct small rays at the rim, which the Roman models do not have, I still find it worth exploring the idea of sun representations. Seventy years after the publication of Lindqvist's corpus there are also other good reasons for re-investigating the early picture stones. New finds point to a necessary revision of the chronology. The new dating consequently leads to new contexts and also opens up a new discussion of both contemporary parallels and older models.

New contexts

When excavating the large burial ground Barshaldershed on southern Gotland in 1984, Peter Manneke found a cremation grave with the lower part of an erected stone still standing in the middle. Judging from the finds, the grave can be dated to AD 200–350. A similar grave, with a lower part of an erected stone, was excavated as early as the late nineteenth century at Bläsnungs in Väskinde, north-western Gotland, giving an even earlier date of AD 100–250 (Manneke 1984). It is not totally clear whether these erected stones had carved images, but they mark the beginning of limestone slabs being erected as grave markers.

The possibility of an earlier start for the first picture stones actually fits well with the design and decorative elements of some early monuments. The overall design of some of the early picture stones, such as Stenkyrka Kyrka I (Lindqvist 1942, fig. 490), bears some resemblance to the so-called swastika fibulas from the third and fourth centuries (Fig. 39). Besides, some of the round figures on the early stones are not whirls, but rosettes with 'leaves' or figures with geometrical pleated and interlaced patterns. Such motifs are known from picture stones from Ire in Hellvi (Lindqvist 1941, figs 1–2), Burs (Lindqvist 1941, fig. 21), and Tofta (Lindqvist 1962). These motifs have good parallels in metalwork from the third and fourth centuries, such as bronze fittings found in the weapon deposits in present-day Denmark (Jørgensen et al. 2003). These links indicate that the early picture stones were erected during a longer period than Lindqvist suggested, probably from the third to the sixth centuries.

A consequence of the longer chronology is that the early picture stones can be placed in a much more prolific social context. They were part of new 'stone enclosure communities' (Sw. *stengrundsbebyggelse*), established on the island from the second and third centuries AD. These communities consisted of houses with stone foundations (Sw. *stengrundshus*) as well as stone enclosures (Sw. *stensträngar*) framing fields and meadows. Even today, more than 1,800 houses and large areas of deserted fields with stone walls are still preserved on the island (Nihlén and Boethius 1933; Stenberger and Klindt Jensen 1955; Carlsson 1979). Some of the ringforts on Gotland, such as the enormous Torsburgen with its perimeter of over 4.5 kilometres, also date from the same time (Engström 1984). Besides, distinct features of this expansive period are the Roman objects found everywhere on Gotland. They include bronze vessels, coins of silver and gold, and even terra sigillata pottery (Lund Hansen 1987; Lind 1981, 1988; Herschend 1980; Fagerlie 1967).

Lindqvist, and later Holmqvist, pointed to Roman gravestones and Roman mosaics as models for the design of the whirls and spirals (Lindqvist 1941:91 ff.; Holmqvist 1952). Davidson later gave further examples of Roman models, such as an altar with whirls and rosettes, found at Hadrian's Wall in northern England (Gelling and Davidson 1969:144). A longer chronology of the early picture stones, starting possibly in the third century, would help to give a much better understanding of the proposed Roman models for these monuments. They

Figure 39. Picture stone from the church at Stenkyrka. This stone is an example of the first phase of the early picture stones, since the central figure has parallels with the so-called swastika fibulas from the third and fourth centuries. (Drawing by Olof Sörling in Lindqvist 1942, fig. 490.)

can be viewed as just one of many cultural traits in Scandinavia that had a Roman background.

Although the early picture stones from Gotland are the best-known Scandinavian pictorial monuments from AD 200–550, they are not unique. In Uppland and Södermanland, around 25 small picture stones with similar images are known (Lindqvist 1941:30 ff.; Ahlberg 1978; Hamilton 2012). Usually they only contain one or two images of a whirl, a spiral, a ship, or two horses and warriors. They were grave markers, as on Gotland, and in one case, at Rällinge in Södermanland, the picture stone still stands on top of a small barrow. These small picture stones are part of a similar expansive period, above all in Uppland, where large houses were built on terraces, stone enclosures were erected around infields, and several Roman objects have been found (Lund Hansen 1987; Olausson 1997; Andersson 1998).

Closer parallels to the Gotlandic pictures stones may also have existed on the neighbouring island of Öland. Large limestone slabs are still standing today in many burial grounds on Öland. In contrast to the Gotlandic picture stones, however, no figures were cut or carved on the slabs, but instead the smooth show sides of the slabs were probably painted with images similar to the pictures on Gotland (Fig. 40). The limestone slabs on Öland can be put in a very similar context to the picture stones on Gotland. They were grave markers raised in a period of expansive settlement, in which houses were built on stone foundations, long stone walls enclosed fields, distinct ringforts were constructed and

Figure 40. Two upright limestone slabs at Ottenby in Ås on Öland. This type of limestone slab are common in burial grounds on Öland, and they usually have smooth show sides facing north. (Photo by the author.)

many Roman objects were deposited (Stenberger 1933; Fallgren 2006; Andrén 2006; Fargelie 1967; Lind 1981, 1988; Herschend 1980; Lund Hansen 1987; see also the previous chapter).

The Roman background of the design of the pictorial monuments, especially in eastern Sweden from the third to the sixth centuries, fits well with Roman connections in general during that time in southern Scandinavia. However, the Roman background of the style of the figures does not necessarily give us a better understanding of the iconography of the early picture stones. In order to reach possible interpretations of these monuments, one has to move beyond style to investigate the content of the images, beginning with the pictorial structure.

An initial pictorial analysis

According to the latest survey, around 70 early picture stones are currently known from about 35 locations on Gotland (Nylén and Lamm 2003:177 ff.). Not one has been found in its original place, and more than half of the monuments have been found in medieval stone churches from the twelfth, thirteenth, and early fourteenth centuries (see Fig. 38). Many of the picture stones were probably still standing as grave markers in the burial grounds until that time when they were incorporated into the fabric of the stone churches. In several cases these parish churches are located near very large burial grounds, where the monuments were probably originally erected. The earliest stones were placed in the centre of graves surrounded by rectangular frames of stones (Manneke 1984). Later, the stones instead formed part of large round cairns built up with dry-stone walls. The upper edges of these walls sometimes had stones with cut decoration, such as lines and spirals (Lindqvist 1942:118 ff.).

The early picture stones varied considerably in size. A few very tall stones can be estimated to have had a height of between two and a half and four metres, and most of them have been found along the west coast of Gotland. Smaller stones had a height of no more than one metre, and were erected in all parts of the island (Nylén and Lamm 2003:177 ff.). The large stones usually contain more images than the smaller ones, and consequently are better suited for analysis of the pictorial structure. Most stones are in fragments, since many of them were broken into pieces to fit into the fabric of the medieval churches, but nevertheless the images on the different fragments fit into an overall structural pattern. The formal interpretation of the different images is not totally clear. The recurring geometrical figures are usually distinct enough, whereas the smaller accompanying images can be more problematic, due to the uneven preservation of the surface of the stones. For instance, on a stone from Vallstena, Lindqvist interpreted two figures as horses with their heads bent backwards, but these figures have later been reinterpreted as two armed riders (Arrhenius and Holmqvist 1960). This means that the overall pictorial pattern is fairly unambiguous, whereas the single image can sometimes be more problematic.

The basic structural pattern of the stones comprises a large round figure at the top, two antithetical smaller figures in the middle, and a ship at the bottom. Above the large round figure, animals or humans

Figure 41. Pictorial structure of the early picture stones, demonstrated by five stones from Ire in Hellvi (A), the church at Martebo (B), the church at Sanda (C), the church at Bro (D), and Vallstenarum in Vallstena (E) (photos A–D by the author and E by Bengt A. Lundberg, Statens Historiska Museum, Stockholm). Compare also Figs. 39, 50 and 54.

are often antithetically placed (Fig. 41). This pictorial pattern is best illustrated by the stone from Sanda, which is the most complete monument of the large stones, measuring fully 3.3 metres. The stone consists of two parts, which were found around 1900 and 1956 respectively (Lindqvist 1962). It has all the main and supplementary elements of the recurring pictorial structure.

The recurring large round geometrical figure is known from about 45 stones. In most cases, this figure is a whirl, but in two early cases it is a rosette or a pleated round figure, and in three late cases it is a complex

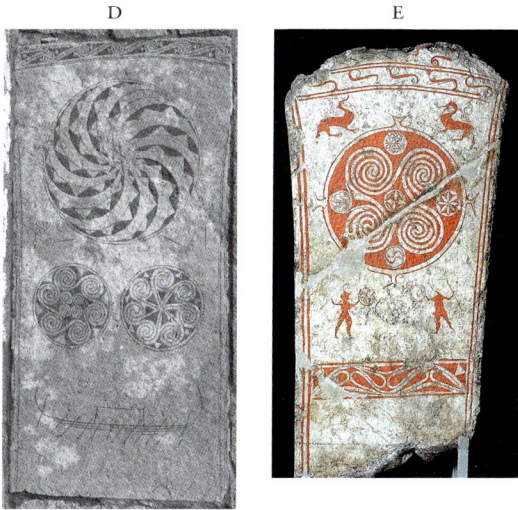

knot. On some smaller stones the whirl is the only image, whereas on most large stones it is accompanied by other figures. The configuration may differ between the stones, but they all follow the same structure.

In eleven cases, there are various creatures above the large whirl. These can include snakes, dragons, animals with horns, armed riders or three-pointed geometrical figures. In one case, a man seems to be placing his hand in the mouth of a multi-legged dragon (see Fig. 54). Beneath the large whirl on twenty stones appear a pair of antithetical figures, either round geometrical figures or humans or animals. In fifteen cases, the images are round geometrical figures, and most of them are spirals, but early rosettes and late knots also occur. In half of the cases, the small spirals end with animal heads and tails or are surrounded by a snake. In seven instances, the antithetical images are pairs of warriors, armed riders, horses, or, in one case, snakes. The riders and warriors have round shields with the same pattern of whirls and spirals as the round figures. Normally, only one pair of antithetical figures is depicted on a single stone, showing that two round figures could be replaced with two warriors, riders, or horses. This in turn, indicates that the figures represented some form of transformation.

Beneath the antithetical pairs, a horizontal line or a horizontal pleated zone is found on five stones. In one case, on the stone from

Sanda, a small tree is standing on the horizontal line, accompanied by some kind of monster below the line. At the bottom of eight stones is a ship, with varying relations to the images above. The ship can be placed beneath the horizontal line/zone or the antithetical pairs, or even directly beneath the large round geometrical figure. The ship is always being rowed to the left, and it has steering oars in the stern as well as in the bow.

The pictorial pattern of the early stones is thus conspicuously uniform, although the different elements are not totally understood. The compulsory large round figure can provisionally be interpreted as a sun representation because of the common rays around the rim, but the other figures are much more difficult to grasp. In order to get a better understanding of the early stones, it is necessary to make several comparisons, chronologically and geographically.

A return trip to Bronze Age iconography

A good starting-point when comparing the early picture stones is the sun-chariot from Trundholm (Fig. 42). As mentioned earlier, the carriage is a ritual object, incorporating the disc and the horse as a mythical representation. The disc and the horse were originally connected by a string or a chain, creating a sun-horse. One side of the bronze disc, the one that is visible when the horse is seen drawing the disc from left to right, is gilded, whereas the other side is not. Ever since the discovery, the gilded side has been interpreted as the day-side, showing how the sun was seen as being drawn across the sky from east to west by a horse, whereas the ungilded side has been understood as the night-side, showing how the horse pulled the invisible sun back through the sky or through the underworld from west to east (Kaul 1998, 2004).

The sun-horse from Trundholm is clearly part of a broader Scandinavian pattern. A more fragmented find, with two similar horses, comes from Tågaborg, in north-western Skåne. A possible sun-chariot, although without the disc, has also been found at Järfälla, north-west of Stockholm (Victor 2007:163 ff.). Several sun-horses, including the connecting string, are depicted on rock carvings in Bohuslän and on bronze razors in Denmark as well. Some of these images are more recent than the Trundholm find, dating to the period 1100–500 BC. However, the solar representations during the Bronze Age include other elements

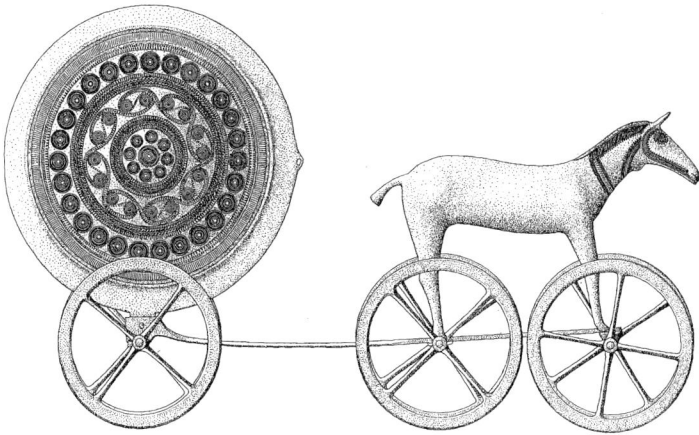

Figure 42. The sun-chariot from Trundholm in north-west Sjælland. (After Aner and Kersten 1976.)

as well, which is most evident from recent studies by Flemming Kaul (1998, 2004). His detailed investigations of sun symbolism are inspired by earlier works by, among others, Ernst Sprockhoff (1954) and Peter Gelling (Gelling and Davidson 1969).

Kaul bases his study on a very thorough analysis of the images on about 420 bronze objects, mostly from the Late Bronze Age (1100–500 BC) that have been found in present-day Denmark (Kaul 1998). The images are preserved above all on asymmetric razors, but also on neck-rings and other objects such as knives and tweezers. Sometimes, he also includes pictures from objects found in present-day Sweden, Norway, and northern Germany in his analysis. Recurring images on these objects are one or several ships, which are sometimes combined with circles, horses, mushroom-shaped figures, fishes, snakes, birds, and occasionally humans. This pictorial world is clearly transformative, including snake-horses, and ship stems with human heads, heads of horses, snakes, birds, and mushroom-shaped figures (Kaul 1998:188 ff.; 2004:271 ff.). Apart from the ship, the most frequently recurring image is the circle. Kaul interprets the circle as a symbol of the sun, because it sometimes has rays and sometimes is connected with a horse, creating a sun-horse like the figure from Trundholm (Kaul 1998:195, 2004:352).

Kaul makes a fundamental distinction between the ships based on their direction of travel, and the images combined with ships sailing to the right or the left. This division offers a parallel to the day-side and the night-side of the disc from Trundholm (Kaul 1998:165 ff.). Since all circle motifs and all pictures of sun-horses are connected to ships travelling to the right, Kaul interprets these ships as images of 'day-ships', transporting the sun across the sky from sunrise in the east to sunset in the west. Consequently the ships travelling to the left are interpreted as images of 'night-ships', passing through the underworld from sunset in the west to sunrise in the east. The mushroom-shaped figure appears only with day-ships and the sun. The snakes, birds and fishes are more ambivalent in their connections to day-ships and night-ships, and are therefore regarded as helpers of the sun at critical transitions, such as sunrise, zenith, and sunset. Kaul argues that all these images represent a solar myth in Scandinavia from the Late Bronze Age (Kaul 1998:257 ff., 2004:241). The sun-horse of Trundholm, as well as early mushroom-shaped figures and fishes, shows that this myth existed already in the Early Bronze Age, although in a slightly different version. In the Late Bronze Age, aquatic birds, snakes, and ships as the main means of transport were introduced into narratives about the eternal journey of the sun (Fig. 43).

Although Kaul reckons on other myths too (Kaul 2004:183 ff.), he regards the solar myth as the fundamental narrative of the Scandinavian Bronze Age. He is, however, very reluctant to acknowledge anthropomorphic gods and goddesses, since very few humans are depicted on bronze objects (Kaul 2004:341 ff.). Instead he interprets most bronze figures and human images on rock carvings as different representations of rituals. Only a few human figures with solar rays around their heads that appear on bronze objects from the end of the Bronze Age are regarded as possible personifications of a solar god or perhaps divine twins, the Dioscuri (Kaul 1998:55 ff., 249 ff., 2004:80). This idea has since been developed by Kristian Kristiansen and Thomas Larsson (Kristiansen and Larsson 2005:262 ff.), who, following other scholars, also interpret the recurring 'pair motif' in figures and objects as expressions of divine twins (Krüger 1940–2; Althin 1945; Sprockhoff 1954; de Vries 1957:244 ff.; Fredell 2003; Kristiansen and Larsson 2005). The earliest double male figures, originally probably with horned hats, come from Stockhult in northern Skåne and are dated to 1500–1300

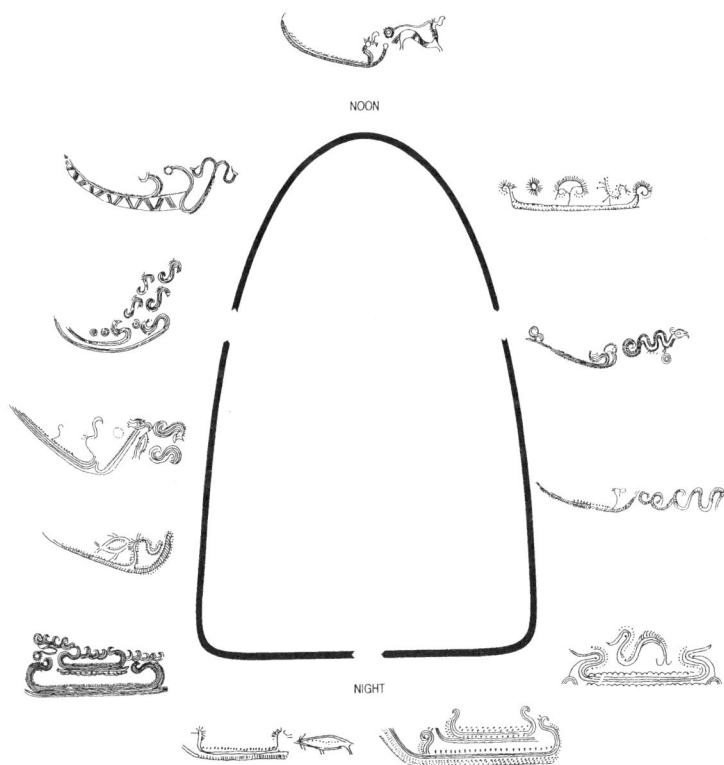

Figure 43. The solar cycle in the Bronze Age, according to Flemming Kaul. (After Kaul 1998:262.)

BC (Fig. 44). In a later version from Grevensvænge in Sjælland, the male pair have horned helmets and large axes, whereas the men from Fogdarp in central Skåne have horned helmets with bird beaks. On a razor from Vestrup Mark in northern Jutland a pair of men, and another accompanying man, are depicted with horned helmets and lurs. Similar pair motifs are also known from the large cairn at Kivik and rock carvings in Bohuslän. Since the pair motif is connected with the ship on the razor from Vestrup mark, it is argued that ideas of divine twins may have been part of the solar myth (Kristiansen and Larsson 2005, cf. Kaul 2004:345).

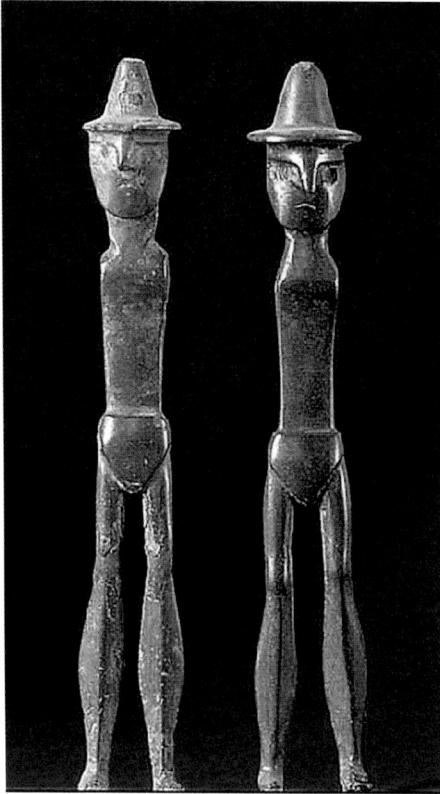

Figure 44. Two standing men from Stockhult in Loshult in Skåne. The two figures are dated to the fifteenth or early fourteenth centuries BC, and are a good example of the recurrent pair motif during the Bronze Age. (Photo by Statens Historiska Museum, Stockholm.)

According to Kaul, the fundamental solar myth was also related to rituals. Some of the images on the bronze objects are placed in ritual contexts on rock carvings, for instance humans holding sun-symbols, bearing ships or mushroom-shaped figures (Kaul 2004:73 ff.). Other images, such as ships, horses, and wheel-crosses are also known from ritual contexts as parts of graves. In the spectacular graves at Kivik in Skåne and at Sagaholm and Hjortekrog in Småland, the images have been carved on specially made slabs or directly on the rock (Kaul 2004:137 ff., cf. Randsborg 1993; Goldhahn 1999; Widholm 1998). Likewise, more humble stones with cut images have been found on or at several grave mounds in Denmark (Kaul 2004:156). Besides, several ritual objects known from the pictorial world have been found as deposited full-scale artefacts. These include ceremonial bronze axes with clay cores, bronze helmets with horns, and bronze lurs. A large imported bronze shield with a wheel-cross may also have been used as a sun symbol carried in rituals (Kaul 2004:352).

Kaul maintains that the mythologies and rituals surrounding the sun were important aspects of Bronze Age religion in Scandinavia. Although he takes into account regional ritual variations in this religion, he argues that the religious traditions were basically the same from the middle of Norway and Sweden to northern Germany, since the pictorial world and the ritual objects are found in all parts of this region (Kaul 1998:274). Within Scandinavia, he suggests that Bohuslän, with the most rock carvings and also the most varied images, should be framed in a Scandinavian context and not in a local context as it usually is (cf. Bertilsson 1987). Instead, he sees this region as a kind of holy district, perhaps visited by people from many different regions on prehistoric 'pilgrimages' (Kaul 2004:98, 281; cf. Kristiansen 2001). Kaul points out two central places around which many of the bronze-objects from the Late Bronze Age containing images have been found. These centres are Voldtofte in south-western Funen, with a large mound adjacent to an unusually large settlement, and Boeslunde in western Sjælland, centred round a probably holy mountain called Borgbjerg (Kaul 2004:87).

This reconstructed religion, according to Kaul, is not only limited to Scandinavia as a region, but is also confined to the Bronze Age, which he sees as a specific 'solar age' (Kaul 1998:273 ff., 2004:407 ff.). The earliest images and ritual objects connected to the religion can be attested at the transition between period IB and period II in the Early Bronze Age (that is, around 1500 BC) in southern Scandinavia. Following other scholars, Kaul maintains that a new religious tradition was created at that time, by a new elite that monopolized the important bronze supply (Kaul 2004:231, 369 ff.; cf. Sprockhoff 1954, Randsborg 1993, Kristiansen and Larsson 2005). Imported objects show that a group of people had contacts with central Europe (the present-day Czech Republic, Slovakia, Hungary, and Romania) through alliances and long journeys (cf. Kristiansen and Larsson 2005). Probably via this region, they had further indirect contact with the eastern Mediterranean, which was the origin of several of the models of the iconography, such as the ship, the mushroom-shaped figure, and the wheel-cross. By combining local elements with selected foreign models, the elite created a new, specifically Scandinavian religious tradition, according to Kaul.

At the transition to the Late Bronze Age, around 1100 BC, the rituals and mythologies partly changed again, with cremations now replacing inhumations, ship symbolism being used more than before, and snakes and birds being introduced into the iconography (Kaul 1998:53, 145, 274 ff., 2004:218). Kaul does not see these changes as a new religion, but rather as a social widening of a former elite religion. Inspiration for these changes came once again from central Europe (the present-day Czech Republic, Slovakia, and Hungary), although imported objects from around 900–800 BC also point towards present-day southern Germany, eastern France, Switzerland, and northern Italy. At the end of the Bronze Age, around 500 BC, the former pictorial world more or less totally disappeared, along with the bronze supply. Like several other Bronze Age specialists, Kaul envisages a profound religious change in direct relation to a collapse of the long-distance travel and alliances that had previously secured foreign bronze. He thinks that the old elite disappeared, and with it the religion that for a thousand years had explained and legitimized its claim to power (Kaul 1998:110, 2004:391 ff.; cf. Jensen 1997; Kristiansen and Larsson 2005).

However, from a landscape perspective the transition around 500 BC is not that dramatic. Instead, a continuity or gradual change from the tenth and ninth centuries BC to the first centuries BC can be attested for land use (Welinder et al. 1998:239 ff.; Arnberg 2007), settlements (Feldt 2005), henged mountains or stone-enclosed hilltops (Olausson 1995), and burials (Wangen 2009). Simpler artefacts, such as pins and needles, did not change very much between the Bronze Age and the Iron Age. These similarities have led Claus Kjeld Jensen to suggest in a recent chronological study (Kjeld Jensen 2005) that the great divide came not around 500 BC but rather c.200 BC.

Still, ritual practice clearly changed in the Pre-Roman Iron Age from about 500 BC, when pottery, animal bones, and humans began to be deposited in bogs (Becker 1971; Kaul 2003; Fischer 2007; Pauli Jensen 2009). In several cases there is a continuity of new ritual sites from the fifth and fourth centuries BC until the fifth century AD and later, for instance, at sites such as Ullevi in Östergötland, Kärringsjön in Halland, and Skedemosse on Öland (Nielsen 2005; Carlie 1998, 2009a; Monikander 2010). Due to these ritual patterns, Kaul reckons there were two fundamental religious changes, one about 500 BC, when the solar myth disappeared, and another around 500 AD, when he supposes that an 'Æsir religion' was established. Consequently, Kaul believes that Bronze Age religion has very little in common with Old Norse religion, although he is open for a few transformed elements, linking up with later periods, such as the snake motif (Kaul 1998:14). However, irrespective of these ritual changes, elements of a solar iconography can be traced in the Early Iron Age as well. Instead of disappearing, it seems as if the sun was placed in new ritual contexts, leading to re-definitions of its role.

Bridging the gap between Eskelhem and Sanda

At Eskelhem on western Gotland, a large deposit with horse bits and bronze fittings as well as a large bronze disc (Fig. 45) was found in 1866 (Montelius 1887). The bronze disc originated from central Europe, whereas some of the other objects came from south of the Baltic Sea (Larsson 1994:119–20). The deposit can be dated to the very end of the Bronze Age, around 500 BC. The disc, which for good reasons has been interpreted as a sun-disc, consists of five rings connected by many small spikes, giving an impression of many small rays, radiating from a wheel-cross in the centre. On one of the rings are two loops with four hanging bronze pieces of tin. At the top of the disc are three loops surrounded by two antithetically placed birds, similar to some of the birds in Kaul's study. Judging by the loops, the disc must have been hung, either from the neck of a horse or from the shaft of a carriage making the dangling pieces of tin tinkle. This gives us an unusual illustration of a sun symbol in its functional, and probably ritual, context. A similar bronze disc has been found at Kurum in Tjust on the east coast of mainland Sweden. This disc seems to have been locally produced, showing that the motif was still actively used in Scandinavia (Goldhahn et al. 2012).

The sun-disc from Eskelhem, and its parallel at Kurum, represent the very end of Kaul's proposed 'sun age', being a millennium later than the sun-disc from Trundholm, but still connected to horses. The main question here is whether it is possible to bridge the following centuries from the sun-disc at Eskelhem to the early picture stones on Gotland. The best-preserved early picture stone, from Sanda, was raised only

Figure 45. The sun disc from Eskelhem, dated to *c.*500 BC. (Photo by Gunnel Jansson, Statens Historiska Museum, Stockholm.)

five kilometres from Eskelhem, but about 900 years later. Davidson proposed some continuity between the Bronze Age and the Iron Age, but she based her studies on simple comparisons of images and symbols in time and space, without any considerations of context (Gelling and Davidson 1969:139 ff.) Nonetheless, bridging this gap between the two locations concerns not only traces of possible sun representations, but also issues of figurative expressions and questions of context.

The problem with discussing the division between the Bronze Age and the Iron Age is partly that there are few pictures from the Early Iron Age, and partly that the conventions of image representations changed. Much of the pictorial world that Kaul analyses actually disappeared at the end of the Bronze Age. Few figurative images are known from the end of the Bronze Age to the early Roman Iron Age, that is, 500 BC – AD 200. Those images that were created during these 700 years were nonetheless made according to other pictorial conventions from central Europe, first inspired by the Hallstatt culture, later by the Celtic world, and finally by early Roman models. This means that images have to be interpreted from their content rather than from their style.

Images from the earliest Iron Age (500–200 BC) can best be described as low-key expressions of Bronze Age origin, partly cast in new forms inspired by the Hallstatt culture in central Europe, such as the disc from Eskelhem. Kaul himself mentions that some rock carvings were still cut during this period in Bohuslän, Østfold, Trøndelag, Uppland, and Bornholm. A new motif in this final phase was the armed rider (Kaul 1998:87). This means that the rituals of cutting images on rocks survived in many parts of Scandinavia until the first centuries BC. Besides, new investigations of rock carvings have shown that rituals were conducted around the images long after the cutting itself had stopped. In some cases, it is possible to follow rituals at the site of rock carvings into the second and third centuries AD (Nilsson 2010). At Himmelstalund in Östergötland, an early runic inscription from the third or fourth centuries was even added to a rock with older rock carvings (Krause and Jankuhn 1966:121 ff.), showing a continued interest in or return to a historically important site. Kaul also points out that the Hjortspring boat from southern Jutland, dated to around 350 BC, seems to have had a ring as a sun symbol at the top of its stem, strongly resembling some of the ship images on earlier rock carvings (Kaul 1998:87 ff.).

Kaul, along with Kristiansen and Larsson, have convincingly argued that the wheel-cross was established as an alternative sun symbol already in the Early Bronze Age (Kaul 2004:352 ff.; Kristiansen and Larsson 2005:194 ff., 240 ff., 298 ff.). After 500 BC, the sun-motif was only represented in this formalized way, as more or less elaborate wheel-crosses or concentric rings, partly resembling the sun-disc from Eskelhem. Some bronze needles and pins had simple wheel-crosses at the top, whereas larger bronze buckles were designed as complex wheel-crosses with several rings, including small round discs. Another element of Bronze Age origin is the spiral, which was used to decorate some fibulas and pins (Nylén 1955; Arrhenius and Eriksson 2006). Some ritual aspects from the Bronze Age were also preserved during this period. Pairs of neck-rings were deposited in wetland, echoing the earlier twin motif (Kaul 2009). On Gotland, small ship-formed graves were still built for inhumations during the Early Iron Age. More or less complex wheel-crosses built from small stones were used as grave markers during the Early Iron Age in Norway (Wangen 2009) and eastern Sweden (Äijä 1999), as well as on Gotland (Nylén 1969; Arnberg 2007). Even the importance of the razor was preserved, since iron razors are known from Denmark, but without known or preserved images.

The following period from about 200 BC to AD 200, however, from a Scandinavian point of view is more or less aniconic, making it a pictorial 'Dark Age'. There are some figurative objects, such as the overwhelmingly richly decorated silver cauldron from Gundestrup in Jutland, but due to its foreign origin it has very little to say about the Scandinavian pictorial world (Kaul 1991). At the same time, some locally produced objects have whirls, triskeles, and aquatic birds inspired by decorated objects from the Celtic world (Kaul 2009). Further, wheel-crosses, concentric rings, rosettes, and rings with elaborate spokes of different shapes were still used as grave markers in Norway, mainland Sweden, and on Gotland (Äijä 1999; Nylén 1969; Arnberg 2007; Fig. 46)

It is only in the third and fourth centuries that a more complex pictorial world of Scandinavian origin can be discerned again, now based on Roman models (Åberg 1925; Holmquist 1952). From that time, images occur on metalwork as well as on stones, the Gotlandic picture stones being the best example of this new pictorial world. Although the links between the picture stones and the iconography of the Bronze Age are thin, I would argue that there is a connection. Above all it is possible to see a continuity of solar images by going beyond style and by using different kinds of archaeological categories. A strong case for continuity on Gotland at least is that wheel-crosses, concentric rings, and rosettes as grave markers were now replaced by cut picture stones with rosettes and whirls.

Bronze Age perspectives on early Gotlandic picture stones

This long return trip to the Bronze Age has basically confirmed older interpretations of the images of the early picture stones as being related to the sun (Lindqvist 1941:91; Gelling and Davidson 1969:141 ff.; Davidson 1988:168 ff.). However, it has also given new insights, which can be used to help understand the images in new ways, as well as offering interpretations for some of the unexplained details of this pictorial world. The complete stone from Sanda is the best starting point for a new interpretation (Fig. 47). Its layout is surprisingly similar to Kaul's reconstructed solar cycle, although a day-ship is lacking, showing that the symbolic importance of the ship has been downplayed since the Late Bronze Age. Like Davidson, I see this stone as a representation of the Old Norse cosmos, although we comprehend some important elements differently.

The large whirl on top of the stone corresponds to the sun at its

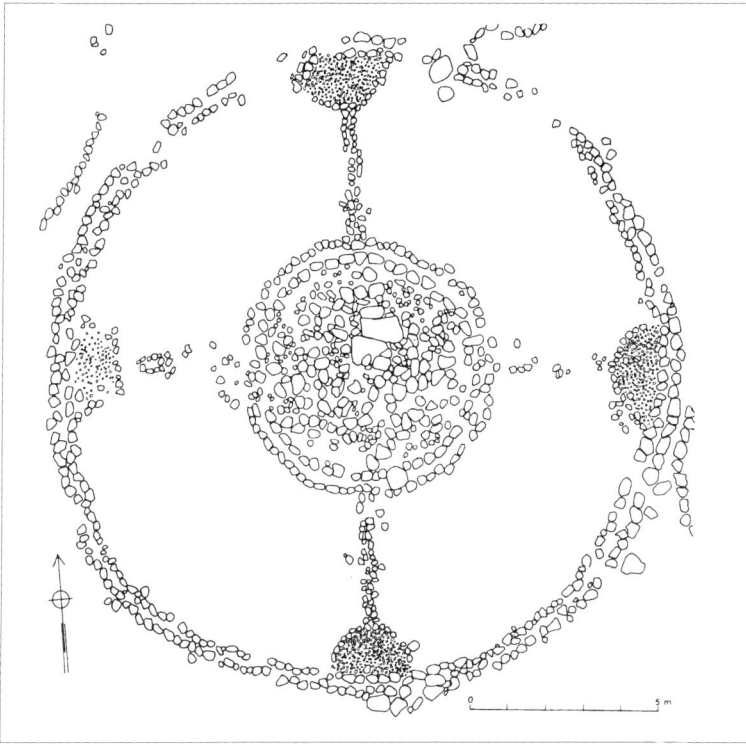

Figure 46. A grave in the form of a wheel-cross at Sälle in Fröjel on Gotland. The grave is dated to the early Roman Iron Age, *c.* AD 1–200. (After Nylén 1969:107.)

zenith, whereas the two smaller spirals with animal heads represent the sunrise and the sunset, respectively. The motif can be directly compared with a rock carving from Askum in Bohuslän (Kaul 2004:277), where two sun-horses are standing in front of each other, with the day-side to the left and the night-side to the right. The ship travelling to the left underneath the horizontal line can best be understood as the night ship of the sun making its voyage through the sea or the rivers of the underworld. The tree standing on the horizon can be interpreted as a world tree standing in the middle of the world, around which the sun makes its daily tour in the sky and the underworld.

The adjacent figures on the Sanda stone and the other early stones

Figure 47. Drawing of the picture stone from the church at Sanda, from *c*.400. This is the best preserved early picture stone on Gotland. (Drawing by the author.)

should in some way be connected with the main solar cycle. They could be regarded as helpers of the sun at critical passages, as in Kaul's interpretations, or as creatures threatening the sun during its daily trip around the world. Monsters or snakes above the large whirl, around the two smaller spirals, and below the horizontal line could be interpreted as sky monsters and sea monsters threatening the sun. Meanwhile, the warriors, riders, and horses, which sometimes replaced the small spirals below the large whirl, could be regarded as representations of sunrise and sunset, or as helpers of the sun at these critical transitions. The pair motif may also recall the idea of divine twins connected with the solar cycle. In this context, it is also interesting to note that the Dioscuri in the Baltic as well as the Greek and Roman traditions were associated with horses (Rosenfeld 1984; Simek 1993:59–60.).

It is not surprising that the motifs on the early Gotlandic picture stones are so close to Kaul's reconstructed solar myth, since iconographic continuity throughout the Early Iron Age is best attested on Gotland. Although the Gotlandic picture stones are comparatively unique, they should not be regarded as expressions of a regional tradition or a religious relict, since there are other contemporary expressions elsewhere in Scandinavia linked into the same pictorial world. Echoes of a similar solar iconography are present in the much smaller picture stones from Uppland and Södermanland. The whirls, spirals, rowing ship, armed rider, and antithetically placed horses and warriors here recall the Gotlandic images (Ahlberg 1978). Contemporary Scandinavian metalwork in bronze, silver, and gold includes aspects of the same iconography, but also extends the pictorial world to other motifs. In order to place the solar cycle of the Iron Age in this broader context, it is therefore necessary to have a closer look at some of the contemporary metalwork.

Metalwork in the Iron Age

The main large round figure on the early picture stones has direct parallels in metal objects from the same period. Some of the large whirls, such as the whirl on the picture stones from Atlingbo and Stenkyrka I, are designed like the so-called swastika fibulas. These fibulas date to the third and fourth centuries, and are found in female as well as male graves in Denmark, southern Sweden, Norway, Finland, and northern Germany (Lund Hansen 1995:214 ff.; see Gelling and Davidson 1969:140). The fibulas can be viewed as developed sun-wheels, with the four main positions of the sun marked out as small round discs at the end of the bent arms, namely sunset, midnight, sunrise, and midday with the sun at its zenith. Some large whirls on early Gotlandic picture stones also have clear parallels in other fibulas, such as a plate fibula from Ejersten

Figure 48. A pelta-shaped gilded silver pendant, dated to the early fifth century, from Vännebo in Roasjö in Västergötland. The image on the pendant can be regarded as a counterpart in metal to the cosmological image on the Sanda stone (Fig. 47). (Photo by Statens Historiska Museum, Stockholm.)

in Vestfold, dated to the early fifth century (see Salin 1904:209; Lindqvist 1941:109) and the so-called shield fibulas from Denmark, Norway, and England, also dated to the fifth century (Magnus 1975:47 ff.)

Another interesting link can be traced to mushroom- or pelta-shaped gilded silver pendants from Fulltofta in Skåne and Vännebo in Västergötland. Both pendants come from extraordinary deposits of horse equipment from the first half of the fifth century. These deposits have repeatedly been used to underline long-distance elite connections between south Scandinavia and south-east Europe, directly or indirectly linked with steppe-nomadic groups (Åberg 1936; Forssander 1937; Fabech 1991a; 2011; Bemmann 2007). The pendant from Fulltofta depicts a large whirl with three small circles on each side of the whirl and bird heads at the two ends, as a kind of abbreviated version of the Gotlandic solar cycle. The piece from Vännebo includes four representation of the sun (Fig. 48). The pendant as a whole can be interpreted as the world tree reaching to the sky as well as the underworld. On top of

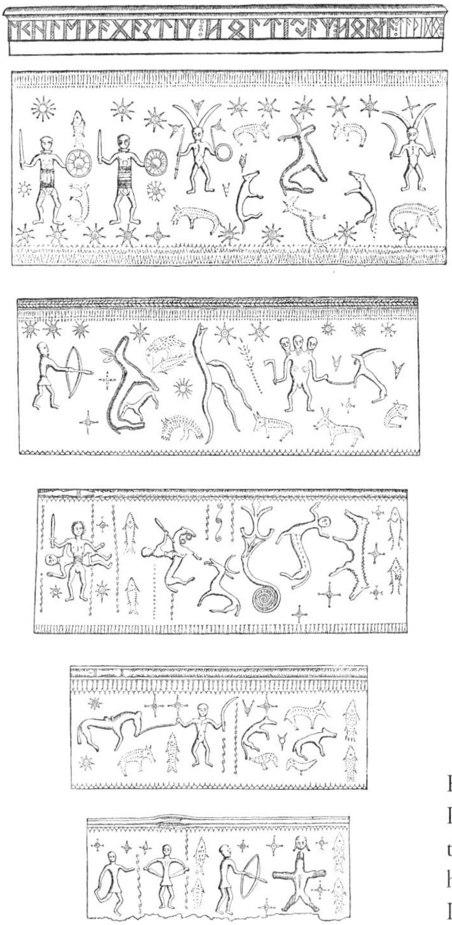

Figure 49. Drawing by J. R. Paulli in 1734 of the shorter of the two gold horns from Gallehus. (After Brøndsted 1954, table II.)

this tree is the sun at its zenith with long rays, flanked by two smaller suns representing sunrise and sunset. At the bottom of the figure is a sun with short rays, representing the sun passing through the roots of the tree in the underworld during the night. At the outer ends of the tree are animal heads, providing links with the antithetically placed figures on the early Gotlandic stones. From this perspective, the pendant from Vännebo can be regarded as a counterpart in metal to the complete cosmological image presented on the Sanda stone. Once again, it is interesting that the solar cycles from Fulltofta and Vännebo can be connected with horses and horse equipment, similar to the much earlier finds from Trundholm and Eskelhem.

In addition to sun representations, the motif of pairs also re-appeared in figurative metalwork. Two horned animals from Solberga on southern Öland have been found in a settlement dating from the third to the fifth centuries (Persson and Rasch 2001:373–4; cf. Fallgren 2008:132). Interestingly, a decorated ring at the withers of one of the animals can be interpreted as a sun symbol, recalling the sun-horse with a string connecting the sun with the neck of a horse (see Fig. 56). Twin motifs were also present on the enigmatic gold horns from Galle-hus in Jutland from the fifth century. Many images on the horns are difficult to interpret, however, because the objects no longer exist and only are known from antiquarian sketches (Brøndsted 1954:64 ff.; cf. Oxenstierna 1956). According a drawing from 1734, the top panel of the shorter horn included two pairs of warriors, one with swords and shields, the other with spears, a shield, and a twig, as well as long horns on their heads. The two pairs of warriors were accompanied by one horned animal, eight small dog-like animals, and a fish (Fig. 49). This panel also included seventeen suns with six or more rays, more than any of the other panels on the horn. On the third panel of the short horn were another horned animal and a monster/snake with a coiling tail (Brøndsted 1954; Oxenstierna 1956). Otherwise the pictorial world of the Gallehus horns is quite different from the picture stones on Gotland, underlining the broad spectrum of possible images – and narratives – that seems to have existed also in the Iron Age.

A special case: the gold bracteates

Another iconographical connection existed, this time between the picture stones and gold bracteates. These gold pendants with stamped images on one side represented a pictorial world with a broader selection of images, but with several parallel motifs. Models for the bracteates were Roman coins and medallions, although the pictorial world of the bracte-ates was clearly changed in relation to the Roman models. Currently about a thousand bracteates and imitations of Roman gold medallions are known, primarily from Scandinavia, but also from Germany, Poland, Hungary, northern France, and England (Heinzmann and Axboe 2011). The gold medallions are usually dated to the fourth century, whereas the gold bracteates are dated from the mid fifth century to the early and mid sixth century (Axboe 2007:65–76). Owing to their coin-like character, the bracteates have been investigated in recurrent chronological studies from the mid nineteenth century (Malmer 1963:215 ff.; Axboe 2007; Behr 2011). Usually the bracteates are interpreted as protective amulets, but they may similarly have functioned as political gifts and signs of a claimed Scandinavian identity outside Scandinavia (Andrén 1991; Seebold 1992:307; Axboe 2007; Pesch 2007).

The iconography of the bracteates has also been a central issue since the mid nineteenth century. Basically, the images have been interpreted in three different perspectives: mythological, heroic, and political. As early as 1855 C. J. Thomsen proposed that the images represented some of the Old Norse gods, whereas Worsaae in 1870 suggested that some of the figures were heroes (Thomsen 1855; Worsaae 1870). Since the Roman models of the gold bracteates were coins depicting emperors, gods, and goddesses, other scholars have interpreted the pictures as ideal portraits of rulers (see Seebold 1992).

Today, the mythological interpretation totally dominates the debate, mainly due to the research by Karl Hauck and his colleagues and pupils (Hauck 1984, 1992; Behr 1991; Axboe 2007; Pesch 2007; cf. Gaimster 1998). However, the identification of specific Old Norse gods and goddesses is still disputed, mainly due to different methods in the iconographical analysis. Hauck's 'contextual iconology' presupposes ideal models, which means that he reckons on broad variations of a very few distinct motifs, whereas some archaeologists instead underline the typological variations, which leads to many more distinct motifs.

Among the undisputed identifications are motifs of the sky god Tyr (Týr) putting his hand in the mouth of the wolf Fenrir (Öberg 1942; Oxenstierna 1956), and Baldr being killed by a twig of mistletoe (Hauck 1970). However, the commonest motif on the so-called C-bracteates, consisting of a horse or a horned animal with a human head at the neck of the animal (head-animal), is much more disputed (see Fig. 51). Since Thomsen's study in 1855, many archaeologists have distinguished between head-animals with runes and birds, and head-animals without these characteristics, instead including a beard and horns on the animals. The first motif is interpreted as the rune-versed Odin with his ravens, whereas the second motif is believed to be Thor with one of his he-goats (Salin 1895:91; Malmer 1963:215 ff.). In a series of studies Hauck has criticized these interpretations as being incoherent, since the motifs are not mutually exclusive, with variants combining both motifs. Instead Hauck regards all variants as different forms of iconographical abbreviations of an ideal model. With references to the Second Merseburg Charm from the tenth century, he interprets the recurring motif on the C-bracteates as Odin curing the horse of Baldr by whispering in the ear of the horse. Hauck connects this interpretation of the motif with the function of the bracteates as protective amulets (Hauck 1992, 2011; overview in Pesch 2007).

Although Hauck's interpretations have been widely accepted, they are not totally convincing, since he has based them mainly on classical and medieval texts and classical and Romanesque art, and to a much lesser extent on contemporary Scandinavian images, and especially the early picture stones from Gotland. It is well known that the picture stones and the bracteates share some common motifs. The bracteates have a broader range of motifs, but they are placed in less complex iconographical contexts. The more complex pictorial structure on the Gotlandic monuments may give new perspectives on the gold bracteates.

Among the parallel motifs are the quatrefoil knot, found on the picture stone from Havor in Hablingbo as well as on the double bracteate from Lyngby on Sjælland (Gaimster 1998:120). Another parallel motif is a triskele of three animals, represented on the picture stone from Smiss in När and on the double bracteate from Trollhättan in Västergötland. On the other side of the same bracteate is another link to Gotland, namely a man putting his hand into the mouth of a monster or wolf. Apart from the Trollhättan bracteate, the motif is known on other bracteates (Pesch 2007:123) and also the picture stone at Austers in Hangvar (see Fig. 54). The images on the bracteates as well as on the picture stone are, as mentioned above, interpreted as the sky god Tyr putting his hand into the mouth of Fenrir (Öberg 1942; Oxenstierna 1956; Ney 2006).

The disputed motif on the C-bracteates of a horned animal with or without a beard has several parallels, which have long been noted. Similar motifs are known from the picture stone at Häggeby in Uppland (Arne 1902:321 ff.; Gjessing 1943), from Gotlandic fibulas from the fifth century (Janse 1922:93; Öberg 1942:62), from one of the gold horns from Gallehus, and from several other Scandinavian sites (Oxenstierna 1956:44 ff.). Recently, the same motif was found in one of the high-rank-

Figure 50. Picture stone from the church at Väskinde. Below the central whirl are two horned animals with beards. These horned and bearded animals have many parallels in the gold bracteates. (Photo by the author.)

ing graves at Hagenow in northern Germany, dated to around AD 100 (Lüth and Vors 2001).

However, it has not been noticed that the motif has an interesting parallel on the picture stone from Väskinde church (Fig. 50) found in 1955 (Lindqvist 1956). Below the large whirl and above the horizontal zone, two antithetical bearded animals are depicted, with some kind of flying figures close to their necks. As mentioned above, this image is connected with the common twin motif of spirals, horses, horned animals, or warriors, which I have interpreted as the sunrise and sunset or as the Dioscuri helping the sun at these transformations. A further argument for linking the image of the C-bracteates with these motifs is the appearance of the two horned animals at Solberga on Öland. The decorated ring on one of these animals is located at the same spot as the head of the C-bracteates, which indicates that a Roman model of a rider was reinterpreted as an already existing Scandinavian iconography of a solar animal with the sun at the mane or in a string from the mane.

Consequently, I interpret the disputed head-animals of the C-bracteates as a motif connected with the divine twins and the sunrise and sunset. Such a general context may explain the variation of the motif as well as the surprisingly uneven distribution of the direction of the animals (Fig. 51). Out of a total of 252 different images, the animals face left in 183 instances (73 per cent) and right in only 69 examples (27 per cent), according to the published corpus of bracteates (Hauck et al. 1985–9; Heizmann and Axboe 2011). This discrepancy cannot be explained by Hauck's idea of a general variation of an ideal motif, but fits well with the idea that sunset – when the sun-horse or one of the twins is turning left – is the most critical part of the solar cycle. This is when the sun is entering the underworld, and a new day is beginning with the night, according to Old Norse time reckoning (see Nordberg 2006). A recurring motif connected with this fundamental and critical transition may also be linked with the protective aspects of the bracteates. Such an interpretation does not exclude a link with Odin, since some of the later motifs of the Dioscuri seem to have Odinic connections (see Hauck 1984; Magnus 2001a). However, the interpretation starts from a more general perspective and is less dependent on the Second Merseburg Charm as a specific and much later text.

Finally, another unnoticed link between the picture stones and the bracteates can be seen in the broad borders surrounding the central image on some bracteates. In contrast to the enormous efforts that have been put into chronological and iconographical studies of the bracteates, including the stamps of the borders (Axboe 1982, 2007; Wicker 1990), very little attention has been paid to the pictorial aspects of these borders. Only Carl-Axel Moberg (1953) has pointed to the star-like character of the pattern of some of the borders, because they consist of one or more zones with triangles and rays. Out of the total corpus of bracteates, about 325 have some kind of border, apart from the central motif and the rim (Hauck et al. 1985–9; Heizmann and Axboe 2011). The borders may consist of one to seven zones with points, circles, strokes, semicircles, spirals, crosses, wave lines, and triangles. Imitations of gold medallions from the third century, such as the finds from Inderøy and Svarteborg, already have star-like patterns around the central head. All types of the later bracteates have borders, but they are most common among the C-bracteates with an animal and a head. Only a small number of bracteates, about 40, have three or more zones, and all of these large bracteates come from Scandinavia,

Figure 51. Two gold bracteates from Åkarp in Burlöv in Skåne. These two bracteates represent the two possible directions of the animal and human head on the
C-bracteates. In 27 per cent of the cases they are facing right and in 73 per cent
of the cases left. (Photos by Ulf Bruxe, Statens Historiska Museum, Stockholm.)

apart from two German finds (Fig. 52). Among these large bracteates,
26 have a central motif of an animal with a head at the neck, and in 24
cases (92 per cent) the figures are facing left. In only two cases (8 per
cent) is the direction right.

The star-like borders combined with human heads and sometimes
horned animals can be linked to the antithetical figures on the Gotlandic
picture stones, such as whirls, spirals, sometimes with heads and tails,
warriors, armed riders, and animals. Due to this parallel, my interpretation is that the borders, or at least the borders with star-like patterns
and several zones, referred to the sun and its rays. It is interesting that
the solar aspects of the broad borders have a very pronounced connection
with the animal and head facing left, which I have interpreted as an
expression of the transformation around sunset. The star-like borders
consequently underlined this important and critical transition as well
as the idea of the divine twins.

Figure 52. An imitation of a Roman gold medallion from Senoren in Blekinge and a gold bracteate from Ravlunda in Skåne. In both cases the central figure is surrounded by a broad star-like border, which can be interpreted as sun rays. (Photos by Ulf Bruxe, Statens Historiska Museum, Stockholm.)

Iron Age perspectives on early Gotlandic picture stones

This short comparison with contemporary metalwork shows that the images on the early picture stones on Gotland were firmly based in a common Scandinavian pictorial world. Different aspects of the solar cycle, such as the sun itself and the divine twins, can also be traced in three-dimensional figures, dress ornaments and bracteates. However, the solar cycle was not the only major motif, but co-existed with other motifs, such as Baldr and Tyr on the bracteates and the uninterpreted images on the horns from Gallehus. This indicates that the sun as a mythological motif coexisted with narratives connected with other mythological figures as well.

A similar pattern is indicated by the names of the runes. As is well known, each of the runic letters had its own name. The names are recorded in different continental manuscripts from the eighth and ninth centuries, but can be indirectly secured through the use of runes as concepts in inscriptions from at least around 600 (Nedoma 2003). The names probably go back to the invention of runes in the second

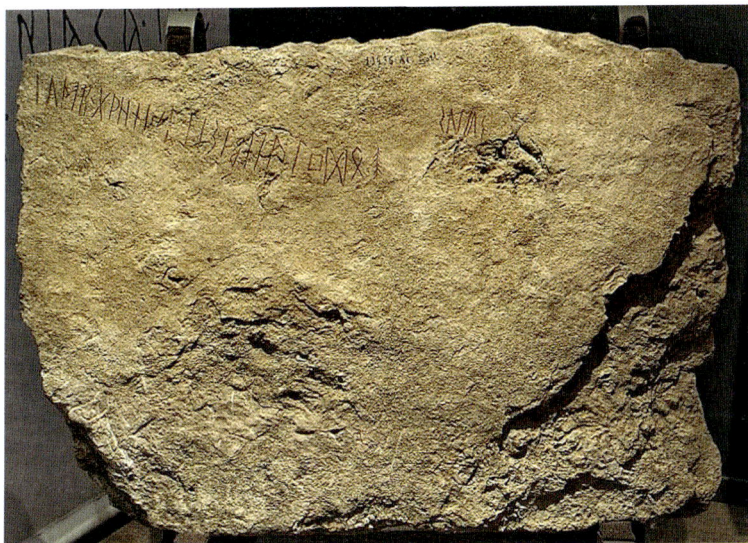

Figure 53. The runic alphabet from Kylver in Stånga on Gotland. This is one of the oldest recorded runic alphabets, and it is carved on a limestone slab that was part of a grave, probably from the first half of the fifth century. (Photo by Christer Åhlin, Statens Historiska Museum, Stockholm.)

century AD, since the order of runes has been unchanged since the first recorded runic alphabet in the fifth century, on a stone from Kylver on southern Gotland (Fig. 53) and on a bracteate from Vadstena in Östergötland (Nedoma 2003). The names were probably used as a mnemonic device to help in remembering the rune characters. For each runic character, a word was selected with the same initial sound value. Although the words for each character could have been selected from an enormous range, the final choice of the names points towards fundamental concepts which existed in the northern world in the second century AD. It is therefore interesting that we find rune names referring to concepts that can be directly or indirectly linked to the images on the Gotlandic monuments. The fundamental concepts in question include sun (*sowulo-*), day (*daga-*), water (*lagu-*), horse (*ehwa-*), man/human (*mann-*), birch (*berkana-*), and possibly elk (*algi-*) (Nedoma 2006). Apart from these general concepts, the names of two gods also designated runes, namely the sky-god Tyr (*Teiwa-*) and the chthonic god Yngvi (*Ingwa-), possibly linked to the later known god Freyr (Nedoma 2003). At least Tyr can be clearly linked with the solar cycle on the picture stone from Austers in Hangvar.

Another early example of the sun and its relation to other mythological figures is seen in the Germanic translations of the Roman names of the days of the week. The Germanic adoption of the Roman days of the week was probably completed in the fourth century. Through the names it is possible to see how the sun as a mythological figure coexisted with the moon, Tyr, Odin, Thor, and Frigg during this century, at least in the southern Germanic world, where the translation probably took place (Simek 1993:371).

Finally, the external views of classical authors point towards a similar pattern, with the sun being an important part of a broader mythological world. Tacitus in his *Germania* from AD 98 claimed that the main Germanic gods in general were Mercury, Mars, and Heracles, which have usually been equated with Odin, Tyr, and Thor (Tacitus 1999:42). However, when he is describing specific groups in the Baltic Sea region and in the far North, he actually mentioned the fertility goddess Nerthus, divine twins, and the sun. According to Tacitus, the Germanic tribe of the Naharnavali living south of the Baltic Sea worshipped the twin gods Alcis, which he directly equated with the Roman Dioscuri, Castor and Pollux (Tacitus 1999:59; cf. Simek 1993:240, 316, 337). The name Alcis probably means 'elk', associating the gods with horned animals (Vikstrand 2001:199 ff.). As noted, *AlgiR* ('elk') may have been the name of the a-rune in the futhark, giving further indications of Dioscuri in Scandinavia in the third and four centuries. Tacitus' information may also be compared with that of the Greek historian Timaios, who as early as the third century BC reported that the 'Celts' along the North Sea coast were particularly devoted to the Dioscuri (de Vries 1957:247).

Tacitus also states that in the far North, beyond the *sviones*, is another sea at the end of the world, where 'popular belief holds that the sound of the sun emerging from the sea can be heard and the shape of his horses and the ray of his head can be seen' (Tacitus 1999:60; see de Vries 1956:355 ff.). Here, the connection between the sun and horses is mentioned in writing for the first time, although the motif had been known since the sun-horse of Trundholm. According to Tacitus, the sun in northern Europe was an anthropomorphic male figure with rays around his head. He had at least two horses that drew him across the sky. In this Roman interpretation, the sun was accordingly interpreted as a sun god, probably based on interpretative Mediterranean models such as Helios.

The parallels in metalwork, the names of the runes, and the days of the week as well as notices by classical authors clearly show that the early picture stones on Gotland formed part of a mental world that was in many ways common throughout the northern Europe during the Early Iron Age. The sun and the solar cycle with the divine twins were important parts of a broad mythological world, alongside other divinities such as Tyr, Thor, Odin, Ingwaz/Freyr, Frigg, Baldr, and Nerthus.

The sun in later mythological contexts

The solar cycle is well attested on the early picture stones, and some of the other divine powers are indirectly known from other sources. In spite of this, it is difficult to understand the more specific mythological context of this cycle, but possible fragments of a mythological context may be glimpsed from different later analogies. Because the analogies come from different times and places there is always a risk of reconstructing too homogeneous a mythological background. However, using the analogies in a dialogue with the Gotlandic pictorial world makes it possible to sketch a more specific background (cf. Wylie 1985).

Some aspects of the way the sun was understood can be gained from late references in Eddic poetry, and especially the metaphors for the sun in this poetry. According to *Grímnismál* 38 the sun is called 'the shining god' (*scínanda goði*), in front of which was a shield called Svalin, which protected the mountains and sea from burning up. *Sigdrífumál* 15 states that runes should be cut on the shield 'which stands before the shining god'. In *Alvíssmál* 16, we read that 'Sun it is called by men, and sunshine by the gods, for the dwarfs it is Dvalin's deluder, the giants call it everglow, the elves the lovely wheel, the sons of the Æsir all-shining' (*Sol heitir með mǫnnom, enn sunna með goðom, kalla dvergar Dvalins leica, eygló iǫtnar, álfar fagrahvél, alscír ása synir*). Snorri also mentions in *Skáldskaparmál* that the sun could be called the 'day star' (*sunna*), 'elf-disc' (*alfrǫðull*), 'the doubt disc' (*ifrǫðull*), and 'the stained' (*mýlin*). The idea of the sun as a wheel echoes the symbols of the sunwheels, whereas the shield in front of the sun carries associations with the images of warriors bearing shields with whirls and spirals on some early picture stones. In the Icelandic narrative tradition, the sun and the day, as well as the moon and the night, were also regarded as anthropomorphic powers. As noted above, the sun could be called 'the shining god'. However, according to Snorri's *Gylfaginning* 34, Sól ('sun') was one of the Æsir goddesses. In *Gylfaginning* 10, which Snorri based in part on *Grímnismál* 37–39, *Sigrdrífumál* 15, and *Vafþrúðnismál* 23, he mentioned that Sól and Máni ('moon') were children of Mundilfari ('the one moving according to particular times'). Sól drove a chariot pulled by two horses, Árvakr ('early awake') and Alsvíðr ('very quick'), across the sky by day, and was pursued by a wolf called Skǫll ('mockery'). Similarly, according to *Gylfaginning* 10, Máni drove another chariot pulled by two horses across the sky by night, and was chased by the wolf Hati ('despiser'). Both of these wolves are probably poetic embellishments of Fenrir (Simek 1993:201, 222, 297).

Snorri also stated in *Gylfaginning* 9, which he partly based on *Alvíssmál* 29 and *Vafþrúðnismál* 12, 14, and 25, that a giant in Jǫtunheim called Nǫrr ('narrow') had a daughter call Nótt ('night'), who married three times, among others a man called Naglfari. From these marriages, she had a son Auðr ('prosperity'), a daughter Jǫrð ('earth'), and a son Dagr ('day'). Snorri adds that Nótt drove a chariot pulled by Hrímfaxi ('frostmane'), who dripped dew from his bit at dawn. Nótt was followed by Dagr ('day'), who crossed the sky in a chariot pulled by Skinfaxi, ('shining-mane'), who illuminates the world with his mane (Simek 1993:55, 235, 238). Although this story is only known in Snorri's version, it contains several interesting aspects. The notion that the day is born from the night fits well with the Old Norse time-reckoning, which was based on the idea that the day ended at sunset, when a new night and day started (Nordberg 2006). Naglfari could possibly be connected with the ship Naglfar ('nail-ship', or ship of the dead), which appears in *Vǫluspá* 50, and is described by Snorri in *Gylfaginning* 42 and 50 as the biggest of all ships, which is used by the powers of chaos at the end of the world, Ragnarok (Simek 1993:226). Jǫrð is usually regarded as mother of the thunder-god Thor (Simek 1993:179), giving associations with the earth as well as the sky. At the same time, the personification of the day seems to have had a broader mythological context, since Snorri describes Dagr in *Skáldskaparmál* 62 as the divine ancestor of the Dǫglingar, to which the Eddic hero Helgi Hundingsbani is said to belong (Simek 1993:55).

The sun also has a central position in *Sólarljóð*, which is a late and clearly Christian poem. Many of the references to the sun in this poem have convincingly been interpreted as expressions of the Christian God (Fidjestøl 1979). However, in *Sólarljóð* 55 a sun-deer (*sólar hjǫrt*), with its hoofs on the earth and antlers in the sky, is mentioned. This figure could be a Christian symbol, but in view of the horned animals in Iron Age iconography, it could also be an older motif, and in that case possibly an alternative to the idea of a sun-horse.

Although the Eddic poems and Snorri describe the sun, the moon, the day, and the night as personifications, they do not play any particular role in the mythological narratives preserved in medieval Iceland. It is therefore difficult to determine whether the personifications are late inventions, possibly by Snorri himself, or echoes of older worldviews. Nonetheless, Tacitus' account of an anthropomorphic sun god could indicate a deep history behind the personifications. Other arguments for early personifications can be taken from the Sámi and the Old Baltic religions, where the sun played a much more central role in mythological tradition (Nesheim 1971; Biezais 1975; Vaitkevicius 2004; Mebius 2003). Admittedly, these mythologies were collected at a later date, usually after the Middle Ages, but the geographical distance from the Sámi and Baltic regions to southern Scandinavia is very short, making them interesting as analogies nonetheless. After all, the distance between Gotland and the coast of Curonia is only 150 kilometres.

In the later Sámi tradition, the sun was regarded as a female being, from whom all living animals descended. The symbol of the sun was a cross, often inserted into a square or a rhomb. This symbol was painted in the middle of many shamanistic drums from the southern Sámi area (Nesheim 1971; Mebius 2003:75). In the Old Baltic mythological traditions from Latvia, Lithuania, and Old Prussia, recorded in the seventeenth and eighteenth centuries, the sun goddess Saule played a central role (Biezais 1975:329 ff.; Vaitkevicius 2004:12 ff.). She drove her horsedrawn chariot over the celestial mountains by day and returned in a boat through the underworld by night. She was accompanied by Dieva deli, that is, the sons of the sky god Dievas. A solar tree as well as Saules meitas, or Saule's daughters, were also important parts of the solar myth. The goddess Saule was one of the main figures in the Old

Baltic pantheon, which also included divinities such as the moon god Meness, the morning star god Auseklis, the sky god Dievas who lived in the celestial mountains, the thunder god Perkunas who wielded a bolt, the goddess of fate Laima, and Mother Earth (Biezais 1975). Most of the divine figures in the Old Baltic mythology are functionally and linguistically recognizable in the narrative tradition from Iceland, although their importance differed quite considerably. Saule can be equated with Sól, Meness with Máni, Auseklis possibly with Aurvandill, Dievas with Tyr, Mother Earth with Jǫrð, and Perkunas with Thor. However, no clear counterparts to Dievas deli existed in the Icelandic narratives, although they represented an Old Baltic version of the Dioscuri motif. In the Baltic tradition, they were sons of the sky god, just as the classical Dioscuri were sons of the sky god Zeus, literally *dios kuroi* ('Zeus' sons').

Although no apparent Dioscuri motif is preserved in the Icelandic literature, several scholars have interpreted the references to two brothers of Haddingjar (*tveir Haddingjar*) in *Hyndluljóð* 23, *Qrvar-Odds saga* 29, *Hervarar saga* 3, and *Saxo Grammaticus* 5:13:4 as echoes of a Dioscuri motif, with Odinic associations (Ward 1968; Dumézil 1973; Simek 1993:127). Another possibility is to regard the two sons of Odin – Vidar and Vale – as echoes of the divine twins (Magnus 2001a). As mentioned above, there are also some references to twin motifs in earlier written sources and images until the eighth century regarding northern Europe (Krüger 1940; de Vries 1957:247 ff.; Ström 1975; Hauck 1984; Magnus 2001a). Apart from the earlier noted references by Tacitus to 'Alcis' and by Timaios to the 'Celtic' Dioscuri, the twin motif is present in several Germanic origin myths. According to these myths, the Langobards were led by Ibur and Aio, and the Vandals by Raos and Raptos, whereas the Anglo-Saxon conquest of Britain was led by the twins Hengist and Horsa, literally 'stallion' and 'horse'. A twin motif may also be present in the Swedish royal brothers Alrik and Erik as well as Alf and Yngve mentioned in *Ynglingatal* (de Vries 1957:251 ff.; Hauck 1984). The sources on north European Dioscuri are thus sparse, but the names are connected with a semantic field of twin warriors, horses, and elk, which fits very well with the images of two men, warriors, armed riders, horses, and/or horned animals in Scandinavia from the third to the seventh centuries AD. The position of these images on the early Gotlandic picture stones shows that the Scandinavian Dioscuri were seen as helpers of the sun at sunrise and sunset, just like the Dieva deli of the Old Baltic tradition. The transformative character of these men/riders/horses/deer/elk can best be explained by their functions during the daily trip of the sun.

As mentioned above, Tyr can be identified on the picture stone at Austers in Hangvar (Fig. 54) as well as on some of the gold bracteates (Öberg 1942; Oxenstierna 1956; Ney 2006). In the much later Icelandic narrative tradition, Tyr is a very vague figure, except for the story about how he lost his hand (Simek 1993:337). According to Snorri's *Gylfaginning* 24, the wolf Fenrir grew too strong for the gods and threatened the world. Therefore the wolf had to be tied by strong fetters made by the dwarfs. The wolf only allowed the chain to be put on if Tyr put his hand in the mouth of the wolf. When the beast noticed that he could not break free he bit the god and Tyr lost his hand. This narrative has been interpreted as a divine sacrifice to secure the cosmic order (de Vries 1957:24). Regardless of this divine sacrifice, Tyr will finally be killed by the hound of Hel at Ragnarok, and the wolf will eventually eat the sun as well as the moon, according to *Gylfaginning* 50 (see Simek 1993:80).

Another god that may have been connected with the solar cycle is Thor, who was indirectly mentioned by Tacitus as early as AD 98. He is not depicted as a figure on the early Gotlandic monuments, but animal attributes connected with him can be traced. On the picture stone from Väskinde two horned animals are depicted above the whirl (see Fig 50). They seem to represent two he-goats, offering associations with Thor, who drove a chariot drawn by two he-goats (*Hymiskviða* 37; *Gylfaginning* 20, 43). Thor was the thunder god, but also a fertility god and a defender of the cosmic order against powers of chaos. One of his antagonists was the large snake surrounding the world, which Snorri called the Midgard serpent (*Hymiskviða* 18–25; *Gylfaginning* 47). This monster is probably depicted between the horizontal line and the ship in the underworld on the picture stone from Sanda, providing further links to Thor on the picture stones (see Fig. 47).

Another possible link between the solar cycle and a divine figure is Freyr. He has not been identified with any certainty on the picture stones, but he is known in the Icelandic narratives as a fertility god connected with sunshine, water, seafaring, ships, and carriages (Simek 1993:31 ff., 379 ff.). According to Snorri, Freyr rules over 'rain and sunshine' (*Gylfaginning* 23) and owns the ship Skíðblaðnir (*Gylfaginning*

Figure 54. Picture stone from Austers in Hangvar. Above the central whirl is a monster and a human putting a hand into the mouth of the monster. The image, which has parallels among the gold bracteates, calls to mind the myth of Fenrir and Tyr. (Photo by the author.)

42–43, *Skáldskaparmál* 7 and 33), with its associations with the sun as well as the night-ship on the early Gotlandic picture stones.

Summarizing the different analogies, it is possible to outline certain basic elements in the Gotlandic solar cycle, although the specific mythological context is not known. The sun could have been regarded as a sun goddess, comparable with the Icelandic Sól or the Baltic Saule. According to Tacitus and the Icelandic tradition of a 'shining god', however, the sun may also have been viewed as a sun god. In the later Icelandic narratives there are many candidates for a possible transformed sun god. Among the candidates are Freyr, who was the divine lord and ruler of sunshine; Ull (Ullr), whose name probably derives from a word meaning 'lustrous' (de Vries 1957:159); Baldr, whom Snorri describes as 'so bright that light shines from him' (*Gylfaginning* 21); and possibly Odin, who Snorri says was the Allfather of the gods and whose one-eyed-ness is a characteristic of many other sun gods (cf. West 2007:194 ff.).

The sun, whether it was considered a female or male being, was helped at sunrise and sunset by divine twins in the shape of warriors, riders, horses, or horned animals. As noted above, no clear Dioscuri are known in the Icelandic literature, but some of the gods with solar aspects may have included elements from the divine twins, such as Baldr and Odin, especially since the character of the two Haddingjar was Odinic. At its zenith, the sun passed through the sky, where the sky god Tyr ensured the cosmic order. He did this by sacrificing his hand in the mouth of a chained wolf, which would otherwise devour the sun. The cosmic order was also secured by the thunder god Thor, who fought the powers of chaos in the sky and the world serpent in the sea around the world. During the night, the sun travelled in a night-ship in the underworld. The ship could also have been regarded as a ship of the dead, associated with a chthonic god and goddesses, such as Niord (Njǫrðr), Freyr, or Freyja.

The early Gotlandic solar cycle thus seems to have included some of the divinities known from the later Icelandic narratives. However, the context was different in the sense that the gods were part of a solar cycle that later disappeared. This means that their character, and consequently the narratives about them, must have changed fundamentally in most cases.

Tracing sun rituals

The pictorial world, as well as the rune-names and some written sources, indicate that solar traditions, resembling the Bronze Age solar myth that Kaul has reconstructed, still existed in the Iron Age until the sixth century. Kaul has also presented good evidence that the solar cycle was linked to rituals during the Bronze Age. In the Iron Age, there are obvious links between the sun and mortuary practice, since ship-forms, wheel-crosses, and other geometrical rings as well as the picture stones were directly connected with graves in many areas. The daily trip of the sun through the sky and the underworld, and possibly the annual solar cycle, must have still been regarded as being closely related to issues of life and death and the question of time. Indeed, as noted above, the night-ship could also have been associated with a death ship.

Sun rituals in general are more difficult to trace during the Iron Age, although there are indications from written sources as well as place-names. A few written sources about central and northern Europe underline the ritual importance of the sun in the Iron Age. According to Caesar's *De Bello Gallico* 4:21, the Germanic tribes that he encountered in central Europe worshipped the sun (de Vries 1956:355 ff.). This statement has been viewed as a classical topos, making his enemies more primitive, because they did not have named gods. However, the details of a sun god given by Tacitus in AD 98 actually indicate the importance of the sun in northern Europe. As mentioned above, he writes that in the sea north of the *sviones*, the sound of sunrise could be heard and the shape of the sun god and his horses could been seen (Tacitus 1999:60; cf. de Vries 1956:355 ff.). Later on the sun is also mentioned by Procopius in his description of Scandinavia in the sixth century. He writes that people in Thule celebrated the return of the sun, after it had disappeared for 35 days during midwinter. Judging by his description of the five weeks without sun, this ritual must have taken place north of the polar circle in northern Scandinavia (de Vries 1956:355 ff.; cf. Nordberg 2006).

Another indication of the ritual importance of the sun during the Iron Age could be different place-names with the compound *sol-* ('sun'), such as Solberga, Solheim, and Solstad. In earlier place-name studies these names were regarded as sacral (see Lindroth 1918; Kiil 1936), but they have, for quite some time, usually been explained away as non-sacral designations of sunny places. In a survey of the literature, Lars Hellberg underlines that many of the *sol-* names seem to be recent, and consequently should be regarded as profane. He does not exclude, however, that some older names could be interpreted in ritual terms (Hellberg 1967:193–6). For instance, the compound *-berga*, as in Solberga, is in several cases combined with names of divinities such as Freyja, Niord,

Odin, Thor, and Ull (Vikstrand 2001), pointing to possible sacral aspects of hills (Fig. 55). Besides, many of the *sol-* names are securely attested as names for old, large settlements that can be linguistically dated before the Viking Age. The compound was not commonly used for place-names dated to the Viking Age and the early Middle Ages, such as -*by*, -*torp*, and -*ryd*, and if the *sol-* element only designated sunny places one would expect many more examples to be found among these younger place-names. Recently, the place-name Tungelunda in Östergötland has also been interpreted as a sacral name connected to the sun or the moon, because *tungl* means 'celestial body' (Strid 2009:85).

The best archaeological evidence for a ritual interpretation of the compound *sol-* in place-names comes from two bronze figures of horned animals from Solberga on Öland (Fig. 56), found on a large farm dated from the third to the fifth centuries (Persson and Rasch 2001:373–4, cf. Fallgren 2008:132). As mentioned above, one of the animals has a decorated ring at the neck, which resembles the remark by Snorri that the horse of Dagr, Skínfaxi, illuminated the world from his shining mane. The horned animals from Solberga can thus be interpreted as sun-animals, possibly used in rituals at the site. A ritual interpretation of the *sol-*names may also be supported by analogies with the Baltic region. In Latvia and Lithuania a common place-name is Saulekalns, meaning 'sun hill', a direct equivalent to the Scandinavian place-name Solberga. In many cases, midsummer rituals are recorded from places called Saulekalns (Vaitkevicius 2004:12 ff.).

This is not the place to thoroughly explore all the possible ritual aspects of the *sol-*names, but some general comments may be added. The names are known from all parts of the Scandinavian agrarian settlement, from the middle of Norway and Sweden to southern Denmark (see Fig. 55). Usually a few *sol-*names are known from each region or province – on Öland and Gotland there are two Solberga on each island, for example. The names occur in onomastic environments with old place-names, and sometimes designate regions and islands as well. Two good examples just north of Stockholm are Solland, a regional name surviving in the place-name Sollentuna (*de Solendatunum*, 1287), and Solna (*Solnø*, 1305) which originally was a name for an island (Wahlberg 2003:287–8).

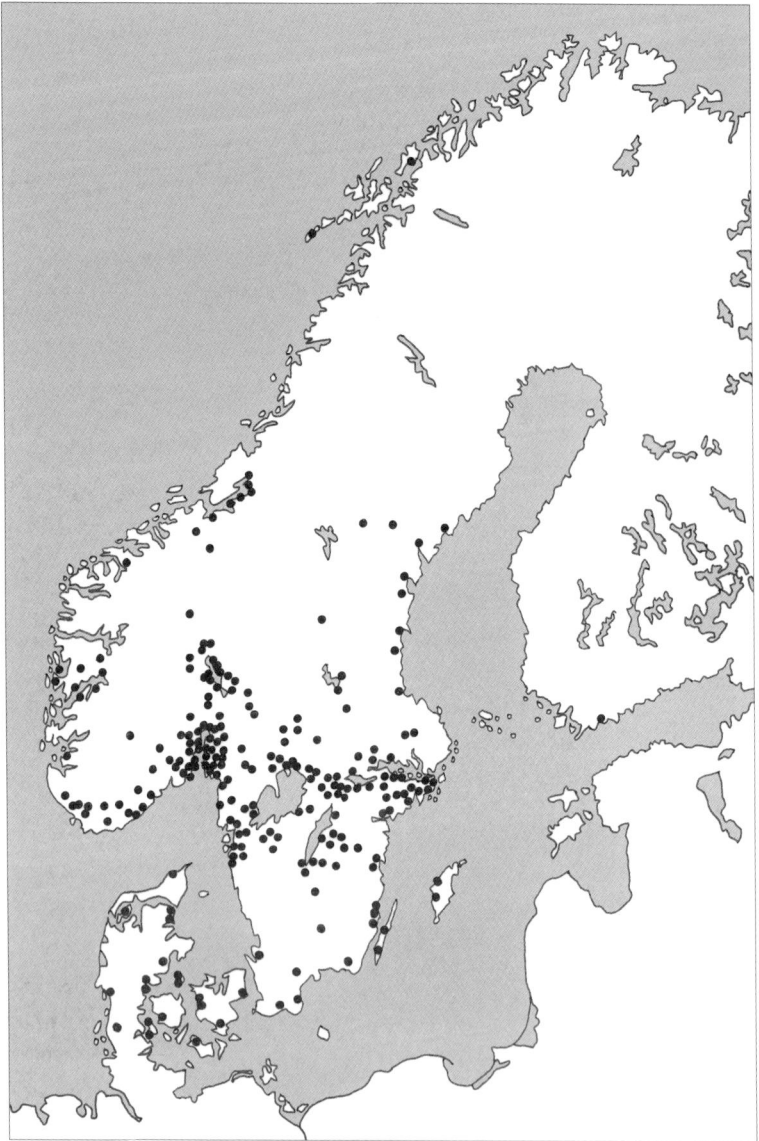

Figure 55. Distribution of the place-names Solberg, Solberga, and Solbjerg in Scandinavia. Kiil emphasizes that his survey is not comprehensive, and probably the Norwegian examples are over-represented in relation to Denmark and Sweden. Nevertheless, the map gives an idea of the regions where these sun-related names are found. (Map by the author, based on Kiil 1936.)

Figure 56. Horned animals of bronze from Solberga in Gräsgård on Öland. One of the animals has a decorated ring at the neck, placed in the same way as the head on C-bracteates. This and the pair motif indicate that the animals were used in sun rituals at Solberga. (Photo by Pierre Rosberg, Kalmar Länsmuseum, Kalmar.)

The disappearance of solar symbols and sun rituals in the sixth century

As noted above, the early picture stones on Gotland were all surprisingly similar in structure and motifs, always including a whirl. However, a few late examples of these monuments, probably from the sixth century, contain some new expressions. The usual large whirl is replaced by a quatrefoil knot on two stones from Austers in Hangvar (see Fig. 54) and Havor in Hablingbo (Lindqvist 1941, fig. 23), and by a three-pointed figure, triskele, of three different animals on a stone from Smiss in Närr (Lindqvist 1962; Arrhenius 1994). Apart from the triskele, the Smiss stone also contains a totally new motif, namely a human in a sitting position holding a snake in each hand. These monuments mark the transition to an intermediate group of small picture stones, which are generally dated to the seventh and eighth centuries (Lindqvist 1941; Nylén and Lamm 2003).

There are about 70 intermediate picture stones, usually not exceeding one metre in height (Fig. 57). They are often found in the burial grounds, where they were once erected, and not in medieval churches like the early large picture stones (Lindqvist 1941; Nylén and Lamm 2003). Not a single monument of this group of small stones contains a whirl or a spiral. Instead, the motifs are reduced to a few recurring images; ships with or without sails, horses, aquatic birds, snakes, riders, horned animals, and chess-formed patterns possibly representing sails. Sometimes the horses and birds are placed antithetically, sometimes they appear as pairs cut on both sides of a monument (Ragnarsson 2007). This means that the twin motif was partly preserved, whereas the sun disappeared. However, there is no recurring structure in the images found on these stones. Sometimes the ship is at the top of a stone, sometimes at the bottom.

In the ninth and tenth centuries, these intermediate stones were followed by the classic Gotlandic picture stones, which contain vivid and varied images. Some of these pictures can also be connected with Old Norse mythology and the heroic narratives known from Old Icelandic literature, but apart from the monument at Bote in Garda (Lindqvist 1941, fig. 41) none of the stones contain references to the sun. A few stones once again depict antithetically placed warriors, which may echo the former twin motif, and many of these later monuments also depict a ship at the bottom of the stone, as a parallel to the early picture stones (Myrberg 2005), but in contrast to the early stones the direction of the ship varies. However, it is quite clear from the later picture stones on Gotland that the sun symbolism, which was so dominant from the very first monuments in the third century, suddenly disappeared during the sixth century.

In central Sweden it is not possible to follow the changes in the same way, since picture stones on the whole ceased to be erected after the sixth century. However, some of the older pictorial monuments were destroyed and reused in later burials. This destruction has led some scholars to suggest a kind of iconoclasm, again mirroring fundamental religious changes (Hamilton 2012)

Images on metalwork followed the same pattern. Gold bracteates fell out of use in the mid sixth century (Axboe 2007:65–76). Only on Gotland did bracteates made of above all silver and bronze continue to be produced in the seventh and eighth centuries. The central figures on these bracteates were often simple triquetra motifs (Gaimster 1998). In order to follow the fate of the solar images in the sixth century and later

Figure 57. Picture stone from Smiss in Garda. This monument is an example of the intermediate picture stones of the sixth and seventh centuries. (Photo by the author.)

it is therefore necessary to use other metalwork in Scandinavia from the Merovingian and Viking ages. Metalwork, such as decorated weapons and dress ornaments, gold-foil figures, and small three-dimensional figures, depict animals and human figures that can be provisionally related to the Icelandic narratives by their more distinct attributes. In many cases, the pictures from the sixth century onwards are more or less disguised in complicated animal art, but once again the sun seems to disappear in this context (Arrhenius 1994; cf. Price 2006). Twin motifs continued to be used in the seventh and eighth centuries, but later also disappeared (Magnus 2001a). Once again, there is a clear parallel to the images on the Gotlandic picture stones after the sixth century.

In short, after the sixth century, the solar cycle disappeared from the pictorial world of Scandinavia, and probably many of the sun rituals as well. Place-names with the compound *sol-* do not seem to have been coined in the Viking Age or later. In the Viking Age, we only find echoes of the former importance of the sun. A late sun ritual in burial context may be inferred from a site called Rösaring in southern Uppland, discovered only 25 years ago. It is a road, 540 metres long, running from a small house to a grave mound. The road bank is built in a straight line from north to south, and is flanked on the eastern side by a row of about 120 post-holes. The monument, which is dated to the ninth and tenth centuries, has been interpreted as a ritual road used in connection with funerals, and is said to have solar associations (Damell 1985; Pásztor et al. 2000). Another late reference to the sun comes from Cnut the Great's Anglo-Saxon laws from the 1020s, partly directed at Scandinavians in the Danelaw. According to this code, rituals addressing the heathen gods as well as the sun, the moon, and the stars were prohibited (de Vries 1956:356–7). It is probably these remaining solar aspects of the Viking Age that can explain why the sun is mentioned in the later Icelandic texts. However, the sun plays no active role in the *Eddas* and the sagas, which shows that only distant echoes of the former role of the sun were left in the twelfth and thirteenth centuries. In the late Sámi tradition, on the other hand, the female sun was still worshipped in the seventeenth and eighteenth centuries. There are references to offerings of food and burnt sacrifices at midsummer, and also the slaughter of white female animals, honouring the female character of the sun (Nesheim 1971). Similarly, in the Baltic traditions, the sun preserved much of its importance until the seventeenth and eighteenth centuries (Biezais 1975).

Solar traditions through time

The sun has shone on us since the beginning of time. The metaphorical potential of the sun as the source of light and warmth is endless, and the sun has consequently been important in many cultures around the world. In the European Neolithic, it is evident from the layout of Megalithic monuments as well as henge monuments that the sun played a fundamental role (Kaul 2004:379). In several cases the sunrise and the sunset at midwinter and midsummer were the main orientations of these monuments. However, the solar myths and rituals that Kaul has reconstructed are much more specific and detailed. They probably built on the old importance of the sun, but show that many new elements were introduced and reinterpreted. Groups in southern Scandinavia, with some form of long-distance relations across Europe, seem to have created a new religious tradition around 1500 BC. Many elements were taken from central Europe and ultimately from the eastern Mediterranean, but they were brought together in a new specific context, shaping an early form of a Scandinavian narrative and ritual tradition concerning the journey of the sun.

At the start, the solar myth included the sun being drawn across the sky and the underworld by one or two horses. The divine twins may have been part of the tradition from the beginning, their transformative functions being expressed through images of men with horned helmets, axes, and lurs. A mushroom-shaped figure also formed part of the tradition. It is clear from the Trundholm sun-chariot as well as rock carvings and graves that the solar myth was not only a narrative but also connected to rituals associated with the sun. The solar myth nonetheless changed gradually over time. Due to local reinterpretations of new models from central Europe, the image of the ship as a main form of transport for the sun was introduced, together with images of serpents and aquatic birds around 1100 BC. The narrative tradition was still connected to rituals, which must likewise have changed. Above all, ships, models of ships, and ship symbols became important parts of the rituals.

Around 500 BC, many of the representations of the solar myth disappeared. The expressions were reduced to formalized symbols such as wheel-crosses, concentric rings, and ship-forms, used in metalwork as well as external grave markers. Only burial rituals and deposits of neck-rings in pairs can be connected to the narrative tradition from that time. Three hundred years later, around 200 BC, even these sparse sun symbols disappeared, apart from some objects involving images of aquatic birds, triskeles, and more or less complex wheel-crosses and concentric rings as grave markers in Norway and Sweden. From an archaeological point of view the four centuries years between about 200 BC and AD 200 are the most obscure. Nonetheless, it is from this very period that the earliest classical sources actually describe the continuing mythological importance of the sun and its horses, as well as the divine twins in central and northern Europe.

From around AD 200 to 550 the existence of solar myths is once again clearly visible in images and objects. The narratives now appear to have involved the sun moving around the world tree, across the sky, and then through the underworld in a night-ship. At sunrise and sunset, the sun was helped by divine twins in the form of warriors, armed riders, horses, or horned animals. Possibly some of the gods in the Icelandic narratives have their roots in transformed sun divinities and the idea of divine twins. The sky god Tyr and the thunder god Thor secured the cosmic order by controlling forces of chaos in the form of monsters or serpents. As in earlier narratives, the late versions of the Scandinavian solar myths were also related to rituals. The narratives are visible in the burial context of the picture stones on Gotland and in Uppland and Södermanland, but the horned sun-animals from Solberga and the place-name compound *sol-* in general indicate other rituals, too.

The solar cycles in the Iron Age seem to have had many similarities to the old solar myths from the Bronze Age. However, the ship had lost much of its importance as a means of transport. It is also possible that the old solar myths were renewed with inspiration from the contemporary Roman world (Gelling and Davidson 1969:182). The Roman Dioscuri as well as the imperial cult of Sol Invictus, which was introduced in the early third century, may have stood as models for local reinterpretations of earlier mythologies. One argument for such Roman impulses is that the best formal parallels to the early Gotlandic picture stones come from Roman altars, mosaics, and gravestones (Lindqvist 1941:91 ff.; Holmqvist 1952; Gelling and Davidson 1969:144).

Above all the gold bracteates, and their parallels with some motifs on the Gotlandic picture stones, indicate that Scandinavian rulers, at least since the fourth and fifth centuries, ruled through a divided leadership legitimized through the divine twins as supporters of the sun. However, the important solar cycles with their sun symbols rapidly disappeared from images in the sixth century. Instead, the narratives and rituals about the divine and celestial world were thoroughly transformed during the sixth and seventh centuries. Only faint echoes of the solar cycles survived into the medieval Icelandic literature, probably due to the sun remaining an important natural phenomenon. To sum up, the solar myths and sun rituals of ancient Scandinavia show a great deal of continuity, with variations and successive changes being based on incorporations and reinterpretations of foreign models. It is a complex tradition that is largely outside the reach of the later Icelandic narratives, but was still an important part of Old Norse religious tradition.

Figure 58. Gamla Uppsala with its 'royal mounds' and the remains of the cathedral. The large mounds have been dated to the late sixth and seventh centuries, and can be regarded as symbols of a new social order emerging after a crisis in the mid sixth century. (Photo by the author.)

CHAPTER 5

Placing Old Norse cosmology in time and space

The study of Old Norse religious traditions is a multidisciplinary field of research. Due to its complexity, the perspectives adopted in the field vary quite considerably, resulting in research that is conducted in fundamentally different ways. One example of this, as mentioned above in the introduction, is the various approaches to the Icelandic texts as sources of Old Norse religious traditions. The Icelandic texts are regarded by some as Christian interpretations of an imagined pagan homeland created in a diaspora culture. For others, the Icelandic narratives are viewed as an important source for fundamental pagan worldviews and practices with a very long history. Yet others see the Icelandic texts as mirrors of a more recent pagan past, at most going back to the sixth century AD.

The three perspectives seem incompatible, but the paradox is that all three of them are in some sense correct. The Icelandic texts, which contain the main written sources about Old Norse religion, are certainly fundamentally Christian. However, they also contain important references to pagan practice and pagan worldviews, as has been confirmed by recent archaeological research. In contrast to the Christian frame of the texts, it seems plausible that some elements in the texts are very old indeed. Classical authors, as well as linguistic and archaeological indications, point to a time perspective reaching beyond a millennium. However, a close correlation between the texts and material culture can only be maintained during the last centuries before the conversion, above all from the sixth and seventh centuries onwards.

Different trajectories

In the three main chapters of this book, I have tried to show how this paradox can be solved, by following three different cosmological elements through time and space. The notions of the world tree, the world, and the sun were all aspects of Old Norse cosmology, but had partly different trajectories over time. Although a possible representation of a world tree is known already at Seahenge in England as early as around 2050 BC, this motif remains elusive in Scandinavia for a long time. There are hardly any trees in the rock carvings from the Bronze Age. It is only from the fifth and fourth centuries BC that triangular stone settings, which can be regarded as tree representations, appear. The tree motif then became more distinct, with the three-pointed stone settings appearing around AD 200, and images of a cosmic tree from around AD 400, and ritual trees from the ninth and tenth centuries known from archaeology and written descriptions. Probably early place-names with names of different trees as their first element can be connected with early ritual trees, in turn associated with the idea of a world tree. The motif of the world tree seems to have been built up through the centuries until the time of the conversion. This is also reflected in the tree having a very strong position in the later Icelandic written tradition.

The notion of Midgard, or the world in its totality, is much more difficult to follow in material representations, because of the complexity of such a figure of thought. There are indications from around 1000 BC that hill forts, or so-called henged mountains, were built and used in central Sweden in accordance with anthropocentric worldviews. Otherwise, representations of the world can only be traced in circles of erected stones. Usually the numbers of stones are odd, often seven or nine. Sometimes the height of the stones varies according to the location of the stones in the circle, the tallest being placed in the north and the shortest in the south (Fig. 68). These monuments are difficult to date; some are probably as old as the first centuries BC, whereas others are from AD 200–550. The motif reflected in these circles of erected stone was transformed into complex ringforts on the island of Öland. In at least three cases, these ringforts were built with nine edges or gates, Ismantorp being the best preserved. After the sixth and seventh centuries these representations disappeared. Instead expressions of Old Norse worldviews became much more associated with central places, and the large halls that dominated these locations. These cosmological ideas probably go back to the third century, but became more dominant through time (Hedeager 2001; Sundqvist 2004). Ideas about Midgard consisting of several different worlds, sometimes numbering nine, survived in the later written Icelandic tradition, but a much stronger emphasis was put on gods and goddesses having different divine abodes in large halls.

In contrast, the solar cycle has a very different history. The sun, as a fundamental natural phenomenon, had a clear role already in the Neolithic. Sunset and sunrise at different times of the year were used as points of orientation for large monuments in many parts of Europe. However, at the start of the Bronze Age in the seventeenth and sixteenth centuries BC, a more specific Scandinavian solar tradition was created, with the sun-horse and the divine twins serving as central figures. In the eleventh century BC, this tradition was transformed, with ships, snakes, and aquatic birds becoming new elements. Later, from the fifth century BC, many elements of the solar cycle disappeared, and the sun was represented symbolically in the form of sun-wheels or as concentric circles only. In a final phase, AD 300–550, the sun, the divine twins, and the ships were again clearly expressed in metalwork and on picture stones. Place-names with a *sol-* prefix probably also date from this period, indicating sun rituals as well. After the sixth centuries, the sun more or less disappeared as a cosmological and ritual element, and only faint echoes were preserved in the Icelandic narrative tradition.

In all the three studies, changes over time have been interpreted as hybridizations in the form of variations, incorporations, and reinterpretations. These interpretations are based on the idea of culture as a gradually changing patchwork. Although hybridizations were constantly taking place, it seems that some periods as well as some regions were more decisive than others. Clusters of changes occur in specific periods, followed by other phases with fewer changes. Since these clusters of changes have geographical locations as well, they also tend to create more homogeneous regions for longer or shorter periods. In my three cases such clusters of changes can above all be located in the Early Bronze Age, probably the Early Iron Age, the first part of the late Roman Iron Age, and the Migration Period. In order to indicate how such a cluster of changes worked out, I will in this context dwell on the Migration Period. I have selected this time frame since it is decisive for several of my case studies, and since a number of archaeologists have argued that a new form of 'Æsir religion' was introduced in Scandinavia during the Migration Period (Bennett 1987; Hedeager 1997, 2007, 2011; Kaul 1998, 2004). Irrespective of whether the changes that took place during this time should be framed in such a way, the transformations in the Migration Period undoubtedly had fundamental consequences for Scandinavian society in general as well as for the later Icelandic narrative tradition.

The Migration Period as a cluster of changes

The Migration Period (AD 400–550) has for a long time been an enigmatic period in Scandinavian archaeology. The turbulent political events in central and southern Europe are well known, for instance the short-lived Hunnic realm, the replacement of the West Roman Empire with a number of Germanic kingdoms, the expansion and contraction of the Byzantine Empire, and the final expansion of Slavonic rule in eastern and south-eastern Europe (see Fig. 60). Many Scandinavian archaeologists have assumed that these fundamental changes must have affected Scandinavia in different ways. Above all, the Roman gold coins, the *solidi*, and other gold objects found in southern Scandinavia indicate long-distance connections with the late Roman army as well as different barbarian groups that received huge gold tributes from the Romans. However, the extent to which Scandinavia was part of the turbulent European history has remained uncertain.

An aspect of this enigmatic character of the Migration Period is whether this archaeological period should be regarded as the start of a new era of as the end of an old phase in Scandinavia. In Danish archaeology, the Migration Period is usually regarded as the start of the Late Iron Age, since the division of periods is basically defined from objects. Since the distinct animal art was created in the fifth century and used well into the twelfth century, the Migration Period is regarded as the beginning of a new era. However, in Swedish and Norwegian archaeology, the Migration Period is usually viewed as the end of the Early or Middle Iron Age, because the archaeology is much more concerned with studies of settlements and land use. The distinct stone-enclosed settlements were gradually abandoned at the end of the Migration Period, as were many of the hillforts and ringforts. Many settlements and some burial grounds were also relocated in the sixth century. Therefore, the Migration Period is viewed as the end of an expansive period, starting in the Roman Iron Age.

I have no intention to analyse all the problems of the Migration Period in full, but I will illuminate the paradoxical character of the period by using two recent discussions. One concerns a possible Hunnic conquest of Scandinavia in around 400 and the other a possible climatic disaster in the 530s. Moreover, these studies view the Migration Period from different perspectives, as a start or as an end of an era.

The Huns

In a recent provocative study, Lotte Hedeager argues that the Huns conquered southern Scandinavia in the late fourth or early fifth centuries (Hedeager 2011, cf. 2007). According to her, this conquest triggered the creation of animal art and was decisive for the late Old Norse religion, above all regarding the character of Odin, who she sees as modelled on the Hunnic king Attila. In many ways, she is returning to older discussions on eastern influences in Scandinavia during the Migration Period (see Salin 1904; Janse 1922), but her ideas have been ignored, met with scepticism (Ramqvist 2012), or firmly criticized (Näsman 2008b, 2009). However, I find her ideas interesting for two reasons of principle. Firstly, Scandinavian archaeologists usually underline the Scandinavians as active in long-distance connections. Kerstin Cassel has recently criticized this standard motif – that it is always Scandinavians 'returning home' from distant foreign regions who introduce new ideas to Scandinavia (Cassel 2008). Although we know that Scandinavians 'returned home', for instance during the Viking Age, Hedeager's ideas open up for foreigners of non-Scandinavian origin having had a decisive influence on the Scandinavian past. Secondly, most Scandinavian archaeologists today look south or south-east, and ultimately to the Mediterranean when looking for foreign models and inspirations. Instead, Hedeager's ideas are much more connected to older archaeological and art-historical discussions, where south-east Europe, the Black Sea, and ultimately central Asia and China are underlined (see Salin 1904; Janse 1922; Holmqvist 1980). It is also interesting that her Hunnic thesis adds a possible non-Indo-European aspect to Old Norse religion.

However, the empirical basis of Hedeager's thesis is somewhat elusive. Her best argument for a Hunnic conquest of south Scandinavia is the late Roman author Priscius, who mentioned that Attila 'ruled even the islands of the Ocean', which can be interpreted as islands in the Baltic as well as the Scandinavian peninsula (Hedeager 2011:192, but cf. Näsman 1984:99 ff.). The archaeological remains in Scandinavia of a possible Hunnic conquest are more difficult to discern, and consequently an issue that has been critically examined (Näsman 2008b; Ramqvist 2012). No material culture that has been labelled as 'Hunnic' (cf. Werner 1956; Anke and Externbrink 2007) – such as deformation of heads, large copper cauldrons for cooking meat, pendant bronze mirrors, and plain gold earrings – have been found in secured contexts from the Migration Period in Scandinavia (Hedeager 2007, 2011; Näsman 2008b; Ramqvist 2012; cf. Ljungkvist 2005).

Since objects may have been moved over long distances for several reasons, the best arguments for some kind of Hunnic connection are a few distinct grave deposits of riding equipment from around AD 400. Such deposits have been found in present-day southern Romania, eastern Austria, western Ukraine, southern Poland, and southern Sweden, at Sösdala and Fulltofta in Skåne and at Vännebo in Västergötland (Fig. 59). For a long time now, these finds have been used in the discussion of a Gothic connection to southern Scandinavia (Norberg 1931; Åberg 1936; Forssander 1937), but Charlotte Fabech has demonstrated that they represented groups of mounted warriors in south Scandinavia that practised a specific form of ritual otherwise known in central and south-east Europe (Fabech 1991a; 2011). These grave deposits are not Hunnic in a narrow sense (see Werner 1956), but rather expressions of a hybrid culture created in the Hunnic realm, in the forced encounter between steppe nomads, Germanic groups, and a Romanized population. Whether the grave depositions represent a Hunnic conquest (Hedeager 2011:203), or returning Scandinavians from 'multicultural barbarian societies beyond the disintegrating Roman empire' (Fabech 2011:34) is a matter of minor differences. The rituals may even have been carried out by foreign, including Hunnic, mercenaries, enrolled by local Scandinavian rulers (see Andrén 2011b). What is important in this context is that they clearly express connections between southern Scandinavia and the Hunnic political centre in south-east Europe (Bemmann 2009).

Figure 59. The hoard from Sjörup in Häglinge in Skåne. The objects are dated to the first half of the fifth century, and are decorated with an early form of animal art, sometimes called the Sjörup style after the hoard. The mount in the middle, with four bird heads, has parallels in south-east Europe and the Caucasus (see Werner 1956, table 47), thereby showing links with central and south-east Europe, dominated by the Huns. (Photo by Sören Hallgren, Statens Historiska Museum, Stockholm.)

The Hunnic conquest of Scandinavia will remain a hypothesis, but it is not a necessary precondition for Hunnic elements in Scandinavian animal art and late paganism. Since the Huns clearly dominated east and central Europe from the 370s to the 450s (Anke and Externbrink 2007), Scandinavians had to accommodate to this political entity as they had done with the Roman Empire previously, and continued to do with the Byzantine Empire. Since Roman models were incorporated and reinterpreted in Scandinavia without a Roman conquest, similar processes may have been at work during the short Hunnic dominance of east and central Europe.

Early animal art clearly has a hybrid character, which means that there will never be any definite model as a single origin. It includes Roman chip-carved design, which in itself was a hybrid expression, including Roman motifs as well as 'barbarian features' with animal heads as end motifs (Böhme 1986:48). The design is interpreted as an expression of the 'barbarization' of the late Roman army during the period 375–425 (Böhme 1986), with a large proportion of non-Roman soldiers, of Germanic, Sarmatian, and Armenian but also Hunnic origins (Elton 1996). However, the Roman chip-carved design was only 'one root' of animal art (Böhme 1986:25), and other models may have been of Germanic (Werner 1966; Roth 1979:44), Sarmatian (Lund Hansen 2003b), or Hunnic origin. Especially a possible central Asian background needs further consideration, because the standard survey of animal art (Haseloff 1981) was written long before central Asia was opened to new excavations, yielding very interesting results concerning animal art in the Xiongnu empire (Erööl-Erdene 2011; Leus 2011). It is disputed whether Xiongnu (reconstructed as 'Hunnu' in Old Chinese) was linked with the Huns, but central Asian sources equate the two names. Besides, both groups used similar copper cauldrons, and deposited them in similar ways in riverbanks (Miklos 1993). If the Huns partly originated from Xiongnu, a further important aspect can be added to the issue of Huns. The Xiongnu empire was an urbanized society, clearly influenced by China (Brosseder and Miller 2011), meaning that the Hunnic invasion of central Europe was not just a 'barbaric storm', but an invasion of urbanized steppe nomads.

The enigmatic divine figure of Odin has been discussed for over a century. Although most scholars agree that Odin is an old figure with ecstatic aspects, indirectly mentioned as the Germanic high god Mercury by Tacitus as early as AD 98, the complex character of Odin is difficult to explain and is without counterpart in other comparable religious traditions. Therefore, aspects of the god have been regarded as modelled on the Gallo-Roman cult of Mercury, the Roman cult of emperors, the Roman Mithras cult, or a nomadic shaman-god incorporated by Germanic warrior groups in south-east Europe (Kaliff and Sundqvist 2004; Hultgård 2007a).

Hedeager adds new arguments to this debate, but little is known directly about Hunnic religion, which means that she has to use fairly weak Mongol analogies in her arguments for a Hunnic origin of the shamanistic traits of Odin (Hedeager 2011:196). However, if we accept that the Huns spoke a Turkic language (see Heather 1995) a few other aspects of Hunnic religion may be added. The Hunnic personal names of two high-ranking men, Atakam and Eskam, are probably based on the

Turkish word *qam*, which means shaman. Therefore, 'shamans seem to have belonged to the upper stratum of Hun society' (Maenchen-Helfen 1973:269). There are also indications that the Huns regarded Attila as a sun, possibly with inspiration from the Roman imperial cult of Sol Invictus (Maenchen-Helfen 1973:272). Therefore, shamanistic and solar aspects may have been added from Hunnic sources to Odin's already complex divine figure.

Hedeager has clearly renewed the debate about the Migration Period, animal art, and late Old Norse religion, although the issues need further consideration, not least the possible central Asian connections. However, in one respect I cannot agree with her, namely that the animal styles represented a *longue durée* from 400 to 1200 that 'consciously or un/sub-consciously reflect cosmological structures in pre-Christian Nordic societies' (Hedeager 2011:75). Her perspective is based on current ideas that animal styles were not neutral decorations, but had fundamental meanings (see Kristoffersen 1995, 2000; Hedeager 1997). Generally speaking, I agree with this perspective, but I find that this close connection between animal styles and pre-Christian religion gives animal art too specific a pagan meaning. Hedeager uses figurative representations on metal, above all from the Merovingian Period, to interpret the animal styles in one *longue durée* (Hedeager 2011:66 ff.), but the Gotlandic picture stones clearly indicate more varied contexts. The picture stones were erected from probably the fourth to the early twelfth centuries and included figurative representations as well as animal art. As I have argued above and elsewhere (Andrén 1993), the figures can be associated with solar aspects as well as more classical Old Norse traditions and Christianity.

Following earlier scholars, I rather see animal art as a parallel to writing and skaldic poetry (Andrén 2000a; cf. Söderberg 1905; Lie 1952; Gurevich 1985). As a consequence, I regard animal art as a figurative discourse, with a much more open and contextual meaning. Each style has to been interpreted on its own terms. The early styles are very different from late styles, such as the Ringerike and Urnes styles. The late styles lack the divided humans and animals, and are dominated by motifs that have been convincingly interpreted as Christian symbols (Horn Fuglesang 1986). Only such open and contextual interpretations can explain the fact that animal art was used for 200 years in obviously Christian contexts (see Staecker 2011).

A good analogy is skaldic poetry, which was clearly linked to Old Norse mythology. At the same time it could be used without problems in Christian contexts (Clunies Ross 2007). Another analogy of a similar open discourse is runic writing. As mentioned above, the names of the runes clearly show that runic writing was embedded in pagan worldviews from the start. In the long run, however, runes were used in many different contexts, thereby transcending the pagan origin of the writing system (Jansson 1977:166 ff.; Benneth et al. 1994; Fischer 2005). Besides, the runes represent an even longer Scandinavian *longue durée* than animal art, covering in general 1,200 years from the second century to the fourteenth century – and in some regions continuing well into the sixteenth, seventeenth, and eighteenth centuries. Consequently, I think that Hedeager puts too much weight on animal art when trying to frame late pagan Scandinavia as a continuum from about 400.

The dust veil

For a long time Scandinavian archaeologists have discussed a possible crisis in the sixth century, at the transition between the Migration Period and the Merovingian Period. The background to this debate was that many of the houses built on terraces or stone foundations on Öland and Gotland and in Hälsingland and Rogaland seem to have been abandoned at the end of the Migration Period. Moreover, many of the Swedish and Norwegian hillforts and ringforts fell out of use at the same time. In several regions the number of graves in the Merovingian Period declined considerably as well. Usually the crisis was regarded as an expression of warfare and political unrest, leading to plundered and destroyed settlements and a decreasing population (see, for instance, Stenberger 1933, 1955). This conventional perspective has been repeatedly criticized for taking the material remains at face value. The number of buried people in a certain period does not need to have had any relation to the size of the population, but is dependent on different burial customs. Settlements and forts were not always abandoned in the middle of the sixth century and ruins of farms and villages could be the result of a new social order, moving settlements, and changing land use as well (Näsman and Lund 1988; Myhre 2002:170 ff.; Näsman 2012).

However, ideas about a crisis in the middle of the sixth century have recently reappeared, prompted by a sudden disappearance of the sun behind a dust veil in 536. This event has been debated in the last fifteen years (Baillie 1999; Axboe 1999, 2001, 2007), and has most recently been summarized and developed by Bo Gräslund (2008), who sees a major population crisis as a result of the dust veil. A meteor impact or an enormous volcanic eruption took place in 536, resulting in a thick cloud covering the sky for years. The cloud had a global effect on the climate, as is visible in ice cores from Greenland and the Antarctic as well as in dendrochronology from Europe, Siberia, and north and south America. The cloud is also mentioned by several classical authors. John of Ephesus wrote in 536 that 'the sun became dark and its darkness lasted for one and a half years. Each day it shone for about four hours, and still this light was only a feeble shadow' (Gräslund 2008:103). Cassiodorus wrote in the same year about the fearful and terrifying experience of the darkened sun in Italy, leading to crop failure, hardened fruit, and bitter grapes. In northern Europe, dendrochronology shows even more drastic effects. From 536 to 545 the growth of tree-rings nearly stopped, indicating several years without real summers. The effects of the cloud must have been more pronounced than in the Mediterranean (Gräslund 2008), although the local consequences may have varied. Communities growing cereals must have been more hit than communities that were dependent on fishery (Widgren 2012).

Recently, Daniel Löwenborg has argued that the event in 536 was a shock that profoundly changed the economy as well as the social and political organization in central Sweden (Löwenborg 2012). He refers to extensive desertion, followed by relocated settlements and burial grounds, and new burial customs, such as large mounds. Using analogies from the late medieval agrarian crisis, he envisages profound changes in property rights as a result of the dust veil in 536 and the decline in population that followed the cold summers in the 530s and 540s. Löwenborg has been criticized for exaggerating the consequences of the event in 536, and for not taking into account other contemporary aspects such as warfare (Näsman 2012).

The dust veil will never explain all changes in the sixth century. Apart from warfare, another series of important events was sparked by the collapse of Byzantine rule in many parts of the Mediterranean, when the Byzantine Empire was reduced to Constantinople, a few

Figure 60. Ruin of Basilica A in Nikopolis, founded by Bishop Alkyson, who died in 516. This basilica is just one example of over 300 large churches that were ruined or abandoned in Greece during the 'dark ages', from the end of the sixth century to the late eighth century (see Zakynthinos 1966; Pallas 1977). These church ruins represent a clear 'system collapse', when the Byzantine Empire lost its political and religious control over most of its European regions to different Slavic groups. (Photo by the author.)

Greek ports, and some heavily fortified sites in Anatolia (Fig. 60). An aspect of the Byzantine collapse was that Avarian and Slavonic groups conquered large parts of the Balkans and Greece (Hendy 1985:69 ff.; Gregory 1994; Andrén 1997). In this process, Scandinavia lost its old connections with south-east Europe and the Byzantine Empire, as well as its sources of gold. No new gold coins, *solidi*, entered Scandinavia after the mid sixth century (Fagerlie 1967), which must have had huge consequences because gold had been used as a social and political medium by Scandinavian elite groups since the first century AD (Andersson 1995:9 ff.).

However, the dust veil as a global phenomenon needs more consideration, not least with respect to possible consequences and reactions. Löwenborg used a few analogies with the late medieval agrarian crisis, but these can be expanded to other illuminating parallels. For a long time, the Black Death in 1347–51 has been explained away as a main source of the late medieval agrarian crisis, since its non-human background made it historically 'meaningless' (Gissel et al. 1981). The same reactions can be indirectly found in the discussion concerning the dust veil (Wickham 2005:548 ff.; Näsman 2012). However, in recent years the devastating consequences of the Black Death have become more and more obvious (Harrison 2000; Myrdal 2003), and probably a similar reorientation will be visible regarding the dust veil.

It is practically impossible to estimate how many people died in Scandinavia during the Black Death, but the consequences of the population decline are quite visible (Myrdal 2003). According to dendro-chronological dates, no new blockhouses were built in northern Sweden between 1350 and 1490, since the surviving population used and reused abandoned houses. The desertion is above all visible in marginal land, since whole settlements were abandoned in those regions. In central agrarian regions, a depopulation is much more difficult to trace, since the land of the deserted farms was used by the surviving farms. However, a recent study of western Östergötland shows considerable desertion and depopulation, although the arable land continued to be used (Karsvall 2011).

The late medieval desertion of agrarian settlements hit large parts of the minor landowning nobility, which more or less disappeared. In contrast, a small group of aristocratic families became large landholders, with political aspirations (Benedictow et al. 1971; Christensen 1976). From a material point of view, this change in property holding is visible in the abandonment of many small castles and fortified settlements during the fourteenth century (Olsen 2011). Due to the disappearance of the many smaller feudal families, the population decline in the long run led to larger political units in many parts of Europe.

The population decline affected the towns as well. Some small towns disappeared as urban settlements, several larger cities were partly deserted, no new towns were established from 1350 to about 1400, and from the early fifteenth century the ranking between the larger cities changed (Andrén 1985:100 ff.). From a religious point of view, the Black Death resulted in a new image of God. The earlier view of a triumphant Christ was replaced more generally by an image of the sacrificial Christ, at the same time as religious practice became more personal (Nilsén 1991:107 ff.; Pernler 1999). In European philosophy, a distinct empirical and critical turn is also visible from the mid fourteenth century, basically because the old scholastic scholars died in the plague, and were replaced by a whole new generation of young teachers (Nordin 1995:221). It is generally important to understand how the word crisis is used in the late medieval case. It was a crisis for the old social and political order. For most people who survived the plague, however, living conditions improved. New opportunities opened for a few landowning families, and the crisis led to a distinct ideological and religious creativity.

From a late medieval point of view, I see many similarities between the crisis in the fourteenth century and the profound changes in the sixth century. A non-'man-made' phenomenon led to a relatively pronounced population decrease. The desertion of settlements, following the population decease, is most visible in marginal regions, such as the interior of Småland (Fig. 61), where new comparative pollen analysis shows a distinct decrease in agrarian activities and signs of reforestation during the sixth century (Berglund et al. 2002; Häggström 2007; Lagerås 2007). The results clearly correspond to other pollen analyses in Sweden (Welinder 1975) as well as in other parts of northern Europe (Andersen and Berglund 1994). Besides, large-scale excavations show that the number of houses declined considerably in the sixth century, even in a central agrarian region such as Uppland (Göthberg 2007:440).

At the same time as the population declined, an old social and political order, based on ringforts, hillforts, and weapon deposits, was successively replaced by new or renewed elites that expressed their power through large halls and mounds (Skre 1998; Myhre 2002:170 ff.; Zachrisson 2011). In the long run, small political units, such as the *gentes* mentioned by Jordanes in the mid sixth century, were replaced by larger political coalitions of Danes, Svear, and Northmen mentioned from the ninth century onwards. There were no urban settlements in the sixth century, but the so-called central places were affected in the same way as the late medieval towns. Old centres such as Gudme and Högom disappeared (Jørgensen 2009:332 ff.; Ramqvist 1990:13 ff.), whereas other centres were newly established or became more important at the end of the sixth century, such as Lejre, Tissø, Järrestad, and Uppsala (Jørgensen 2009:337 ff.; cf. Ljungkvist 2005; Zachrisson

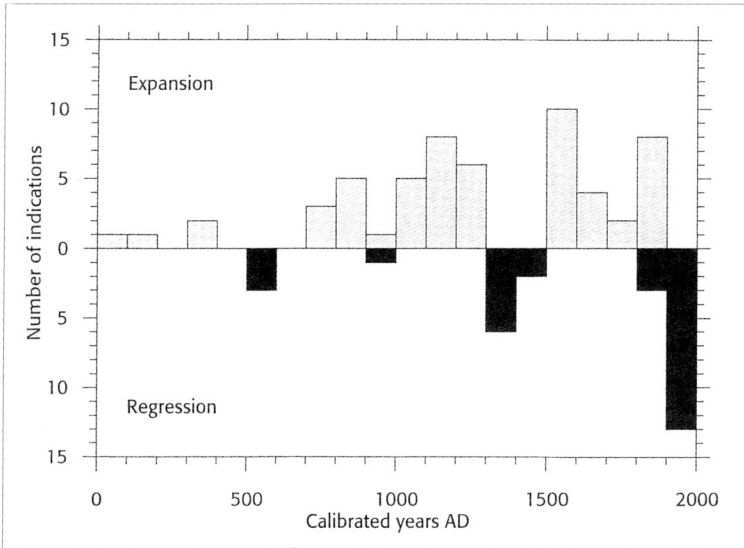

Figure 61. Indications of agricultural expansion (grey) and regression (black) in twenty high-quality pollen diagrams from upland areas in southern Sweden. Apart from decreasing agricultural activities in the last century and the late medieval agrarian crisis, the agrarian regression in the sixth century is clearly visible. (After Lagerås 2007:90.)

2011). The religious traditions changed as well, most notably with the disappearance of the sun-oriented traditions during the sixth century.

The profound changes in the sixth century must be related to the economy, social order, and political relations at that time. However, I have no doubts that the dust veil in 536 and the following depopulation were important aspects of these changes. This is especially true of the religious changes that occurred during that period.

The disappearance of the sun-oriented traditions in the sixth century

Different versions of solar myths and sun rituals existed in Scandinavia for two millennia, from 1500 BC to the sixth century AD, but the question is why the sun was venerated for such a long period and why it disappeared as an image after the sixth century, although some motifs ended up surviving in use until the thirteenth century. There are probably several answers to these two questions. Firstly, the metaphorical potential of the sun is quite obvious. The general idea of the sun moving across the sky in the day and through the underworld at night was a fundamental and natural element of many pre-modern worldviews, before the heliocentric cosmology was established in the sixteenth and seventeenth centuries. Since the idea of the sun's daily journey across the sky was shared by many pre-modern societies, different foreign aspects of this trip could easily be incorporated in local traditions. However, the general aspects of the journey of the sun cannot explain the special traits in the narrative tradition, such as the divine twins, or the disappearance of the solar narrative in the sixth century.

From a specific Scandinavian point of view, other factors must also be accounted for. A possible explanation is that the solar narrative was some kind of political discourse, following the changes to the social order. Kristiansen and Larsson have explored this aspect in the Bronze Age, with analogies from Greece (Kristiansen and Larsson 2005:262 ff.). Sparta, being the mythological home of the Greek *dios kuroi*, was ruled in the sixth and fifth centuries BC by two leaders in a literal parallel to the divine twins. Likewise, the Mycenaean palaces in the fourteenth and thirteenth centuries BC seem to have been ruled by two leaders, a ritual ruler called *wanax* and a military leader called *lawagetas* (Palaima 1995). Kristiansen and Larsson argue for a similar divided leadership in Bronze Age Scandinavia, based on and legitimized through the idea of twin gods supporting the sun on its eternal tour around the world (Kristiansen and Larsson 2005:271 ff.).

We must account for distinct differences in the social order of the Bronze Age and the Iron Age, but still a similar divided leadership seems to have existed in some places during parts of the Iron Age. Several Germanic origin myths mention twins or two brothers as being the original leaders of the tribes. As I have argued above, the marginal location and temporary use of the ringforts on Öland also indicate temporary military leaders ruling for short periods. And according to the *Vita* of St Saba, describing a Visigothic village in the 370s, the Visigothic tribes were actually ruled in the fourth century by a chieftain (*reiks*) and a temporary leader (*kindins*). However, the account states that in the long run the chieftains managed to take control of the Visigoths (Thompson 1966; Näsman 1988).

Such a political background to the solar myth may partly explain why the sun narratives were transformed and later disappeared. The divided leadership, which is clear in many Germanic myths of origin, disappeared during the Migration Period, when large parts of Europe and the late Roman world were transformed into early medieval kingdoms (Wickham 2005, 2009; Hedeager 2011). In Scandinavia, above all the broad star-like borders on the imitations of Roman medallions and bracteates indicate that rulers in the fourth and fifth centuries legitimized their power through the sun or the divine twins as supporters of the sun. These ideas were old, but may have been renewed with inspiration from the Roman imperial cult of Sol Invictus as well as a possible Hunnic notion of a solar king.

However, in 536 the sun literally disappeared in a global dust veil. It is easy enough to link the darkened sun with the vanishing of the solar symbol, but climate change in itself cannot directly explain why the sun symbol disappeared in Scandinavia. After all, the sun remained a central mythological figure in the Baltic and Sámi religions, although these regions must have been as much affected as Scandinavia by the darkened sun. Instead, the clouds in front of the sun must have hit specific aspects of Old Norse religion, above all its eschatological and political basis.

Gräslund has underlined the link between the darkened sun in 536 and the myth of the Fimbul Winter (*fimbulvetr*, 'the mighty winter') mentioned in *Vafþrúðnismál* 44 and Snorri's *Gylfaginning* 50 (Gräslund 2008). The Fimbul Winter is described by Snorri as being a terribly cold period of three winters and two non-existent summers. It marked the start of Ragnarok, the end of the world, when all the gods died in battle with the powers of chaos, and the world eventually was destroyed in a gigantic fire. Elements of this myth may have been inspired by the experience of the darkened sun in the 530s, as Gräslund proposes. However, Anders Hultgård has argued from Iranian parallels that the idea of a Fimbul Winter was part of an older eschatology (Hultgård 2004). If this suggestion is correct, the disappearance of the sun in 536 must have been terrifying, a sign of the imminent destruction of the world.

The clouds in the sky may also have posed a profound political challenge. If my interpretation of the star-like border zones of the bracteates and imitations of medallions is correct, the ideological link between the rulers and the sun must have made the rulers in some sense responsible for the climatic disaster in the 530s. Consequently, the sun could no longer be used in political discourse, which meant that the important solar cycles with their sun symbols rapidly disappeared from images in the sixth century. Instead, the narratives and rituals about the divine and celestial world were thoroughly transformed during the sixth and seventh centuries.

A golden age

The Migration Period will remain an enigma. In one sense it is the start of the distinct animal art and the distant mythical past of the Icelandic narrative tradition. In another sense it marks an end of weapon deposits, most hillforts and ringforts, most stone-enclosed settlements, and the solar cycle. As I have argued elsewhere (Andrén 1998b), the fifth and sixth centuries stand out as a literal golden age, not only in Scandinavia but also in the Byzantine and Carolingian empires of the eighth and ninth centuries. However, the changes in the sixth century were so profound that these retrospective tendences or 'renaissances' from about 800 were placed in very different social realities. From a Scandinavian point of view, this change can be framed as people thinking of gold but dealing in silver (Zachrisson 1998:29 ff.).

For several reasons, I see the final *longue durée* of pagan Scandinavian culture as starting in 550 rather than 400. The social and ritual continuity from the late sixth century to the eleventh century is quite clear in central elite places such as Tissø, Lejre, and Järrestad, as well as in high-ranking burial grounds such as Vendel, Valsgärde, and Borre (Jørgensen 2009:337 ff.; Myhre 2002:170 ff.). In all these places, the same kind of buildings were built and the same kind of burial rituals were used for more than four centuries. In Sweden and Norway most large mounds were built from the late sixth century to the tenth century, although a few older mounds are known in western Norway and northern Sweden. In the politically important Mälaren region alone, about 270 large mounds were erected from the late sixth century to the tenth century. The largest mounds are dated to the late sixth and seventh centuries (Bratt 2008:29 ff.).

Several scholars have underlined that the social and ritual continuity seen from the late sixth century onwards indicate the start of a new type of aristocracy, one that based its power on control of land and legitimized its role as divine descendants (Skre 1998; Myhre 2002; Zachrisson 2011). It seems as the former division between more temporary ritual and military leaders disappeared, and was replaced by permanent ruling lineages that combined the ritual and military aspects of lordship (Schjødt forthcoming). This idea fits well with the royal lineages of the Ynglingar and the Skjoldungar, since they are connected with Gamla Uppsala and Lejre respectively, which were established as central places in the late sixth century (see Fig. 58). The older central places, such as Gudme and Uppåkra, are interestingly enough not known in the later Icelandic narrative tradition.

The new land-controlling elite must have claimed a divine origin through partly new mythological traditions. When the sun and the divine twins as central mythological motifs disappeared in the mid sixth century, many of the narratives of the other divine figures were transformed into versions that are recognizable in the much later Icelandic narrative tradition. The life of the new ruling elite was in many ways projected on to a divine world, where gods and goddesses lived in large halls and lived an aristocratic life in much the same way. This transformation explains why most of the motifs on the bracteates are difficult to interpret from an Icelandic point of view, and why most of the divine figures can, at least provisionally (cf. Price 2006), be identified in representations from only the Merovingian and Viking Age (550–1050).

Outlines of a new context

To conclude, I would maintain that Old Norse religion was not a coherent tradition, with a specific origin. Instead, different elements had different trajectories. I have argued earlier there were some very old elements in Scandinavian cosmology, which can be traced back to the fifteenth century BC. These include the sun-horse, the divine twins, and the night-ship. Possibly these old elements also include a version of the sky-god Tyr, since his name is cognate with other Indo-European sky-gods, such as Greek Zeus, Baltic Dievas, and Sanskrit Dyaus.

All these figures can be directly or indirectly traced in Scandinavian iconography running from the Early Bronze Age to the Middle Iron Age, including the early picture stones on Gotland. Interestingly enough, these are basically the same figures that Martin West, in a recent survey of Indo-European poetry and myth, labels as Indo-European (West 2007:166–237). Although he criticizes Georges Dumézil's structural Indo-European mythology, he points out that these very general cosmological elements can actually be found cross-culturally in many Indo-European languages. It is therefore possible to interpret the new solar iconography in the Early Bronze Age as reflecting new Indo-European elements in Scandinavia, created in cultural interactions with continental Europe and indirectly with the eastern Mediterranean.

Although ideas of a world tree or a world pillar as well as an ordered world might be very old, it is not possible to trace these notions firmly in material culture until the Early Iron Age. It is also during this period that the fundamental figure 'nine' starts appearing in material culture for the first time. The central solar cycle survived the end of the Bronze Age, but new elements came to be included in the cosmology, or became more formalized.

In this context, I have not discussed a possible cultural encounter with the Celtic world, but the central European oppida culture from the third to the first centuries BC undoubtedly played an important role in Scandinavia (Rieckhoff and Biel 2001). The linguistic links between the thunder-god Thor and the Celtic god Taranis point to some shared history (Simek 1993:322), and aspects of the Scandinavian world tree might also be connected to the Celtic holy trees.

I have argued for the fundamental importance of cultural interaction with the Roman world, for instance, the expression of the idea of Midgard consisting of nine worlds and the distinct figure of an Old Norse world tree. In the last phase of the solar tradition, around 400–550, the incorporation of some kind of solar ruler is probably based on foreign models, such as the Roman Sol Invictus, the Byzantine emperor by God's grace, and a possible Hunnic notion of a solar king.

Transformations in the wake of the dust veil in the 530s had very different effects on the cosmological elements. The sun lost all its central mythological role, although echoes of solar myths are still found in the later Icelandic written tradition. The divine twins, in the form of two horses or two warriors, were still found in images from the seventh and eighth centuries, but later disappeared or were transformed. Tyr was an important god in the first centuries AD, which is clear from Tacitus mentioning him as one of the three main Germanic gods, from the Germanic translation of *dies Martii*, from the votive inscription of *Mars Thingsus* from the third century, and from early place-names (Simek 1993:337–8). However, after the sixth century, Tyr faded away to become a shadowy god, only mentioned in connection with the myth of how he saved the cosmic order by putting his hand in the mouth of the wolf Fenrir. In contrast, the importance of the god Thor remained unchallenged after the sixth century, and he actually seems to have been even more important at the end of paganism. This is above all visible in Thor's hammer, which was introduced in the eighth century as a symbol of Thor and of paganism, offering a contrast to the Christian cross.

Some of the other Old Norse gods and goddesses may be more or less securely attested through the descriptions of Tacitus in AD 98, by the Germanic translations of the Roman days of the week and possibly also through some of the images on the bracteates. However, new attributes appearing from the sixth and seventh centuries clearly show how the mythological narratives have changed, and consequently how the character of the divinities has also changed (Fig. 62). Judging from the later written Icelandic tradition, it seems as if these new narratives of the gods in some cases actually included transformed solar elements from the earlier cosmology.

Among these transformed figures are Freyr, who according to *Gylfaginning* 23 ruled over 'sunshine and rain', and Ull, whose name probably derives from a word meaning 'lustrous' (de Vries 1957:159). Heimdall, who in *Gylfaginning* 27 was described as 'the white As', was said to have been born from the waves, thereby giving associations with the sun rising from the sea. In contrast, Baldr, who according to *Gylfaginning* 21 was 'so bright that light shines from him', is said in *Gylfaginning* 48 to have been cremated in a burning ship that sank into the sea, like the setting sun. Snorri also tells in *Gylfaginning* 53 that, after Ragnarok, Baldr would return from the dead and the underworld, coming back to the living world, as did the sun every morning. Odin's ability to move between different worlds and transcend borders certainly fits the Dioscuri motif. Several late expressions of the Dioscuri motif from the sixth and seventh centuries have Odinic features, including elements such as spears and helmets with two birds (see Hauck 1984; Magnus 2001a).

As is clear from this very short overview, Old Norse religion and cosmology were not a coherent tradition with a single origin. Instead, the tradition was much more like a patchwork, with motifs and threads from different times and places. There were local and regional as well as social variations in this tradition, and there were more or less profound religious changes over time. One of these religious transformations occurred in the sixth century, but I will not label this transformation as a change to a new 'Æsir religion'. Instead, it was a religious transformation where some old elements disappeared, some old aspects were remoulded into new contexts, and some new elements were introduced. It was this reworked patchwork of old and new threads that formed the mental background for the Christian authors who lived in Iceland centuries later.

Figure 62. Silver figure from a grave mound at Aska in Hagebyhöga in Östergötland. The figure has been interpreted as an image of the goddess Freyja with her necklace Brísingamen (Arrhenius 1969). Such an interpretation must remain provisional (see Price 2006), but the important point is that this figure, like other contemporary images, can be related to the mental world in the later Icelandic literary tradition in ways that older images cannot. (Photo by Gabriel Hildebrand, Statens Historiska Museum, Stockholm.)

References

Primary Old Norse sources

Old Norse names are rendered in conventional English forms, but Icelandic forms are added in brackets when the names are first introduced. Quotations from Old Norse texts in Icelandic and in English translations are taken from the following editions.

Edda 1962. *Die Lieder des Codex Regius nebst verwandten Denkmäler.* Edited by G. Neckel and H. Kuhn. Heidelberg: Carl Winter Universitätsverlag [including the poems *Alvíssmál, Fjǫlsvinnsmál, Grímnismál, Hávamál, Helgakviða Hundingsbana* II, *Hymiskviða, Hyndluljóð, Sigdrífumál, Sólarljóð, Vafþrúðnismál,* and *Vǫluspá*].

The Poetic Edda 1996. Translated with an introduction and notes by C. Larrington. Oxford: Oxford University Press [including the poems *Alvíssmál, Fjǫlsvinnsmál, Grímnismál, Hávamál, Helgakviða Hundingsbana* II, *Hymiskviða, Hyndluljóð, Sigdrífumál, Sólarljóð, Vafþrúðnismál,* and *Vǫluspá*].

Snorri Sturluson. 1987. *Edda.* Translated and edited by A. Faulkes. London: M. Dent [including *Gylfaginning* and *Skáldskaparmál*].

— 1987. *Edda: Prologue and Gylfaginning.* Edited by A. Faulkes. London: Viking Society for Northern Research.

— Snorri Sturluson. 1991. *Edda: Háttatal.* Edited by A. Faulkes. Oxford: Clarendon Press.

— 1998. *Edda: Skáldskaparmál.* Edited by A. Faulkes. London: Viking Society for Northern Research.

Other primary sources and secondary literature

Aannestad, H. L. 2004. 'Her haver det i Fortiden været et mærkeklig Sted' – Om bygdeborger og Folktro. *Primitive Tider* 1998–2003:31–42.

Åberg, N. 1925. *Förhistorisk nordisk ornamentik.* Uppsala: Lindblad.

— 1936. Till belysande av det gotiska kulturinslaget i Mellaneuropa och Skandinavien. *Fornvännen* 31:264–77.

Adam av Bremen. 1984. *Historien om Hamburgstiftet och dess biskopar.* Translated into Swedish by E. Svenberg with comments by C. F. Hallencreutz. Pro fide et christianismo 6. Stockholm: Proprius.

Adam Bremensis. 1917. *Gesta Hammaburgensis ecclesiae pontificum.* Edited by B. Schmeidler. Hamburgische Kirchengeschichte. Hannover: Hahnsche Buchhandlung.

Ahlberg, B. 1978. Mälardalens bildstenar. Seminar paper in archaeology. Stockholm: Stockholms universitet.

Äijä, K. 1999. Jordbrogravfältet – rumsliga och sociala dimensioner. In K. Andersson, A. Lagerlöf, and A. Åkerlund (eds), *Forskaren i fält – en vänbok till Kristina Lamm*, pp. 67–76. Stockholm: Riksantikvarieämbetet.

Albrethsen, S. E. 1997. Logistical problems in Iron Age warfare. In Nørgård Jørgensen and Clausen 1997:210–19.

Alcock, L. 2003. *Kings and warriors, craftsmen and priests in northern Britain AD 550–850.* Edinburgh: Society of Antiquaries of Scotland.

Alkarp, M. 1997. Källan, lunden och templet. Adam av Bremens Uppsalaskildring i ny belysning. *Fornvännen* 92:155–61.

Almqvist, B. 1984. *Jämtlands medeltida kyrkor.* Fornvårdaren 19. Östersund: Jämtlands läns museum.

Althaus, S. 1993. *Die gotländischen Bildsteine: Ein Programm.* Göppinger Arbeiten zur Germanistik 588. Göppingen: Kümmerle.

Althin, C.-A. 1945. *Studien zu den bronzezeitlichen Felszeichnungen von Skåne.* Lund: Gleerup.

Ambrosiani, B. 1964. *Fornlämningar och bebyggelse: Studier i Attundalands och Södertörns förhistoria.* Uppsala: Almqvist & Wiksell.

Andersen, S. H., Lind, B., and Crumlin-Pedersen, O. 1991. *Slusegårdsgravpladsen* iii: *Gravformer og gravskikke. Bådgravene.* Jysk Arkæologisk Selskabs Skrifter XIV:3. Århus.

Andersen, S. T. and Berglund, B. E. 1994. Maps for terrestial non-tree pollen (NAP) percentages in north and central Europe 1800 and 1450 yr BP. *Paläoklimaforschung* 12:119–34.

Andersson, C. 2001. Gotländska bildstenar: Folkvandringstida samhällsmarkörer och religiösa indikatorer. Seminar paper in archaeology. Umeå: Umeå universitet.

Andersson, G. 1996. Valsta gravfält: Arkeologisk undersökning av RAÄ 59, Norrsunda Sn, Up. *UV-Stockholm, Rapport* 1997:9/1–2. Stockholm.

Andersson, G. and Skyllberg, E. 2008 (eds). *Gestalter och gestaltningar: Om tid, rum och händelser på Lunda.* Stockholm: Riksantikvarieämbetet.

REFERENCES

Andersson, K. 1995. *Romartida guldsmide i Norden* iii: *Övriga smycken, teknisk analys och verkstadsgrupper*. Aun 21. Uppsala. Institutionen för arkeologi.

Andersson, K. 1998 (ed.). *Suionum Hinc Civitates: Nya undersökningar kring norra Mälardalens äldre järnålder*. Occasional Papers in Archaeology 19. Uppsala: Institutionen för arkeologi och antik historia.

Andrén, A. 1985. *Den urbana scenen. Städer och samhälle i det medeltida Danmark*. Acta Archaeologica Lundensia 80, no. 13. Bonn: Habelt Verlag.

— 1989. Dörrar till förgångna myter – en tolkning av de gotländska bildstenarna. In A. Andrén (ed.), *Medeltidens födelse*, pp. 287–319. Symposier på Krapperups borg 1. Nyhamnsläge: Gyllenstiernska Krapperupstiftelsen.

— 1991. Guld och makt: En tolkning av de skandinaviska guldbrakteaternas funktion. In Fabech and Ringtved 1991:245–56.

— 1993. Doors to other worlds: Scandinavian death rituals in Gotlandic perspectives. *Journal of European Archaeology* 1:33–56.

— 1997. I Platons skugga – intryck av den efterantika arkeologin i Grekland. *META – Medeltidsarkeologisk tidskrift* 1997(3):3–36.

— 1998a. *Between artifacts and texts: Historical archaeology in global perspective*. New York: Plenum Press.

— 1998b. Från antiken till antiken. Stadsvisioner i Skandinavien före 1700. In S. Thorman and M. Hagdahl (eds), *Staden, himmel eller helvete. Tankar om människan i staden*, pp. 142–84. Stockholm: Informationsförlaget.

— 1999. Landscape and settlement as utopian space. In C. Fabech and J. Ringtved (eds), *Settlement and landscape*, pp. 383–93. Jutland Archaeological Society. Aarhus: Aarhus University Press.

— 2000a. Re-reading embodied texts: An interpretation of rune-stones. *Current Swedish Archaeology* 8:7–32

— 2000b. Ad sanctos: De dödas plats under medeltiden. *Hikuin* 7–26.

— 2002. Platsernas betydelse: Norrön ritual och kultplatskontinuitet. In K. Jennbert, A. Andrén, and C. Raudvere (eds), *Plats och praxis: Studier av nordisk förkristen ritual*. pp. 299–342. Vägar till Midgård 2. Lund: Nordic Academic Press.

— 2004. I skuggan av Yggdrasil: Trädet mellan idé och realitet i nordisk tradition. In Andrén et al. 2004:389–430.

— 2006. A world of stone: Warrior culture, hybridity, and Old Norse cosmology. In Andrén et al. 2006:33–8.

— 2007a. Behind *heathendom*: Archaeological studies of Old Norse religion. *Scottish Archaeological Journal* 27(2):105–38.

— 2007b. A petrified patchwork: The rune-stone at Karlevi and the early history of Öland. In B. Hårdh, K. Jennbert, and D. Olausson (eds), *On the road: Studies in honour of Lars Larsson*, pp. 295–300. Acta Archaeologica Lundensia 40, no. 26. Stockholm: Almqvist & Wiksell International.

— 2010. Vem lät bygga kyrkorna på Gotland? *Saga och Sed* 2009:31–59.

— 2011a. *Det medeltida Gotland: En arkeologisk guidebok*. Lund: Historiska Media.

— 2011b. Betydelsen av främmande unga män. In A. Andrén 2013:31–43.

— 2011c. (ed.) *Förmodern globalitet: Essäer om rörelse, möten och fjärran ting under 10000 år*. Lund: Nordic Academic Press.

— 2012a. Servants of Thor? The Gotlanders and their gods. In M. Kaplan and T. R. Tangherlini (eds), *News from other worlds: Studies in Nordic folklore, mythology and culture in honour of John F. Lindow*, pp. 92–100. Berkeley & Los Angeles: North Pinehurst Press.

— 2012b. From sunset to sunset: An interpretation of the early Gotlandic picture stones. *Gotländskt Arkiv* 84:49–58.

Andrén, A. and Carelli, P. 2006 (eds). *Odens öga: Mellan makter och människor i det förkristna Norden*. Helsingborg: Dunkers kulturhus.

Andrén, A., Jennbert, K., and Raudvere, C. 2004 (eds). *Ordning mot kaos: Studier av nordisk förkristen kosmologi*. Vägar till Midgård 4. Lund: Nordic Academic Press.

Andrén, A., Jennbert, K., and Raudvere, C. 2006 (eds). *Old Norse religion in long-term perspectives: Origins, changes, interactions*. Vägar till Midgård 8. Lund: Nordic Academic Press.

Aner, E. and Kersten, K. 1976. *Die Funde der älteren Bronzezeit des nordischen Kreises in Dänemark, Schleswig-Holstein und Niedersachsen*, iii: *Holbæk, Sorø und Præstø Amter*. Copenhagen: Nationalmuseet.

Anjou, S. 1935. Fornborgarnas betydelse ur etnografisk synpunkt. *Rig* 1935:1–12.

Anke, B. and Externbrink, H. 2007 (eds). *Attila und die Hunnen*. Stuttgart: Theiss.

Arbman, H. 1940 *Birka: Untersuchungen und Studien*, i: *Die Gräber*. Stockholm: Kungliga Vitterhets- Historie- och Antikivitets Akademien.

Arnberg, A. 2007. *Där människor, handling och tid möts: En studie av det förromerska landskapet på Gotland*. Stockholm Studies in Archaeology 42. Stockholm: Institutionen för arkeologi och antikens kultur.

Arne, T. J. 1902. Huru gammal är ristningen å Häggebystenen? *Svenska fornminnesföreningens tidskrift* 11:321–6.

— 1938. Domarringar äro gravar. *Fornvännen* 33:165–77.

Arrhenius, B. 1969. Zum symbolischer Sinn des Almandin im frühen Mittelalter. *Frühmittelalterliche Studien* 3:47–59.

— 1994. Järnåldern. In *Signums svenska konsthistoria* I:163–225. Lund: Signum.

Arrhenius, B. and Eriksson, G. 2006. *Gulldens hög i Husby-Långhundra*. Stockholm: Rapporter från Arkeologiska forskningslaboratoriet 6.

Arrhenius, B. and Holmqvist, V. 1960. En bildsten revideras. *Fornvännen* 55:173–92.

Asad, T. 1993 *Genealogies of religion: Discipline and reason of power in Christianity and Islam*. Baltimore: Johns Hopkins University Press.

Aveni, A. 2008. *People and the sky: Our ancestors and the cosmos*. London: Thames & Hudson.

Axboe, M. 1982. The Scandinavian gold bracteates. Studies on their manufacture and regional variations. With a supplement to the catalogue of Mogens B. Mackeprang. *Acta Archaeologica* 52:3–87.

— 1999. The year 536 and the Scandinavian gold hoards. *Medieval Archaeology* 43:186–8.

— 2001. Året 536. *Skalk* 2001(4):28–32.

— 2007. *Brakteatstudier*. Nordiske fortidsminder B25. Copenhagen: Det Kongelige Nordiske Oldskriftselskab.

Bachrach, B. S. 1997. The imperial roots of Merovingian military organization. In Nørgård Jørgensen and Clausen 1997:25–31.

Bäck, M. and Hållans Stenholm, A.-M. 2012. *Lilla Ullevi – den heliga platsens geografi*. Stockholm: Riksantikvarieämbetet.

Baillie, M. G. L. 1999. *Exodus to Arthur: Catastrophic encounters with comets*. London: Batsford.

Baitinger, H. 1999. Waffen und Bewaffnung aus der Perserbeute in Olympia. *Archäologischer Anzeiger* 1999:125–39.

Bauchhenss, G. and Noelke, P. 1981. *Die Iupitersäulen in den germanischen Provinzen*. Cologne: Rheinland-Verlag.

Beck, H. 1986. Das Problem der bitheriophoren Personennamen im Germanischen. In Roth 1986:303–15.

Becker, C. J. 1971. 'Mosepotter' fra Danmarks jernalder: Problemer omkring mosefundne lerkar og deres tolkning. *Aarbøger for Nordisk Oldkyndighed og Historie* 1971:5–60.

Beckmann, B. 1995. Die germanischen Funde in der Kastellen des Taunuslimes und ihre Beziehungen zum Fundgut in der Germania libera. In U. Lund Hansen 1995:410–13.

Behr, C. 1991. *Die Beizeichen auf den völkerwanderungszeitliche Goldbrakteaten*. Europäische Hochschulschriften, Reihe 38, Archäologie 38. Frankfurt am Main: Lang.

— 2011. Forschungsgeschichte. In Heizmann and Axboe 2011:153–229.

Bell, C. M. 1992. *Ritual theory, ritual practice*. Oxford: Oxford University Press.

Bemmann, J. 2007. Hinweise auf Kontakte zwischen dem hunnischen Herrschaftsbereich in Südosteuropa und dem Norden. In Anke and Externbrink 2007:177–81.

Benedictow, O., Dahlerup, T., and Lindholm, K.-G. 1971 (eds). *Den nordiske adel i senmiddelalderen: Struktur, funktioner og internordiske relationer.* Copenhagen: Nordiska historikermötet 15.

Benneth, S., Ferenius, J., Gustavson, H., and Åhlén, M. 1994 (eds). *Runmärkt från brev till klotter: Runorna under medeltiden.* Stockholm: Carlssons.

Bennett, A. 1987. *Graven: Religiös och social symbol. Strukturer i folkvandringstidens gravskick i Mälarområdet.* Theses and Papers in North-European Archaeology 18. Stockholm: Arkeologiska institutionen.

Berglund, B. E. 1991 (ed.). *The cultural landscape during 6000 years in southern Sweden.* Ecological Bulletins 41. Copenhagen: Munksgaard International.

Berglund, B. E., Lagerås, P., and Regnéll, J. 2002. Odlingslandskapets historia i Sydsverige – en pollenanlytisk syntes. In B. E. Berglund and K. Börjesson (eds), *Markens minnen: Landskap och odlingshistoria på småländska höglandet under 6000 år*, pp. 150–74. Stockholm: Riksantikvarieämbetet.

Bergström, E. 1979. Bäcka stenar – om domarringsfrågan. *Västergötlands fornminnesförenings tidskrift* 1979–80:289–95.

Bertell, M. 2003. *Tor och den nordiska åskan: Föreställningar kring världsaxeln.* Stockholm: Religionshistoriska institutionen.

— 2006. Where does Old Norse religion end? Reflections on the term Old Norse religion. In Andrén et al. 2006:298–302.

Bertilsson, U. 1987. *The rock carvings of northern Bohuslän: Spatial structures and social symbols.* Stockholm Studies in Archaeology 7. Stockholm: Arkeologiska institutionen.

Beskow Sjöberg, M. 1987 (ed.). Ölands järnåldersgravfält I. Stockholm: Statens historiska museum.

Best, W., Gensen, R. and Hömberg, P. R. 1999. Burgenbau in einer Grenzregion. In C. Stiegemann and M. Wernhoff (eds), *799 – Kunst und Kultur der Karolingerzeit: Karl der Grosse und Papst Leo III in Paderborn. Beiträge zum Katalog der Ausstellung Paderborn 1999*, pp. 328–45. Mainz: Zabern.

Bevan-Jones, R. 2002. *The ancient yew: A history of Taxus baccata.* Macclesfield: Windgather Press.

Biezais, H. 1975. Baltische Religion. In Å. V. Ström and H. Biezais (eds), *Geramische und Baltische Religion.* Die Religionen der Menschheit 19,1. Stuttgart: Kohlhammer.

Birge, D. 1994. Trees in the landscape of Pausanias' Periegesis. In S. E. Alcock and R. Osborne (eds), *Placing the gods: Sanctuaries and sacred space in ancient Greece*, pp. 231–45. Oxford: Clarendon Press.

Boessneck, J. von, Driesch, A. von den and Stenberger, L. 1979 (eds), *Eketorp: Befestigung und Siedlung auf Öland/Schweden. Die Fauna.* Stockholm: Kungl. Vitterhets historie och antikvitetsakademien.

Böhme, H. W. 1986. Bemerkungen zum spätrömischen Militärstil. In Roth 1986:25–49.

Boman, Å. 1982. Fornborgar i Västmanlands län. *Västmanlands fornminnes-förenings och Västmanlands läns museums årsskrift* 60:98–120.

Borg, K. 1998 (ed.). *Eketorp III. Den medeltida befästningen på Öland. Artefakterna.* Stockholm: Kungl. Vitterhets- historie- och antikvitetsakademien.

Borg, K., Näsman, U., and Wegraeus, E. 1976 (eds), *Eketorp: Fortification and settlement on Öland/Sweden. The monument.* Stockholm: Kungl. Vitterhets-historie- och antikvitetsakademien.

Bourdieu, P. 1990. *The logic of pratice.* Stanford: Stanford University Press.

Bradley, R. 2000. *An archaeology of natural places.* London: Routledge.

Bratt, P. 2008. *Makt uttryckt i jord och sten: Stora högar och maktstrukturer i Mälardalen under järnåldern.* Stockholm Studies in Archaeology 46. Stockholm: Institutionen för arkeologi och antikens kultur.

Brinch Madsen, H. 1975 En nordjysk kvindegrav fra omkring 400 e. K. *Hikuin* 2:123–30

Brink, S. 2001. Mythologizing landscape: Place and space of cult and myth. In M. Strausberg, O. Sundqvist, and A. van Nahl (eds), *Kontinuitäten und Brücke in der Religionsgeschichte*, pp. 76–112. Ergänzungsbände zum Reallexikon der Germanischen Altertumskunde. Berlin: de Gruyter.

— 2004. Mytologiska rum och eskatologiska föreställningar i det vikingatida Norden. In Andrén et al. 2004:291–316.

— 2007. How uniform was the Old Norse religion? In J. Quinn, K. Heslop, and T. Wills (eds), *Learning and understanding in the Old Norse world: Essays in honour of Margaret Clunies Ross*, pp. 105–35. Turnhout: Brepols.

Brøgger, A. W. 1916. Borrefundet og Vetsfoldskongenes graver. *Videnskabs-Selskabet i Christiania Skrifter* 2(1):1–67.

Brøndsted, J. 1954. *Guldhornene.* Copenhagen: Nationalmuseet.

Brosseder, U. and Miller, B. K. 2011 (eds). *Xiongnu archaeology: Multidisciplinary perspectives of the first steppe empire in inner Asia.* Bonn Contributions to Asian Archaeology 5, pp. 333–40. Bonn: Vor- und Frühgeschichtliche Archäologie.

Bugge, S. 1881–9. *Studier over de nordiske Gude- og Heltesagns Oprindelse.* Christiania: Feilberg & Landmark.

Buisson, L. 1976. *Der Bildstein Ardre VIII auf Gotland: Göttermythen, Heldensagen und Jenseitsglaube der Germanen im 8. Jahrhundert n. Chr.* Abhandlungen der Akademie der Wissenschaften in Göttingen. Philologisch-Historische Klasse, Dritte Folge 102. Göttingen: Vandenhoeck & Ruprecht.

Carlie, A. 1994. *På arkeologins bakgård: En bebyggelsearkeologisk undersökning i norra Skånes inland baserad på synliga gravar.* Acta Archaeologica Lundensia, 80 no. 22. Stockholm: Almqvist & Wiksell International.

— 1998. Käringsjön: A fertility sacrificial site from the late Roman Iron Age in south west Sweden. *Current Swedish Archaeology* 6:17–37.

— 2009a. Käringsjön – en gammal fyndplats i ny belysning. In Carlie 2009b:225–63.

— 2009b (ed.). *Järnålderns rituella platser.* Utskrift 9. Halmstad: Stiftelsen Hallands länsmuseer.

Carlsson, D. 1979. *Kulturlandskapets utveckling på Gotland.* Meddelanden från kulturgeografiska institutionen vid Stockholms universitet B49. Visby: Press.

Carlsson, M. 1990. En studie av undersökta treuddar i Mälardalen och Östergötland. Seminar paper. Stockholm: Stockholms universitet.

Carman, J. 1997 (ed.). *Material harm: Archaeological studies of war and violence.* Glasgow: Cruithne Press.

Carman, J. and A. Harding 1999 (eds). *Ancient warfare: Archaeological perspectives.* Stroud: Sutton.

Cassel, K. 1998. *Från grav till gård: Romersk järnålder på Gotland.* Stockholm Studies in Archaeology 16. Stockholm: Arkeologiska institutionen.

— 2008. *Det gemensamma rummet: Migrationer, myter och möten.* Södertörn Archaeological Studies 5. Huddinge: Institutionen för kultur och kommunikation.

Christensen, A. E. 1976. *Danmark, Norden og Østersøen: Udvalgte afhandlinger.* Copenhagen: Den danske historiske forening.

Clanchy, M. T. 1979. *From memory to written record: England 1066–1307.* London: Edward Arnold.

Clover, C. J. and Lindow, J. 1985 (eds). *Old Norse-Icelandic literature: A critical guide.* Ithaca: Cornell University Press.

Clunies Ross, M. 1994. *Prolonged echoes: Old Norse myths in a medieval northern society,* i: *The myths.* The Viking Collection 7. Odense: Odense University Press.

— 1998. *Prolonged echoes: Old Norse myths in a medieval northern society,* ii: *The reception of Norse myths in medieval Iceland.* The Viking Collection 10. Odense: Odense University Press.

— 2005. *A history of Old Norse poetry and poetics.* Cambridge: Brewer.

— 2007 (ed.). *Poetry on Christian subjects*. Skaldic Poetry of the Scandinavian Middle Ages 7. Turnhout: Brepols.

— 2011. Images of Norse Cosmology. In D. Anlezark (ed.), *Myths, legends, and heroes: Essays on Old Norse and Old English literature in honour of John McKinnell*, pp. 53–73. Toronto: University of Toronto Press.

Cöllen, S. 2011. *Der rätselschafte Gott: Heimdallr im Licht altnordischer Vorstellungen von Ahnen und Ordnung*. Uppsala: Teologiska institutionen.

Collinder, B. 1926. Ett nytt uppslag i den fornnordiska religionsforskningen. *Nordisk tidskrift för vetenskap, konst och industri* 2:220–30.

Coomaraswamy, A. K. 1938. The inverted tree. *Quarterly Journal of the Mythic Society* 29(2):1–38.

Crumlin-Pedersen, O. and Munch Tye, B. 1995 (eds). *The ship as symbol in prehistoric and medieval Scandinavia*. Copenhagen: Nationalmuseet.

Cunliffe, B. W. 1997. *The ancient Celts*. London: Penguin.

Damell, D. 1985. Rösaring and a Viking Age Cult Road. In M. Backe, I. Bergman Hennix, L. Forsberg, L. Holm, L. Liedgren, A.-K. Lindqvist, I.-M. Mulk, M. Nejati, P. Perstrand, and P. H. Ramqvist (eds), *In Honorem Evert Baudou*, pp. 171–85. Archaeology and Environment 4. Umeå: Department of Archaeology.

— 1993. Hillforts and state formation. In G. Arwidsson, A.-M. Hansson, L. Holmquist Olausson, B. M. Johansson, M. Klockhoff, K. Lidén and H.-Å. Nordström (eds), *Sources and resources: Studies in honour of Birgit Arrhenius*. Rixensart: Pact 38:53–64.

Damell, D. and Lorin O. 1985. Om fornborgsundersökningar i nordvästra Södermanland. *Tor* 20:229–36.

Davidson, H. R. E. 1988. *Myths and symbols in pagan Europe: Early Scandinavian and Celtic religions*. Manchester: MUP.

Deichmann, F. W. 1983. *Einführung in die christliche Archäologie*. Darmstadt: Wissenschaftliche Buchgesellschaft.

Dobat, A. S. 2009. En gave til Veleda. Om en magtfuld spåkvinde og tolkningen af de sydskandinaviske krigsbytteofringer. *Kuml* 2009:127–52.

Domeij Lundborg, M. 2006. Bound animal bodies: Ornamentation and skaldic peotry in the process of Christianization. In Andrén et al. 2006:39–44.

Douglas, M. 1966. *Purity and danger: An analysis of concepts of pollution and taboo*. London: Routledge & Kegan Paul.

Drobin, U. 1989. Indoeuropeerna i myt och forskning. In L. Larsson and B. Wyszomirska (eds), *Arkeologi och religion*, pp. 43–55. Report Series 34. Lund: Arkeologiska institutionen.

— 1991. Mjödet och offersymboliken i fornnordisk religion. In L. Bäckman,

U. Drobin and P.-A. Berglie (eds), *Studier i religionshistoria tillägnade Åke Hultkrantz professor emeritus den 1 juli 1986*, pp. 97–141. Löberöd: Plus ultra.

Drobin, U. and Keinänen, M.-L. 2001. Frey, Veralden almai och Sampo. In M. Strausberg, O. Sundqvist and A. van Nahl (eds), *Kontinuitäten und Brücke in der Religionsgeschichte* pp. 136–69. Ergänzungsbände zum Reallexikon der Germanischen Altertumskunde. Berlin: de Gruyter

DuBois, T. A. 1999. *Nordic religions in the Viking Age*. Philadelphia: University of Pennsylvania Press.

Dumézil, G. 1973. *Gods of the ancient Northmen*. Berkeley & Los Angeles: University of California Press.

Düwel, K. 1985. *Das Opferfest von Lade: Quellenkritische Undersuchungen zur germanische Religionsgeschichte*. Wiener Arbeiten zur germanischen Altertumskunde und Philologie 27. Vienna: Halosar.

Dybeck, R. 1865. *Runa: En skrift för Nordens fornvänner*. Stockholm.

Edgren, B. 1979 (ed.). *Eketorp – den befästa byn på Ölands Alvar*. Stockholm: Riksantikvarieämbetet.

Edsman, C.-M. 1944. Arbor inversa. *Religion und Bibel* 3:5–33.

Ekengren, F. 2009. *Ritualization – hybridization – fragmentation: The mutability of Roman vessels in Germania Magna AD 1–400*. Acta Archaeologica Lundensia 40, no. 28. Lund: Institutionen för arkeologi och antikens historia.

Eliade, M. 1958. *Patterns in comparative religion*. London: Sheed & Ward.

Elton, H. 1996. *Warfare in Roman Europe, AD 350–425*. Oxford: Oxford University Press.

Engdahl, K. and Kaliff, A. 1996 (eds). *Religion från stenålder till medeltid*. Riksantikvarieämbetet, Arkeologiska undersökningar 19. Linköping: Riksantikvarieämbetet.

Engström, J. 1984. *Torsburgen: Tolkning av en gotländsk fornborg*. Aun 6. Uppsala: Uppsala University, Institute of North European Archaeology.

— 1991. Fornborgarna och samhällsutvecklingen under mellersta järnåldern. In Fabech and Ringtved 1991:267–76.

Erä-Esko, A 1965. Germanic animal art of Salin's style I in Finland. *Finska fornminnesföreningens tidskrift* 63.

Erööl-Erdene, C. 2011. Animal style silver ornaments of the Xiongnu period. In U. Brosseder and B. K. Miller 2011:333–40.

Fabech, C. 1991a. Neue Perspektiven zu den Funden von Sösdala und Fulltofta. *Studien zur Sachsenforschung* 7:121–35.

— 1991b. Samfundsorganisation, religiøse ceremonier og regional variation. In Fabech and Ringtved 1991:283–303.

— 2009. Fra ritualiseret tradition til institutionaliserede ritualer. In Carlie 2009b:317–42.

— 2011. War and rituals: Changes in rituals and transformations of power. In T. A. S. M. Panhuysen (ed.), *Transformations in north-western Europe (AD 300–1000)*, pp. 27–36. Neue Studien zur Sachsenforschung 3. Hannover: Niedersächsisches Landesmusem.

Fabech, C. and Ringtved, J. 1991 (eds), *Samfundsorganisation og regional variation: Norden i romersk jernalder og folkevandringstid*. Jysk Arkæologisk Selskabs Skrifter 27. Aarhus: Aarhus Universitetsforlag.

Fagerlie, J. 1967. *Late Roman and Byzantine solidi found in Sweden and Denmark*. New York: Numismatic Notes and Monographs 157.

Fallgren, J.-H. 1993. The concept of the village in Swedish archaeology. *Current Swedish Archaeology* 1:59–86.

— 1998. Hus och gård på Öland. *Bebyggelsehistorisk tidskrift* 33:63–76.

— 2006. *Kontinuitet och förändring: Bebyggelse och samhälle på Öland 200–1300 e Kr.* Aun 35. Uppsala: Institutionen för arkeologi och antik historia.

— 2008. Fornborgar, bebyggelse och odlingslandskap. In Tegnér 2008b:119–36.

Feldt, B. 2005. *Synliga och osynliga gränser: Förändringar i gravritualen under yngre bronsålder – förromersk järnåder i Södermanland*. Stockholm Studies in Archaeology 37. Stockholm: Institutionen för arkeologi och antikens kultur.

Fidjestøl, B. 1979. *Sólarljóð: Tyding og tolkningsgrunnlag*. Bergen: Universitetsforlaget.

Fischer, C. 2007. *Tollundmanden – gaven til guderne: Mosefund fra Danmarks forhistorie*. Højbjerg: Hovedland.

Fischer, S. 2005. *Roman imperialism and runic literacy: The westernization of northern Europe (150–800 AD)*. Aun 33. Uppsala: Institutionen för arkeologi och antik historia.

Fischer, T. 1999. *Die Römer in Deutschland*. Stuttgart: Theiss.

Flygare, L. 2000. Fornborgens omvärdering. Seminar paper. Uppsala: Uppsala universitet.

Ford, B., Deakin, P., and Walker, M. 2002. The tri-radial cairns of Northumberland. *Current Archaeology* 182:82–5.

Forssander, J. E. 1937. Provinzialrömisches und germanisches: Stilstudien zu den schonischen Funden von Sösdala und Sjörup. *Meddelanden från Lunds universitets historiska museum* 1937:11–100.

Fredell, Å. 2003. *Bildbroar: Figurativ bildkommunikation av ideologi och kosmologi under sydskandinavisk bronsålder och förromersk järnålder*. Gotarc B 25. Gothenburg: Institutionen för arkeologi.

Freeden, U. von, Friesinger H., Wamers E. 2009 (eds). *Glaube, Kult und*

Herrschaft: Phänomene des Religiösen im 1. Jahrtausend n. Chr. in Mittel- und Nordeuropa. Kolloquien zu Vor- und Frühgeschichte, 12. Bonn: Habelt.

Fries, S. 1957. *Studier över nordiska trädnamn.* Uppsala: Almqvist & Wiksell.

Fritz, J. M. and Mitchell G. 1987. Interpreting the plan of a medieval Hindu capital, Vijayanagara. *World Archaeology* 19:105–29.

Gaimster, M. 1998. *Vendel period bracteates on Gotland: On the significance of Germanic art.* Acta Archaeologica Lundensia, 80, no. 27. Stockholm: Almqvist & Wiksell International.

Gansum, T. 1999. Mythos, logos, ritus: Symbolisme og gravskikk i lys av gudediktene i den eldre Edda. In I. Fuglestvedt, T. Gansum, and A. Opedal (eds), *Et hus med mange rom*, pp. 439–505. AmS-rapport 11 B. Stavanger: Arekologisk museum i Stavanger.

Geertz, C. 1973. *The interpretation of cultures: Selected essays.* New York: Basic Books.

Gell, A. 1993. *Wrapping in images: Tattooing in Polynesia.* Oxford: Oxford University Press.

Gelling, P. and Davidson, H. E. 1969. *The chariot of the sun and other rites and symbols of the northern Bronze Age.* London: Phoenix House.

Gihl, G. 1918. Upplands fornborgar: En antikvariskt-topografisk beskrivning. *Upplands fornminnesförenings tidskrift* 33:33–88.

Gissel, S., Jutikkala, E., Österberg, E., Sandnes, J., and Teitsson, B. 1981 (eds). *Desertion and land colonization in the Nordic countries, c.1300–1600.* Stockholm: Almqvist & Wiksell International.

Gjessing, G. 1943. Hesten i førhistorisk kunst og kultus. *Viking* 1943:1–143.

Glob, P. V. 1967. *Danske oldtidsminder.* Copenhagen: Gyldendal.

Glørstad, H. and Hedeager, L. 2009 (eds). *Six essays on the materiality of society and culture.* Gothenburg: Bricoleur Press.

Goldhahn, J. 1999. *Sagaholm: Hällristningar och gravritual.* Studia Archaeologica Universitatis Umensis 11 and Jönköpings läns museum, rapport 41. Umeå: Arkeologiska institutionen.

Goldhahn, J., Wikell, R., Broström, S.-G., and Ihrestam, K. 2012. Bronsålderns hällbilder i Tjust. In V. Palm (ed.) Västerviks historia: Förhistoria och arkeologi I. *Årsbok för Tjustbygdens Kulturhistoriska Förening* 68: 35–67.

Görman, M. 1998. Folkvandringstida stenkonst på Gotland: Uttryck för nordisk forntidstro? *Svensk religionshistorisk årsbok* 7:47–75.

Göthberg, H. 2007. Mer än bara hus och gårdar. In H. Göthberg (ed.), *Hus och bebyggelse i Uppland: Delar av förhistoriska sammanhang*, pp. 403–47. Arekologi E4 Uppland, Studier 3. Uppsala: Riksantikvarieämbetet, Societas Archaeologica Upsaliensis and Upplandsmuseet.

Grane, T. 2007 (ed.). *Beyond the Roman frontier: Roman influences on the northern Barbaricum*. Analecta Romana Instituti Danici, Supplementum 39. Rome: Edizioni Quasar.

Granlund, J. 1939. Hartstätning till svepta kärl under äldre järnåldern. *Fornvännen* 34:257–87.

Gräslund, B. 2008. Fimbulvintern, Ragnarök och klimatkrisen år 536–537 e. Kr. *Saga och Sed* 2007: 93–123.

Grav Ellingsen, E. J. 2003. Trekantede og stjerneformede anlegg i Trøndelag: En studie av symbolikk og funksjon. Seminar paper. Trondheim: Vitenskapsmuseet.

Gregory, T. E. 1994. Archaeological and theoretical considerations on the transition from Antiquity to the Middle Ages in the Aegean Area. In N. Kardulias (ed.), *Beyond the site: Regional studies in the Aegean area*, pp. 137–59. Lanham, New York: University Press of America.

Grimm, O. 2001. Norwegian boathouses from the Late Roman and Migration periods: An analysis of their military function. In B. Storgaard (ed.), *Military aspects of the aristocracy in barbaricum in the Roman and early Migration periods*, pp. 55–66. Studies in Archaeology and History 5. Copenhagen: Nationalmuseet.

Guber. S. 2011. *Die Bildsteine Gotlands der Völkerwanderungs- und Vendelzeit als Spiegel frühgeschichtlicher Lebenswelten*. BAR International Series 2257. Oxford: Archaeopress.

Gunnell, T. 2001. Hof, halls, goðar and dwarves: An examination of the ritual space in the pagan Icelandic hall. *Cosmos* 17(1):3–36.

— forthcoming. How high was the High One? The role of Óðinn in Pre-Christian Icelandic society. In S. Brink (ed.), *Myth and theory in the Old Norse world*. Turnhout: Brepols.

Gurevich, A. J. 1969. Space and time in the *Weltmodell* of the Old Scandinavian peoples. *Medieval Scandinavia* 2:42–53.

— 1985. *Categories of medieval culture*. London: Routledge & Kegan Paul.

Gustafsson, G. 1999. *Evocatio deorum: Historical and mythical interpretations of ritualised conquests in the expansion of ancient Rome*. Uppsala: Teologiska institutionen.

Haas, J. 1990 (ed.). *The anthropology of war*. Cambridge: Cambridge University Press.

Habbe, P. 2005. *Att se och tänka med ritual: Kontrakterande ritualer i de isländska släktsagorna*. Vägar till Midgård 7. Lund: Nordic Academic Press.

Hagberg, U.-E. 1967a. *The archaeology of Skedemosse I. The excavations and finds of a Öland fen, Sweden*. Stockholm: Almqvist & Wiksell International.

— 1967b. *The archaeology of Skedemosse 2. The votive deposits in the Skedemosse fen and their relation to the Iron Age settlement on Öland, Sweden.* Stockholm: Almqvist & Wiksell International.

Häggström, L. 2007. Den folkvandringstida 'krisen' i ett lokalperspektiv. In L. Häggström (ed.), *Öggetorp och Rogberga: Vägar till småländsk förhistoria*, pp. 183-200. Jönköping: Jönköpings läns museum.

Hållans Stenholm, A.-M. 2006. Past memories. Spatial returning as ritualized remembrance. In Andrén et al. 2006:341–5.

Hallberg, G. 1985. *Ortnamn på Öland.* Stockholm: Almqvist & Wiksell.

Hallberg, P. 1952. Världsträdet och världsbranden: Ett motiv i Völuspá. *Arkiv för nordisk filologi* 67:145–55.

Halsall, G. 1989. Anthropology and the study of pre-conquest warfare and society: The ritual war in Anglo-Saxon England. In S. Chadwick Hawkes (ed.), *Weapons and warfare in Anglo-Saxon England*, pp. 155–77. Oxford University Committee for Archaeology, Monograph. Oxford: Oxbow Books.

— 2003. *Warfare and society in the barbarian West.* London: Routledge.

Hamilton, J, 2012. Bildstenar i mälarområdet: Uppställning, destruktion och övertäckning. *Gotländsk arkiv* 84:161–70.

Hårdh, B. and Larsson, L. 2002 (eds). *Central places in the Migration and Merovingian Periods: Papers from the 52nd Sachsensymposium, Lund, August 2001.* Uppåkrastudier 6, Acta Archaeologica Lundensia, 80, no. 39. Stockholm: Almqvist & Wiksell International.

Harrison, D. 2000. *Stora döden: Den värsta katastrof som drabbat Europa.* Stockholm: Ordfront.

Haseloff, G. 1981. *Die germanische Tierornamentik der Völkerwanderungszeit: Studien su Salin's Stil I.* 3 vols. Berlin: de Gruyter.

Hastrup, K. 1985. *Culture and history in medieval Iceland: An anthropological analysis of structure and change.* Oxford: Clarendon Press.

Hauck, K. 1970. *Goldbrakteaten aus Sievern: Spätantike Amulett-Bilder der 'Dania Saxonica' und die Sachsen-'origo' bei Widukind von Corvey.* Münstersche Mittelalter-Schriften 1. Munich: Wilhelm Fink.

— 1984. Dioskuren. 4. Dioskurendarstellungen des Nordens seit den Goldhörnern von Gallehus. *Reallexikon der germanischen Altertumskunde* 5:484–94. Berlin: de Gruyter.

— 1992. Der religions- und sozialgeschichtliche Quellenwert der völkerwanderungszeitlichen Goldbrakteaten. In H. Beck, D. Ellmers, and K. Schier (eds), *Germanische Religionsgeschichte: Quellen und Quellenprobleme*, pp. 229–69. Ergänzungsbände zun Reallexikon der germanischen Altertumskunde 5. Berlin: de Gruyter.

— 2011. Die Bildformeln der Goldbrakteaten in ihren Leitvarianten. In Heizmann and Axboe 2011:61–152.

Hauck, K., Axboe, M., Düwel, K., and Padberg, L. von 1985–9. *Die Goldbrakteaten der Völkerwanderungszeit: Ikonographischer Katalog 1–3*. Münstersche Mittelalterschriften 24:1–3. Münster: Fink.

Hauptman Wahlgren, K. 2002. *Bilder av betydelse: Hällristningar och bronsålderslandskap i nordöstra Östergötland*. Stockholm Studies in Archaeology 23. Lindome: Bricoleur Press.

Hawkes, C. 1954. Archaeological theory and method: Some suggestions from the Old World. *American Anthropologist* 56:155–68.

Heather, P. 1995. The Huns and the end of the Roman Empire in the Western Europe. *English Historical Review* 110:4–41.

Hedeager, L. 1979. A quantitative analysis of Roman imports in Europe north of the Limes (0–400 AD) and the question of Roman-Germanic Exchange. In K. Kristiansen and C. Paludan-Müller (eds), *New Directions in Scandinavian Archaeology*, pp. 191–216. Lyngby: National Museum of Denmark.

— 1997. *Skygger af en anden virkelighed: Oldnordiske myter*. Copenhagen: Samleren.

— 2001. Asgard reconstructed? Gudme – a 'central place' in the North. In M. de Jong and F. Theuws (eds), *Topographies of power in the early Middle Ages*, pp. 467–507. Leiden: Brill.

— 2004. Dyr og mennesker – mennesker og andre dyr: Dyreornamentikkens transcendentale realitet. In Andrén et al. 2004:219–52.

— 2007. Scandinavia and the Huns: An interdisciplinary approach to the Migration era. *Norwegian Archaeological Review* 40(1):42–58.

— 2011. *Iron Age myth and materiality: An archaeology of Scandinavia AD 400–1000*. Oxford: Routledge.

Hedenstierna-Jonson, C. 2006. *The Birka warrior: The material culture of martial society*. Thesis and Papers in Scientific Archaeology 8. Stockholm: Department of Archaeology and Classical Studies, Stockholm University.

Hegardt, J. 1991. Patrilateralt samhälle, hemliga sällskap och monumentala byggnader: En analys av en gotländsk fornborg. *Tor* 23: 55–84.

Heizmann, W. and Axboe, M. 2011 (eds). *Die Goldbrakteaten der Völkerwanderungszeit. Auswertung und Neufunde*. Berlin: de Gruyter.

Hellberg, L. 1967. *Kumlabygdens ortnamn och äldre bebyggelse. Kumlabygden. Forntid – nutid – framtid*, iii: *Ortnamn och äldre bebyggelse*. Kumla: Kumla kommun.

Hendy, M. F. 1985. *Studies in the Byzantine monetary economy c.300–1450*. Cambridge: Cambridge University Press.

Hermann, P. 2005 (ed.). *Literacy in medieval and early modern Scandinavian culture*. The Viking Collection 16. Odense: Syddansk universitetsforlag.

Hernæs, P. 1999. *Dommedagssteinen ved Avaldsnes kirke*. In I. Fuglestvedt, T. Gansum, and A. Opedal (eds), *Et hus med mange rom* pp. 121–34. AmSrapport 11 A. Stavanger: Arkeologisk Museum i Stavanger.

Herschend, F. 1980. *Myntat och omyntat guld: Två studier i ölandska guldfynd*. Uppsala: Gustavianum.

— 1985. Fällgallerporten i Eketorp II, Öland. *Tor* 20:165–216.

— 1997. *Livet i hallen: Tre fallstudier i den yngre järnålderns aristokrati*. Occasional Papers in Archaeology 14. Uppsala: Institutionen för arkeologi och antik historia.

— 2003. Krig, offerfynd och samhälle i 200-talets Sydskandinavien. *Fornvännen* 98:312–16.

— 2011. *The early Iron Age in south Scandinavia: Social order in settlement and landscape*. Occasional papers in archaeology 46. Uppsala: Institutionen för arkeologi och antik historia.

Hildebrand, H. 1872. Tors hammare. *Kongliga Vitterhets-, historie- och antiqvitetsakademiens Månadsblad* 1:49–55.

— 1898–1903. *Sveriges Medeltid* iii. Stockholm: P. A Norstedt & söner.

Hildebrandt, M. 1985. En kyrka byggd på hednisk grund? *Populär arkeologi* 1985(4):9–13.

— 1989. Frösö kyrka byggd på hednisk grund? In O. Hemmendorff (ed.), *Arkeologi i fjäll, skog och bygd*, ii: *Järnålder och medeltid*, pp. 153–66. Fornvårdaren 24. Östersund: Jämtlands läns museum.

Hill, J. D. 1993. Can we recognise a different European past? A contrastive archaeology of later prehistoric settlements in southern England. *Journal of European Archaeology* 1:57–75.

Hodder, I. 1986. *Reading the past: Current approches to interpretation in archaeology*. Cambridge: Cambridge University Press.

— 2012 (ed.). *Archaeological theory today*. 2nd edn. Cambridge: Polity Press.

Hofrén, M. 1948. Ölandska byar och gårdar. In B. Palm (ed.), *Öland 1*, pp. 399–475. Kalmar: Dillbergska Bokhandeln.

Hofsten, N. von 1957. *Eddadikternas djur och växter*. Skrifter utgivna av Kungliga Gustav Adolfs Akademien 30. Uppsala: Lundequistska.

Høilund Nielsen, K. 1991. Centrum og periferi i 6.–8. årh. Territoriale studier af dyrestil og kvindesmykker i yngre germansk jernalder i Syd- og Østskandinavien. In P. Mortensen and B. M. Rasmussen (eds), *Fra stamme til stat 2. Høvdingesamfund og kongemagt*, pp. 127–71. Højbjerg: Jysk Arkæologisk Selskab.

Holmbäck, Å. and Wessén, E. 1943 (eds). *Skånelagen och Gutalagen*. Svenska Landskapslagar 4. Stockholm: Geber.

Holmberg (Harva after 1927), U. 1922–3. *Der Baum des Lebens*. Annales Academiae Scientiarum Fenniae B XVI:3. Helsinki: Finnish Academy of Science.

Holmquist Olausson, L. and Olausson, M. 2009. (eds) *The martial society: Aspects of warriors, fortifications and social change in Scandinavia*. Theses and Papers in Archaeology B:11. Stockholm: Arkeologiska forskningslaboratoriet.

Holmqvist, W. 1951. *Tauschierte Metallarbeiten des Nordens aus Römerzeit und Völkerwanderungszeit*. Kungliga vitterhets-, historie- och antikvitetsakademien, handlingar 70:2. Stockholm: Almqvist & Wiksell.

— 1952. De äldsta gotländska bildstenarna och deras motivkrets. *Fornvännen* 47:1–20.

— 1980. *Guldhalskragarna*. Stockholm: Statens historiska museum.

Holst, M. 2004. The Syntax for the Iron Age Village. Transformations in an Orderly Community. Unpublished thesis in archaeology. Aarhus: University of Aarhus.

Hope-Taylor, B. 1977. *Yeavering: An Anglo-British centre of early Northumbria*. London: Her Majesty's Stationary Office.

Horn Fuglesang, S. 1986. Ikonographie der skandinavischen Runensteine der jüngeren Wikingerzeit. In Roth 1986:183–210.

Hultgård, A. 1997 (ed.). *Uppsala-kulten och Adam av Bremen*. Nora: Nya Doxa.

— 2004. Fimbulvintern: Ett mytmotiv och dess tolkning. *Saga och Sed* 2003:51–69.

— 2007. Wotan-Odin. *Reallexikon der germanischen Altertumskunde* 35:759–85. Berlin: de Gruyter.

Hultkrantz, Å. 1996. A new look at the world pillar in Arctic and sub-Arctic religions. In J. Y. Pentikäinen (ed.) *Shamanism and northern ecology*, pp. 31–49. Berlin: de Gruyter.

Humphrey, C. and Laidlaw, J. 1994. *The archetypal action of ritual: A theory of ritual illustrated by the Jain rite of worship*. Oxford: Clarendon Press.

Hvass, S. 1985. *Hodde: Et vestjysk landsbysamfund fra ældre jernalder*. Copenhagen: Akademisk forlag.

— 1988. Jernalderens bebyggelse. In P. Mortensen and B. M. Rasmussen (eds), *Fra stamme til stat i Danmark*, i: *Jernalderens stammesamfund*. pp. 53–93. Jysk Arkæologisk Selskabs skifter 22. Aarhus: Aarhus Universitetsforlag.

Hyenstrand, Å. 1974. *Centralbygd – randbygd: Strukturella, ekonomiska och administrativa huvudlinjer i mellansvensk yngre järnålder*. Studies in North-European Archaeology 5. Stockholm: Arkeologiska institutionen.

— 1981. *Excavations at Helgö VI. The Mälaren area*. Kungl. Vitterhets-, historie-och antikvitetsakademien. Stockholm: Almqvist & Wiksell International.

— 1984. *Fasta fornlämningar och arkeologiska regioner*. Stockholm: Riksantikvarieämbetet.

Hygen, A.-S. and Bengtsson, L. 1999. *Hällristningar i Gränsbygd: Bohuslän och Östfold*. Sävedalen: Warne.

Ilkjær, J. 1997. Gegner und Verbündete in Nordeuropa während des 1. bis 4. Jahrhunderts. In Nørgård Jørgensen and Clausen 1997:55–64.

— 2000. *Illerup Ådal, et arkæologisk tryllespejl*. Moesgård: Moesgård Museum.

— 2001. *Illerup Ådal*, ix: *Die Schilde*. Højbjerg: Jysk arkæologisk selskab.

— 2003. Danke krigsbytteofringer. In Jørgensen et al. 2003:44–64.

Ingemark, D. 2003. *Glass, alcohol and power in Roman Iron Age Scotland: A study of the Roman vessel glass from non-Roman/native sites in north Northumberland and Scotland*. Lund: Lunds universitet.

Insoll, T. 2004. *Archaeology, ritual, religion*. London: Routledge.

Iregren, E. 1989. Under Frösö kyrka – ben från en vikingatida offerlund. In L. Larsson and B. Wyszomirska (eds), *Arkeologi och religion*, pp. 119–33. Report series 34. Lund: Arkeologiska institutionen.

Jaanusson, H. 1966. Hur gamla är domarringar i Bohuslän? *Bohusläns fornminnesförenings tidskrift* 1966:45–54.

James. E. 1997. The militarisation of Roman society, 400–700. In Nørgård Jørgensen and Clausen 1997:19–24.

Janse, O. 1922. *Le travail de l'or en Suède à l'epoque mérovingienne: Études précédées d'un mémoire sur les solidi romains et byzantins trouvés en Suède*. Orléans: Paul Pigelot.

Janson, H. 1998. *Templum nobilissimum: Adam av Bremen, Uppsalatemplet och konfliktlinjerna i Europa kring år 1075*. Avhandlingar från Historiska institutionen i Göteborg 21. Gothenburg: Historiska institutionen.

Jansson, S. B. F. 1977. *Runinskrifter i Sverige*. Stockholm: Almqvist & Wiksell.

Jennbert, K. 2004. Människor och djur: Kroppsmetaforik och kosmologiska perspektiv. In Andrén et al. 2004:183–217.

— 2011. *Animals and humans: Recurrent symbiosis in archaeology and Old Norse religion*. Vägar till Midgård 14. Lund: Nordic Academic Press.

Jensen, J. 1997. *Fra Bronze- til Jernalder*. Nordiske Fortidsminder 15. Copenhagen: Det Kongelige Nordiske Oldskriftselskab.

— 2002. *Danmarks Oldtid. 2, Bronzealder, 2000–500 f. Kr.* Copenhagen: Gyldendal.

Johansen, B. 1997. *Ormalur: Aspekter av tillvaro och landskap*. Stockholm: Stockholm studies in archaeology 14. Stockholm: Arkeologiska institutionen.

Johansen, B. and Pettersson, I.-M 1993 (eds). *Från borg till bunker: Befästa anläggningar från förhistorisk och historisk tid*. Stockholm: Riksantikvarieämbetet.

Johansen, O. S. and Søbstad, T. 1978. De nordnorske tunanleggene fra jernalderen. *Viking* 41:9–56.

Johnson, S. 1983. *Late Roman fortifications*. London: Batsford.

Jørgensen, L. 2001. The 'warriors, soldiers and conscripts' of the anthropology in the late Roman and Migration period archaeology. In B. Storgaard (ed.), 2001. *Military aspects of the aristocracy in barbaricum in the Roman and early Migration periods*, pp. 9–19. Studies in Archaeology and History 5. Copenhagen: Nationalmuseet.

— 2009. Pre-Christian cult at aristocratic residences and settlement complexes in southern Scandinavia in the 3rd–10th centuries AD. In Freeden et al. 2009:329–54.

Jørgensen, L., Storgaard, B., and Gebauer Thomsen, L. 2003 (eds). *Sejrens triumf: Norden i skyggen af det romerske imperium*. Copenhagen: Nationalmuseet.

Josefsson, G. 2001. Var Embla en klängranka? *Arkiv för nordisk filologi* 116:71–96.

Kaliff, A. and Sundqvist, O. 2004. *Oden och Mithraskulten: Religiös ackulturation under romersk järnålder och folkvandringstid*. Occasional Papers in Archaeology 35. Uppsala: Institutionen för arkeologi och antik historia.

Karlsson, K. H. 1900. Några bidrag till Sveriges uppodlingshistoria hemtade från ortnamnsforskningens område. *Svenska fornminnesföreningens tidskrift* 10:38–54.

Karsvall, O. 2011. *Utjordar* and the question of deserted farms – a case study of the parish of Svanshals. *Bebyggelsehistorisk tidskrift* 61:22–38.

Kaul, F. 1991. *Gundestrupkedlen: Baggrund og billedverden*. Copenhagen: Nationalmuseet.

— 1998. *Ships on bronzes: A study in Bronze Age religion and iconography* 1–2. Copenhagen: Nationalmuseet.

— 2003. Mosen – porten til den anden verden. In L. Jørgensen et al. 2003:18–43.

— 2004. *Bronzealderens religion: Studier af den nordiske bronzealders ikonografi*. Copenhagen: Det Kongelige Nordiske Oldskriftselskab.

Keeley, L. H. 1995. *War before civilization*. New York: Oxford University Press.

Kiil, V. 1936. Er de nordiske Solberg minner om soldyrkelse? *Maal og minne* 1936:126–75.

Kivikoski, E. 1963. *Kvarnbacken: Ein Gräberfeld der jüngere Eisenzeit auf Åland*. Helsinki: Finnische Altertumsgesellschaft.

Kjeld Jensen, C. 2005. *Kontekstuel kronologi: En revision af det kronologiske grundlag for førromersk jernalder i Sydskandinavien*. 2 vols. Højbjerg: Kulturforlaget.

Kjellström, A. 2005. *The urban farmer: Osteoarchaeological analysis of skeletons from medieval Sigtuna interpreted in a socioeconomic perspective.* Theses and Papers in osteoarchaeology 2. Stockholm: Osteoarkeologiska forskningslaboratoriet.

Krag, C. 1991. *Ynglingatal og ynglingasaga: En studie i historiske kilder.* Oslo: Universitetsforlaget.

Krause, W., and Jankuhn, H. 1966. *Die Runeninschriften im älteren Futhark*. 2 vols. Göttingen: Vandenhoeck & Ruprecht.

Krautheimer, R. 1942. Introduction to an iconography of mediaeval architecture. *Journal of the Warburg & Courtauld Institutes* 5:1–33.

Kresten, P. and Ambrosiani, B. 1992. Swedish vitrified forts – a reconnaissance study. *Fornvännen* 87:1–17.

Kristiansen, K. 2001. Rulers and warriors: Symbolic transmission and social transformation in Bronze Age Europe. In J. Haas (ed.), *From leaders to rulers*. pp. 85–104. New York: Kluwer Academic.

— 2004. Institutioner og materiel kultur: Tvillingherskerne som religiøs og politisk institution under bronzealderen. In Andrén et al. 2004:99–122.

Kristiansen, K. and Larsson T. B. 2005. *The rise of Bronze Age society: Travels, transmissions and transformations*. Cambridge: Cambridge University Press.

Kristoffersen, S. 1995. Transformation in Migration Period animal art. *Norwegian Archaeoloigcal Review* 28(1):1–17.

Krüger, E. 1940–42. Die gallischen und germanischen Dioskuren. *Trierer Zeitschrift* 15:8–27 & 16–17:1–66.

Kure, H. 2002. Emblas ask. *Arkiv för nordisk filologi* 117:161–70.

— 2006. Hanging on the world tree: Man and cosmos in Old Norse mythic poetry. In Andrén et al. 2006:68–71.

Kyriakidis, E. 2007. Archaeologies of ritual. In E. Kyriakidis (ed.), *The archaeology of ritual*, pp. 289–308. Los Angeles: Cotsen Institute of Archaeology, University of California.

Lagerås, P. 2007. *The ecology of expansion and abandonment: Medieval and post-medieval agriculture and settlement in a landscape perspective*. Stockholm: Riksantikvarieämbetet.

Larsson, L. 2004 (ed.). *Continuity for centuries: A ceremonial building and its context at Uppåkra, southern Sweden.* Uppåkrastudier 10. Acta Archaeologica Lundensia, 80, no. 48. Stockholm: Almqvist & Wiksell International.

Larsson, T. B. 1994. Bronsålder. In *Signums svenska konsthistoria* i:69–161. Lund: Signum.

— 1997. *Materiell kultur och religiösa symboler: Mesopotamien, Anatolien och*

Skandinavien under det andra förkristna årtusendet. Umeå: Institutionen för arkeologi.

Lassen, A. 2011. *Odin på kristent pergament: En teksthistorisk studie.* Copenhagen: Museum Tusculanums Forlag.

Lauffer, S. 1989. *Griechenland: Lexikon der historischen Stätten von den Anfängen bis zur Gegenwart.* Munich: Beck.

Leus, P. M. 2011. New finds from the Xiongnu period in central Tuva. Preliminary communication. In U. Brosseder and B. K. Miller (eds), *Xiongnu Archaeology. Multidisciplinary perspectives of the first steppe empire in inner Asia*, pp. 515–36. Bonn Contributions to Asian Archaeology 5. Bonn: Vor- und Frühgeschichtliche Archäologie.

Leube, A. 1979. Eisenzeitliche Steinsetzungen im nördlichen Mitteleuropa. *Zeitschrift für Archäologie* 13:1–19.

Lie, H. 1952. Skaldestilstudier. *Maal og Minne* 1952:1–92.

Liestøl, A. 1975. Borrehaugene. Kart 1:2500, ekv. 1. m. Flyfotografert 1966. Synfart av A. Liestøl 1973. Universitetets Oldsaksamling. Oslo.

Liljeholm, N. 1999. Gravfält kontra kyrkogård – Bysans kontra Rom? Diskussion kring det senvikingatida begravningsskicket på Gotland utifrån gravfältet Stora Hallvards och Silte kyrkas kyrkogård. *Fornvännen* 94:145–60.

Lind, L. 1981. *Roman denarii found in Sweden,* ii: *Catalogue text.* Stockholm Studies in Classical Archaeology 11:2. Stockholm: Institutionen för antikens kultur och samhällsliv.

— 1988. *Romerska denarer funna i Sverige.* Stockholm: Rubicon.

Lindow, J. 1997a. *Murder and vengeance among the gods: Baldr in Scandinavian mythology.* Helsinki: Suomalainen tiedeakatemia, FF communications 262.

— 1997b. Baldr and Lemminkäinen. *Journal of Finnish Studies* 1:37–47.

— 2001. *Handbook of Norse mythology.* Santa Barbara, Calif: Abc-Clio.

Lindquist, S.-O. 1968. *Det förhistoriska kulturlandskapet i östra Östergötland. Hallebyundersökningen 1.* Studies in North-European Archaeology 2, Meddelanden från kulturgeografiska institutionen vid Stockholms universitet B11. Stockholm: Almqvist & Wiksell.

Lindqvist, S. 1941–42. *Gotlands Bildsteine* 1–2. Stockholm: Kungliga Vitterhets- Historie- och Antikvitetets Akademien.

— 1945. *Vår svenska guldålder.* Uppsala: Lindblads.

— 1956. Bildstensfynd vid kyrkorestaureringar. *Gotländskt Arkiv* 28:19–30.

— 1962. Jättestenen från Sanda och andra nyfunna bildstenar. *Gotländskt Arkiv* 34:7–22.

Lindroth, H. 1918. *Bohusläns härads- och sockennamn.* Gothenburg: Institutet för ortnamns- och dialektforskning vid Göteborgs högskola.

Ljungkvist, J. 2005. Uppsala högars datering: Och några konsekvenser av en omdatering till tidiga vendeltiden. *Fornvännen* 100:245–59.

Lomborg. E. 1973. *Die Flintdolche Dänemarks: Studien über Chronologie und Kulturbeziehungen des südskandinavischen Spätneolitikums.* Nordiske Fortidsminder B1. Copenhagen: Universitetsforlaget.

Lönn, M. 1999. *Fragment av samtal: Tvärvetenskap med arkeologi och ortnamnsforskning i bohusländska landskap.* Kungsbacka: Riksantikvarieämbetet.

Lönnroth, L. 1965. *European sources of Icelandic saga-writing.* Stockholm: Thule.

Löwenborg, D. 2012. An Iron Age shock doctrine – Did the AD 536–7 event trigger large-scale social changes in the Mälaren valley area? *Journal of Archaeology and Ancient History* 4:3–29.

Lund, A. A. 1993. *Det etnografiske kilder til Nordens tidlige historie.* Århus: Aarhus universitetsforlag.

Lund, J. 2009. *Åsted og vadested: Deponeringer, genstandsbiografier og rumlig strukturering som kilde til vikingetidens cognitive landskaber.* Acta Humaniora. Oslo: Universitetet i Oslo, Det humanistiske fakultet.

Lund Hansen, U. 1987. *Römischer Import im Norden: Warenaustausch zwischen dem Römischen Reich und dem freien Germanien während der Kaiserzeit unter besonderer Berücksichtigung Nordeuropas.* Nordiske Fortidsminder serie B, 10. Copenhagen: Det Kongelige Nordiske Oldskriftselskab.

— 1995 (ed.). *Himlingøje – Seeland – Europa: Ein Gräberfeld der jüngeren römischen Kaiserzeit auf Seeland, seine Bedeutung unter internationalen Beziehungen.* Nordiske Fortidsminder B13. Copenhagen: Det Kongelige Nordiske Oldskriftselskab.

— 2003a. Våbenofferfundene gennem 150 år – forskning og tolkninger. In L. Jørgensen et al. 2003:84–9.

— 2003b. Die Sarmaten aus südskandinavischer Sicht. In C. von Carnap-Bornheim (ed.), *Kontakt – Kooperation – Konflikt. Germanen und Sarmaten zwischen dem 1. Und dem 4. Jahrhundert nach Christus.* Schriften des Archäologischen Landesmuseums, Ergänzungsreihe, 1. Veröffentlichungen des Vorgeschichtlichen Seminars Marburg, Sondeband 13. Neumünster: Wachholtz.

Lundström, I. 1976. Skagervik – gravfält med domarringar. *Västergötlands fornminnesförenings tidskrift* 1975–6:87–101.

Lundström, P. 1965. *Gravfälten vid Fiskeby i Norrköping*, ii: *Fornlämningar och fynd.* Stockholm: Almqvist & Wiksell.

— 1970. *Gravfälten vid Fiskeby i Norrköping*, i: *Studier kring ett totalundersökt komplex.* Stockholm: Almqvist & Wiksell.

Lüth, F., and Voss, H.-U. 2001. Neue Römergräber aus Hagenow – ein Vorbericht. *Bodendenkmalpflege in Mecklenburg-Vorpommern* 48:149–214.

Maenchen-Helfen, O. J. 1973. *The world of the Huns: Studies in their history and culture*. Berkeley & Los Angeles: University of California Press.

Magnus, B. 1975. *Krosshaugfunnet: Et forsøk på kronologisk og stilhistorisk plassering i 5. århundrede*. Stavanger Museums skifter 9. Stavanger: Stavanger Museum.

— 2001a. Om tvillinger. In B. Magnus, C. Orrling, M. Rasch, and G. Tegnér (eds), *Vi får tacka Lamm*. Museum of National Antiquities, Stockholm, Studies 10, pp. 119–27. Stockholm: Statens historiska museum.

— 2001b. Reliefspenner fra Uppåkra og andre funnsteder i Skåne. In B. Hårdh (ed.), *Uppåkra – centrum och sammanhang*, pp. 175–85. Uppåkrastudier 3. Acta Archaeologica Lundensia, 80, no. 34. Stockholm: Almqvist & Wiksell International.

— 2003. Krigerens insignier. En parafrase over gravene II og V fra Snartemo i Vest-Agder. In P. Rolfsen and F.-A. Stylegar (eds), *Snartemofunnene i nytt lys*, pp. 33–52. Oslo: Universitetets kulturhistoriske museer.

— 2004. Brooches on the move in Migration Period Europe. *Fornvännen* 99:273–82.

Magnusen, F. 1825. *Eddalæren og dens oprindelse eller Nøjaktig fremstilling af de gamle nordboers digtninger*, iii: Copenhagen.

Maier, B. 1997. *Dictionary of Celtic religion*. Woodbridge: Boydell Press.

Malmer, M. P. 1963. *Metodproblem inom järnålderns konsthistoria*. Acta Archaeologica Lundensia, 80, no. 13. Bonn: Habelt.

Manneke, P. 1984. En tidig bildsten i Grötlingbo? *Gotländskt Arkiv* 60:81–8.

Mannhardt, W. 1875–7. *Wald- und Feldkulte*. 2 vols. Berlin: Borntraeger.

Marinatos, N. and Hägg, R. 1993 (eds). *Greek sanctuaries: New approaches*. London and New York: Routledge.

Mårtenson, J. 1987. *Djävulens hand*. Stockholm: Legenda.

Mårtensson, A. W. 1976. Gravar och kyrkor. In A. W. Mårtensson (ed.), *Uppgrävt förflutet för PK-banken i Lund*, pp. 87–134. Archaeologica Lundensia 7. Lund: Kulturhistoriska museet.

McKinnell, J. 1994. *Both one and many: Essays on change and variety in late Norse heathenism*. Rome: Il Calamo.

— 2008. 'Völuspá' and the Feast of Easter. *Alvíssmál* 12:3–28.

Mebius, H. 1968. *Värrō: Studier i samernas förkristna offerriter*. Skrifter utgivna av religionshistoriska institutionen 5. Uppsala: Almqvist & Wiksell.

— 2003. *Bissie: Studier i samisk religionshistoria*. Östersund: Jemtlandica.

Meulengracht Sørensen, P. 1977. *Saga og samfund: En indføring i oldislandsk litteratur*. Berlingske leksikon bibliotek 116. Copenhagen: Berlingske.

— 1993. *Fortælling og ære: Studier i islændingesagaerne*. Aarhus: Aarhus universitetsforlag.

Miklos, E. 1993. Hun and Xiongnu type cauldron finds throughout Eurasia. *Eurasian Studies Yearbook* 67:5–94.

Mitlid, Å. 2003. Bygdeborgene – synlige spor fra forhistorien: En analyse av borgens funksjon og plass i det tidlige jernaldersamfunnet med vekt på deres forsvarsrelaterte oppgaver. Hovedfagsoppgave i arkeologi. Oslo: Universitetet i Oslo.

— 2004. Bygdeborgerna i rollen som forsvarsobjekt. *Primitive Tider* 6:7–20.

Moberg, C.-A. 1953. Über die Rahmenverzierung der Goldbrakteaten. *Acta Archaeologica* 23:115–31.

Modée, J. 2005. *Artifacts and supraphysical worlds: A conceptual analysis of religion*. Lund: Centrum för teologi och religionsvetenskap.

Moltke, E. 1976. *Runerne i Danmark og deres oprindelse*. Copenhagen: Forum.

Monikaner, A. 2010. *Våld och vatten: Våtmarkskult vid Skedemosse under järnåldern*. Stockholm Studies in Archaeology 52. Stockholm: Institutionen för arkeologi och antikens kultur.

Montelius, O. 1887. Bronsåldersfyndet från Eskelhem. *Vitterhetsakademiens månadsblad* 16. Stockholm: Historiska Förl. [1993].

Montgomery, J. 2000. Ibn Fadlan and the Rusiyyah. *Journal of Arabic and Islamic Studies* 3:1–25.

Müller, D. 1968. Germanische Tiersymbolik und Namenbegung. *Frühmittelalterliche Studien* 2:202–17.

Müller, W. 1975. *Die Jupitergigantensäulen und ihre Verwandten*. Beiträge zu klassischen Philologie 66. Meisenhem am Glan: Hain.

Müller-Wille, M. 1999. *Opferkulte der Germanen und Slawen*. Archäologie in Deutschland, Sonderheft. Stuttgart: Theiss.

— 2001. Offerplatser på kontinenten: Några exempel från förkristen tid. In K. Jennbert, A. Andrén., and C. Raudvere (eds), *Plats och praxis: Studier av nordisk förkristen ritual*. pp. 135–66. Vägar till Midgård 2. Lund: Nordic Academic Press.

Myhre, B. 1966. Bygdeborger på Nord-Jæren. *Fra haug ok heidni* 1966:181–93.

— 1972. *Funn, fornminner og ødegårder: Jernalderens bosetning i Høyland Fjellbygd*. Stavanger: Stavanger Museums skrifter 7.

— 1997. Boathouses and naval organization. In Nørgård Jørgensen and Clausen 1997:169–83.

— 2002. Landbruk, landskap og samfunn 4000 f. Kr–800 e. Kr. In B. Myhre and I. Øye. *Norges landbrukshistorie I. 4000 f. Kr–1350 e.* Kr. Oslo: Det norske samlaget.

—— 2005. Krossane på Ullandhaug, Døds-sjødno på Sele og fem dårlige jomfruer på Norheim. Symboler for Yggdrasil – livets tre? *Frá haug ok heidni: Tidsskrift for Rogalands arkeologiske forening* 2005 (3):3–10.

Myhre, B. and Gansum, T. 2003. *Skipshaugen 900 e. Kr. Borrefunnet 1852–2002.* Borre: Midgard historisk senter.

Myrberg, N. 2005. Burning down the house: Mythological chaos and world order on Gotlandic picture stones. *Current Swedish Archaeology* 13:99–119.

Myrdal, J. 2003. *Digerdöden, pestvågor och ödeläggelse*: *Ett persepktiv på senmedeltidens Sverige.* Runica et mediævalia, Scripta minora 9. Stockholm: Sällskapet Runica et mediævalia.

Näsman, U. 1976. The settlement of Eketorp II. In Borg et al. 1976:117–50.

—— 1981. Borgenes ø. *Skalk* 1981(1):18–27.

—— 1984. *Glas och handel i senromersk tid och folkvandringstid: En studie kring glas från Eketorp II, Öland, Sverige.* Uppsala: Institutionen för arkeologi.

—— 1988. Analogislutning i nordisk Jernalderarkæologi: Et bidrag til udviklingen af en nordisk historisk etnografi. In P. Mortensen and B. M. Rasmussen (eds), *Jernalderens stammesamfund*, pp. 123–40. Fra stamme til stat i Danmark 1. Aarhus: Jysk Arkæologisk Selskab.

—— 1989. The gates of Eketorp: To the question of Roman prototypes of the Öland ringforts. In K. Randsborg (ed.), *The birth of Europe: Archaeology and social development in the first millennium AD*, pp. 129–139. Analecta Romana Instituti Danici, 16. Rome: L'Erma di Bretschneider.

—— 1997. Strategies and tactics in Migration Period defence. On the art of defence on the basis of the settlement forts of Öland. In Nørgård Jørgensen and Clausen 1997:146–56.

—— 2001. Tabell över Ölands fornborgar. In G. Aldestam (ed.), *Ölands guldålder: Romersk jänrålder och folkvandringstid med en liten öländsk historiebok*, p. 93. Kalmar: Bildningsförlaget and Kalmar läns museum.

—— 2008a. Från Attila till Karl den store: Skandinavien i Europa. In M. Olausson (ed.), *Hem till Jarlabanke: Jord, makt och evigt liv i östra Mälardalen under järnålder och medeltid*, pp. 19–47. Lund: Historiska Media.

—— 2008b. Scandinavia and the Huns: A source-critical approach to an old question. *Fornvännen* 103:111–18.

—— 2009. Paradigm misused: A de-railed debate. *Fornvännen* 104:45–7.

—— 2012. Comments on 'An Iron Age shock doctrine. The 536–7 event as a trigger of large-scale change in the Mälaren valley area' by Daniel Löwenborg. *Journal of Archaeology and Ancient History* 4.

Näsman, U. and Lund, J. 1988 (eds). *Folkvandringstiden i Norden: En krisetid mellem ældre og yngre jernalder*. Århus: Universitetsforlaget.

Näsström, B.-M. 1996. Offerlunden under Frösö kyrka. In S. Brink (ed.), *Jämtlands kristnande*, pp. 65–85. Projektet Sveriges kristnande, 4. Uppsala: Lunne böcker.

— 2001. *Fornskandinavisk religion: En grundbok*. Lund: Studentlitteratur.

— 2006. *Bärsärkarna: Vikingatidens elitsoldater*. Stockholm: Norstedts.

Nedoma, R. 2003. Runennamen. *Reallexikon der germanischen Altertumskunde* 25:556–62. Berlin: de Gruyter

Nerman, B. 1935. *Die Völkerwanderungszeit Gotlands*. Stockholm: Kungliga Vitterhets- Historie- och Antikvitets Akademien.

— 1941. *Sveriges rikes uppkomst*. Stockholm: Skoglunds.

Nesheim, A. 1971. Soldyrkelse. *Kulturhistorisk lexikon för nordisk medeltid* 16:409–12. Malmö: Allhem.

Ney, A. 2006. The edges of the Old Norse world-view: A bestiary concept? In Andrén et al. 2006:63–7.

Nicklasson, P. 1997. *Svärdet ljuger inte: Vapenfynd från äldre järnålder på Sveriges fastland*. Acta Archaeologica Lundensia, 40 no. 22. Stockholm: Almqvist & Wiksell International.

Nielsen, A.-L. 1997. Pagan cultic and votive acts at Borg: Expressions of the central significance of the farmstead in the late Iron Age. In H. Andersson, P. Carelli and L. Ersgård (eds), *Visions of the past: Trends and traditions in Swedish Medieval Archaeology*, pp. 372–92. Lund Studies in Medieval Archaeology 19 & Riksantikvarieämbetet, Arkeologiska undersökningar. 24. Stockholm: Almqvist & Wiksell International.

— 2005. Under Biltema och Ikea: Ullevi under 1500 år. In A. Kaliff and G. Tagesson (eds), *Liunga. Kaupinga. Kulturhistoria och arkeologi i Linköpings-bygden*, pp. 204–35. Riksantikvarieämbetet, Arkeologiska undersökningar, 60. Stockholm: Riksantikvarieämbetet.

Nihlén, J., and Boethius, G. 1933. *Gotländska gårdar och byar under äldre järnåldern: Studier till belysning av Gotlands äldre odlingshistoria*. Stockholm: Seelig.

Nilsén, A. 1991. *Kyrkorummets brännpunkt: Gränsen mellan kor och långhus i den svenska landskyrkan. Från romanik till nygotik*. Stockholm: Kungliga Vitterhets- Historie- och Antikvitets Akademien.

Nilsson, B. 1992. Till frågan om kyrkans hållning till icke-kristna kultfenomen: Attityder under tidig medeltid i Europa och Norden. In B. Nilsson (ed.), *Kontinuitet i kult och tro från vikingatid till medeltid*, pp. 9–47. Projektet Sveriges kristnande, publikationer 1. Uppsala: Lunne böcker.

REFERENCES

Nilsson, P. 2010. Reused rock art: Iron Age activities at Bronze Age rock art sites. In J. Goldhahn, I. Fuglestvedt, and A. Jones (eds), *Changing pictures: Rock art traditions and visions in Northern Europe*, pp. 154–69. Oxford: Oxbow Books.

Nilsson Stutz, L. 2003. *Embodied rituals and ritualized bodies: Tracing ritual practices in late mesolithic burials.* Acta Archaeologica Lundensia, 40, no. 46. Stockholm: Almqvist & Wiksell International.

Norberg, R. 1931. Moor- und Depotfunde aus dem 5. Jahrhundert nach Christus in Schonen. *Acta Archaeologica* 2:104–11.

Nordberg, A. 2003. *Krigarna i Odens hall: Dödsföreställningar och krigarkult i fornnordisk religion.* Stockholm: Religionshistoriska institutionen.

— 2006. *Jul, disting och förkyrklig tideräkning: Kalendrar och kalendariska riter i det förkristna Norden.* Acta Academiae Regiae Gustavi Adolphi 91. Uppsala: Kungliga Gustav Adolfs akademien.

Nordén, A. 1929. *Östergötlands järnålder,* i: *Ringstad och Bråbygden.* Stockholm: Författarens förlag.

— 1938. *Östergötlands järnålder,* ii: *Kolmården – V. Husbydalen – Fornborgarna.* Stockholm: Författarens förlag.

Nordin, F. 1881. Om Gotlands fornborgar. *Kungl. Vitterhets-, historie- och antikvitetsakademiens månadsblad* 1881:97–147.

Nordin, S. 1995. *Filosofins historia: Det västerländska förnuftets äventyr från Thales till postmodernism.* Lund: Studentlittartur.

Nordqvist, B. 2007. Der Kriegsbeuteopferplatz von Finnestorp in Schweden. *Offa* 61–2:221–38.

Nørgård Jørgensen, A. 1997. Sea defence in Denmark AD 200–1300. In Nørgård Jørgensen and Clausen 1997:200–209.

— 2009. Weapon-offering types in Denmark, 350 BC to 1200 AD: Definitions, chronology and previous interpretations. In Freeden et al. 2009:37–51.

Nørgård Jørgensen, A. and Clausen, B. L. 1997 (eds). *Military aspects of Scandinavian society in a European perspective, AD 1–1300.* Studies in Archaeology and History 2. Copenhagen: Nationalmuseet.

Norling-Christensen, H. 1957. Haraldstedgravpladsen og ældre germansk jærnalder i Danmark. *Aarbøger for Nordisk Oldkyndighed og Historie* 1956:14–143.

Nylén, E. 1955. *Die jüngere vorrömische Eisenzeit Gotlands: Funde, Chronologie, Formenkunde.* Uppsala: Uppsala universitet.

— 1969. Hjulet och hjulkorsgravarna. *Tor* 13:98–128.

Nylén, E. and Lamm, J.-P. 1978. *Bildstenar.* 1st edn. Visby: Barry Press.

Nylén, E. and Lamm, J.-P. 2003. *Bildstenar.* 3rd edn. Stockholm: Gidlunds.

Öberg, H. 1942. *Guldbrakteaterna från Nordens folkvandringstid.* Kungliga

Vitterhets-, historie- och antikivitetsakademiens handlingar 53. Stockholm: Wahlström & Widstrand.

Olausson, M. 1995. *Det inneslutna rummet – om kultiska hägnader, fornborgar och befästa gårdar I Uppland från 1300 f Kr till Kristi födelse.* Arkeologiska undersökningar, skrifter 9. Stockholm: Riksantikvarieämbetet.

— 1997. Fortified manors during the Migration Period in eastern middle Sweden – a discussion of politics, warfare and architecture. In Nørgård Jørgensen and Clausen 1997:157–67.

— 2009. At peace with walls – Fortifications and their significance AD 400–1100. In Holmquist Olausson and Olausson 2009:35–70.

— 2011 (ed.). *Runnhusa: Bosättningen på berget med de många husen.* Skrifter från projektet Runsa borg, Eds socken, Uppland 1. Stockholm: Archaeologica.

Oldenstein, J. 2009. Kastell Alzey. Archäologische Untersuchungen im spätrömischen Lager under Studien zur Grenzverteidigung im Mainzer Dukat. Mainz: online-edition of Habilitationsschrift 1992.

Olsen, B. 2003. Material culture after text: Remembering things. *Norwegian Archaeoloigcal Review* 36(2):87–104.

— 2010. *In defense of things: Archaeology and the ontology of objects.* Lanham: Altamira Press.

Olsen, O. 1966. Hørg, hov og kirke: Historiske og arkæologiske vikinge-tidsstudier. *Aarbøger for nordisk Oldkyndighed og Historie* 1965:1–307.

Olsen, R. A. 2011. *Danske middelalderborge.* Aarhus: Aarhus universitetsforlag.

Olsson, I. 1976. *Gotlands stavgardar: En ortnamnsstudie.* Visby: Barry Press.

Ong, W. 1982. *Orality and literacy: The technologizing of the word.* London: Methuen.

Ørsnes, M. 1988. *Ejsbøl I. Waffenopferfunde des 4.-5. Jahrhundert nach Christus.* Copenhagen: Det Kongelige Nordiske Oldskriftselskab

Östenberg, I. 2009. *Staging the world: Spoils, captives, and representations in the Roman triumphal procession.* Oxford: Oxford University Press.

Österman, K. 1994. Insjögravar: Minnen efter samiska fångstmän eller sydsven-ska bönder? Seminar paper. Stockholm: Stockholm universitet

Österman, P. 2001. *Svenska jätteträd och deras mytologiska historia.* Kverrestad: Artbooks.

Otto, T., Thrane, T., and Vandkilde, H. 2006 (eds). *Warfare and society: Archaeo-logical and social anthropological perspectives.* Aarhus: Aarhus University Press.

Oxenstierna, E. 1956. *Die Goldhörner von Gallehus.* Lidingö [printed Mainz]: the author.

Palaima, T. 1995. The nature of the Mycenaean wanax. Non-Indo-European origins and priestly functions. In P. Rehak (ed.), *The role of the ruler in the prehistoric Aegean*, pp. 119–38. Liège: Aegaeum 11.

Pallas, D. 1977. *Les monuments paleochrétiens de Grèce découverts de 1959 à 1973*. Rome: Sussidi allo studio delle antichità cristiane 5.

Palm, T. 1948. *Trädkult: Studier i germansk religionshistoria*. Lund: Gleerup.

Palm, V. 2008. Lyx och vardag i Gråborg. In Tegnér 2008b:89–108

Pásztor, E., Roslund, C. Nässtöm, B.-M., and Robertson, H. 2000. The sun and the Rösaring ceremonial road. *Europan Journal of Archaeology* 3(1):57–67.

Pauli Jensen, X. 2009. From fertility rituals to weapon sacrifies: The case of south Scandinavian bog finds. In Freeden et al. 2009:53–64.

Pauli Jensen, X., Jørgensen, L., and Lund Hansen, U. 2003. Den germanske hær: Krigere, soldater og officerer. In L. Jørgensen et al. 2003:310–28.

Pernler, S.-E. 1999. *Sveriges kyrkohistoria,* ii: *Hög- och senmedeltid*. Stockholm: Verbum.

Persson, I. and Rasch, M. 2001. Gräsgård socken. In M. Rasch (ed.) *Ölands järnåldersgravfält,* iv. Stockholm: Riksantikvarieämbetet and Statens historiska Museum.

Pesch, A. 2007. *Die Goldbrakteaten der Völkerwanderungszeit: Thema und Variation*. Ergänzungsbände zum Reallexikon der germanischen Altertumkunde 36. Berlin: de Gruyter.

Petersen, H. 1876. *Om nordboernes gudedyrkelse og gudetro i hedenold: En antikvarisk undersøgelse*. Copenhagen: Reitzel.

Petré, B. 1980. Björnfällen i begravningsritualen – statusobjekt speglande regional skinnhandel? *Fornvännen* 75:5–14.

— 1984. *Arkeologiska undersökningar på Lovö,* iv: *Bebyggelsehistorisk analys*. Studies in North-European archaeology 10. Stockholm: Stockholms universitet.

Pitts, Lynn F., and St Joseph. J. K. 1985. *Inchtuthil: The Roman legionary fortress. Excavations 1952–65*. Gloucester: Alan Sutton.

Price, N. S. 2002. *The Viking way: Religion and war in late Iron Age Scandinavia*. Aun 31. Uppsala: Department of Archaeology and Ancient History.

— 2006. What's in a name? In Andrén et al. 2006:179–83.

Pryor, F. 2001. *Seahenge: New discoveries in prehistoric Britain*. London: Harper Collins.

Ragnarsson, A. 2007. Vingslag från gotländsk vendeltid: En studie av bildstenar med fågelmotiv. Seminar paper in archaeology. Visby: Gotlands högskola.

— 2011. Stridens symboler och maktens märken – En studie av Gotlands äldsta bildstenar. Seminar paper in archaeology. Visby: Gotlands högskola.

Ramqvist, P. H. 1990. *Högom*. Stockholm: Riksantikvarieämbetet.

— 2007. Fem Norrland: Om norrländska regioner och deras interaktion. *Arkeologi i Norr* 10:153–80.

— 2012. Two perspectives on Iron Age southern Scandinavia. *Antiquity* 86: 561–5.

Ramskou, T. 1951. Viking Age Cremation Graves in Denmark: A Survey. *Acta Archaeologica* 21:137–82.

— 1976. *Lindholm høje: Gravpladsen*. Copenhagen: Nationalmuseet.

Randsborg, K. 1993. Kivik: Archaeology and Iconography. *Acta Archaeologica* 64(1):1–147.

— 1995. *Hjortspring: Warfare and sacrifice in early Europe*. Aarhus: Aarhus University Press.

Rappaport, R. A. 1999. *Ritual and religion in the making of humanity*. Cambridge: Cambridge University Press.

Raudvere, C. 2004. Delen eller helheten: Kosmologi som empiriskt och analytiskt begrepp. In Andrén et al. 2004:59–95.

Renfrew, C. 1987. *Archaeology and language: The puzzle of Indo-European origins*. London: Cape.

Rentzhog, S. 1987. Frösön under järnålder: En bebyggelsehistorisk studie med utgångspunkt från det äldsta kartmaterialet. Seminar paper in archaeology. Uppsala: Uppsala universitet.

Riddersporre, M. 1995. *Bymarker i backspegel: Odlingslandskapet före kartornas tid*. Trelleborg: Förlagshuset Swedala.

Rieck, F., Jørgensen, E., Vang Petersen, P., and Christensen, C. 1999. '… som samlede Ofre fra en talrig Krigerflok': Status over Nationalmuseets Nydamprojekt 1989–97. *Nationalmuseets Arbejdsmark* 1999:11–34.

Rieckhoff, S., and Biel, J. 2001 (eds). *Die Kelten in Deutschland*. Stuttgart: Theiss.

Rival, L. 1998 (ed.). *The social life of trees: Anthropological perspectives on tree symbolism*. New York: Berg.

Rosenfeld, H. 1984. Dioskuren. *Reallexikon der germanischen Altertumskunde* 5:482–4. Berlin: de Gruyter.

Roth, H. 1979. *Kunst der Völkerwanderungszeit*. Propyläen Kunstgeschichte 4. Frankfurt am Main: Propyläen.

— 1986 (ed.). *Zum Problem der Deutung frühmittelalterlicher Bildinhalte*. Sigmaringen: Jan Thorbecke.

Rundkvist, M. 1996. Järnålderns ringamuletter med knoppar eller vulster. *Fornvännen* 91:13–25.

— 2001. Knoppringar och vulstringar än en gång. In B. Magnus, C. Orrling, M. Rasch, and G. Tegnér (eds), *Vi får tacka Lamm*, pp. 173–82 Museum of

National Antiquities, Stockholm, Studies 10. Stockholm: Statens historiska museum.

Rüpke, J. 1990. *Domi militiae: Die religiöse Konstruktion des Krieges in Rom.* Stuttgart: Steiner

Rygh, O. 1882. *Gamle bygdeborge i Norge.* Kristiania: Foreningen til norske Fortidsmindesmerkers Bevaring Aarsberetning.

Rykwert, J. 1988. *The idea of a town: The anthropology of urban form in Rome, Italy and the Ancient World.* Cambridge, Mass.: MIT Press.

Salin, B. 1895. De nordiska guldbrakteaterna. *Antikvarisk tidskrift för Sverige* 14(2):n.p.

— 1904. *Die altgermanische Thierornamentik: Typologische Studie über germanische Metallgegenstände aus dem IV. bis IX. Jahrhundert, nebst einer Studie über irische Ornamentik.* Stockholm: Asher.

Sandvall, A. 1980 (ed.). *Vendeltid.* Stockholm: Statens Historiska Museer.

Santesson, L. 1989. En blekingsk blotinskrift: En nytolkning av inledningsraderna på Stentoftenstenen. *Fornvännen* 84:221–9.

Saxo Grammaticus. 2005. *Gesta Danorum. Danmarkshistorien.* Edited by K. Friis-Jensen and translated into Danish by P. Zeeber. 2 vols. Copenhagen: Det Danske Sprog- og Litteraturselskab.

Schjødt, J. P. 1990. Horizontale und vertikale Achsen in der vorchristlichen skandinavischen Kosmologie. In T. Ahlbäck (ed.), *Old Norse and Finnish religions and cultic place-names*, pp. 35–57. Scripta Instituti Donneriani Aboensis 13. Stockholm: Almqvist & Wiksell International.

— 1992. Nío man ec heima, nío íviði, mjotvið mæran fyr mold neðan: Tid och rum i Vǫluspá 2. *Arkiv för nordisk filologi* 107:156–66.

— 1999a. *Det førkristne Norden: Religion og mytologi.* Copenhagen: Spektrum.

— 1999b. Krigeren i førkristen nordisk myte og ideology. In U. Drobin (ed.), *Religion och samhälle i det förkristna Norden: Ett symposium*, pp. 195–208. Odense: Odense universitetsforlag.

— 2004. Kosmologimodeller og mytekredse. In Andrén et al. 2004:123–33.

— 2008. *Initiation between two worlds: Structure and symbolism in pre-Christian Scandinavian religion.* The Viking Collection 17. Odense: Syddansk universitetsforlag.

— 2009. Diversity and its consequences for the study of Old Norse religion. What is it we are trying to reconstruct? In L. Słupecki and J. Morawiec (eds), *Between paganism and Christianity in the North.* Rzeszów: Wydawn Uniwersytetu Rzeszowskiego.

— forthcoming. Kings. In *Pre-Christian Religions of the North. Histories and Structures*, ii. Turnhout: Brepols.

Schlüter, W. 1997. Archäologische Forschungen zur Örtlichkeit der Varus-schlacht. Die Ausgrabungen und Prospektionen 1987–1996 im Engpaß zwischen Kalkrieser Berg und Großem Moor, Landkreis Osnabrück, Deutschland. In Nørgård Jørgensen and Clausen 1997:65–75.

Schnell, I. 1934. Fornborgar i Västmanlands län. *Västmanlands fornminnes-förenings årsskrift* 22:5–97.

Schnittger, B. 1913. Die vorgeschichtlichen Burgwälle in Schweden. In *Opuscula archaeologica Oscari Montelio septuagenario dicata d. XI m. Sept. a. MCMXIII*, pp. 335–49. Stockholm: Ivar Haeggström.

Schnurbein, S. von 1997. Die Organisation des Römischen Heeres und die Struktur des Limes in Germanien. In Nørgård Jørgensen and Clausen 1997:11–18.

Seebold, E. 1992. Römische Münzbilder und germanische Symbolwelt: Versuch einer Deutung der Bildelemente von C-Brakteaten. In H. Beck, D. Ellmers, and K. Schier (eds), *Germanische Religionsgeschichte: Quellen und Quellenprobleme*, pp. 270–335. Ergänzungsbände zun Reallexikon der germanischen Altertumskunde 5. Berlin: de Gruyter.

Sigvallius, B. 1994. *Ismantorps borg, Långlöt socken, Öland: Undersökning av benmaterial från Inventarienummer 17991:1.* Stockholm: Rapportserie från Osteologiska enheten, Statens historiska museum, Osteologisk rapport 1994:17.

Simek, R. 1993. *Dictionary of Northern mythology.* Cambridge: Brewer.

Sjöborg, N.-H. 1822. *Samlingar för Nordens fornälskare*, i. Stockholm: Nestius.

Skjelsvik, E. 1951. Steinringen på Hunn. *Viking* 15:116–26.

Skre, D. 1998. *Herredømmet: Bosetning og besittelse på Romerike 200–1350 e Kr.* Oslo: Scandinavian University Press.

Słupecki, L. P. 1994. *Slavonic pagan sanctuaries.* Warszawa: Institute of Archaeology and Ethnology, Polish Academy of Sciences.

Slöjdare, Y. 1973. Treuddar i södra Sverige. Seminar paper in archaeology. Stockholm: Stockholms universitet.

Smith, J. Z. 1987. *To take place: Toward a theory of ritual.* Chicago: University of Chicago Press.

Söderberg, B. 2001. Väg 11 – ett pågående arkeologiskt projekt i sydöstra Skåne. *Ale, historisk tidskrift för Skåne, Halland och Blekinge* 2001(1):1–12.

— 2005. *Aristokratiskt rum och gränsöverskridande: Järrestad och sydöstra Skåne mellan region och rike 600–1100.* Riksantikavrieämbetet, Arkeologiska undersökningar, skrifter 62. Stockholm: Riksantikvarieämbetet.

Söderberg, S. 1905. Om djurornamentiken under folkvandringstiden. *Antiqvarisk tidskrift för Sverige* 9(3):1–93.

Solli, B. 2002. *Seid: Myter, sjamanisme og kjønn i vikingenes tid.* Oslo: Pax.

— 2004. Det norrøne verdensbildet og *ethos*: Om kompleksitet, kjønn og kontradiksjoner. In Andrén et al. 2004:253–87.

Southern, P. and Dixon, K. R. 1996. *The late Roman army.* London: Batsford.

Sprockhoff, E. 1954. Nordische Bronzezeit und frühes Griechentum. *Jahrbuch des Römisch-Germanischen Zentralmuseum Mainz* 1:28–110.

Staecker, J. 2004. Hjältar, kungar och gudar: Receptionen av bibliska element och av hjältediktning i en hednisk värld. In Å. Berggren, S. Arvidsson, and A.-M. Hållans (eds), *Minne och myt. Konsten att skapa det förflutna*, pp. 39–78. Vägar till Midgård 5. Lund: Nordic Academic Press.

— 2011. Enigma in Bildform: Die Decodierung des Bamberger und Camminer Schreins. *Offa* 65–6:165–82.

Steinsland, G. 1979. Treet i Völuspá. *Arkiv för nordisk filologi* 94:120–50.

— 1983. Antropogonimyten i Völuspá: En tekst- og traditsjonskritisk analyse. *Arkiv för nordisk filologi* 98:80–107.

— 1991. *Det hellige bryllup og norrøn kongeideologi: En analyse av heirogami-myten i Skírnismál, Ynglingatal, Háleygjatal og Hyndluljóð.* Oslo: Solum.

— 2005. *Norrøn religion: Myter, riter, samfund.* Oslo: Pax.

Steinsland, G. and Meulengracht Sørensen, P. 1994. *Menneske og makter i vikingenes verden.* Oslo: Universitetsforlaget.

Stenberger, M. 1925. En preliminär undersökning av Ismantorps borg. *Fornvännen* 20:358–75.

— 1933. *Öland under äldre järnålder: En bebyggelsehistorisk undersökning.* Stockholm: Kungliga Vitterhets, Historie och Antikvitets Akademiens förlag.

— 1955. The reasons for the abandonment of Vallhagar. In M. Stenberger and O. Klindt Jensen 1955:1161–85.

Stenberger, M. and Klindt Jensen, O. 1955 (eds). *Vallhagar: A Migration Period settlement on Gotland, Sweden.* 2 vols. Copenhagen: Munksgaards.

Storli, I. 2000. 'Barbarians' of the North: Reflections on the establishment of courtyard sites in north Norway. *Norwegian Archaeological Review* 33(2):81–103.

— 2001. Tunanleggenes rolle i nordnorsk jernalder. *Viking* 64:87–111.

Stout, M. 1997. *The Irish ringfort.* Irish Settlement Studies 5. Dublin: Four Courts Press.

Strid, J. P. 2009. Försvunna sjöars land – om ortnamnen i västra slättbygden. In A. Kaliff (ed.), *Skuggor i ett landskap: Västra Östergötlands slättbygd under järnålder och medeltid*, pp. 47–101. Riksantikvarieämbetet, Arkeologiska undersökningar, Skrifter 75. Stockholm: Riksantikvarieämbetet.

Ström, Å. V. 1975. Germanische Religion. In Å. V. Ström and H. Biezais, (eds), *Germanische und Baltische Religion*. Die Religionen der Menschheit 19,1. Stuttgart: Kohlhammer.

Ström, F. 1980. Björnfällar och Oden-religion. *Fornvännen* 75:266–70.

Strömberg, M. 1963. Kultische Steinsetzungen in Schonen. *Meddelanden från Lunds universitets historiska museum* 1962–3:148–85.

Stylegar, F.-A. 1999. Rikssamling, statsoppkomst og ujevn utvikling: Regional variasjon i tidlig middelalder. In J. Goldhahn and P. Nordquist (eds), *Marxistiska perspektiv inom skandinaisk arkeologi*, pp. 111–34. Arkeologiska studier vid Umeå universitet 5. Umeå: Umeå universitet.

— 2006. Store-Dal – en studie i horisontaltstratigrafi. In T. Østigård (ed.), *Lik og ulik: Tilnærminger til variasjon i gravskikk*. UBAS nordisk 2, pp. 159–70. Bergen: Arkeologisk institutt, Universitetet i Bergen.

Stylegar, F.-A. and Grimm, O. 2003. Das südnorwegische Spangereid – Ein Beitrag zur Diskussion archäologischer Zentralplätze und norwegischer ringförmiger Anlagen. *Offa* 59–60: 81–124.

Sundqvist, O. 1998. Kultledare och kultfunktionärer i det forntida Skandinavien. *Svensk religionshistorisk årsskrift* 7:76–104.

— 2002. *Freyr's offspring: Rulers and religion in ancient Svea society*. Historia religiorum 21. Uppsala: Teologiska institutionen.

— 2004. Uppsala och Asgård. Makt, offer och kosmos i forntida Skandinavien. In Andrén et al. 2004:145–79.

— 2007. *Kultledare i fornskandinavisk religion*. Occasional Papers in Archaeology 41. Uppsala: Institutionen för arkeologi och antik kultur.

— 2010. Om hängningen, de nio nätterna och den dyrköpta kunskapen i Hávamál 138–145 – den kultiska kontexten. *Scripta Islandica – Isländska Sällskapets Årsbok* (61):68–97.

Sundqvist, O. and Hultgård, A. 2004. The Lycophoric Names of the 6th to 7th Century Blekinge Rune Stones and the problem of their Ideological Background. In A. van Nahl, L. Elmevik, and S. Brink (eds), *Namenwelt: Orts- und Personennamen in historischer Sicht*, pp. 583–602. Ergänzungsbände zum Reallexikon der germanischen Altertumskunde, 44. Berlin: de Gruyter.

Svanberg, F. *Death Rituals in south-east Scandinavia AD 800–1000. Decolonizing the Viking Age*, ii. Acta Archaeologica Lundensia, 40 no. 24. Stockholm: Almqvist & Wiksell International.

Svensson, K. 2012. Götavi – en vikingatida kultplats. In A. Hed Jakobsson (ed.), *På väg genom Närke – ett landskap genom historien*, pp. 85–110. Skifter från Arkeologikonsult 2. Upplands Väsby: Arkeologikonsult.

Taavitsainen, J.-P. 1990. *Ancient hillforts of Finland: Problems of analysis, chronology and interpretation with special reference to the hillfort of Kuhmoinen*.

Finska fornminnesföreningens tidskrift 94. Helsinki: Finska fornminnes-
föreningen.

Tacitus, C. 1999. *Agricola and Germania*. Translated with an introduction and
notes by A. R. Birley. Oxford: Oxford University Press.

Tegnér, G. 2008a. Gåtan Gråborg. In Tegnér 2008b:39–58.

— 2008b (ed.). *Gråborg på Öland: Om en borg, ett kapell och en by*. Stockholm:
Kungliga Vitterhets-, Historie- och Antikvitets Akademien.

Thompson, E. A. 1966. *The Visigoths in the time of Ulfila*. Oxford: Clarendon
Press.

Thomsen, C. J. 1855. Om Guldbracteaterne og Bracteaternes tidligste Brug
som Mynt. *Annaler for Nordisk Oldkyndighed og Historie* 1855:265–347.

Thomsen, T. 1929. *Egekistefundet fra Egtved, fra den ældre Bronzealder*. Nordiske
Fortidsminder II:4. Copenhagen: Gyldendal & Nordisk forlag.

Thordeman, B. 1939–40. *Armour from the battle of Wisby 1361*. Monografier
27. Stockholm: Kungliga Vitterhets-, historie- och antikvitetsakademien.

Törnqvist, O. 1993. Fornborgarnas betydelse under ekonomisk expansion,
politiskt paradigmskifte och social segregering. En studie med utgångspunkt från Vikbolandet, östra Östergötland. Seminar paper in archaeology.
Stockholm: Stockholm University.

Trigger, B. G. 2006. *A history of archaeological thought*. 2nd edn. Cambridge:
Cambridge University Press.

Vaitkevicius V. 2004. *Studies into the Balts' sacred places*. BAR International
Series 1228. Oxford: Hedges.

Vandkilde, H. 2003. Commemorative tales: Archaeological responses to modern myths, politics, and war. *World Archaeology* 35(1):126–44.

— 2006. Archaeology and war: Presentations of warriors and peasants in
archaeological interpretations. In T. Otto et al. 2006:57–73.

Viberg, A., Victor, H., Fischer, S., Lidén, K., and Andrén, A. 2012. A room
with a view – archaeological geophysical prospection and excavations at
Sandby ringfort, Öland, Sweden. In A. Viberg (ed.), *Remnant echoes of the
past: Archaeological geophysical prospection in Sweden*. Theses and Papers in
Scientific Archaeology 13. Stockholm: Arkeologiska forskningslaboratoriet.

Victor, H. 2007. Vägen till andra sidan: Med vagn genom bronsåldern i
Mellansverige. In M. Notelid (ed.), *Att nå den andra sidan: Om begravning
och ritual i Uppland*. pp. 145–71. Arkeologi E4 Uppland. Studier 2. Stockholm: Riksantikvarieämbetet, Uppsala: Societas Archaelogica Upsaliensis,
and Uppsala: Upplandsmuseet.

Vikstrand, P. 2001. *Gudarnas platser: Förkristna sakrala ortnamn i Mälar-*

landskapen. Studier till en svensk ortnamnsatlas 17, Kungliga Gustav Adolfs Akademien för svensk folkkultur. Uppsala: Swedish Science Press.

— 2004. Berget, lunden och åkern: Om sakrala och kosmologiska landskap ur ortnamnens perspektiv. In Andrén et al. 2004:317–41.

— 2006. Ásgarðr, Midgarðr, and Útgarðr: A linguistic approach to a classical problem. In Andrén et al. 2006:354–7.

— 2007. *Bebyggelsenamnen i Mörbylånga kommun.* Sveriges ortnamn, Ortnamnen i Kalmar län 7. Uppsala: Institutet för språk och folkminnen.

Vries, J. de 1956. *Altgermanische Religionsgeschichte,* i. Grundriss der germanischen Philologie 12/1. Berlin: de Gruyter.

— 1957. *Altgermanische Religionsgeschichte,* ii. Grundriss der germanischen Philologie 12/2. Berlin: de Gruyter.

Voss, O. and Ørsnes-Christensen, M. 1949. Der Dollerupfund: Ein Doppelgrab aus der römischen Eisenzeit. *Acta Archaeologica* 19:209–71.

Wahlberg, M. 2003 (ed.). *Svenskt ortnamnslexikon.* Uppsala: Språk- och folkminnesinstitutet.

Wall, Å. 2003. *De hägnade bergens landskap: Om den äldre järnåldern på Södertörn.* Stockholm Studies in Archaeology 27. Stockholm: Institutionen för arkeologi.

Wangen. V. 2009. *Gravfeltet på Gunnarstorp i Sarpsborg, Østfold: Et monument over dødsriter og kultutøvelse i yngre bronsealder og eldre jernalder.* Norske Oldfunn 27. Oslo: Kulturhistorisk museum.

Ward, D. 1968. *The divine twins: An Indo-European myth in Germanic tradition.* Folklore Studies 19. Berkeley & Los Angeles: University of California Press.

Warmind, M. 2004. '…á þeim meiði, er mangi veit, hvers hann af rótom renn'. Kosmologi og ritualer i det førkristne Norden. In Andrén et al. 2004:135–44.

Weber, K. 1976a. The ring-wall around Eketorp-I. In Borg et al. 1976:61–6.

— 1976b. The Gateways of Eketorp II. In Borg et al. 1976:97–116.

Wegraeus, E. 1976. The Öland ring-forts. In Borg et al. 1976:33–44.

Welinder, S. 1975. *Prehistoric agriculture in eastern middle Sweden: A model for food production, population growth, agricultural innovations, and ecological limitations in prehistoric eastern middle Sweden 4000 BC–AD 1000.* Lund: Gleerup.

Welinder, S., Pedersen, E. A., and Widgren, M. 1998. *Jordbrukets första femtusen år, 4000 f.Kr.–1000 e.Kr.* Det svenska jordbrukets historia I. Stockholm: Natur och Kultur.

Wellendorf, J. 2006. Homogeneity and hetrogeneity in Old Norse cosmology. In Andrén et al. 2006:50–3.

Werner, J. 1949. Zu den auf Öland und Gotland gefundenen byzantischen Goldmünzen. *Fornvännen* 44:256–86.

— 1956. *Beiträge zur Archäologie des Attila-Reiches*. Munich: Verlag der bayerischen Akademie der Wissenschaften.

— 1963. Tiergestaltige Heilsbilder under germanische Personennamen. *Deutsche Vierteljahresschrift für Litteraturwissenschaft und Geisteswissenschaft* 37:377–83.

— 1966. *Das Aufkommen von Bild und Schrift in Nordeuropa*. Bayerische Akademie der Wissenschaften. Philosophisch-historische Klasse, Sitzungsberichte 4. Munich.

West, M. L. 2007. *Indo-European poetry and myth*. Oxford: Oxford University Press.

Wheatley, P. 1971. *The pivot of the four quarters: A preliminary enquiry into the origins and character of the ancient Chinese city*. Edinburgh: Edinburgh University Press.

Wicker, N. L. 1990. *Migration period bracteates: Art historical constructs and the archaeology of crafts production and distribution*. Minneapolis: University of Minnesota.

Wickham, C. 2005. *Framing the early Middle Ages: Europe and the Mediterranean 400–800*. Oxford: Oxford University Press.

— 2009. *The inheritance of Rome: Illuminating the Dark Ages 400–1000*. London: Penguin.

Widengren, G. 1969. *Religionsphänomenologie*. Berlin: de Gruyter.

Widgren, M. 1983. *Settlement and farming systems in the early Iron Age: A study of fossil agrarian landscapes in Östergötland, Sweden*. Stockholm Studies in Human Geography 3. Stockholm: Almqvist & Wiksell International.

— 2012. Climate and causation in the Swedish Iron Age: Learning from the present to understand the past. *Geografisk Tidskrift: Danish Journal of Geography* 112(2):126–34.

Widholm, D. 1998. *Rösen, ristningar och riter*. Acta Archaeologica Lundensia 40, no. 23. Stockholm: Almqvist & Wiksell International.

Wiegels, R. 2007 (ed.). *Die Varusschlacht: Wendepunkt der Geschichte?* Stuttgart: Thiess.

Wijkander, K. 1983. *Kungshögar och sockenbildning: Södermanlands administrativa indelning under vikingatid och tidig medeltid*. Sörmländska handlingar 39. Nyköping: Södermanlands museum.

Wikander, S. 1978. *Araber, vikingar, väringar*. Svenska Humanistiska Förbundet 90. Nyhamnsläge: Svenska humanistiska förbundet.

Worsaae, J. J. A. 1870. Om Forestillingerne paa Guldbracteaterne. *Aarbøger for Nordisk Oldkyndighed og Historie* 1870:382–419.

Wylie, A. 1985. The reaction against analogy. In M. B. Schiffer (ed.), *Advances in archaeological method and theory*, viii. pp. 63–111. Orlando: Academic Press.

Ystgaard, I. 1998. *Bygdeborger i Trøndelag: En forskningshistorisk og empirisk undersøkelse av et begrep og en kulturminnekategori.* Hovedfagsoppgave ved NTNU. Trondheim: Norges tekniske og naturvitenskaplige universitet.

— 2003. Bygdeborgerne som kilde til studiet av samfunns- og maktforhold i eldre jernalder. *Primitive Tider* 6:21–30.

Zachrisson, I. 1997. *Möten i gränsland: Samer och germaner i Mellanskandinavien.* Stockholm: Statens historiska museum.

Zachrisson, T. 1994. The odal and its manifestation in the landscape. *Current Swedish Archaeology* 2:219–38.

— 1998. *Gård, gräns, gravfält. Sammanhang kring ädelmetalldepåer och runstenar från vikingatid och tidig medeltid i Uppland och Gästrikland.* Stockholm Studies in Archaeology 15. Stockholm: Institutionen för arkeologi.

— 2004a. The holiness of Helgö. *Excavations at Helgö 16. Exotic and sacral finds from Helgö*, pp. 143–75. Stockholm: Kungliga Vitterhets-, historie- och antikvitetsakademien.

— 2004b. Det heliga på Helgö och dess kosmiska referenser. In Andrén et al. 2004:343–88.

— 2011. Property and honour – social change in central Sweden, 200–700 AD, mirrored in the area around Old Uppsala. In L. Boye (ed.), *Det 61. Internationale Sachsensymposion 2010 Haderslev, Danmark.* Arkæologi i Slesvig, pp. 141–56. Neumünster: Wachholtz.

Zakynthinos, A. 1966. La grande brèche dans la tradition historique de l'hellénisme du septième au neuvième siècle. *Charisterion eis A. K. Orlandon*, iii. pp. 300–27. Athens: Vivliothiki tis en Athines Archeolojikis Eterias 54.

Index

An index of concepts, names, modern place-names, and relevant Old Norse concepts and names.